A RECKLESS PASSION

A sheltered but impetuous young beauty, Lindsay Somerset would risk anything for a succulent taste of wild adventure—and Jared Giles, the dashing Earl of Dovercourt, is the answer to her prayers. A gallant and fearless gentleman, he is rumored to be a spy— and the ideal man to fulfill Lindsay's most cherished, unspoken desires.

MY RUNAWAY HEART

But once aboard ship on a high, raging sea, Lindsay realizes the folly of her rash actions—and the truth about the bold hero to whom she has entrusted her love. For Jared is no servant of the Crown, but a lusty scoundrel with a dark secret and passions that know no bounds. And Lindsay is a hostage to his dangerous will—trapped on a sensuous adventure that will imperil her life . . . and her innocent heart as well.

"A GIFTED WRITER
WHOSE BOOKS BELONG ON EVERY
ROMANCE READER'S SHELF."
Romantic Times

MIRIAM MINGER

MY RUNAWAY HEART

An Avon Romantic Treasure

AVON BOOKS ◆ NEW YORK

MY RUNAWAY HEART is an original publication of Avon Books. This work has never before appeared in book form. This work is a novel. Any similarity to actual persons or events is purely coincidental.

AVON BOOKS
A division of
The Hearst Corporation
1350 Avenue of the Americas
New York, New York 10019

Copyright © 1995 by Miriam Minger
Published by arrangement with the author
Library of Congress Catalog Card Number: 95-94428
ISBN: 0-380-78301-0

First Avon Books Printing: November 1995

AVON TRADEMARK REG. U.S. PAT. OFF AND IN OTHER COUNTRIES, MARCA REGISTRADA, HECHO EN U.S.A.

Printed in the U.S.A.

RA   10   9   8   7   6   5   4   3   2   1

Prologue

"**D**o we set her ablaze, Cap'n? She's listing so far to port already, it won't take long—"

"Light the torches."

The damning words were spoken so low that they were almost sucked up by the roar of the wind, but the captain made no effort to repeat them. And the stumpy Irishman scrambled to obey his command. As another howling gust tore at the captain's hair, the icy sting of salt spray plastering his shirt to his body, he gripped the starboard railing and peered through the gathering dusk at the doomed merchantman, *Superior*.

Galleys loaded with officers bobbed around the crippled ship like ducklings reluctant to leave their mother's side, although one longboat had turned into the wind to head for England. A harsh smile touched his face. "What do you say, Walker? Think they'll see the flames in London?"

"Ha! With all those munitions aboard? Damned if they don't hear the explosion all the way to Boston."

1

The captain didn't respond, falling as grimly silent as the raven-haired American standing behind him. Torches hissed to life along the quarterdeck. Bright orange flames curled and clawed at the wind with malevolent fingers. First one, then another, then a dozen torches were hurled across pewter-dark waves to the *Superior*, her billowing white sails soon writhing like tortured souls in a maelstrom of hellish fire and heat.

Within moments the upper decks were a roaring pyre of flame and the captain smiled again, his face as tight as his grip on the railing. Hoarse cries of alarm carried to him from the galleys, plaintive wails to the Blessed Virgin careening to the heavens.

"Yes, pray, damn you," he said under his breath, watching as the frantic officers rowed like fiends to get themselves clear of the burning ship. "Pray as if God had any time for man's piteous affairs."

Blasphemy, he knew, but he was already damned. He didn't flinch when an earsplitting explosion suddenly rocked the night, the merchantman's foredeck blown to bits into the darkening sky. Red-hot sparks and shards of burning wood pelted the sea like blistering rain. It was only then that he gave the signal to unfurl the sails, and the sleek schooner cut cleanly through the waves, leaving the merchantman to its watery fate. But he kept his eyes riveted upon the flames even as another thunderous explosion ripped in two what remained of the British ship.

Boiling, seething flames that only fed the inferno in his soul, faces appearing to him against a backdrop of crimson fire and acrid black smoke. The faces of beloved ones long dead and the faces of those he lived to hate. He had lost so much, and what of the years that had been stolen from him? Precious, irretrievable years . . .

Such fierce rage swept over him that his knuckles whitened, his splayed fingers digging into the railing. A great hiss cut through the wind, hot steam rising like a mist. The sea churned and bubbled around the glowing carcass of what had once been a mighty trading vessel. Then the merchantman was gone, dragged beneath the debris-strewn waves, and with its disappearance he felt the rage begin to subside within him.

But the soul-deep chill remained. As icy cold as the salt spray stinging his flesh. He turned from the railing, his hands cramped, his fingers numb, and met Walker's gaze.

"See that the prisoners are fed, blankets all around. The sea is up. It'll be a hard crossing to the Isle of Wight."

"True, but what better end to a tale they'll be telling their children and grandchildren for years to come? It isn't every day a ship's crew is escorted safely to land while their officers are made to row home. Think they'll place wagers on their captain's skill at the oar?"

He made no reply to the American's wry response, having grown accustomed long ago to Walker's grim humor. But right now he had no stomach for it. He wanted to be alone. He wanted a brandy. He wanted an entire bottle.

"Aye, it's him, the cap'n of this ship, didn't I tell you?" A young sailor's excited voice carried from mid-deck, where the *Superior*'s crew stood surrounded by guards. "The scourge o' the entire Channel fleet! 'Tis the Phoenix himself, and wearin' a gold mask to boot, just like they been sayin' in London!"

"Crimey, lad, hold your tongue! This ain't a blasted Sunday picnic. Can't you see he's lookin' our way?"

The man they called the Phoenix was looking their way, his jaw growing hard when he saw the older sailor nearly knock the youth to his knees with a harsh cuff to the ear. His strides strong and furious across the listing deck, he had the man by the throat before the astonished fellow could blink.

"Strike him again and you're over the side to swim back to England," he growled, his fingers tightening mercilessly around a leathery neck. "Am I understood?"

Bulging blue eyes stared back at him in raw fear, an Adam's apple gulping beneath his hand. "A-aye, sir, but I meant no harm to the boy. No harm at all, I'd swear on me mother's grave! I-I can't breathe, sir, please . . ."

"Cap-tain."

Jarred by the deep, slurred bass which held the faintest note of reproach, he bit back the memories of vicious blows raining upon his own head and ears. With a vehement curse he released the sailor to crumple gasping at his feet, while the other prisoners stared openmouthed at the fair-haired, bearded giant whose height and breadth of shoulder cast a hulking shadow across the deck.

A gentle giant—half his wits and most of his speech lost to a metal ball still lodged in his brain— who helped to remind him of what shreds remained of his conscience whenever it seemed he possessed none at all.

"Help Walker with the prisoners, Dag."

His low command greeted with a solemn nod, the captain made for the hold while the deck erupted with activity, blankets being handed out, the savory smell of beef stew tingeing the air. A grim laugh escaped him.

Warm blankets. Beef stew. Safe passage back to England. Hardly inhospitable treatment from the dreaded Phoenix, legendary plague of the Channel fleet. But, of course, no ship's officers could say such gracious things about him; even now those men pulling for their lives upon wet, slippery oars were probably cursing his name.

Just as the British Admiralty would be cursing and rattling their shiny dress swords when they heard of the *Superior*'s fate. And the ton, always so quick to grow bored, would have fresh fodder to add to the latest society gossip and scandal. Blast them to hell; he could already hear them.

Oh, dear, how monstrously wicked! What a horror! Another King's ship burned to ashes upon the sea! Ladies would swoon. Men would bluster. Commotion would reign.

Blast them all to hell; he would enjoy every bloody minute of it.

Chapter 1

“**O**h, Corie, I can hardly believe you're here in London! The party was lovely tonight, wasn't it? And you looked so beautiful in that green gown—no, no, sea foam sounds so much better—yes, your exquisite sea-foam gown, and how perfectly it complemented your auburn hair! And Lord Donovan looked so handsome and I'm so happy that everything has worked out for the best—”

“Lindsay Somerset, you're making me breathless!” her best friend replied. “Aren't you beginning to feel sleepy at all?”

Lindsay rolled onto her stomach, a sheepish grin on her face as she met Corisande Easton's exasperated gaze.

No, no, not Corisande Easton anymore, but Lady Donovan Trent, Lindsay reminded herself as she swept white-blond strands from her eyes. And it was all so romantic, so wonderful, she would never tire of hearing the story, never—

“Lindsay?”

“No, I'm not sleepy, not a bit. How could I be? Tell me everything again, will you, Corie? From beginning to end—how you first met Lord Donovan, when he first kissed you, when you knew you were in love with him. Everything!"

Fully expecting to be obliged, Lindsay eagerly rose to a cross-legged sitting position in the middle of the huge four-poster bed and tucked her linen nightgown around her knees. She hoped Lord Donovan's last-minute business would keep him from Corisande's side just a little while longer, although from the pink flush on Corisande's cheeks, Lindsay imagined her friend was already anticipating his return. As she followed Corisande's expectant brown-eyed gaze to the door, Lindsay felt a poignant tug at her heart.

She was so happy for Corisande, truly happy. She thought back to the last afternoon, four weeks ago, they had spent together in Cornwall, just before she had left for London. They had clambered onto a rock and shouted their secret pact to the four winds: neither of them could wed anyone less than the man of her dreams. Had it been only a month ago?

And now Corisande was already happily married to a man who couldn't be more perfect for her, Lord Donovan. And, from everything Lindsay had seen and heard, one of the most good and honorable gentlemen she had ever met. He had even found it within himself to overlook Corisande's fearsome temper, which made Lindsay smile. She had never known anyone more impassioned than Corisande about helping those less fortunate, her legendary ability to exercise her lungs only rising with the intensity of her beliefs. And knowing Corisande, poor Lord Donovan must have gotten a splitting earful of that temper, but he had fallen in love with her all the same.

Lindsay closed her eyes, fresh longing tugging deep at her heart. How long before she found the man of *her* dreams?

It was already weeks into the Season and still she hadn't met anyone who came close to the husband she envisioned for herself. The dull, self-absorbed, heiress-seeking gentlemen Aunt Winifred kept steering her way were no more valiant adventurers than she was a young woman merely interested in making a suitable marriage. She wanted more, so much more.

She wanted someone to show her the world, a bold, daring man who would want an equally adventurous woman by his side. And they would be so hopelessly, utterly, in love, nothing would be more important to him than their life together . . .

"Are you thinking of him?"

Lindsay opened her eyes, Corisande's soft question making her smile wistfully. "Always. I'm just beginning to wonder if he exists at all."

"Exists at all? That doesn't sound like the indomitable Lindsay Somerset I know." Corisande drew her knees up beneath the embroidered counterpane and studied her friend, even while her skin seemed to grow more heated at the thought of Donovan's imminent return. "I noticed several agreeable-looking young gentlemen ogling you at the party tonight—"

"A boring, ridiculous bunch, the whole lot of them. Olympia has poor Aunt Winnie so cowed she doesn't dare allow any but the most spineless sort near me—just the sort Olympia would absolutely adore as a son-in-law. Someone she'd have no trouble tying into an obliging, sniveling, intimidated knot. Well, I'll have none of my step-mother's plans for me. None of it!"

"That's good to hear." Corisande couldn't help smiling at the indignant look on Lindsay's face—amazing, that even a frown couldn't mar her friend's flawless beauty—and the defiance spark-ing her brilliant blue eyes. "I almost feared your leaving Cornwall had sapped that adventuresome spirit I recall so well. I'm pleased to see that I was wrong."

"Sapped it?" Lindsay gave an unladylike snort. "I feel as if I'm about to burst! I simply can't wait to strike out on my own, I told you that in my letters. There must be so much more to this city than balls and assemblies and seeing the same peo-ple night after night." Lindsay uncrossed her legs and leaned earnestly toward Corisande, a sudden look of regret in her eyes. "Not that your party tonight wasn't lovely, Corie."

"I'm not offended."

"No, no, it was wonderful, and so very kind of Lord Donovan's friends to give you both a proper wedding ball. But what would be even more won-derful is if you could stay in London for just a while longer, even a few more days, and you and Lord Donovan could chaperone me instead of Aunt Winnie—"

"Our ship sails in the morning, Lindsay, you know that," Corisande broke in gently. "Donovan is so eager to reach Lisbon, to see his daughter, Paloma, again. It's a miracle that the child was found. Donovan spent nearly everything he had to find her. It's so hard to believe that I'll soon have a little daughter to care for, to love."

"Oh, dear, how ridiculously selfish of me." Lindsay sat back on her heels, feeling doubly ashamed. "I'm sorry, Corie. I've waited so long to come to London and it is wonderful being here, but Aunt Winnie is so determined to honor all of Olympia's wretched demands—where I'm to go, who I'm to meet, what I must wear—"

"And you haven't thought of clever ways to thwart that old termagant before?"

Lindsay met Corisande's gaze, a gamine's grin spreading over her face. "Oh, I can recall a time or two."

"Like sneaking from your father's manor around midnight to come and help me land smuggled brandy and lace handkerchiefs? Lord, if Lady Somerset knew her stepdaughter had a knack for fair trading that any man in Cornwall could hope to boast of—"

"Or for filching a bit of food from the pantry to help you feed the tinners and their families."

"A *bit* of food? Sacks of grain, buckets of potatoes, loaves of fresh baked bread?"

Lindsay shrugged nonchalantly, her grin widening. "Any way I could help you, I was glad to do it."

"And you'll be able to help yourself, too; you just have to keep your eyes open for the right moment. You weren't gifted with that wild imagination to let it go to waste. You'll soon think of something."

"And so I will, but enough of me, Lady Donovan. I believe you were going to tell me again how you and your husband met, and only three days after I left Porthleven. Threatened him with a pitchfork, as I recall?"

"Well, I was waving one around, but it was his

family's agent, Henry Gilbert, I was aiming for and—''

"And I would have thought to find my beautiful wife asleep at this late hour considering we're to set sail first thing tomorrow morning."

Lindsay gasped at the sight of Lord Donovan leaning casually against the door, the man so tall and strapping she was astounded she and Corisande hadn't heard his footsteps down the hall. Her face burning, she snatched up the fringed India shawl she had worn to the guest chamber, whirling it around her shoulders as she scooted off the bed.

"Oh, dear, it's all my fault," Lindsay hastened to explain, her eyes darting from Lord Donovan's amused gaze to Corisande's face. Her dearest friend was positively beaming, Corisande looked so happy to see her husband. "We were talking and I kept asking Corie so many questions. Truly, she would have been asleep long ago if not for me."

And truly, Lindsay realized with chagrined relief as she hurried barefoot to the door, her shawl clutched modestly under her chin, she could have been back in her room already for all the notice Lord Donovan gave her. Tall and as swarthily dark as a Gypsy, he moved to the bed even as Lindsay darted past him, his near-black eyes settling warmly upon his wife. Lindsay felt her face grow hotter, her wish thundering more fervently deep inside her breast that someday soon she might meet a man who had eyes only for her.

"Good night, Corie. Lord Donovan."

She hadn't expected a response and none came but the softest exhalation of delight. Lindsay glanced over her shoulder to see Donovan bend to kiss Corisande's smiling mouth. Her heart aching all the harder, she closed the door quietly behind her and fled to her room.

Her best friend had progressed beyond her.

By the next evening, Lindsay was back in a social mode, her flustered aunt clutching at her arm.

"Oh, dear, oh, dear, this ballroom is dreadfully stuffy, such a crush of people. Where's my fan? Matilda! Oh, my, where could she have gone? Just when I need her most, she disappears—"

"Here's your fan, Aunt Winnie, dangling from your wrist," Lindsay said with indulgent gentleness. She caught her aunt's fluttering right hand and popped open the prettily painted silk fan. At once the plump older woman began to beat vigorously at the air, her dimpled cheeks crimson with agitation as she searched the huge second-floor room for the lady's maid who accompanied her everywhere, even to balls.

"But Matilda—"

"I'm sure Matilda will return at any moment. She told me she wanted to fetch you a glass of lemon punch."

"Oh, my, yes, punch would be very nice. She must have known just how peaked I was feeling. Such a dear, my Matilda."

"Yes, she is a dear, but how about if we move closer to that window where you might catch a breath of fresh air?" Without waiting for a reply, Lindsay carefully steered her beloved aunt through the thronged room, the Dowager Baroness Penney nodding greetings to acquaintances even as she turned and whispered with exasperation into Lindsay's ear.

"I don't understand why Lady Oglethorpe had to invite the whole of London to this ball! Even three marriageable daughters shouldn't warrant such a crowd, and not a beauty among them, no, no, not like you."

"Aunt Winnie . . ."

"It's the truth," the lady protested. "But with so many guests, why, there'll be little room for dancing and that would be such a disappointment, not only for yourself, my dear, but for all the nice young men whom you've met since you came to London. Yes, such a pity."

More a relief, Lindsay thought with a small sigh, grateful when at last they had reached the window. An impeccably dressed older gentleman in buff-colored breeches and a stiff white cravat at once vacated a chair, Lady Penney plopping onto the crimson brocade cushion with an audible groan. As her aunt continued to fan herself with an energetic vigor that negated any real cause for concern, Lindsay surveyed the brilliantly lit ballroom, which was indeed as crowded as any she had seen.

Bejeweled ladies dressed in stylish gowns of every hue—though lavender seemed to be especially favored tonight—and gentlemen dapper in formal evening wear milled around the room in an ever-changing kaleidoscope of colorful confusion, the pitch of conversation sounding to Lindsay like an agitated swarm of bees. She and Aunt Winifred had only just arrived at the fashionable assembly and already Lindsay wished they could return home.

Other than the mad crush of people, it appeared a ball just like any other she had attended: formal, stuffy, hopelessly predictable and with the same faces. And she wasn't feeling very festive, not since Corisande and Donovan had left that morning.

Their ship had to be well into the Channel by now, forging its way to Lisbon, Portugal. How she wished she were aboard, too. It would have been so exciting, so much more than enduring night after night of these interminable balls. She had even packed a bag in the hope that at the last moment she might persuade Aunt Winifred to allow her to accompany Corisande, but she had never carried it from her room. Her aunt might have succumbed to a swoon that even Matilda's ever-present smelling salts wouldn't remedy, and Lindsay couldn't do that to the poor dear. Aunt Winifred was trying so wretchedly hard to accommodate Olympia, damn that ridiculous woman!

Lindsay spun around to the open window, suddenly needing fresh air herself. Her face felt hot, her chest constricted. How long was she to be a prisoner of her stepmother's plans for her?

She could at least be thankful that Olympia's vanity hadn't allowed her to come to London as well, the woman preferring instead to stay in Porthleven, where she was the high priestess of society and not just another baronet's wife in a sea of glittering nobility. Although Lindsay wouldn't have minded at all to have her father here. Instead he was still with her stepmother . . .

Forcing Olympia from her mind, Lindsay was startled by a nearby outburst.

"Zounds, I owned stock in that ship! The *Superior* was top of the line from foremast to keel, only two years at sea. That bloody bastard must be caught and hanged! No, no, better yet, drawn and quartered!"

Chapter 2

"**O**h, Lord." Lindsay rested her forehead on the cool pane and closed her eyes, finding some comfort in one of Corisande's favorite expressions as she willed the blustering fellow nearby to find another topic of conversation. He didn't. For the past three days, the talk among the ton had been of little else.

"Damned if that scoundrel didn't make the officers row to Wight, the poor blokes half drowned and chilled to the marrow by the time they dragged themselves ashore. Made them row, mind you!"

"Yes, indeed, like common sailors—and one of my own nephews among them!" piped up another gentleman. "Said the *Superior* was blown to bits and sank like a stone while that devil's ship disappeared into the night as if swallowed by hell itself!"

Lindsay shivered, imagining the scene. Crackling flames, deafening explosions and frightened men crying out in the dark. She thought of Corisande and Donovan sailing at this moment to Lisbon aboard the brig *Industry*, and was grateful Donovan had arranged for a sixteen-gun King's cutter to escort them safely through the Channel. But once it had rounded the northwestern tip of France, the *Industry* would be left to its own defenses.

Another man added his voice to the mounting uproar. "The name Phoenix suits him well enough, I'm deuced to say. Every time the villain fires a ship, he rises from the ashes to burn again—bloody constant as the sun and laughing at us all, I'd wager! Forty-two British merchantmen and nine warships in three years, and our esteemed navy hasn't come close to stopping him. An American privateer, no less, making his home in our fair waters! It's an outrage! Something must be done!"

"The Phoenix?" A sharp tug came at Lindsay's skirt. "Oh, dear, are they talking about that dreadful pirate again? Where's Matilda? Where's my punch? My smelling salts!"

Lindsay sank down next to her aunt's chair, the poor woman's silk fan fluttering triple time. Aunt Winifred looked ashen, which was exactly what Lindsay had feared. When a young bride, her aunt had lost her first husband, an official with the East India Company, to a pirate attack in the Bay of Bengal.

"You mustn't let them distress you so, Aunt Winnie. Their conversation has nothing to do with us."

"But your friend Corie and Lord Donovan. Oh, dear, oh—"

"You saw how they shrugged off such talk at their party last night. Corie's very brave, you know. And Lord Donovan arranged for an armed cutter to accompany them just in case. He would be the last to take any heedless chances with his new wife aboard. So you mustn't worry for them—ah, look, here's Matilda with your lemon punch."

Lindsay rose and threw a grateful look at the sweet-faced lady's maid whose stout girth so matched that of her mistress, whispering the word "pirates" as Matilda held out a brimming crystal punch cup to Aunt Winifred.

"Frantic about pirates, are ye?" the old Scotswoman chided softly while her mistress took a shaky gulp. "Nonsense, now, milady. They're far out to sea and far away from ye, ye can be sure. And if any comes near, they'll have to contend with Matilda MacDougal first, don't ye forget it. Now drink up yer punch, it'll calm ye."

"Yes, Aunt Winnie, drink your punch, and if you don't feel better soon, we could always lea—"

"Miss Somerset! Oh, Miss Somerset!"

Lindsay stiffened, groaning inwardly as she told herself if she didn't move, didn't make a sound, the russet-haired, earnest-faced apparition plunging toward her through the crowd would surely disappear. She even blinked, once, twice, but Lord Ambrose Lamb, the twenty-four-year-old son of an impoverished marquis and one of her most determined suitors, didn't stop his headlong rush until he was virtually upon her, a black buckled shoe trodding upon her slippered toe.

Lindsay tried to stifle a wince, but it was too late. Lord Ambrose reddened from his snowy starched cravat to the roots of his neatly combed hair and immediately took her elbow to support her, his expression stricken.

"Oh, my, Miss Somerset, I'm so terribly sorry! So clumsy of me. Does it hurt? Perhaps we should find a physician."

"Please, my lord, I'm fine. Really." Lindsay groaned to herself again as she tried unsuccessfully to disengage her arm, Lord Ambrose Lamb no doubt fearing she might topple. "I'm made of quite sturdy stuff, I assure you. No, no, that really isn't necessary . . . oh, dear."

Lindsay felt her face growing hot as flame as Lord Ambrose dropped to one knee, awkwardly groping for her foot.

"But we should really call for a physician—I say, bones could be broken. Perhaps if I rubbed—"

"Lord Ambrose, please!" Lindsay jumped back a step, bumping into the window ledge as she glanced up to see a host of shocked faces turned toward them, Aunt Winifred's fan frozen in midair. It was all so ridiculous she couldn't help but laugh, and at once Lord Ambrose ceased his fumbling and looked up at her, relief shining in his hazel eyes. But just as quickly came mortification, the young gentleman's shiny scrubbed face glowing even redder as he realized the immodest impropriety of his actions.

"Miss Somerset, f-forgive me. I fear I've made quite a mess of things."

"No, no, don't be silly—you were simply concerned about my welfare and I'm very grateful." Summoning a reassuring smile, Lindsay knew she now risked enduring his company for much of the evening, but Corisande had always said she was too kindhearted for her own good. Lord Ambrose's deep chagrin had been too pitiful to bear. Yet as the first strains of music, a minuet, filled the air, she couldn't help thinking that there still might be an escape . . .

"Miss Somerset, I was hoping to ask you for a dance, but now that your toe—"

"Truly, my toe is fine, my lord, but I fear that Aunt Winnie is feeling indisposed this evening. We were planning to call our carriage as soon as she finished her punch."

"Oh, my, no, I never said a word about leaving," Aunt Winifred announced with surprising vigor after her recent complaints. "It appears there's going to be dancing after all, my dear. See, they're making room this very moment. Lady Oglethorpe is leading the way with her daughters and their escorts. How absolutely delightful for you!"

"Yes, delightful," Lindsay said under her breath, the night suddenly looming long and drearily before her. And to think only weeks ago a glittering ball would have thrilled her, being so new to London and the Season. But after eleven such assemblies and not one trip to the theater or pleasure gardens, thanks to Olympia's deeming such amusements entirely too frivolous and unnecessary in securing a husband, she felt as doomed as a prisoner bound for Tyburn.

"May I have the pleasure, Miss Somerset?"

Forcing a bright smile, Lindsay nodded and allowed herself to be led to the dance floor, Lord Ambrose beaming so broadly she wondered if his face might split as they joined the minuet.

Of course, she could always pretend a swoon and claim later that she had underestimated the injury to her toe. She was very good at swoons, her flair for the dramatic having come in quite handy on several occasions in Cornwall as a way to thwart her stepmother. And swooning was particularly useful when telling tales of damsels in distress, as she had done for Corisande's three younger sisters, Marguerite, Linette and Estelle Easton. Twelve-year-old Linette had especially liked her stories—

"Y-you look very lovely tonight, Miss Somerset. Simply exquisite."

Lindsay pushed away warm memories of many happy hours spent at the Easton parsonage as a refuge from her stepmother, and tried to ignore, too, Lord Ambrose's persistent squeezing of her fingers. Grateful that the dance wasn't a waltz for the bruised ribs she might suffer, she politely inclined her head. "It is kind of you to say so, sir."

"Not kind at all. I say, Lindsay, you're the most beautiful woman in the room—in all of London! Forgive my boldness, but may I call you Lindsay?"

Somehow she managed a nod, not sure what she might say if he insisted that she call him Ambrose. And he had voiced his effusive compliment so loudly, she was certain that there were many guests who might have overheard. As they circled around each other, Ambrose's expression growing all the more earnest, she began to hope fervently that the minuet would soon end.

"Your gown is all the crack, too. If you were my wife I'd shower you with dozens like it. Yellow truly suits you—"

"Jonquil."

"I'm sorry?"

"Not yellow. Jonquil," Lindsay repeated nervously, fearing suddenly that Lord Ambrose Lamb might be considering dropping a second time onto his knee and proposing marriage to her right there on the dance floor. His *wife*? Kindheartedness be damned. It was definitely time for a swoon. Pulling her fingers free of Ambrose's, she pressed them to her forehead and rolled her eyes heavenward. "Dear Lord, the room is positively swimming. I feel

the most horrible pain in my foot—quite dreadful—"

"Lindsay? Lindsay!"

Lord Ambrose's stricken cry echoed around
them as Lindsay spun and collapsed to the floor,
not as gracefully as she would have wanted, but
effective all the same. She heard several gentlemen
command loudly for the guests to stand back and
make room, ladies gasping and a few complaining
that they felt faint as well; then she felt herself being lifted.

"You heard them, damn you. Stand back and
give the young woman air."

Damn you? That profane command didn't sound
like Ambrose at all, Lindsay never having heard
him use anything but the most impeccable speech.
And she would never have imagined Ambrose pos-
sessing such strength to lift her so effortlessly, the
marquis's son being somewhat on the slender side.
Tempted beyond measure to open her eyes, Lindsay had to will herself to remain limp, although she
was finding these strange inconsistencies quite disconcerting.

"Oh, dear God, what has happened to my niece?
Lindsay? Can you hear me? Set her down—set her
down in this chair! Matilda, my smelling salts!"

Deposited just as easily as she'd been swept up
from the floor, Lindsay prepared herself for the dis-
agreeable smell of ammonia and started appropri-
ately when the vile stuff was waved under her
nose. Fluttering open her eyes, she smiled weakly
at Aunt Winifred and Matilda, the two women
hovering over her.

"Lindsay? Oh, my dear child, you've given me
such a fright. Matilda, fetch some punch—hurry!"

"I believe the good gentleman already went to the refreshment table, milady."

"Good gentleman indeed," Aunt Winifred said in outrage, to Lindsay's surprise. "I'll have none such as he fetching punch for my niece—why, it's bad enough he had to come to her rescue, carrying her so brazenly from the dance floor—"

"Who carried me, Aunt Winnie?" Lindsay did a fair impression of shaking the cobwebs from her head while her aunt seemed intent upon half lifting her from the chair.

"Never you mind. Matilda, help me support her! I want us gone before that blackguard returns."

"What blackguard? I thought it was Lord Ambrose—"

"I'm here, my dearest, right here!" cried a familiar tenor voice. Lindsay focused upon Ambrose's flushed face as he tried unsuccessfully to squeeze his way past Aunt Winifred and Matilda's girth to come to her side. There was such a crush of concerned guests around her chair that it was a wonder the two older women could maneuver at all, but together they drew Lindsay to her feet, each gripping an arm, and she could do nothing but walk with them.

"Aunt Winnie, I'm feeling better, really," she said with some embarrassment, stunned by her aunt's strange behavior. "We don't have to rush so."

"And I tell you we do! Some say he's a spy against Napoleon himself, but we'll have no part of that notorious fellow, oh, my dear, no. A rake he is, not to be trusted with any young girl, and certainly not with my—"

"Did you say a spy?" Suddenly heedless of the

curious faces as they hastened across the room, Lindsay threw a glance behind her but saw only a distraught-looking Lord Ambrose gazing forlornly after them. She glanced wildly to the left and right, gooseflesh dimpling her skin as she recalled the sheer strength of her rescuer. He had gallantly gone to fetch her punch, but who . . . ?

"Oh, dear, it certainly won't look very gracious of me if we leave without bidding Lady Oglethorpe good night," Aunt Winifred said with clear frustration, her fan fluttering crazily. "I'll only be a moment, Lindsay. Stay right here by the door with Matilda."

"Never ye fear, I'll protect the lass," the Scotswoman intoned briskly, looping her plump arm through Lindsay's. But as Aunt Winifred bustled back into the crowd, Matilda leaned to whisper into Lindsay's ear, "Pity he's a rogue. I've ne'er seen so handsome a gentleman as that one, no, not even in the Highlands, where fine, strapping men are as common as rain."

Lindsay felt her heart plummet into her slippers, her disappointment so keen she could taste it.

A spy against Napoleon? She had been so close to so noble and heroic a gentleman, and she wasn't going to be allowed to meet him? If only she had peeked! She would have known then it wasn't Lord Ambrose carrying her but another man altogether—

"I'm pleased to see you so remarkably recovered, Miss Somerset. I trust you no longer need a glass of punch?"

Chapter 3

⟨⌒⟨⌒⟨⌒⟨⌒⟩⌒⟩⌒⟩⌒⟩

Lindsay spun around, her heart suddenly in her
throat as she met a pair of amused blue eyes.

And not just any blue, but a deep turbulent blue
that held her mesmerized, at least until a wry smile
drew her gaze reluctantly away. She was staring,
she knew, but she couldn't help herself, the man
truly as handsome as Matilda had said—even more
so. And to think he had held her in his arms, had
come to her rescue like a gallant knight, had—

"Your lemon punch, Miss Somerset?"

Lindsay blinked. Lord, what a ninny she must
appear! Her face as warm as if she'd stood in front
of a hot oven, she groped for something to say.

"I-I, uh, yes, the punch—so kind of you, truly,
but I'm afraid we're leaving, my aunt Winifred and
I. And—and Matilda, of course, Aunt Winnie's
maid, she came with us—and she's leaving,
too . . ." Lindsay fell helplessly silent, incredulous
that she was stammering such nonsense.

"Aye, milord, 'tis true we're leaving, and Lady
Penney bade that we wait right here while she gives
her good-nights." Matilda's firm voice filled the
awkward pause, Lindsay realizing that the feisty
Scotswoman still held fast as a bulldog to her arm.

"A pity. I noted during your headlong flight to

27

the door, Miss Somerset, that your foot appears to have mended nicely—no limp, no injury apparent at all. Is that true?"

The husky timbre of his voice making her shiver, Lindsay once more lost her tongue. But when his smile grew more amused, the speculative look in his eyes clearly daring her to deny she felt right as rain, she realized with a jolt that he was teasing her. Teasing her! He must know she had feigned her swoon, he had to—he was a spy, after all. Surely accomplished spies could recognize such things.

A strange, giddy elation suddenly swept through Lindsay and she smiled up at him, believing she might have found a kindred soul. "Yes, amazingly it is true. Whatever afflicted me passed quite quickly."

"A certain persistent young gentleman, perhaps?"

Wondering if other guests had seen so easily through her ruse to fend off Lord Ambrose, Lindsay gave him a small nod.

"So I suspected. But no matter; at least you're smiling again . . . a most entrancing smile. I can't allow you to leave without first asking the most beautiful woman in London for a dance."

Lindsay scarcely heard Matilda's gasp for the wild thundering of her heart; he had obviously heard Lord Ambrose's gushing compliment, too. But the words this time hadn't sounded inappropriate at all, thrilling her to her toes. In the next instant she was being led to the dance floor, Matilda holding a glass of punch and gaping after them.

Lindsay thought her heart might burst from her

breast when he turned to face her, the chamber orchestra striking up a waltz as he took her in his arms. And suddenly she seemed aware of everything and nothing as the room began to spin around them in a dizzying blur more heady than any swoon.

The strength of his arm at her waist, the powerful breadth of his shoulder beneath her trembling hand. Her gloved fingers seemed to burn in his strong warm ones, though she shivered as with cold. His burnished dark blond hair gleamed in the chandelier's brilliant light, the faintest gold stubble of a beard along his jaw. Was it soft, she wondered, or prickly? The altogether disconcerting scent of him, masculinity and the subtle warmth of bay rum.

He was so tall, too, towering a full head above her, and athletically lean; his face, so dangerously handsome, wasn't pale at all like so many other gentlemen's but browned from the sun, showing clearly he spent time out of doors. And always there was the incredible blue of his eyes, so unusual a shade she had no idea how to name it. Name it . . . oh, Lord, here she was, waltzing with a man whose name she didn't even know while Matilda was probably alerting Aunt Winifred and perhaps the house guards as well!

"I fear, sir . . ." Lindsay swallowed, the intensifying of his gaze upon her the moment she had spoken quite overwhelming. "I fear we haven't been properly introduced. You know my name, but I—"

"Jared. Jared Giles, the Earl of Dovercourt."

"Jared," she said softly, thinking it was the most

wonderful of names. "I-I mean Lord Giles. After all, we've only met—"

"Ah, but we share a secret, don't we? I've seen few women swoon as expertly and prettily as you. And that secret makes us co-conspirators who should clearly call each other by their given names. Would that suit you, Lindsay?"

He spun her then and she couldn't answer, his low, intimate rendering of her name making her feel strangely light-headed, the crowded ballroom flying past her as if they danced on air. For she felt as if she were truly dancing on air, her silken slippers barely touching the floor, Jared held her so closely.

Dear heavens, so closely that her breasts brushed his chest, the rough velvet of his black evening coat rubbing as if against her bare flesh and not the delicate satin of her gown. Stunned by such a wanton thought and how decadent they must appear to the assembled guests, she nonetheless did not try to pull away from him; in fact could not, as if captured by some enchanted spell.

A spell she hoped would last and last forever. Lindsay suddenly felt certain deep in her heart that she had found the hero of her dreams. Her imagination as fired as her senses, she believed this man must know everything about London—everything about the world, for that matter. As a spy, no doubt well traveled, how could he not?

"You smile so beguilingly, Lindsay. What are you thinking?"

His teasing half whisper filling her with reckless abandon, she tilted her head and said very softly, "Only that I hope I will see you again."

Heaven help her, she had said it, truly said it!

Lindsay exulted to herself even as nervousness gripped her, Jared's eyes darkening to an unfathomable blue. Fearing she might have been too bold, too brazen, she made to apologize for her forwardness, but his arm drawing her possessively against him stopped her breath.

"Oh, I fully intend that we'll be seeing much of each other," came his low reply, his gaze raking her face and then falling to her breasts. But his eyes didn't linger there, once more meeting hers. "Tomorrow afternoon, two o'clock. A ride in Hyde Park, with a chaperone, of course—"

"Oh, no, Aunt Winnie would never allow it." The waltz nearly done, Lindsay rushed on breathlessly, sensing at last a chance for adventure. "I suspect she doesn't particularly like you. I'm not sure why, but I have another—"

"My notorious reputation?"

Reddening a bit, Lindsay nodded. "But I don't think you're at all as she described."

"And how was that?"

Lindsay sighed, their conversation not progressing at all as she would have liked, and there was so little time. "A blackguard and a rake and—"

"A seducer of innocents."

"No, no, I was going to say a spy." Seeing his expression suddenly harden, Lindsay felt an undeniable tension in his embrace. "I'm sorry. I'm sure that's not something you wish to hear spoken of so freely, but I think it's wonderful! How noble to serve your country in such heroic fashion—how thrilling it must be for you!"

"If I were a spy, I'm sure it would have its moments," came the dry response. Lindsay took heart that she actually saw a glimmer of amusement re-

turning to his eyes, although his face remained
oddly grim. Hoping she might further cheer him,
she kept her voice light and engaging.

"Well, I'd love to hear about your adventures—
and I hope you still want to see me again no matter
the dreadful things my aunt said about you. But it
can't be during the day; that won't do at all. Evening would be better—yes, half-past midnight
would be perfect. We're always home by eleven.
Aunt Winnie doesn't like staying out too late, and
that would allow plenty of time for everyone to
retire. Then I could meet you outside my aunt's
town house at Sixteen Piccadilly."

"Meet me alone?"

"Of course, it's the only way. Oh, dear, I know
it's very presumptuous of me to even ask—" It was
the most outrageous thing she'd said since she'd
been in London, but . . .

"Half-past midnight will be fine."

Lindsay met his eyes, exhilaration filling her.
"Truly? Tomorrow night?"

His only answer was a brusque nod as the final
strains of the waltz surged around them. Lindsay
wondered if she might have broached every rule
of etiquette, because he stepped so stiffly away
from her when the dance was done. But he still
held her hand, and her hopes soared that she
hadn't made an utter fool of herself when he lifted
her gloved fingers to his lips and gentle kissed
them. Yet his gaze was anything but gentle, burning into hers even as Lindsay heard an unmistakable voice cut through the rising din of conversation.

"Oh, dear, oh, dear, whatever am I to tell Olympia if she hears news of this night? She'll never forgive me, I'm certain of it! Never!''

Lindsay grimaced, imagining the carriage ride home. She turned to flee to her aunt's side, then glanced back to bid Jared good night. But he had already disappeared into the throng filling the dance floor, nowhere to be seen, leaving Lindsay to wonder if she had only imagined the last incredible moments that had been the most exciting of her life.

"Will you 'ave another drink, luv?"

Jared narrowly eyed the tavern keeper's wife, the woman's huge, pendulous breasts close to spilling out of her too-tight bodice as she leaned over the table. A plump white hand slid suggestively along his arm. Sooty eyelashes lowered over dark, sultry eyes. The tavern keeper himself having gone upstairs to bed some time ago, his wife clearly meant to make Jared's stay at their establishment as comfortable as possible.

And perhaps he might have accepted her lusty offer, indeed had fleetingly considered taking her right here on the table as he had last night, all the other guests gone to bed, too, but he had no stomach for the woman's generous proportions this evening. Shrugging off her hand, he swallowed the last of his wine and rose, barely giving her a glance as he walked to the stairs.

"Wot, you mean I stayed up all this time for nothin' to show for me trouble?"

Jared turned to see the woman's face flushed with outrage in the dying firelight. Digging into his pocket, he found a coin and flipped it onto a nearby table. She fell upon the silver crown like a vulture, her expression ingratiating as she tucked the coin deep into her bodice.

"That was sweet of you, luv, but I would have liked another tumble, if you want the truth of it. I'd risk splinters in me bum at any hour for the likes o' you."

Smiling grimly, Jared offered a slight bow and turned back to the stairs, but she made it there before him, her ample rump switching from side to side as she made one last obvious attempt to entice him. But he was already thinking again of another woman's figure, a younger woman with such delectable hourglass curves that waltzing with her tonight had been the worst sort of torture.

A torture, by God, that would end tomorrow night, his burning thoughts of seduction having kept him up even later than usual, the first pale rays of dawn sneaking glimpses through the Boar's Head tavern's closed shutters. With a low groan he pushed open the door to his room and kicked it shut behind him, not caring about the noise or whom he might awaken.

He made short work of his evening clothes, tossing them onto a threadbare stuffed chair before dropping naked onto his bed. No matter that this room was the best offered by the tavern; the air was chill, the mattress lumpy, the blankets scratchy and thin, but he had slept in worse in his day. And the place suited him more than any elegant Mayfair town house he could have rented for the Season where busybody neighbors and fellow members of the ton might watch his every move.

Suited, too, his notorious reputation, Jared thought with a humorless laugh, throwing an arm over his eyes. What better place for a rake such as he other than some latest conquest's boudoir? He could imagine the furtive talk about his choice of lodging when he could easily afford the finest of London's accommodations, and that suited him as well. Such speculation kept idle, frivolous minds and tongues well occupied and thankfully diverted from more serious matters so a man could go about his work.

Another low, grim laugh broke the silence. Jared closed his eyes and allowed the beauteous Miss Lindsay Somerset to once more overwhelm his thoughts. She had been on his mind already, he hadn't been able to think of much else since first setting eyes upon her at the Oglethorpes' ball, so it came as no surprise to him that focusing upon her could so completely and quickly enflame his senses.

He wanted her.

And he would have the minx tomorrow night, perhaps even inside the carriage if she teased him as mercilessly as she had done tonight. Her beguiling smiles, her willingness to allow him to hold her so closely in his arms, her brazen suggestion that he meet her alone, that feigned swoon which had clued him at once that Lindsay Somerset was a shrewd young woman who knew how to manipulate and entice men.

He had met her kind before, his association in the past with several comely chits fresh from the countryside having earned him the reputation of a seducer of innocents. But those young women, not a blushing virgin among them, had proved themselves from the first to be not so pure and innocent and had welcomed his advances as skillfully as married ladies of the ton offered him their sexual favors.

A fat purse and paid coach back to the country had soothed conniving mothers and cuckolded papas, the cunning wantons quite happy to settle down with a local squire or baronet once their fortunes were either enriched or assured. But that hadn't improved his reputation, not that he gave a damn. And seducing Lindsay Somerset wouldn't make matters any worse, and would certainly ease his present discomfort . . .

Jared groaned to himself, almost wishing he had accepted the tavern keeper's wife's lusty invitation. With great difficulty he forced away tantalizing thoughts of Lindsay's breasts pressed against him, breasts so creamy and full and perfectly rounded he could already feel their ripe weight in his hands.

In mute agony, he forced away a heart-stopping vision of her straddling him in the carriage, her slim white thighs gripping his hips, his fingers slipping into the wet heat of her body while her silky blond hair drifted over them like silver gossamer and her beautiful sky-blue eyes begged him to take her.

With a low curse he threw himself onto his side and yanked a blanket over his shoulder, Lindsay Somerset's soft red mouth yielding utterly to his, her whimpers and breathless pants of sweet release echoing in his ears even as he prayed somehow to get some sleep.

Chapter 4

"Lord, another ten minutes to go. Could this
night possibly drag on any slower?"

Lindsay's frustrated whisper was answered by
the low, rhythmic ticking of the mantel clock,
which only made her pace her bedchamber with
mounting impatience.

She had been ready since half-past eleven, the
town house gradually falling still as a tomb, Aunt
Winifred tucked into bed with her nightly cup of
hot chocolate, Matilda and the other servants re-
tired to their attic rooms. Truly, she had begun to
wonder if that blessed hurdle might even be
breached!

Somehow she had endured an endless card party
at the Whimseys' home, elderly neighbors of Aunt
Winifred's, Lindsay feeling through countless
hands of whist as if her excitement might very well
kill her, and now she truly felt as if she were about
to burst. At last an adventure! But where was Jared? Oh, dear, had he forgotten?

Lindsay stopped abruptly at a window over-
looking the broad avenue and swept aside ivory
lace curtains to take another peek, but still no coach
had slowed at the Piccadilly address.

The dull clip-clop of horses' hooves had drawn

her to the window a dozen times, and each time her disappointment had been almost painful, making her wonder again if meeting Jared Giles, the Earl of Dovercourt, had been nothing but a dream. But Aunt Winifred's frantic lecture all the way home had been quite real, as well as her pronouncement in a stricken voice that there would be no more balls for several days, the smelling salts passed more than once under the poor woman's nose.

"Please, please, don't be a dream," Lindsay said fervently to herself, her breath fogging the windowpane. A soft drizzle tapped at the glass, wispy strands of mist creeping over the gaslit thoroughfare. She turned back to the clock. Almost half-past midnight . . .

No longer able to contain herself, Lindsay drew the hood of her cloak over her hair as she quietly left her room, pausing only to close the door behind her before she flew down the hall. Her slippers barely made a sound upon the thick Oriental runner, but she knew the staircase would be a different story. Nearly each step creaked, so she fled down them as quickly as she could, her heart pounding for fear she might awaken one of the servants.

Aunt Winifred, fortunately, slept as soundly as the dead, as did her docile Welsh corgis, Ignatius and Primrose; Lindsay almost imagined she could hear their buzzing snores following after her. But Matilda was known to be a light sleeper—she had to be with such a mistress—yet Lindsay couldn't worry about the Scotswoman now. She raced across the vaulted center hall, nearly slipping on the polished pink marble floor, which only made her heart beat faster.

Made her smile, too, Lindsay once more swept with nervous excitement. Her last obstacle the imposing double front doors, she nearly laughed with relief once she stepped outside into the chilly night air, but her smile faded when she saw that no carriage and snorting horses awaited her at the street. Shrouded from head to foot in her black cloak, she hesitated, not sure whether to venture out closer to the road or resign herself unhappily to bed.

"I was beginning to think perhaps you had reconsidered our rendezvous."

Lindsay spun around as a tall shape materialized from the shadows, her heart settling into her throat when she recognized Jared in the hazy golden halo emanating from the lamplight in the street. "No, no, I didn't see the carriage . . ." She fell silent, gaping as a glossy black coach drawn by four magnificent matched bays eased into motion from where it had been waiting several houses away, only to stop at the head of Aunt Winifred's walk, the burly coachman jumping down from the driver's box to open the door.

"Come."

Lindsay didn't tarry when Jared took her by the elbow and hastened her to the coach, his one simple word making her feel as wondrously elated as she had last night when she had waltzed in his arms. He hadn't forgotten after all! She scarcely set a foot upon the steps when she felt his strong hands encircle her waist to lift her inside, her face growing warm with pleasure that he would be so gentlemanly. A few low words were spoken to the coachman and then Jared joined her, settling into

the empty space beside her as the carriage jolted
into motion.

"I thought we might drive around the city."

"Oh, yes, that would be lovely!" Lindsay knew
she was grinning like an utter fool, but she couldn't
help herself. An adventure at last! With a man who
must know London inside and out, a true hero of
the realm! Her imagination whirling as fast as the
spokes of the carriage wheels, she paid little heed
when Jared pulled a soft plaid blanket from the
opposite seat and draped it over their legs.

"It's a damp night. I don't want you to be cold."

"Oh, it could be freezing, truly, and I doubt I'd
even notice. I've so wanted to see more of London
ever since I arrived here."

"When was that?"

"Just over three weeks ago. That's why I'm surprised I'd never seen you before—at any of the
balls I attended. Twelve, to be exact—well, eleven
if we don't count last night."

Oh, dear, she was uttering nonsense again, Lindsay thought when Jared didn't readily answer, his
handsome face half cloaked in shadow. But her excitement was so great she could barely contain herself, and she decided then and there she wasn't
going to worry how she might or might not appear.

She had considered, since the Oglethorpes' ball,
that it might be rash to sneak out of the house and
meet a gentleman she hardly knew, a notorious
rake, no less, if she believed even an ounce of what
Aunt Winifred had had to say—which she did not.
More likely, jealous tongues had created false ru-
mors about so daring and valiant a man. And how
else would Jared discover that he had found a perfect match for himself if she didn't demonstrate

that she could be as bold and fearlessly adventurous as he?

"Tell me about London, please," she blurted, glancing excitedly out the window. "You must know everything about it—certainly more than Mayfair. That's all I've seen and scarcely much of it, since poor Aunt Winnie is so determined to obey Olympia's demands to the letter."

"Olympia?"

Even hearing the woman's name on Jared's lips made Lindsay wish she hadn't mentioned it. "My stepmother, Lady Somerset. She gave strict instructions that I was to attend balls and little else, no trips to the theater or pleasure gardens, no visits to Hyde Park—"

"We're passing Hyde Park right now. It's dark, but if you'd like, I'll have the driver—"

"Could we?" Lindsay craned her neck to get a glimpse of the broad expanse of green beyond the gaslights along the way, elated that Jared had seemed to read her mind. "At least then I can say I've been there. Then could we pass by Covent Garden, and afterward maybe Vauxhall Gardens?" She felt breathless as she settled back in the seat and pushed her damp hood off her hair. "And you must tell me everything about what we see along the way, will you? And about the places you've traveled? It must be so exciting to be a spy—oh, but I'm not asking that you tell me any military secrets. I've just never been anywhere else but Cornwall, and it's so wonderful that you agreed to meet me tonight and show me the city . . ."

Lindsay suddenly fell still, realizing as heat crept up her face that Jared was studying her intently, his expression the strangest mix of bewilderment and irritation.

"I-I'm sorry. Did I say something to offend?"

Offend? Jared knew he was staring at her like a simpleton, but suddenly he felt like a blind fool.

Damnation, if she hadn't said as much, then *he* would have been the one likely to offend—a bloody virgin's honor, no less! Muttering an oath, he yanked the blanket from across their laps and flung it upon the opposite seat, and would have followed himself if not for the hand suddenly at his arm.

"Jared? Have I done something wrong?"

"No, Miss Somerset, you haven't, but I damned well have." He leaned forward and rapped on the front shell of the carriage. "Back to Piccadilly, man! And make haste!"

"Back to Piccadilly?"

He heard the disappointment in her voice but said nothing, his own displeasure more akin to utter frustration as he shoved all thoughts of seduction from his mind.

How could he have so misread the chit? Sitting rigidly beside her, he glanced at her lovely face and felt another raw stab of regret for his foiled plans.

Big blue eyes stared at him in confusion; a silken tendril of white-blond hair loosened from its comb and brushed against a flawless cheek that he had ached to touch, the tip of her tongue running uncertainly across tempting red lips that he had fully intended to ravage and kiss. But that was before he had realized—as if a doubled fist had slammed into his jaw—that Miss Lindsay Somerset was no cunning wanton accustomed to enticing men, but a young woman both reckless and dangerously naive.

"Jared—Lord Giles, please. Don't take me back to my aunt's, not yet! I can't imagine what could have brought on your sudden change of heart, but I can assure you, no one knows I'm here. I'm very good at sneaking out of houses—I did it all the time in Porthleven—"

"Ah, so this is a common thing for you?" Jared had spoken sharply and he felt another pang of regret, Lindsay's face growing pink with consternation. But the careless wench had to realize the danger in which she had placed herself, her wide-eyed innocence suddenly reminding him so vividly of Elise . . .

"N-not common so much as a necessity, truly. Olympia didn't like that I spent so much time with my friend Corie—she didn't like Corisande Easton at all, or her father and three sisters, for that matter, so what could I do? And, of course, late at night, I couldn't simply announce that I was leaving and then skip out the front door. Everyone had to be sleeping first, and then I would climb out my window and down the elm tree—"

"So you're accustomed to being about when most young ladies are tucked safely in their beds? That might have caused you no ill effect in a village in bloody Cornwall, but traipsing about alone at night in London is another—"

"But I'm not alone, Jared. I'm with you."

Jared grimaced, Lindsay's simple statement hitting him like a blow to the stomach.

Yes, so she was with him, and if she knew how closely she had come to . . .

Shaking his head, he glanced out the window

and realized Hyde Park was fading from sight behind them, the very place where he had hoped to indulge himself in Lindsay Somerset's obvious charms.

He was no saint, but he was no ravager of innocents, either, no matter his soiled reputation. But how many other "proper" gentlemen with spotless reputations would have turned the coach around if in the company of such a tempting companion? And perhaps an heiress to boot, given Lord Ambrose Lamb's ardent pursuit—that spendthrift family making no secret of its need to refill empty pockets in exchange for a lofty title—which made her all the more vulnerable to masculine birds of prey. Not many, dammit, which caused his gut to knot.

If he didn't indulge her insatiable curiosity about London, no doubt she'd find another man more willing, which made Jared once again think of Elise. His beautiful, trusting, younger sister, so vivacious and full of life and its bright promise before she was laid waste by—

"Enough!" Jared bit off to himself, doubting a razor twisting in his belly could give him more pain.

"Jared?"

The small voice, hopeful yet uncertain, was like a poignant echo calling to him from the past. He met Lindsay's lovely eyes, deciding then and there he must teach her not to entrust herself so completely to a man she didn't know. It was time he could ill afford, a night's easy seduction all he had originally had in mind, but for that very reason he resolved to somehow impress upon her that she must take care and guard herself against not only ruthless fortune hunters, but notorious rakes as well . . . if not for her sake, at the very least for the memory of his sister.

"Driver, to Covent Garden!" His shout clearly startling his delectable companion as Lindsay jumped in her seat, Jared nonetheless was amazed at how quickly a brilliant smile overcame her look of astonishment. He smiled, too, trying to ignore the unsettling effect her transformation had upon him. "Forgive my odd behavior; you're absolutely right. I was struck for a moment about your reputation—how things might look to have you out so late, but, of course, you couldn't be in safer hands than mine."

"So you're going to show me London? Truly?"

Finding it difficult to fathom that she wasn't as concerned about her reputation as he professed to be, Jared suppressed a frown and nodded. "As much as you wish to see—with the thought, of course, that we must have you home well before dawn."

"Oh, this is wonderful!"

It was Jared's turn to be startled as Lindsay threw her arms around his neck and hugged him, but she pulled away quickly as if embarrassed, although her happily glowing face gave no sign of it.

"I've so wanted to see Covent Garden. But isn't it a bit late for a performance?"

"Upon the stage, yes, but I thought you might enjoy visiting another place that's very close to the theater . . . a favorite place of mine."

"Lovely! Anything you enjoy I'm sure I will, too."

Jared couldn't help smiling grimly at Lindsay's

utter faith in him; it was easy to imagine the shocked look on her face that was certain to come once they had arrived at their destination. By the end of their time together, he imagined she would be more than glad to remain snuggled safely in her bed, rather than sneaking out at night to partake in the side of London he intended to show her.

"Does this place have a name?"

His grim smile only deepened. "Oh, yes. Tom's."

Chapter 5

"Look at the carriages, dozens of them!" Lindsay eagerly accepted Jared's assistance as she descended from the coach, excitement bubbling inside her. "And surely it's past one o'clock. I would never have thought so many people—"

"This part of London rarely sleeps. Take care to keep your hood pulled down around your face, just as I told you. It would be a pity if someone recognized you and word flew back to your aunt."

Lindsay nodded, thinking it would be more than a pity. Yet she quickly shoved away a worrisome vision of Aunt Winifred clamoring for her smelling salts and took Jared's proffered arm, her hand settling comfortably in the crook of his elbow as if meant to be there.

Just as she felt as if she were meant to be at his side as they proceeded down the crowded walk, the strange yet wonderful sensation of gliding on air once more enveloping her.

The ride to Covent Garden had passed like a dream, Jared pointing out the sights, although Lindsay was chagrined that she had been more entranced by the masculine warmth of his voice than by what he had been saying. And now the strength of his arm and the pressure of his hand covering hers were proving as disconcerting, which made her wonder if Corisande had felt as much about Lord Donovan. Surely she had—

"Wot 'ave you got there, milord, a little mouse hidden under that fine cloak? Ha, it's not even rainin' any longer! Is she afraid she'll melt? Send 'er off and come while away the hours with a woman sure t' please a strappin' gentl'man like yourself."

Lindsay's eyes grew round at the stylishly dressed beauty posed beneath a streetlamp, several other unaccompanied young women casting admiring glances at Jared as they tittered at their friend's brazen remarks.

"Was she—did she call me a mouse?"

"Pay no mind. They're women of the night."

"I *know* what they are," Lindsay said stiffly, not noticing the look of surprise in Jared's eyes. Affronted not because of their carnal profession, but because the lovely redhead had spoken so rudely about her, Lindsay watched the woman saunter toward a bearded gentleman signaling to her from a parked carriage. The two exchanged brief words; then the woman spun around with a bold laugh and called after Jared.

"Too late, luv. Come 'round tomorrow night and I'll be sure to save you a good bit o' my time!"

Then she was gone, disappearing with a swish of bright green silk into the carriage, which set off at a noisy rumble down the street. Sighing, Lindsay glanced up to find a deep frown on Jared's face.

"Oh, dear, please don't be angry for my sake— it was no large insult. I don't know why I allowed her to upset me. It's charity I should be feeling;

Corie taught me that. Charity and compassion. She
saved several girls in Porthleven from such a life—
found them good, honest work, and one even a
husband.''

"Sounds like a saint."

"Funny, that's exactly what I said after Corie
described the man of her—well, the sort of man
she hoped one day to marry, though I told her he
sounded dull as well. Mind you, Corie isn't dull,
oh, no, and I wouldn't call her a saint, either, not
with that temper. But she has a heart of gold—
I'm sure you'll like her when you meet, though
right now she and her husband are—''

"So your friend has married."

"Oh, yes, shortly after I arrived in London. And
it's the most incredible story—oh, look! There's a
sign for Tom's Cellar up ahead. Is that the place?''

Jared gave a brusque nod, still disgruntled that
Lindsay hadn't seemed shocked at all by the loose
women plying their trade on the street, a bawdy
sight he had hoped might send her scurrying back
to their carriage to demand immediate escort
home.

It was clear that the freedom she had enjoyed in
Cornwall had perhaps gained her a wider view of
the world than other young women of her station
shared, and her saintly friend Corisande had obviously helped things along. Yet Tom's, well, that
was another matter.

"Don't forget about your hood," he reminded
her, the sound of raucous singing growing louder
as they approached a rather nondescript brick
building at one side of which was an archway leading down a flank of stone steps. He found some

comfort that the entrance stank of cider and urine, but if Lindsay had noticed, she gave no note of it, her eyes wide with curiosity.

"Tom's is down there?"

Again he nodded, the breathless excitement in her voice suddenly making him want to shake her. Did the chit imagine they were about to come upon some regal ballroom? A fashionable coffeehouse? Couldn't she see the dinginess all around them?

Almost angrily, he drew her down the damp steps, holding her arm firmly so she wouldn't slip. Dank moist air clouded with tobacco smoke enveloped them, hazy light spilling from a half-opened door at the bottom of the stairs. The singing had grown so boisterous that he couldn't have heard anything Lindsay said unless she shouted.

And she was trying to get his attention, raising her voice to ask him what manner of place was Tom's even as she was drawn into a long, low-ceilinged room that was clearly a cellar, just as the painted sign outside had read. But her words were drowned out by the noise—truly, the cacophony couldn't be described as anything but noise—of more than a hundred men's voices raised in singsong, the barking of dogs and a constant outcry for refills of cider and ale.

She blinked, dense whorls of smoke making her eyes tear, and saw that women moved freely among the clamorous throng, most dressed quite shabbily, unlike the stylish courtesans on the street, but laughing and smiling just as boldly. Lindsay tried to smile, too, but she felt her enthusiasm flagging as she scanned the plainly furnished room, the long trestle tables and side booths filled with drunken revelers, the feeble light cast from three iron chandeliers suspended from rustic beams making her surroundings appear fuzzy and indistinct.

"Come. I see an empty box near the back."

Jared had shouted, startling her, but she accompanied him with as much eagerness as she could muster, grateful for his guiding hand at her arm.

He seemed very much at ease no matter the bedlam, and she reminded herself that he had said Tom's Cellar was one of his favorite places. Perhaps as a military spy, his life constantly fraught with danger, he felt he could drop his guard amidst such pandemonium. Either that or it suited his adventurous nature, which made her resolve to relax and enjoy herself as well.

Actually, Tom's was little different from Oliver and Rebecca Trelawny's quayside inn in Porthleven. Perhaps not as rowdy, Lindsay told herself as she slid onto a bench Jared pulled out for her, but she had been there with Corisande on nights when the village fishermen had celebrated a record catch of pilchards.

Sea chanteys and lively conversation had drowned out talk of the next smuggling run from France, Lindsay always listening silently while Captain Trelawny and Corisande plotted where it might be safest to land his ship, the *Fair Betty*. Of course, she couldn't tell Jared about how she'd sometimes helped with the landings—at least not until they knew each other better. He worked for King and country, after all, and fair trading couldn't be more illegal.

"What do you think?"

Lindsay smiled brightly as Jared sat down beside her, a pretty serving woman plunking two brimming mugs of ale on the table in front of them. In this far corner the singing seemed not half so loud, so she didn't have to shout.

"It's lovely—everyone is so merry. I can see why you enjoy it so much." Gamely she took a sip of ale, trying not to grimace. "Oh, this is very good. You should try yours."

He did, but his sip—more a draught—lasted much longer than hers. And when he set the mug down with a thunk, Jared looked so displeased that Lindsay wondered if it was something she had said. "Is the ale not to your liking?"

"It's fine. Perfect."

"Yes, mine, too." Wondering at the irritation in his voice, Lindsay took another small sip, her cheeks heating under his close scrutiny. Lord, had a man's eyes ever been so blue? "If the truth be known, I've never tasted the drink before—oh!"

She had nearly dropped her mug, Jared moving so close to her on the bench that his thigh pressed into her leg . . . a hard, wholly masculine thigh, the heat of him burning through her cloak. Suddenly feeling as light-headed as she had at the ball, Lindsay glanced around them, her laughter a shade too bright. "Heavens, look up there! Do you see them? Two little boys peering down from the beams?"

She pointed, and thankfully Jared's gaze followed her finger, which presented a chance for her to ease away from him, if only to relieve the fierce beating of her heart. Yet his low chuckle distracted her; truly, she couldn't recall hearing him laugh before.

"Pickpockets, I'd wager, keeping a sharp lookout over the room. Watch."

She did, her eyes widening as one of the boys

pointed wildly at an inebriated gentleman who had just toppled off his chair, a flurry of hands reaching out to help him. Meanwhile, a third boy, no more than seven or eight and wearing the dirty rags of a street urchin, scurried as if out of nowhere and availed himself of the commotion by fleecing the pockets of all those bending to help the drunken fellow back to his seat. In a flash the young thief was gone, slipping into the throng.

"Shouldn't we do something? Say something?" Lindsay began to rise, but Jared stopped her, his hand at her arm.

"Why? I've always admired anyone who can survive by his wits. Let them be."

The singsong abruptly ending couldn't have been more jarring to Lindsay than the harshness in Jared's voice, his expression grown hard, too. As different as night and day from the charming gentleman at the Oglethorpe ball. She stared at him, stunned. But in the next instant he was smiling at her, wry amusement in his deep blue eyes, leaving Lindsay to wonder if perhaps the ale was tampering with her perception.

"It's all part of an evening's entertainment, wouldn't you say? Look over there."

Lindsay did, following Jared's gaze to an opposite box where a noisy group of four gentlemen appeared to be poking fun at a fifth companion, a sullen old fellow who sat slumped against the wall with a mug balanced upon his prodigious belly.

"By Jove, have you ever seen such a sour face?" exclaimed one of the men, mimicking a dour expression. "If I was a new babe born into the honorable Dr. Foote's hands, I'd take one look at that frightful puss and turn 'round to climb right back into my mother's womb!"

Uproarious laughter erupted, although the old doctor appeared unconcerned that he was the butt of the joke, his expression not lightening a whit. He yawned and closed his eyes, in fact, as if to take a short snooze right there in the box, and therein lay his mistake. Lindsay watched fascinated as the doctor's comrades appeared to conspire among themselves in whispers and choked glee; then one of the men rose and disappeared into the crowd.

"Jared, what—"

She was silenced as Jared raised a finger to his lips and inclined his head toward the opposite box. The men there were elbowing one another and grinning as they saw their companion returning. And with the fellow was as robust a woman as any Lindsay had seen, a grin on her plain face, too, until she stopped at the table and gave the smirking gentlemen a broad wink. Then she spread her feet wide and propped her big fists on her hips, her indignant voice filling the cellar.

"Well, well, Arthur Foote, did you think you could hide from me forever? Spread me legs and left me nine months later with a bawlin' babe, you did, and now I've bloody well found you!"

"A babe? Me? What?" blustered the hapless doctor, fully awake and struggling to his feet while his companions could barely contain their mirth around him. "I say, young woman, you've got the wrong—"

"Don't be speakin' to me like a child, you rummy bastard! Deny it if you will, but you're the father sure as I'm standin' here! The poor thing even looks like you!"

"But that cannot be, dear lady. I've never seen you before!"

"Wot, now? You're calling me a liar?"

Lindsay gasped, the woman's outraged shriek hanging in the air.

"No, no—well, yes, yes, I am—God in heaven! Fend her off me! Fend her off!"

Lindsay watched the wild melee in amazement. The woman shook her fists and tried to reach the doctor cowering across the table, and the poor man's friends appeared to be doing their best to hold her back. Finally a cry went up from one of the gentlemen for the doctor to give the woman a half guinea to appease her, which the stricken fellow did at once, although he dared only to flip the coin onto the floor. The woman swept up the silver with a triumphant laugh, and again perched her hands on her broad hips.

"Aye, well, mayhap 'twas a mistake and you're not the man I'm seekin'. Here, I'll give you a kiss and be gone."

Under much protestation the doctor was made to come forward, the woman catching him by his protruding ears and planting her lips upon his cheek in a noisy smack that sent everyone near into howls of laughter. But another howl joined theirs, the doctor's eyes grown wide with horror.

"She bit me! The wench bit me! Good God, what shall I do? She's mad, surely, like a rabid beast! I'm going to die! I'm going to sicken and die!"

"I say, Foote, a red-hot poker could be used to cleanse the wound," cried one of the conspirators.

"No, no, I'll use the point of my sword to cut out the affected part—Dr. Foote? Dr. Foote?"

Lindsay felt a pang for the poor man as he fled

from his company, a pudgy hand pressed to his cheek, his pitiful complaints drowned out as revelers all around burst into another bawdy song.

"I'm sorry. I pointed them out to you only because I thought you would be amused."

Lindsay turned to find Jared studying her, and she quickly smiled, although she didn't feel quite as enthusiastic about Tom's Cellar as she had a few moments ago. "It was amusing, in a way . . ."

She fell silent, a flicker of something in Jared's eyes making her stop.

Oh, dear, she didn't want him to think she was having a dreadful time, and she wasn't, truly. Her outing thus far had been so much more interesting than another insufferable ball, and, of course, she wouldn't rather be anywhere else than with him.

"Actually, I found their prank very clever, although I'm sure that unlucky doctor doesn't think so." A delicious thought struck her, making her grin. "I could see using such a ruse on my stepmother, but with a bit of a twist—perhaps someone claiming to be her bastard son or daughter. Now, *that* would straighten her sausage curls."

Jared found himself chuckling, mesmerized by the mischievous glint in Lindsay's eyes. Yet in the next instant he felt his exasperation return, for nothing seemed to be upsetting her.

He had thought that he'd seen some measure of distress on her face a moment ago, which had made him hopeful that she might wish to return home, having stomached enough of Tom's Cellar. But now she couldn't appear more merry, as if being in such a raucous place was as common as teatime in the afternoon. Obviously a more drastic course of action was needed; dammit, the chit was having too much fun. He lifted his mug and drained it, which gave him a sudden idea.

"Drink up and I'll order us another."

Chapter 6

"Drink up?" Lindsay glanced at her mug, still brimming with dark amber ale, as she had taken only a few sips.

"You said you liked it, didn't you?"

"Oh, yes, it's quite good," she fibbed, not wanting to offend. Lifting her mug, she took a healthy swallow just to prove how much she enjoyed it and, surprisingly enough, found she had grown slightly more accustomed to the tangy, somewhat bitter taste. She took another deep swallow, a pleasant warmth working all the way down to her toes even before she had set the half-empty mug upon the table.

Either that or it was the disconcerting sensation of Jared sitting so close to her, Lindsay thought, his hard thigh still pressed against her leg. Yet he stood in the next instant to beckon a serving woman and the warmth remained, making her reach for the embroidered silk frogs of her cloak. It was growing quite stuffy down here, so many people, the smelly tobacco smoke, the noise, her cheeks feeling as flushed as the rest of her.

Lindsay started as strong fingers covered hers, gently pulling her hands from the frog at her throat. She met Jared's eyes, not aware until now that he had sat back down beside her.

"I'm sorry, Lindsay, you'll have to keep your cloak on, remember? We can't risk anyone recognizing—"

"Oh, please, it's grown so warm. I just want to loosen it a bit, not take it off."

She smiled with sheer gratitude as he nodded, but once more he caught her hands when she started to lift them.

"Let me."

The rich baritone of his voice catching her breath, Lindsay could only stare at him. She tilted her chin a notch as his hands moved to the fastening at her throat; when his fingers grazed her flesh, she began to tremble.

He undid the first frog and slid his hand along the inside of her cloak to the next, his fingers skimming the curve of her breast and making her wonder if he could feel how wildly her heart was beating. By the third she was more than ready for the fresh mug of ale plunked down in front of her, anything to cool the searing flame in her cheeks.

"That's fine—thank you," she somehow managed to whisper when Jared unfastened the fourth and last frog, certain he couldn't have heard her for the thunderous voices raised in song. It seemed in the past moments that Tom's Cellar had grown even rowdier. Patrons slammed their mugs upon tables to keep time with the bawdy tumble of verses. Women squealed as they were drawn by drunken gentlemen into the center of the room to dance.

Lindsay barely waited for Jared to move away from her before she lifted her full mug and drank deeply, hoping the ale might calm her reeling senses. He seemed to be studying her again, and she noticed he wasn't touching his fresh mug, while she had nearly emptied hers. Chagrin overwhelmed her. At once she lowered the mug from her mouth, and so quickly that ale dribbled down her chin. It made her giggle—how ridiculous she must look—and she lifted her hand to swipe the stuff away.

"Let me, Lindsay."

His warm fingers were cupping her chin before she could blink, his thumb caressing away the spill.

He leaned closer. She sucked in her breath, mesmerized by the indescribable blue of his eyes.

Mesmerized by his angular features, any one of them enough to call a man handsome ... broad cheekbones; a straight, almost hawkish nose; a boldly curved mouth ... all combined to forge a countenance of devastating masculinity unlike any she'd seen.

Oh, Lord, mesmerized by the wondrous sensation of his thumb gliding from her chin to gently trace her lower lip, then the curve of her cheek. His hand cradling her face, she inclined her head as if fitting herself to his palm, not a smooth, aristocrat's palm, but one roughened and callused as a working man's might be.

And he *was* a working man after all, a spy who had no doubt risked his life countless times for his country—the thought suddenly hitting her like a bolt that she really knew so little about him. And she so desperately wanted to know him, to know everything about him ...

"Oh, Jared, tell me—" Her eyes widened, a most unladylike belch bursting from her throat that shattered the breathless spell that gripped her. Mortified to her toes she looked away, but Jared's gentle fingers at her chin drew her gaze back to his face, his eyes, to her relief, filled with studied humor.

"It's the ale, Lindsay, nothing more. And do you know the best way to stop it from happening again?"

She shook her head, the crowded room around her still moving when she grew still and tried to focus upon his face.

"You must drink some more."

"More?" This time a loud hiccup erupted, Lindsay clapping her hand over her mouth to repeat in a muffled voice, "Truly, Jared? More?"

"Truly. Finish your ale; then you must have mine."

"Yours, too?"

In answer he placed his brimming mug in Lindsay's hand; she looked doubtfully at the frothy brew, but another noisy hiccup made her take a long draught, so long and deep that it was Jared who finally coaxed the mug away from her.

"I think that should do it."

"Really?" Suddenly feeling quite woozy, Lindsay gripped the edge of the table, which seemed to be moving as well. She held very still for a moment, waiting, waiting, a self-satisfied smirk breaking over her face when no further hiccups were heard. "Ha! You were right! I feel so much—"

Lindsay gaped at Jared, her second belch so loud that he broke into a laugh. She giggled, too, shrugging her shoulders and spreading her hands wide, which proved a grave mistake as she let go of the table.

Suddenly she felt herself falling backward and she would have tumbled altogether from the bench if Jared hadn't caught her around the waist. Throwing her arms around his neck as he drew her back up beside him, Lindsay couldn't seem to stop giggling even as she fought to catch her breath.

"I . . . I guess I'll just have to drink some more ale—"

"No, I think instead it's time I take you home."

"Home?" She shook her head vigorously, so vigorously that the cellar spun around her and she held onto Jared for dear life. "Oh, dear, why is everything moving?"

"Yes, Miss Somerset, I'd say it's well past your bedtime."

Lindsay gasped as she felt herself being lifted in the air, a fresh burst of giggles overwhelming her. "Oh, Jared, let's waltz, shall we? Just like last night—it was so wonderful, like a dream—whoops!"

The world had suddenly become topsy-turvy. Lindsay was aware in a foggy corner of her mind that she had been thrown over Jared's shoulder, but she couldn't see a thing, her ample hood covering her face. Hiccuping in between giggles, she began to swing her dangling arms in time with the ribald song resonating around her, doing her best to sing along with the lively tune:

What shall we do with a drunken sailor?
What shall we do with a drunken sailor?
What shall we do with a drunken sailor,
    Early in the morning?

Shave him on the belly with a rusty razor,
Shave him on the belly with a rusty razor,
Shave him on the belly with a rusty razor,
    Early in the morning!

She even went so far as to drum upon something lean and hard until a gentleman's voice startled her.

"I say, man, will you look at that? There's a fellow due for some spirited sport tonight, the lucky bastard."

"Oh, yes, the lucky bastard!" she roared, sputtering at the blond hair in her mouth. In the next moment she was jounced so soundly that she lost her breath, Jared's shoulder digging into her stomach.

"Dammit, woman, be still!"

"Shhh, Lindsay, he says be still," she admonished herself, inhaling deeply of the clear, cool air seeping under her hood.

It had grown very dark, too, the boisterous singing becoming dim, other sounds cutting through the blurry cobwebs cluttering her mind. The sharp clip-clop of hooves, the clatter of carriage wheels, Jared's deep voice calling out for a coach to be brought 'round. Then she felt herself being dumped gently onto something soft and velvet, Lindsay grinning as a strong hiccup rocked her.

"You better . . . order more ale for me, Jared. I can't . . . stop."

"So I see," Jared muttered, wondering how he was ever going to get Lindsay tucked into her bed without her waking the entire household.

It appeared his idea to get her soused had

worked too well; he could imagine the wretched headache she would suffer come morning. But if that would keep the reckless chit from venturing out again late at night, then it had been worth it, and he hoped she would be so sick, she wouldn't wish to see him again, either. Not when she realized he had lied to her, encouraging her to drink to quiet her hiccups, no less.

Jared drew Lindsay under his arm as the coach jolted around a corner, a pang of regret hitting him as she snuggled blearily against him, her cheek pressed against his overcoat, her breath smelling like a drunken sailor's. But he suppressed the rare feeling and drew back her hood, that stifling black hood which she had endured without complaint and which had so completely hidden the exquisite riot of blond hair that spilled out over his lap.

He fingered a silken strand, the unusual shade a striking mix of platinum and spun silver. He hadn't realized how long it was until tonight, down to her waist; she had worn it wound in a fashionable chignon last evening. She had looked so lovely, as brilliant as a sunny day in her yellow gown, her magnificent hair coiled by a creamy strand of seed pearls. But he much preferred it streaming loose around her as it was now—

Jared cursed. "Blast it, man, what the hell does it matter if the stuff is loose or the wench is bald?" he bit out, turning to stare through the window.

"Jared? Did you say something?"

Her voice was as silky-soft as her hair; nonetheless, he steeled himself against its bewitching effect and ignored her. Yet that did not prevent him from recalling how smooth her skin had been beneath his fingers when he'd unfastened her cloak, his hand grazing the tender ripeness of her breasts, her heart beating crazily beneath his fingertips, the delicate scent of her perfume—lily of the valley—growing headier from the warmth of her body.

Dammit, his own physical reaction at that moment had been anything but gentlemanly, his thoughts straying now as with a will of their own to how close he had come earlier that night to ravaging her. Even knowing of her innocence did not ease the sudden tightness in his lower body and he groaned, dropping his head back against the cushion and shutting his eyes.

At least her hiccups had ceased, which would aid him in getting her into the house. But if she—by God, had a woman ever looked so beautiful even in belching?

"Jared?"

He glanced down to find her staring up at him, her sleepy eyes luminous in the glow from passing lamplights. If she had been dizzy before, he imagined now she was simply exhausted, the ale having taken its toll. But still she gazed at him as if waiting for him to speak.

"Go to sleep, Lindsay," he bade her, but she stubbornly shook her head.

"No, no, tell me things."

"Things?"

She snuggled closer, one hand dropping into his lap, making Jared groan again.

"Places . . . where you've been . . . so lucky . . ."

He threw his head back, his jaw growing tight. Lucky? If the chit only knew. Yet he couldn't blame her for an innocent request, or for the tension coiling like a poisonous snake in his gut. Why not indulge her? She wouldn't remember a thing come morning.

"Very well. I once called India my home."

She made no sound, her fingers curled in his coat, and he imagined when he saw her lashes droop that she might have even fallen asleep.

"We lived in Calcutta, in a huge house with so many servants I couldn't name them." Yet that wasn't true; he had known all the servants, even considered most his friends, never imagining that . . .

Jared grimaced as the snake inside him sank its fangs into his flesh, a deep chill coming over him.

Was he a bloody fool? Did he think for a moment that the past had eased its death grip enough to permit him to talk casually of the life he had known?

"Calcutta . . . India. More, Jared."

More? His bitter laugh made Lindsay start, her eyes fluttering open to stare once more into his. Just as he stared down at her, suddenly feeling cruel and even more a fool for taking this reckless little bird under his wing.

So she reminded him of Elise. Did he truly think he could save her if fate had already decreed that she would suffer as wretchedly as his sister had suffered?

His gaze swept her face, her lovely features unmarred by care or woe, her blue eyes clear as a crystal pool and offset by dense lashes and delicate winged brows as dark as her hair was light. And her lips, bespeaking innocence yet generously full and provocative as sin. He had indulged her. Why not indulge himself if, indeed, she had already been chosen through her rash nature to be a victim of the brutality that was life?

"You want to hear more, Lindsay?" he taunted

her in a half whisper, fixing his gaze upon her mouth even as she nodded sleepily. "More about Calcutta, where we dined in the morning on pine-apple and at night drank sweet cherry brandy as red as your lips?"

"Sweet . . ." came her soft murmur.

"Yes, sweet," he echoed, drawing her roughly against him as he crushed his mouth upon hers.

He heard a gasp, felt her hands fisting in his coat, then thought of nothing else but the warmth of her lips, the pliant softness of them. Her mouth opened to his fierce onslaught like a fragile flower to rain, her captured breath meeting his, filling him.

As he filled her mouth with his tongue, plundering, ravishing, the lingering taste of ale melding with a sweetness that seemed her very own, an essence so intoxicating that he feared wildly that he might not be able to stop—

"Piccadilly, milord!"

The coachman's voice a welcome warning bell in his brain, Jared tore himself from Lindsay's mouth and gathered her limp form in his arms, for her lush body had gone so slack as to lead him to think she had fainted.

"Just as bloody well." The door was barely opened before Jared lunged from the carriage, Lindsay's weight so slight that he felt as if he bore no burden at all. "Wait here, man. I'll be no more than a moment."

So Jared hoped, taking note that the town house remained dark, no one aware that the beauteous Miss Somerset had been out sampling the seamier side of London. Treading light as a thief once he entered the front double doors, he suddenly realized that he had no idea where Lindsay's bedchamber might be.

"Lindsay, wake up." He shook her, but the chit slept on within his arms as peacefully as a newborn kitten. "Lindsay," he hissed, a bit louder this time. "I need you to show me—"

"I'll lead the way, milord, but on one condition."

Jared spun around, his low oath hanging in the air as a stout apparition swathed in a prim white night-robe came out from behind the open door. Matilda, Lady Penney's maid, set her hands squarely on her hips.

"Swear to me ye haven't touched the lass—on pain that yer soul writhe in eternal hellfire if ye lie—and I'll say nothing of this night's odd business to my mistress. Do ye understand me well, milord?"

Jared gave a nod, feeling like a green schoolboy under the Scotswoman's stern scrutiny.

"So do ye bring her back as pure as she left here or no?"

He swallowed a twinge of anger, wholly unused to explaining himself to anyone. But he could see, in this instance, that he had no choice.

"I haven't touched her, or compromised her in any fashion. On that I give you my word."

Silence reigned for what seemed an interminable moment; then Matilda finally nodded. "Very well, then, follow me. And take care ye step where I do, for the stairs squeak like the devil."

Having no idea what this woman's knowledge might portend for Lindsay, Jared also told himself firmly that it was none of his concern as he followed Matilda up an imposing staircase. Then came a long hallway, their little trio passing by a closed door from which emanated the most outrageous snores, until they came at last to a room at the front of the house.

"This'll be Miss Somerset's bedchamber, not that I imagine ye'll be seeing it again after this night."

Making no reply to Matilda's thinly veiled reprimand, Jared carried Lindsay into the decidedly feminine apartment with its lace curtains and pastel pink wallpaper and laid her on the canopied four-poster, the bedclothes already turned down as if awaiting her return, a lamp burning brightly on a side table. Imagining no matter his sworn oath what the Scotswoman must be thinking to see Lindsay in such bedraggled condition, the smell of ale and tobacco clinging to her cloak and tousled hair, he decided it was time he left.

Perhaps even London, he thought darkly, though he knew that must wait until his business was accomplished.

"Good night to ye, then, Lord Giles," came Matilda's voice, her back to him as she began to divest a limp Lindsay of her soiled slippers. "I take it ye can find yer way out?"

He could tell from the Scotswoman's tone that she didn't expect an answer, and he didn't give one. His face as grim as she had sounded, he couldn't wait to leave the house, and when he did, he closed the door firmly behind him.

As firmly as he trusted Lindsay Somerset was well out of his life, although, settling once more into the carriage, he couldn't help thinking that his oath to Matilda hadn't been entirely true.

So he had kissed the chit. Did that make him a liar? God knows he already had enough transgressions heaped upon his soul to send him straight to hell.

"Driver, the Boar's Head tavern!" he commanded the coachman, his gaze drawn to the pale light streaming from the windows of Lindsay's room even as he made himself look away.

Chapter 7

"**O**h, Lord."

Lindsay slumped onto her side and gripped her head, her low groan sounding as loud to her as the crashing of cymbals. She wondered weakly if she could open her eyes. She wanted to, but it seemed her eyelids were stuck to her lower lashes, either that or the sensation was some dire warning that she should keep her eyes firmly closed.

She could tell it was daylight. Her bedchamber was always bright in the morning, especially on sunny mornings. And she knew it was brilliant outside for the warm rays slanting across her face, which made her slit her eyes to take a peek.

"Oh . . . oh, no." Her fresh groan like a banshee's shriek inside her aching head, Lindsay now knew why she should well keep her eyes shut, the sunlight blinding her. She rolled onto her stomach and lay there limp as a rag, wishing she had something to drink to wash the unpleasant taste of ale from her mouth. Oh, Lord, ale . . .

"Good morning, miss, and a fine morning it is, too! I've brought yer breakfast."

Lindsay didn't move except for a feeble flutter of her hand, Matilda's cheery voice making her wince.

"My, my, miss, ye're looking a bit peaked—wan as a ghost, I'd say. I hope ye're not coming down with a cold."

Anything, Lindsay thought miserably, a nasty cold, a fever, *anything* would be better than how she felt at that moment.

"I-I'm fine, Matilda—well, not truly," she somehow managed, attempting a second time to open her eyes. "I fear something I ate or drank at the Whimseys' card party last night didn't agree with me."

"Aye, that tiny bit of sherry, no doubt."

Matilda had spoken so sharply that Lindsay lifted her head, but the stout Scotswoman was busy sprinkling what appeared to be loose tea into a cup of steaming water.

"Is . . . is that for me?"

"Ha! Surely not for me, lass. I've no headache such as the one plaguing ye this bright morning."

"Headache . . . how—"

"Never ye mind. Just roll yerself over and sit up so ye can drink." Matilda cut her off sternly, her deep brown eyes fixed on Lindsay as she held out the cup. "Ye'll feel better after a sip or two of my willow bark tea, but, Lord knows, mayhap I should just let ye suffer."

Lindsay was so stunned she couldn't but obey, no matter that her head seemed to pound all the more as she lifted herself to a sitting position. With trembling hands she took the cup and brought it to her lips, which made the Scotswoman cluck her tongue disapprovingly.

"Aye, from the look of ye when Lord Giles carried ye into the house at three this morn, I'd say ye're lucky to be awake before noon. Stunk like a drunken sailor, ye did—"

"You saw the Earl of Dov—I mean me? Both of us?"

Matilda's brusque nod made Lindsay gulp, fragmented memories of the night before falling together like a puzzle in her mind.

What shall we do with a drunken sailor? What shall we do—

She grimaced and shoved the bawdy drinking song from her thoughts even as she was struck by another foggy recollection of her drumming on Jared's lower back and his . . . his—oh, dear, she hadn't, had she?

Her face burning, Lindsay slumped against the headboard.

"Now, now, miss, drink yer tea. The world hasn't come to an end. Lord Giles assured me he laid no hand upon ye—I made him swear an oath ye're a virgin still."

"Matilda!"

"Aye, and rightly so I did! 'Tis not my place to be judging yer actions, but I can't imagine what possessed ye to traipse so late from the house, and ye being a proper-brought-up young lady! Certainly the earl's a fine-looking man, but ye heard well what Lady Penney thinks of him."

"Oh, no, Aunt Winnie!" Lindsay had nearly dropped the cup, the hot tea she gulped scalding her throat. "She doesn't know about last night, does she?"

"Know? Have ye any sense in yer head, lass? If I told my mistress of yer doings, she'd fall to her bed with the vapors and mayhap never arise!"

Relief flooding through her, Lindsay set the teacup on the bedside table and looked earnestly at Matilda. "And she must never know, you must promise me, please promise me. I wouldn't want to hurt her, she's been so kind."

"Aye, so she has. But if I hold my tongue, what will ye promise me then?"

"Promise . . . me to you?" As the Scotswoman nodded firmly, Lindsay felt a sinking sensation in her stomach. "If . . . if you mean will I say I won't see Jared again—"

"Jared, is it?" Looking wholly exasperated, the Scotswoman flung up her hands. "Heavens, lass, ye've only just met him and already ye're calling him by his given name?"

"Of course. What else would I call the man I plan to marry? 'Lord Giles' seems silly, and besides, he asked me to call him Jared . . . Matilda?"

The old Scotswoman's face had gone chalk-white. Lindsay threw aside the bedclothes in alarm, but Matilda had already sought the comfort of a chair, plopping down as Lindsay rushed to her side. Her head was throbbing, her stomach suddenly queasy, but she couldn't think of her discomfort now. She took the maid's plump hand in her own.

"Matilda, what's wrong—"

"Wrong? Lord in heaven, lass, are ye so determined to bring Lady Somerset's wrath down upon yer poor aunt?"

At the Scotswoman's poignant dismay, Lindsay had to grit her teeth, just as she had done so many times in Porthleven because her domineering stepmother wielded such power to distress people. For years she had watched Olympia belittle and browbeat her father, Randolph Somerset finally turning to strong drink as a refuge from the second wife he had brought to his home not long after Lindsay's mother had succumbed to a fever.

Lindsay couldn't count the occasions she had wanted to rail at the ridiculous woman—double that number the times she had prevented Corisande from venting her legendary temper on her best friend's behalf—but Lindsay's love for her father had kept her from making his life any more miserable than it already was. Yet somewhere this tyranny had to stop, if not for her father, at least for herself. It had to!

That was why she would wed no man who would allow that woman to govern their lives. And if once married she was adventuring far, far away from Cornwall, so much the better. But no matter if near or far, she knew in her heart that a bold spy and hero of the realm like Jared Giles wouldn't hesitate to stand up to the likes of Olympia Somerset.

"Matilda, you don't have to fear for Aunt Winnie, I promise you. Jared will see to my stepmother. But I won't promise not to see him again."

"Aye, so I thought ye'd say."

"And he's not anything at all like Aunt Winnie described—surely not a rogue, but gallant and brave and daring, everything I've always dreamed for a husband."

"Very well, then, if he's all these fine things, what does Lord Giles say to yer plans to wed? Not that it's any of my business, mind ye, but my dear mistress and her welfare is my affair."

"Well . . ." Lindsay paused, not wanting to admit that Jared was as unaware of her fond hopes as she was determined to make them become reality. "He wouldn't have agreed to meet me last night if his

intentions weren't honorable. What true gentleman
would risk dire censure from his peers by misleading me? After all, you said he did swear."

"Aye, he did, and I believed him. But he's won
a notorious reputation for himself, lass."

"No more than jealous gossip, Matilda, surely,
and I refuse to believe it. And Jared made no move
toward me last night that was anything but gentlemanly and respectable."

As Matilda sighed and looked away, Lindsay
didn't elaborate further, her face grown quite warm
as more memories flooded upon her—Jared unfastening her cloak, his fingers grazing her breasts.
Jared caressing the ale from her chin. And there
was another vision that came to her, more sensation than memory, making her cheeks flame hotter.

A sensation of power . . . power and searing possession in a kiss so dark and hungry that she felt
her breath falter, her hands fisting in the white
linen of her nightgown. Oh, Lord, had Jared really—

"All right, lass, yer secret is safe with me, but for
one week, no longer."

Lindsay blinked, wrenched back rudely to reality. "One—one week?" she echoed, confused.

"Aye, and no more. If Lord Giles's intentions are
as honorable as ye say, and he's willing to escort
ye about the city with no proper chaperone, then I
expect he'll soon be making a formal proposal to
Lady Penney about taking ye for his wife. Mayhap
this very morning he's even posted a letter to Sir
Randolph asking for yer hand in God's holy mat-
rimony—to my mind a prudent thing to do, given
last night."

With that Matilda rose from the chair and bustled to the door, leaving Lindsay so stunned that she merely stared after her.

"Back to bed with ye, miss, and finish yer willow bark tea," came a final admonishment right before Matilda disappeared into the hall. "I'll call for a bath so ye can wash the last of that stench from yer hair."

Lindsay barely heard her, her head pounding twice as hard.

One week.

One week to show Jared she was as bold and adventuresome as he could hope for in a bride— and surely last night she had impressed upon him that she wasn't like most other marriageable young women in London for the Season. Would any of them have dared venture out late at night to see more of the city? Dared to enter a place called Tom's Cellar and down enough ale to—

Lindsay didn't finish the thought, her stomach lurching so crazily that she knew she was going to be sick. She barely made it to the chamber pot . . . so much for Matilda's willow bark tea making her feel any better. When she was done she collapsed upon the bed, wondering weakly how she might contact Jared.

Except she had no idea where in the West End he resided, the realization striking her with fresh intensity that she really knew so little about him. Only that he was an earl and a spy who found some solace in raucous places like Tom's Cellar— making Lindsay groan and roll over onto her side, away from the blinding morning sunlight streaming through the windows.

Yet she indistinctly remembered him saying something about India—yes, she was almost cer-

tain of it, the fuzzy memory becoming more focused. Something about Calcutta and pineapples
and sweet cherry brandy, and then he had . . .

"Lindsay, are you awake? Oh, my dear girl, such
wonderful news! Wonderful news!"

Groaning to herself, Lindsay sat up just as Aunt
Winifred burst into the room in a flurry of pink
silk, her two Welsh corgis, Primrose and Ignatius,
as sturdy as sausages, trotting obediently in her
wake.

"I thought it would never come—what a dreadful slight that would have been—but my dear
friend Lady Sefton didn't fail me. Look!"

As Aunt Winifred excitedly waved an ivory-
colored card, Lindsay forced a smile even though
she felt her spirits sinking. "A letter, Aunt Winnie?" she asked stupidly, knowing better but wishing all the same that Primrose and Ignatius might
transform themselves from docile pets into frenzied
hounds with a penchant for chewing paper.

"A letter? Of course not, dear child, it's a
voucher of admission to Almack's! We'll be attend-
ing a ball there this very night! Oh, this is wonderful. Olympia will be so pleased. Only the very
best sort are invited to join by the Lady Patronesses—you won't fail to make an excellent match
now!"

As Aunt Winifred hurried across the room and
flung open the doors to the wardrobe, Lindsay's
smile faded, the prospect of another ball, especially
this one, making her head doubly ache.

A few weeks ago she might have jumped with
delight at the invitation, but Almack's, well known
as the shrine of the socially unblemished, was hardly a place where she might find Jared. With his

blighted reputation, no matter how unjustly earned, she doubted that he would make it past the hallowed front portal. Yet she could always hope . . .

"Oh, my, yes, this blue silk will be perfect!" Aunt Winifred spun back to the bed, her kind gray eyes misted with tears as she clasped the gown to her ample bosom. "If I'd had a daughter, I would have wished such an honor for her. But that you're my beloved brother Randolph's child and my own dear niece, ah, such a happy day."

Lindsay swallowed hard at her aunt's sincerity, suddenly thinking herself a bit of a traitor to be feeling so ungrateful. "It will be a lovely evening, Aunt Winnie. Truly, I can't wait."

"Aye, and yer bath can't wait, either," Matilda announced briskly from the doorway. "The water's nice and steaming, miss. Up with ye now, before it grows cool."

"Yes, while I must write to Olympia at once." Handing the evening gown to Matilda, Aunt Winifred cooed to her dogs. "Come along, my sweet darlings. Oh, so much to do!"

Lindsay collapsed back onto the pillows to stare numbly at the frilly chintz canopy as soon as her aunt was gone, but that didn't prevent her from stiffening when she heard Matilda clucking her tongue.

"So that might make two letters posted today to Cornwall," the old Scotswoman appeared to say more to herself than to Lindsay, Matilda's slightly bowed back to the bed as she returned the gown to the wardrobe. "One to Sir Randolph and one to his wife. Aye, mayhap this whole tangle will un-ravel itself in a few days' time and not a week, and we'll have a fine spring wedding to plan. If not, well, I suppose my mistress will be writing another letter once she learns . . ."

Lindsay found her heart beating wildly when Matilda fell to clucking again and she lunged from the bed, not wanting to hear any more.

Nor would she consider for a moment that one week wouldn't be enough time to convince Jared that she could be the bride of his dreams. She threw her fringed shawl around her shoulders, her chin rising a notch. "Oh, no, my lord, I've finally found you and I'm not going to lose you now."

"I'm sorry, miss, did ye say something?"

Lindsay didn't answer, her footsteps determined as she flew down the hall thinking of pineapples and cherry brandy and a kiss that made her heart want to leap from her breast.

Chapter 8

"Please, my lords, no, I simply can't dance another step."

Lindsay extricated herself as gracefully as possible from a quintet of disappointed-looking gentlemen, the English country dance she'd just endured barely ended before she and her winded partner, Lord Sotherby, had been surrounded. And Lord Sotherby had even wanted her to dance with him again, although the poor snowy-haired fellow, nearly three times her age, had wheezed and puffed so wretchedly that she had feared he might expire on the dance floor.

"Oh, Lord."

Lindsay veered sharply, ducking into the throng surrounding the refreshment table as she spied Lord Ambrose Lamb heading her way. No wonder she was beginning to feel as if she were caught in a maze! There seemed to be no escape from the constant attention, Almack's proving as much a trial as she had imagined, and with no immediate relief in sight.

Grabbing a small glass of lemonade and retiring to the shadows under the musician's gallery, Lindsay glanced across the huge assembly room to where Aunt Winifred sat conversing merrily with

Maria, Lady Sefton, the Patroness who had granted them a voucher, Matilda sitting patiently behind them. Her beaming aunt was clearly in her glory, the night as much a triumph for her as she had enthused during the carriage ride to King Street that it would be for Lindsay.

But it had become more a torture than anything else, Lindsay thought with a sigh, feeling the same traitorous twinge that she found it so difficult to enjoy herself even for Aunt Winifred's sake. Truly an almost unbearable torture since her fears had been confirmed about Jared.

Almack's had clearly turned its back upon him; she had been looking for him all evening, but to no avail. And within moments the clock would strike eleven; no one would be allowed to join the assembly after that hour, which meant she had no hope of seeing him tonight, no hope of thanking him for the night before and arranging another rendez-vous—

"Ah, Lindsay, there you are!"

As Lord Ambrose bore down upon her, she quickly emptied the tiny goblet so she might press it into his hand and ask him to bring her another, then effect a hasty escape. But frustration filled her when she saw he carried two brimming glasses of lemonade, though she somehow forced a sunny smile.

"How gracious of you, my lord."

"Yes, well, I thought you might enjoy something refreshing after so many dances—though I'd have liked that more of them were with me, I must admit."

The earnest expression on Lord Ambrose's face reminding her uncomfortably of the other night,

Lindsay decided to skip over his wistful comment altogether as she accepted one of the glasses. "This lemonade is lovely, don't you think?" She took a tiny sip, no more, her stomach still feeling a bit uncertain. "So much tastier than ale."

"Ale?"

She nodded, suddenly resolute that if she couldn't escape him, perhaps she could shock him into leaving her in peace. "Oh, yes, we drank quite a bit of ale at home in Cornwall, especially me. But my stepmother has warned me that too much could make me broad as a house one day."

"Oh, no, Lindsay, I doubt that would ever happen. You're so beautiful—"

"Ah, but heftiness runs in my family, I fear." She cast a meaningful look in her aunt's direction, Lord Ambrose's eyes growing wide as he followed her gaze. "Yes, and you should see my father—such a pity, really. If he isn't trussed, his stomach nearly touches his knees—"

"I say, Ambrose!"

Startled by the interruption, Lindsay remained silent as Peter Bench, Lord Bridley, another of the young men who had plagued her for dances all evening, came running up to them to elbow Lord Ambrose in the ribs. A tall, lanky fellow known for his booming voice, he laughed and loosed it upon them.

"Dashed if I haven't just heard the news! You'll never believe it—oh, forgive me, Miss Somerset."

Her curiosity piqued, she inclined her head. "What news, my lord?"

"Actually, I fear it's nothing that would interest a young lady like yourself, Miss Somerset." Lord Bridley ran his hand through a shock of unruly brown hair and glanced excitedly back at his friend. "But there's going to be a mill this very night at Offley's—"

"Offley's?"

This time both men looked at Lindsay, Peter Bench appearing perturbed that he had been interrupted.

"A sporting hotel on Henrietta Street near Covent Garden."

"Ah." She gave a light shrug as if to say the location meant nothing to her, and took another sip of lemonade as Lord Bridley continued with barely contained excitement.

"It could be the match of the decade, Tom Cribb and some young upstart from Wales! Everyone's going to be there—look!"

Lindsay did look, her eyes widening as formally dressed gentlemen began to leave the ballroom in droves. Some even whooped and called out wagers to their friends as they ran down the steps to the street while young damsels, wives and Lady Patronesses clustered in disgruntled groups.

"Well, are you coming, man?"

"By Jove, wouldn't miss it for the world!"

Lindsay jumped as Lord Ambrose grabbed her hand and planted a clumsy kiss on her white-gloved fingers.

"I'm sorry, Lindsay—deuced abrupt, but there it is. I know we'll see each other again."

She had no time to respond as Peter Bench slapped his friend heartily on the back, the two breaking into boyish grins as they seemed to forget her and half ran from the ballroom. But within the next instant she had virtually forgotten them, her mind racing as she spied Aunt Winifred bustling toward her, Matilda in tow.

"Oh, my dear child, such a disgrace!" Aunt Winifred's fan fluttered at double time, and her round face was flushed with indignation. "How could such a thing spoil your lovely evening? A boxing match! Barbaric! Ridiculous! Oh, my, and look, all the men are leaving—"

"It's all right, Aunt Winnie, truly." Hoping she sounded convincing, Lindsay took care to avoid Matilda's eyes. "In fact, I'm so tired. I've been dancing all night."

"So you have, dear girl, as should any belle of the ball! Such a glorious triumph!"

"Yes, well, I thought perhaps you wouldn't mind if we could return home. It's been such a long day—a lovely day, a lovely evening," she quickly amended, "but bed right now sounds just as lovely to me."

"And so we shall return home," proclaimed Aunt Winifred, snapping her fan shut. "Although I was most willing to stay late—anything to see you having such a wonderful time, but a boxing match, of all things! Dreadful business. Ah, well, shall we see to our good-nights?"

"Oh, Aunt Winnie, could you thank Lady Sefton and the other Patronesses for me while I go wait in the carriage? My heels are so blistered I fear I should sit down at once."

Lindsay didn't wait for an answer but headed for the stairs; she doubted she had more than a few precious moments before Aunt Winifred and Matilda would join her. Her heart beating madly, she ignored curious glances as she dashed down the broad marble steps and out the front door. King

Street was clogged with waiting carriages. Most were private, but a few coaches for hire were vying for passengers. Lindsay approached the nearest empty one.

"Need a carriage, miss?" shouted the wiry coachman, flashing her a gap-toothed grin.

She moved close to the driver's box, keeping her voice low. "Yes, I do, but not right now. Sixteen Piccadilly at quarter past midnight—I'll pay you well. Can you be there?"

A speculative look lit his narrow face, making Lindsay feel no small amount of discomfort.

"Yes or no, sir, or I'll find another—"

"I'll be there, right as rain, miss. Sixteen Piccadilly."

Exhilaration gripping her as he tipped his black hat and gave another grin, Lindsay turned without another word and looked for the Penney coach, reaching the vehicle parked on the opposite side of the street just as Aunt Winifred and Matilda stepped from the brick building. In another moment she was settled against the plush seat, smiling so broadly to herself that her face hurt.

Everyone would be there. Yes, that was exactly what Lord Bridley had said, and to Lindsay, such news could mean only one thing.

Jared might be there, too.

Lindsay knew she was at the right location the moment she disembarked from the hired coach, the hearty roar of men's voices spilling from the hotel into the street.

"I ain't one to open me mouth when it's not welcome, miss, but are you sure that you wouldn't rather return 'ome? A boxin' match is no fit place for a lady—"

"I'll be fine, sir, but thank you for your concern," she assured the coachman, adjusting her hood around her face just as she had done last night before she'd entered Tom's Cellar. "And don't forget. I paid you extra—you won't say a word to anyone about bringing me here."

"No, no, not a word. And you've me word on that, Ned King's pledge as good as gold. Shall I wait right 'ere for you, miss, just in case y' change your mind once you're inside?"

"No, that won't be necessary."

But Lindsay wasn't so sure when a trio of drunkards stumbled down the hotel steps as she ascended, one of the men making a bleary comment about her that made her cheeks flame. Something about taking a peek under her cloak . . . ?

The coach clattering noisily down the gaslit street drew her attention from the door, Ned King, if that indeed had been the man's name, obviously having taken her at her word. Lindsay took a deep breath and squared her shoulders, but still kept her head bowed as she entered the hotel.

And once more she allowed the unholy din to lead her, that and the motley swirl of humanity moving in and out of a pair of double doors to her right. Dapper aristocrats and prosperous-looking merchants elbowed aside plainly dressed working men even as shabby young boys, probably pickpockets much as those last night, darted and wove past legs and feet.

Lindsay was relieved to see a few women, their high-pitched, sometimes shrill laughter sounding almost out of place in the predominantly masculine throng. She guessed at once their sort from their garish clothing and easy manner, one woman— more a girl, really—even going so far as to give her male companion a good-natured squeeze between the legs, which made Lindsay blush and look away.

It seemed she had no sooner joined those milling nearest the doors when she was swept inside what appeared to be a huge dining room, darkened but for a well-lit square at its center, yet that wasn't the first thing she noticed. She gasped, her eyes suddenly burning as a smell so intense assailed her that she almost turned around and fled.

Sweat.

Male sweat, pungent and nearly overpowering. And no wonder, with so many men packed into one room, no matter how cavernous.

Keeping close to the wall, she inched her way toward the lighted arena, past onlookers shouting so fiercely that she feared she might become deaf. Belligerent pairs here and there were cursing at one another and even trading punches, and she would have received a vicious blow to her jaw if she hadn't seen one burly fellow's swing go wide and ducked.

"Watch yourself, you bloody fool. Didn't you see the little lady passing by?"

Lindsay sucked in her breath in surprise as she felt two big hands suddenly at her waist, someone lifting her bodily and setting her feet on a table where a few other women had already sought refuge.

"There you go, sweet'eart. That'll keep you out of trouble and give you a fine view, too!"

Lindsay couldn't find her voice to thank the man,

she was so stunned to be virtually on display, the
other women making much of lifting their skirts
and showing white flashes of thigh. She merely
clutched her cloak tighter, her arms hugging her
breasts; she felt tempted to close her eyes and pretend she was anywhere but standing on that table.
Yet she was thankful the hoards of men seemed
more interested in the proceedings in the arena, a
roar of approval going up when one of the two
men hammering away at each other slumped to his
knees.

"Aye, fists like legs of mutton, that's our Tom
Cribb!" cried an onlooker, fresh wagers filling the
air that the famed pugilist's opponent wouldn't
dare to rise and fight on.

And if Cribb was the fighter left standing, as
broad as a barn and towering as an oak, Lindsay
began to pray that his leaner, smaller opponent remained on his knees. She felt like closing her eyes
again when the man—Lord Bridley had said the
young upstart was from Wales—swayed to his feet,
only to be pummeled so mercilessly that he soon
crashed face-first to the floor.

She could only imagine how long the fight had
lasted before she arrived, and now it became clear
to her that it was over, as a roar of such triumph
went up from every throat that she clapped her
hands over her ears. And then it happened, so
abrupt a shift of attention that her gaze grew wide
and fearful.

Suddenly it seemed that all eyes had focused
upon the three other women displaying themselves
atop the table, the boldest of the trio baring her
generous breasts for everyone to see. Grateful that
the room was so dim for whatever cover it offered,

Lindsay at once tried to climb down from the table, but a host of hands reached out to push her back up.

"Oh, no, you don't, wench. Take off yer cloak and give us a look!"

"I say we auction them off, each chit to the highest bidder!"

Lindsay tried desperately to jump again, this time as many hands if not more forcing her back. As tears sprang to her eyes, she felt someone tug roughly at her cloak while bids began to ring out all around.

"Five guineas for the wench with the cloak!"

"No, ten—"

"And I say twenty!"

"One hundred pounds!"

Chapter 9

Lindsay stared incredulously into the aston-ished crowd, daring not to hope as she saw a tall gentleman stride toward the table. The room was so dark she couldn't see his face, but when he drew closer, such relief filled her that she thought her knees might buckle.

"Are you daft, man? One hundred pounds and you don't even know what the wench looks like?" a portly fellow shouted nearby, his cry taken up by other raucous voices as hands reached out once more to wrench at her cloak.

Desperately Lindsay staggered to the center of the table, kicking and striking with balled fists in a futile attempt to fend off her attackers, but she jumped when a deafening blast rocked the room, the smell of gunpowder filling the air. Other on-lookers jumped, too, some men diving to the floor to seek cover, the three women shrieking and scrambling in terror from the table while Lindsay gaped at Jared as he slipped a pistol into his coat. Then he held out his hand to her, a wry smile on his lips, although it didn't reach his eyes.

"I prefer surprises. Come."

She did, holding gratefully onto his broad shoulders as he lifted her from the table, the stunned silence shattered by uproarious laughter and shouts of approval as Jared's words were echoed from man to man.

But sheer bedlam was created when he suddenly drew a thick handful of bank notes from a coat pocket and threw them high into the air. The place went mad. As grown men jumped up and down like frantic children to snatch at the fluttering money, Lindsay was swept off her feet, Jared carrying her from the room.

He didn't speak or scarcely look at her until they had passed through the hotel, and then it was only to set her down almost rudely on the front steps, his face as grim as his gaze as he grabbed her by the hand and yanked her along with him. With a brusque wave he flagged down a passing coach, Lindsay suddenly wondering from his tense silence as he lifted her none too gently inside if he intended not to accompany her but simply to tell the driver where to take her home.

He seemed to hesitate, too, standing there on the street as he glanced over his shoulder at Offley's and then looked back to the coachman, a low curse escaping him when he made his decision and joined her.

"Just drive, man!" he shouted, clearly irritated. He took the opposite seat and shoved his fingers through his hair. Then he leaned back, bracing one lean leg against her seat and staring out the window as if he didn't trust himself further to speak.

The rhythmic clopping of the horses' hooves on the cobbled street and the creaking of the carriage reigned as the only sounds for long moments. Lindsay decided it was best for once that she simply hold her tongue.

She imagined Jared must be angry with her. She had almost found herself overcome by an impossible fix. Certainly her identity would have become known if she had been rudely divested of her cloak, for Lord Ambrose Lamb and Lord Bridley would have recognized her, if not other gentlemen of the ton with whom she was acquainted. It had not occurred to her that things might go so terribly wrong, but she hadn't been to a boxing match before. How could she have known?

"Are you hungry?"

Lindsay met Jared's eyes, startled more that there seemed little anger in his voice than about the unexpectedness of his query. "A bit. Actually, I haven't eaten since dinner at two o'clock, and not much even then. My stomach hasn't felt quite right since . . . well, the ale."

"Ah, yes, the ale."

That bloody useless ale, Jared echoed to himself with frustration, although he did his best to keep his expression calm. The ale he had foisted upon her in the hope that she would drink enough to make her good and sick and reluctant to venture out late again or have anything more to do with him.

But obviously his lesson had failed utterly, for here she was, sitting across from him, as damned lovely as a sinner's dream and looking no worse for whatever ill effects had plagued her, and probably with no idea how close she had come to being devoured by that crowd—blast it all to hell!

"Driver, stop at that tavern ahead." Jared turned back to Lindsay, tempted to grab and shake her hard, which was exactly what he had wanted to do outside Offley's hotel, if he hadn't been so intent upon seeing her safely away from the place.

Even better would be to pull her over his knee and give that pert rump a sound whack or two, yet what good would that do? He wasn't dealing with a child but with a woman, an incredibly foolhardy young woman at that—by God, and what of Matilda? If that feisty old Scotswoman, who'd made him feel more a boy in short pants than a grown man, knew Lindsay had sneaked out again . . .

As the carriage rumbled to a halt, Jared had to tell himself resolutely to stick to his new plan, although his first impulse was to command the driver to set out at once for Piccadilly. But his gut instincts were also telling him that if he didn't follow an admittedly ruthless course of action, Miss Lindsay Somerset might well find herself in another dire situation in which she would have no hope of a rescuer.

And no matter he had thought his hands washed of her last night, Jared considered grimly; given this latest antic, the last thing he wanted on his conscience was her downfall. Elise's already weighed heavily enough upon him.

"The Boar's Head, milord."

As the coachman swept open the carriage door, Jared stepped out and beckoned to Lindsay, her brilliant smile making him think how easily such a look might forgive the chit anything. But dammit, not tonight.

"Are you taking me to another favorite place?"

"Yes, they've good food here. I think you'll like it."

Lindsay felt such relief at the warmth of his answering smile that she could only stare at him for a moment, blinking with some chagrin when the driver cleared his throat to get their attention. As Jared paid the man, even jesting with him when the fellow inquired about the outcome of the boxing match, she felt her spirits soar higher.

He had been so silent in the carriage—other than asking if she was hungry—that she hadn't known what to think. It had been so hard for her to keep still; truly, it wasn't her nature, but she was glad now that she had. She took his proffered arm, elated that he hadn't directed the coach to take her home. If he had been angry, it appeared his ill humor had passed.

"I'm so sorry about the ruckus at Offley's," she blurted out, unable to keep quiet any longer. "We were at Almack's, Aunt Winnie, Matilda and I. Lady Sefton sent us a voucher—oh, but that isn't important. I heard about the boxing match from Peter Bench, Lord Bridley, and I thought perhaps you might be there. I so wanted to thank you for last night and ask if we might arrange another rendezvous—"

"And so things have turned out just as you hoped."

Lindsay looked curiously around her as they entered the near-empty tavern, a simple, unadorned place with sturdy furnishings and timbered walls and a huge stone hearth at one end where a low fire burned. "Oh, yes, well, other than..." She didn't finish, remembering all too clearly her wretched helplessness atop that table. "You've rescued me twice now—"

"Once. Remember our secret? We both know your swoon was a ruse, and quite expertly executed at that."

The low teasing in his voice thrilling her to her

toes, Lindsay was reluctant to let go of his arm as he seated her at a table well away from the few heavy-lidded patrons who appeared to be nodding off into their mugs. She knew she was staring at him again, but she simply couldn't help herself.

He was so handsome, his eyes so blue . . . a deep sea-swept blue; there, she had named the uncommon color at last! Heat raced up her face when he pulled a chair from around the table and sat down next to her; her racing heart lodged in her throat as he reached for her hand, his strong fingers caressing hers.

"Ain't meanin' to interrupt anything, milord, but is there somethin' I could bring you and your fine lady friend? Wine? Mayhap a nice tablecloth to keep you both safe from splinters?"

Lindsay felt Jared stiffen, but she couldn't imagine why as she glanced up to find an attractive, ebony-haired serving woman with the biggest breasts she'd ever seen leaning over the—oh, Lord. Embarrassed, she dropped her gaze even as the woman gave a throaty laugh.

"Aye, you can't help but notice 'em. Quite a nice handful, or so I've been told . . . Ain't that right, milord?"

The woman laughed again, but a door slamming against a wall made her curse softly under her breath.

"Della, wot's takin' you, woman?" came a gruff shout across the room, a strapping fellow with a glistening bald pate peering out at them from what Lindsay imagined was the kitchen. Yet suddenly the man's belligerent tone grew ingratiating as he wiped his hands on a towel and threw it over his shoulder, then forged out to greet them. "Ah, Lord

Giles, welcome! So pleased to see you tonight—and the luvly lady, of course."

Lindsay lowered her head at the man's shrewd and blatantly admiring perusal. She slipped her hand from Jared's to draw her hood closer around her face.

"We'd like supper, Sprigs, and wine."

"Aye, so you shall have it, milord, the best in me house! We've got plain food here, but good—wife, why in blazes are you dallyin'? You heard the gentl'man! Fetch some wine!"

Lindsay winced as Della earned a sound smack on her generous rump for moving too slowly, the tavern keeper spreading his work-reddened hands wide as if to apologize as she sauntered away.

"She's a good girl, Della, aims to please most times. A bit saucy, but I've ne'er heard me customers complain. Well, I'll be off to the kitchen—"

"We'd like to be served upstairs in my room, Sprigs. When everything is ready, have Della knock and leave the tray outside the door. I'd rather we weren't disturbed."

If Jared had said they were thinking of taking an evening dip in the Thames or planning to sup with mad King George himself, Lindsay couldn't have been more astonished. Her eyes were as wide as the tavern keeper's appeared for an instant; in the next there was nothing but a knowing smile on the man's face as he bobbed his shiny head and hustled away. But she had no chance to dwell upon his disconcerting reaction, for Jared once more took her hand.

"Come. It's quieter upstairs. More private."

She could only nod, having lost her voice entirely. She could feel curious eyes boring into her back when Jared drew her from her seat and they made their way to the stairs, but she kept her head lowered, more so Jared couldn't see how red her face felt at that moment, her mind running away with itself.

Jared had a room here? Of course, as a spy, perhaps he found the Boar's Head more suited to the secretive nature of his work, just as Tom's Cellar was a place where he could relax. Oh, dear, everything was suddenly so confusing—she would have much preferred to remain in the dining room. But that wasn't very daring of her, no, not adventurous at all. And, of course, it made perfect sense that he might wish to converse with her in a private place, especially if he intended to share with her some of his heroic exploits . . .

"It's not very elegant, but it suits me."

She made herself smile brightly, pressing her hand to her breast to quiet her thundering heart as he pushed open a door and stepped aside so she could enter. A lamp near the unassuming double bed was burning low and the bedclothes were turned down—an amenity which didn't surprise her, considering how deferential Sprigs had been downstairs—and the room appeared well kempt though a bit threadbare, just as Jared had said.

"You . . . you don't have a town house in the city?" she couldn't help asking, her gaze skipping from a weathered pine wardrobe to Jared's face. He shook his head as he pulled the pistol from his coat and set it upon a table.

"I'm never in London long enough to warrant the trouble—hiring servants and so on. Please, sit."

Glancing from the down-turned bed to the one chair in the room, Lindsay felt herself redden again and nearly tripped over the frayed carpet in her haste to perch herself on a stuffed arm.

"Wouldn't you be more comfortable without that cloak?"

"M-my cloak?"

He had shed his dark navy coat, tossing it onto the bed, a teasing smile on his face as he approached her. She swallowed hard, unable not to notice the expert cut of his waistcoat and how snugly it fit his lean torso, his fawn-colored breeches as close-fitting and hugging his flanks like a second skin, his black riding boots making little sound upon the carpeted floor. Then he was standing in front of her, his fingers unfastening the frogs of her cloak before she could think to do the task herself.

"The stove in the corner offers little heat, but it's not so cool that you need wear this any longer."

Lindsay shivered as he slipped the hood from her hair, his hands lightly skimming her face before they moved to push the cloak gently off her shoulders. He was staring so deeply into her eyes that she had the strangest sensation she was drowning, drowning in something deliciously warm and altogether inviting. Only with great effort was she able to look away, almost giddy as she looked for anything to talk about.

"Do . . . do you always carry a pistol? Of course, as a spy, you must, I'm sure—and—and it was fortunate you had one with you tonight at Offley's. Fortunate for me, I mean."

"Yes, it was very fortunate. And yes"—he reached up to run a callused fingertip slowly along her cheek—"I never go anywhere without a weapon."

The sudden hard glint in his eyes and the harsh timbre of his voice did not go unnoticed. Lindsay was beset by a chill, not of fright, but of vivid empathy. She could imagine the trials he must have endured while in loyal service to the Crown, the trials he still must face. It made her yearn to know that much more about him and she inclined her head, leaning into the strong masculine hand that still cradled her face. But at the sudden knock on the door he left her, Lindsay sinking dizzily from the stuffed arm into the chair.

"Your supper, luv—milord."

She heard Della's throaty laugh, glanced over and saw the buxom tavern keeper's wife give Jared a broad wink, but he said nothing as he took the tray and kicked the door shut.

"Jared . . . shouldn't we have thanked her?"

"She's a woman more fond of coin than words," he said dryly, drawing a small three-legged table to Lindsay's chair and setting down the tray. "I'll compensate her tomorrow—but for now, let's see what she brought us."

Lindsay's mouth was already watering at the savory smells in the air. She gasped with delight when Jared drew aside a white linen napkin.

"Why, it's Cornish pie, surely!" She watched eagerly as he cut into the flaky brown pastry and offered her a generous serving, the steamy filling of ham, leeks and thick cream custard oozing out onto her plate. "Or a dish very much like it. I haven't had anything that looks this good since I left Porthleven. Corie's housekeeper, Frances, makes the most wonderful Cornish pie."

"Obviously Sprigs does, too," came Jared's amused comment as she popped a heaping forkful into her mouth, her mistake not to blow upon it first. At once her eyes began to tear, since the food was so warm. Lindsay threw a grateful look at Jared when he handed her a pewter goblet filled with red wine, and she drank hurriedly.

"Oh . . . oh, that's better." Chagrined with herself, Lindsay returned the goblet to the tray with a sheepish smile. "I guess I was hungrier than I thought. There was food at Almack's. Stale cakes, actually. Not very appetizing even if I had felt like eating."

"So things there haven't changed that much." .

Lindsay stared at Jared as he lifted his goblet and drank deeply, his words surprising her. "You've been to Almack's?"

He nodded, a strange smile on his face. "I haven't been graced with my notorious reputation forever. There was a time when I was granted entrance through those hallowed doors—"

"Oh, Jared, it would have been so wonderful if you could have been there tonight," Lindsay blurted. "I watched for you all evening—none of my partners danced even half as well as you. It isn't fair at all that you should be excluded through no fault of your own, and I intend to post a letter tomorrow morning to Lady Sefton and the other Patronesses, saying just that. I don't believe a word of what my aunt or anyone else has said about you, not a word—oh!"

Lindsay's eyes grew wide as Jared's hand clamped tightly around her wrist, wider still when he drew her roughly up to face him, her plate of food crashing to the floor. His eyes seemed to burn into hers.

"What do you really know of me, Lindsay Somerset? Tell me."

Chapter 10

Lindsay didn't know what to say, wondering wildly what had caused his drastic change of mood. "N-not much, truly, only that you're a spy—"

"Oh, yes, a spy. So it's been rumored. What else?"

"And an earl."

"Yes, the sixth Earl of Dovercourt, the title inherited from my uncle the fifth earl, Alistair Giles. And?"

"And . . ." Lindsay faltered, Jared searching her eyes with such intensity that she felt a blush race to her scalp. "You once lived in India. I . . . I remember that from last night. Calcutta."

"Ah, and what else do you remember?"

He had drawn so close, his face, his lips hovering so near hers, that Lindsay's knees suddenly felt weak. "Only that—that I believe you kissed me."

"Kissed you? Are you sure?"

She bobbed her head, her breath snagged in her throat.

"And what would you have done if one of those men at Offley's had grabbed you from that table and kissed you—a man you didn't know, a man who might mean you harm—"

"I would have slapped him, kicked him."

"And tried to get away?"

"Yes, yes, of course!"

"So what if I told you that I might mean you harm, Lindsay—that perhaps in my personal affairs I'm as disreputable as people say, as your aunt says? A spy, an earl, I've lived in Calcutta. You know so precious little about me, yet here you are, alone, in my room, at a tavern—"

"No, I don't believe you could ever mean me harm!" Lindsay cut him off, her vehemence startling her and, she could see from the darkening of his eyes, clearly startling Jared. "If so, you would have last night in the carriage, but you didn't— only kissed me, and you swore to Matilda that . . . that . . ." She didn't continue, looking down blindly at the mess at her feet, her face burning.

"So Matilda told you she saw us."

"Yes." Lindsay spoke in a half whisper, breathing in the subtle scent of bay rum emanating like heat from Jared's shirt, his skin. "And I told her that you were daring and brave and gentlemanly—"

She gasped, Jared releasing her wrist to raise her chin to face him, his eyes staring deeply into hers.

"Is this so gentlemanly, Lindsay?"

She had no more than an instant to draw breath before his lips found hers, his mouth so warm, warmer than sunlight, devouring her as he drew her roughly against him. She didn't think, couldn't think, his body's lean hardness pressing possessively against her softer form until she no longer felt herself, only him. Then his mouth was gone from hers and she fluttered open her eyes, gasping again when he kissed a trail of heat and fire down her throat.

"Is this gallant, Lindsay?" His voice was thick and hoarse, his powerful arms crushing her against him. "Tell me to stop—strike me, scream for Sprigs, scream for help, woman!"

She shook her head wildly, her jumbled thoughts no match for the sensations overwhelming her until his hand moved to cup her breast—and it was then Lindsay jerked as if stung.

Yes, she should tell him to stop, she should! But such a heat had filled her as his thumb slowly rubbed a nipple through her satin bodice that she felt powerless against it—a breathless inner voice resounding that he wouldn't be touching her so if his intentions weren't honorable.

"Woman, I vow you're in danger . . . scream, damn you!"

His breath was like flame as he dipped his head to her breast. Lindsay, whimpering deep in her throat when she felt his lips touch her flesh, dropped her cheek to his burnished hair and whispered, "I can't . . . I won't. You're everything I've always wanted, everything I've always dreamed for a husband . . . Jared?"

He had frozen, his mouth against the soft, scented curve of her breast, her heart beating frantically against his lips, the heat of her body invading his senses even as he cursed vehemently to himself.

Husband? Had the chit said . . . ?

Trembling feminine fingers entwined loosely in his hair, her voice so hopeful, so trusting. "You're noble and gallant and I will never believe otherwise . . . a true hero, Jared, no matter what anyone

says. You're only saying these things to dissuade
me, because you know the terrible dangers you
face—but I could face them with you. I could—we
could—"

"Blast and damnation, woman!"

Jared disengaged himself so abruptly from her
that she nearly toppled backward, but he didn't
reach out a hand to help her. He could only stare
at her, realizing with utter disbelief that nothing—
no, not even a full-blown seduction—would convince her that he meant her harm. Which he didn't,
but he had done his damned best to make her believe it, nigh thrown her onto the bed if he'd gone
a moment longer—by God, could any one woman
be not only foolhardy and impossibly naive, but
such a romantic fool?

He thrust his fingers through his hair, realizing,
too, that he must appear a crazed lunatic as he circled the room, stopping to glance at her only to
resume pacing in utter frustration, until at last he
threw up his hands.

There was only one bloody thing to do. With a
low curse he grabbed up her cloak and strode to
the door, where he turned and held out his hand.

"Come, I'm taking you home."

Beautiful blue eyes stared at him in confusion.
"Home?"

He gritted his teeth and nodded, doing his best
to shove all thought of the silken texture of her
breasts, the perfumed taste of her skin, from his
mind. "Yes, right now. You've read me too well. I
cannot lie to you. All this"—he swept his arm
around the room—"was done to dissuade you, just
as you say."

He nearly growled aloud at her sudden smile, its brilliance hitting him like a blow.

"Oh, Jared, then you have thought of the possibility—I mean, that we might be togeth—"

"No more, Lindsay; now is not the time to speak of it. I have to think—what is proper and right for us. Now come."

She did, flying to him with such elation in her eyes that Jared could have kicked himself right then and there.

How could he have not seen it? Not understood? Damn *him* for a bloody fool!

Grateful that her obvious delight had left her speechless, Jared quickly led her from his room, down the hall, down the stairs and through the tavern—sleepy patrons, Della and Sprigs staring curiously after them—then outside into the street, where he was grateful, too, that it wasn't yet so late that finding transport might have proved impossible. As he flagged an oncoming coach, the driver thankfully giving him a nod, he felt a hand upon his arm.

"Jared, you've forgotten your coat—"

"Don't trouble yourself," he muttered, flinging her cloak around her shoulders. He waved the driver to stay in his seat and helped Lindsay alight himself; he could feel that she was shivering in the cool night air.

After a terse command to make all haste to Piccadilly for double the wage, he joined her inside the dark interior and, seeing no help for it, drew her close once he had settled next to her. She immediately snuggled against him, her head resting on his shoulder, her hand splayed innocently upon his chest, making Jared groan to himself and pray that the driver knew the meaning of haste.

It seemed the fellow did when the coach careened around a corner, Jared bracing a foot upon the opposite seat to keep his balance while Lindsay was thrown nearly into his lap. With her rump perched atop his thigh, he groaned again as she laughed, the merry sound tugging strangely upon him while he thought that she must consider their mad dash through London's streets some grand adventure.

"I can't believe how fast we're going!" she cried above the clattering hooves, her hand slipping between his legs as she tried to right herself. But another jarring turn only made matters worse, Jared catching Lindsay when she tumbled backward, her bottom now soundly resting upon a mutinous part of him which had grown swollen and heavy as with a mind of its own.

And suddenly he was clenching his teeth for a miracle, that Sixteen Piccadilly was no more than a moment ahead, while Lindsay giggled in his lap with no thought to her peril . . . her cloak fallen open, her creamy breasts straining against her bodice as she tried futilely to right herself despite the coach's furious rocking, her lovely face flushed with laughter.

"Jared, could . . . you help . . . ?"

She was breathless and giggled some more even as she managed to throw her arms around his neck, and Jared felt something snap inside him. Why the hell not help?

Help himself, he amended, drawing her hungrily against him and capturing her smiling red lips with his own. He felt her start, only to relax a second later into utter acquiescence in his arms, which made him kiss her all the harder, her softness, her warmth intoxicating him.

Why not enjoy one last moment of the reckless Miss Lindsay Somerset's charms, when he would never see her again after tonight? The Season would be over before he planned to return to London again, and by then she would be safely betrothed or even married and ensconced in the country, where she would give little thought to the bastard who had lied to her and disappeared without a word.

She was limp, her arms fallen from his shoulders, when Jared finally raised his head, and he wondered if she might have fainted. Then, as the carriage rumbled to a stop next to a lamppost, he saw that she was staring up at him dreamily, her lips slack and swollen from his kiss.

Struck by more than a twinge of regret, Jared had only to remind himself that the foolish chit wished to make a husband of him—damnation, would she shackle herself to the devil?—and it wasn't hard for him to stifle the unwanted emotion. His harsh self-appraisal reminded him, too, of the business he'd left half finished at Offley's—business he would not be distracted from any longer. Frowning, he lifted her almost roughly from his lap.

"Lindsay, you're home."

"Home?" Feeling as if she had awoken from a wonderful dream, Lindsay attempted to clear her reeling senses as Jared brushed past her and shoved open the carriage door.

"Yes. Now, gather your cloak and I'll help you down."

She did as he bade, his gallantry thrilling her, his husky baritone and the strength of his hands closing around her waist thrilling her, the ease with which he lifted her thrilling her, everything about Jared Giles, the Earl of Dovercourt, thrilling her. She knew she was smiling like a lovesick fool, but she couldn't help herself, her joy so great that her dream was at last coming true.

"Go on, Lindsay. I'll wait here with the coach until you're safely inside."

"You're not going to walk to the front door with me?"

Disappointment filled her when he shook his head, but she felt relieved at once when he drew her into his arms.

"I'll call upon you in three days, Saturday—"

"So long?"

"Shhh, I told you I must think—make the right plans for us. You must be patient and not try to find me, no more sneaking from your aunt's house, no excursions at night by yourself into the city, nothing of the kind. Do I have your word?"

She nodded, thrilled that he had said it again— *us. Us!*

"Promise me, Lindsay. Say it."

"Yes, yes, I promise!"

"Good. I don't want to find myself having to rescue you again. Now go."

He released her, Lindsay feeling instantly bereft. But when he inclined his head almost sternly to the walk, she knew he was thinking of her welfare and that it was best to oblige him.

Warmed to her toes by his concern, she turned, but then she spun back to him and, standing on tiptoe, pressed her lips briefly to his. She saw a flicker of something in his eyes, but she didn't linger, instead gathering her cloak around her and flying down the walk, closer to floating on air than ever before.

Once inside the house, she leaned upon the door, listening with equal measures of longing and excitement as the carriage rumbled away, her heart pounding in her ears.

Three days. It would feel like forever. But what was that to a lifetime of happiness?

Hugging herself, she hurried upstairs, paying no mind to the creaky steps. She wished so desperately that Corisande were here to share her wonderful news—but then again, she could rouse Matilda if the plucky Scotswoman wasn't already awake and up waiting for her. On Saturday Jared would be back, well under a week!

With a jubilant laugh, Lindsay raced to the attic door.

Chapter 11

"**A**unt Winnie, were you ever acquainted with Alistair Giles, the fifth Earl of Dovercourt?"

Lindsay continued stirring two lumps of sugar into her cup of chamomile tea, hoping she looked and sounded more nonchalant than she felt as Aunt Winifred glanced up from patting Primrose and Ignatius, the Welsh corgis snoring contentedly at her feet.

"Alistair Giles? Oh, my, yes, I knew him, as did my beloved Rupert, God rest his soul. They both had a great fondness for hunting grouse. A fine man, too, but why, dear girl, would you be asking—"

"No reason," Lindsay fibbed, a very real purpose on her mind. "I chanced to hear his name in passing conversation last night at Lady Butler's masquerade . . ."

"How strange. The poor man's been dead now eight years, although he was quite a dashing figure—so handsome and a staunch widower for the last decade of his life. Broke many a lady's heart, I'd imagine. Was it perhaps a woman you overheard speaking of him?"

"Yes, yes, a woman," Lindsay fibbed again, sti-

fling a pinch of guilt. She took a sip of tea, the
conversation progressing even better than she had
hoped. "But I didn't recognize her—only thought
it curious she was speaking so well of a gentleman
whose nephew is so . . . notorious."

"And a pity it is, too!" Shaking her head, Aunt
Winifred brushed some crumpet crumbs from her
lap. "At least for the poor man's memory. Such a
tragic story. Such a tragic family."

Lindsay leaned back casually in her chair, trying
not to show her excitement that her idea had
worked. She hadn't been quite sure how to broach
the subject of Jared, but with Saturday fast approaching—dear Lord, grant her patience; could it
really be tomorrow?—she hoped by discussing him
somehow, or at least his family, that his appearance
at their door wouldn't be such a complete shock to
her aunt.

"Tragic?" she prodded lightly. "How so?"

"In every way, truly, especially what that—that
rogue has done since to his family's good name.
Disgraceful!"

Lindsay winced, but she covered her reaction
with another sip of tea while Aunt Winifred tipped
the porcelain teapot to pour herself a fresh cup.

"Ah, me, it's been three years since much was
said of the family's misfortunes, but as I recall,
that's when Lord Giles—the present Lord Giles,
mind you—returned from India, where he had run
off to seven years before and left his younger sister—what was her name? Ah, yes, Elise. Broke her
poor heart and his uncle's, left them with no more
than a note saying he had no wish to remain in
England. And the two had come from India only a
few weeks before to live with Alistair, their parents

dying in Calcutta of some strange fever."

"Jar—I mean, Lord Giles abandoned his orphaned sister?" Incredulous, Lindsay found it impossible to imagine Jared doing such a terrible thing.

Aunt Winifred poured a generous amount of cream into her tea and began to stir furiously.

"He did," she replied, "but thankfully, the girl had her uncle to care for her—at least until Alistair passed away quite suddenly, no doubt of grief and despair at his nephew's cruelty. That left the wretched girl alone in the world, well, alone but for Alistair's mistress—hmm, I've forgotten her name, Sally, Susan, ah, no matter. And her son became master of Dovercourt Manor when he married Elise a short time later."

"Dovercourt Manor . . . ?"

"Yes, the ancestral home in West Sussex, near Seaford. I know little else save that Elise died shortly after her brother's unexpected return, and it's rumored the poor dear's husband—oh, yes, Potter was his surname—treated her most abominably, for which that scoundrel Jared Giles has no one but himself to blame!"

"But, Aunt Winnie, you told me yourself Lord Giles is a spy and therefore highly trusted—"

"Yes, and it's a travesty, too, that affairs of a baser nature have no bearing upon affairs of state, even when such notoriety so bespeaks a lack of character—oh, my, Lindsay, enough, enough! How did we ever begin such a distasteful topic? I feel a sudden pain in my head. Where's Matilda?"

Her own thoughts spinning, Lindsay rose from her chair to open one of the tall windows in the sunny drawing room.

"No, no, dear, fetch Matilda, will you? And be quick! Oh, dear, my head is pounding."

As Primrose and Ignatius began to whine and whimper at Aunt Winifred's feet, clearly sensing her distress, Lindsay raced from the drawing room.

Now *her* head was aching and she almost wished she hadn't mentioned Alistair Giles. How would Jared ever favorably press his suit for her hand when her aunt thought so little of him? Of course, it wasn't Aunt Winifred's decision, but her father's, and Lindsay imagined Olympia would demand her say. That might mean two negative votes raised against one—oh, Lord . . .

"Matilda!"

Lindsay stopped her flight on the third step, relieved to see the Scotswoman hurrying down the stairs with smelling salts already in hand.

"Ye don't have to tell me, lass, I can hear it in yer voice. Sensed it in my bones, too—after serving the same mistress for twenty-five years, I always know when she needs me. The drawing room?"

Lindsay nodded, sinking with a sigh onto the step as Matilda bustled past her and disappeared around the corner.

She had only wanted to somehow prepare Aunt Winifred for tomorrow, and now she'd simply made matters worse. If Jared even approached the front door, she imagined the poor woman would be thrown into such a nervous frenzy that a physician might have to be called, either that or Aunt Winifred might go so far as to summon a constable to remove him. There had to be some way she could warn Jared. The last thing she wanted was for his proposal of marriage to be tossed back into his face!

Lindsay rose to her feet. It was only a few hours until dark. She could try to find him then, yet she had promised no sneaking from the house, no excursions into the city at night.

Lindsay sank back onto the stair with a sigh of pure frustration, but she started when she felt a light hand upon her shoulder.

"Anything wrong, miss?"

She glanced up, shaking her head at Gladys, a pretty young chambermaid who was very close to her own age. "No, no, I'm—" She stopped, looking at Gladys as if seeing her for the first time. Of course!

"Gladys, I need you to accompany me."

"B-but I'm not finished dusting yet, miss—"

"Oh, please, Gladys, the dusting can wait. I need you right now as my chaperone—it's very important!"

Lindsay grabbed the young woman's hand without another word and drew her down the stairs and toward the back of the house, imagining Matilda would be kept busy with her aunt for the rest of the afternoon. She hoped Aunt Winifred would need to lie down until supper, which would be even better; Matilda always attended to mending then and Lindsay wouldn't be missed.

Gladys's hazel eyes were round as saucers when Lindsay pulled her out the back door into the tidy garden, the perfumed scent of spring flowers heavy in the air. But Lindsay scarcely noticed them, not even her favorite bluebells brushing against her skirt, as she urged the chambermaid to hurry.

"Where are we going, miss?" Gladys asked when they entered the Penney stable, the young woman skipping to one side as Lindsay set to work hitching a docile bay gelding to a light two-wheeled carriage, since no grooms or Benjamin the coachman was there to help them.

Not that Lindsay needed any assistance; she'd learned many practical things from Corisande, who was nothing if not resourceful. "Don't worry, Gladys, we won't be gone very long."

A few breathless moments later, they were heading out the alley and onto the busy boulevard, Lindsay glad for the leather hood which would offer them protection from the brilliant April sunshine and curious glances. She was so intent upon maneuvering the carriage through the bustle of afternoon traffic that it wasn't until she had turned off Piccadilly that she realized she had no clear idea as to the Boar's Head's address. But she supposed when they drew closer to Covent Garden she could ask for directions if need be.

Truly, she felt exhilarated by her sense of freedom, and it was evident from the pink bloom on Gladys's cheeks that the chambermaid was beginning to enjoy their little adventure as well. And it was broad daylight and she hadn't exactly sneaked away from the house—Lindsay had broken no promise there.

All she wanted to do was tell Jared, or leave him a note if he wasn't at the tavern, that they must think of another course, rather than meeting first with her aunt; perhaps a letter to her father or even a journey themselves—with proper chaperones, of course—to Porthleven. It was all so exciting, yet she felt a slight shadow over her joy.

Aunt Winifred's recollection of events in Jared's family had been quite sobering, but Lindsay didn't doubt for a moment that he must have had good reason to return to India and leave his younger sister, Elise. She resolved to ask him, too, but right now that wasn't the first of her concerns, as finding the Boar's Head was forefront in her mind.

Nearly a half hour had passed before she decided to stop and have Gladys run into a millinery shop to ask directions. To her relief, they were very close, Lindsay's heart beating harder when she saw the familiar tavern ahead at the next corner. A vivid memory of Jared pulling her against him in his room to kiss her made her blush and smile, her fingers trembling slightly at the reins.

"Miss Somerset, mayhap I should go inside for you," Gladys suggested quietly as Lindsay drew the cabriolet to a stop. The young woman looked uncertainly toward the tavern, then back at her mistress. " 'Tis no matter for me, a workin' girl, but a lady like yourself—"

"I'll be fine, Gladys, truly."

Yet Lindsay wished she had her dark cloak, her pale lilac-colored gown and matching pelisse offering no anonymity at all as she entered the tavern, its interior looking so much brighter with sunlight streaming through the small paned windows. Fortunately, the place had only a few more patrons than it had had the other night, though they all turned to stare at her wide-eyed, as if she were some unlikely apparition.

She supposed she was, Lindsay thought uncomfortably, her gaze skipping from the table she and Jared had shared to where Della burst from the kitchen with a platter of sizzling sausages in one hand and a huge mug of ale in the other. A platter that nearly toppled to the floor, three sausages flying into the air, when the woman stopped abruptly to stare at her.

"Wot in heaven's name? Aren't you the same—"

"Yes, and I won't keep you." Lindsay glanced around to see that the patrons were watching with blatant interest, so she lowered her voice to a near whisper. "I've come to see Lord Giles—Jared. Is he—?"

"Here, miss? No, and wot a pity. I'm sure he'd be sorry to have missed you, but he left this early morn."

"Oh. Then I'd like to leave him a note, if I may."

"Aye, you may, but you'd best leave a shilling to post your little note as well. He's gone from London, far as I can tell. Paid his bill and took 'imself off—said he'd return in a few months or so."

Stunned, Lindsay could only stare as Della bent down under a chair and plopped the errant sausages back onto the platter.

"Damned slippery things . . . ouch! Hot, too."

As Della rose and faced her, the woman's smile curiously mocking, Lindsay somehow found her voice. "Did . . . did you say a few months?"

"Aye, and Lord knows I'll miss 'im. From the looks of it, so will you."

Her heart thundering in her ears, Lindsay tried to swallow the huge lump building in her throat. "Do you have any idea where . . ." She faltered, tears misting her eyes. "I have to find—"

"And I told you he left London, at least from the sound of it. Said somethin' to the driver about takin' him to Sussex and he was gone. Poof! Now if you'll excuse me, I've got me payin' customers to think of."

"Yes, yes, of course." Lindsay turned to leave, but then she stopped, glancing back at Della as her heart seemed to pound even louder within her breast. "Are you sure he said Sussex?"

"Aye, that and Seaword, I recall, or Seafirth."

Seaford! Lindsay suddenly felt as if she couldn't breathe, and she fled from the tavern without another word.

"Oh, Miss Somerset, I was growin' so worried," Gladys cried out, scrambling over in the seat even as Lindsay alighted.

"I'm sorry, Gladys, but you'll have to climb down."

"Wot, miss?"

"You'll have to find your way home by yourself—I can't explain. But I promise I'll make amends as soon as I can. I'm so terribly sorry. *Please*, Gladys."

Feeling absolutely wretched for having had to ask, but knowing no way around it, Lindsay could only watch as the chambermaid jumped down from the carriage and looked uncertainly around her.

"Just follow the way we came—there's plenty of daylight left."

"It's not me I'm worried for, miss, but you. I don't think Lady Penney will be happy—"

"I'm truly sorry, Gladys—take care on your way!" With a last guilty glance, Lindsay veered the cabriolet out into the traffic and quickly left the Boar's Head behind her.

Her feelings of wretchedness didn't lessen, but comingled with the restrained excitement and sense of purpose now driving her, one thought burning bright in her mind.

Jared must have been ordered upon another mission, surely! Why else would he not have taken the time to see her first and explain himself if he did not require such haste, such secrecy, such seeming deception?

It must be a dangerous mission, too. Hadn't Della said a few months? If Jared had gone to his ancestral home in Seaford, she doubted his stay would be but brief before he disappeared on some daring adventure. Dear God, she had to hurry. She was not going to be left behind without him, not when she could do so much to help!

By the time Gladys found her way home, Lindsay would be miles and miles away, with no chance of anyone finding her or even knowing where to look. Not Matilda or Aunt Winifred . . .

Fresh guilt stabbed at Lindsay, but she tamped it down. Instead she thought of Jared, her heart leading the way as she threw all caution to the wind and turned the carriage into a crowded thoroughfare wending south from London.

Chapter 12

"**H**ow long will it take to transport the supplies?"

"From the look of it, mayhap fifteen minutes, no more."

"Good. Let's move, then. We've ample cover with the fog, but I want to be gone as soon as everything's loaded." Wiping sweat from his eyes, Jared turned from the squat Irishman to a trio of silent figures whose faces were smudged with coal, wool caps upon their heads and their clothes soot-dark, even though the moon was no more than a hazy sliver through the mist, the night black as tar. "You three, come with me. I've a few kegs of fine Scotch whiskey I'd rather we didn't leave behind."

Low laughter erupted, but it died when Jared motioned for the three men to follow him, all four of them clambering along the steep path leading from the narrow secluded cove known as the Devil's Den. At the top of the rise Jared glanced back at the beach, the efficient skeleton crew hard at work ferrying foodstuffs to the men waiting aboard ship, two heavily laden galleys scraping against rocks and sand as they were pushed out into the waves.

Cowan had judged right. It wouldn't take long for them to unload the galleys and then send one back to help with the last boat loaded and still waiting on the shore. And that suited Jared more than he could say. He wanted to be gone from this windswept scrap of Sussex coastland with its ghosts and bitter memories.

If he hadn't brought the Scotch whiskey all the way from London, he would have said to hell with the stuff and already been aboard the ship, but he'd won it in a wager, after all.

He'd never seen a merchant as proud of the quality of his brew as he was misguided about his bets, the fellow gambling four kegs that the champion, Tom Cribb, was past his prime and due for a sound trouncing. The merchant had lost, but that hadn't kept him from good-naturedly offering to half the onlookers at Offley's a sample of the same batch of whiskey he claimed would soon be bound for Portugal and Lord Wellington himself.

And if that rowdy throng had enjoyed a taste, so would his crew, Jared thought grimly; the kegs that had been delivered to the Boar's Head yesterday morning were marked for export, just as the merchant had boasted.

"First man to the whiskey wins the first drink once we're under sail," Jared goaded his compatriots, the three matching his hard sprint toward a thick copse of elms where he'd hidden the kegs earlier in the day, before heading to Dovercourt Manor. He could barely see the lights of the main house for the thick mist billowing in from the sea, but he didn't miss them. He missed nothing about that hated place where his sister had suffered—Blast and damnation, what was that?

"Shhh, get down, all of you!"

The three men threw themselves onto their stomachs. Jared dove beside them into the damp grass, cocking his head and listening. He could have sworn he heard a horse whinnying very near, so near that he judged they might have run directly across its path. But the fog was becoming so thick that he couldn't see anything more than fifteen feet away.

"Cap'n, do you think Simon—?"

"No, there was only the one wagon of supplies." Yet Jared wondered if the loyal old codger who served as caretaker of Dovercourt Manor during his long absences and butler during his brief stays might have forgotten to include some foodstuffs and had decided to ride back out to this desolate spot.

But no, Simon Tuft would have made himself known to them by now; to do otherwise might risk a metal ball in the gut. Jared listened for another long, silent moment, then lunged to his feet.

"Let's go. Cowan and the rest are waiting—we can't risk a delay."

Keeping low, Jared signaled for the three men to run ahead of him into the trees even as he kept scanning the fog.

Lindsay slipped and slid down the rock-strewn path, her heart pounding so fiercely that she felt its throb in every fiber of her being.

She knew she had to hurry. Jared and those three men would surely return at any moment, and who could say how soon those other men might row back to the beach? She couldn't see the ship for the dense fog—dear Lord, to think she had stumbled so innocently upon Jared in this remote place!—but she could hear low bursts of command and pulleys creaking as supplies were hoisted aboard, and it was all so exciting she could barely contain herself.

She had been almost in despair, the night grown so late and she had yet to reach Dovercourt Manor. The directions she had received from a sleepy innkeeper in Seaford had taken her along a rutted coastal road which seemed to lead to nowhere when the fog had arisen. And her poor horse had been so exhausted from the long journey, she feared he might collapse, so she had disembarked and tethered him to a tree just short of the cove and begun to walk, hoping someone from the house could come back for him.

It was only then she'd heard male voices drifting to her as if from the sea, one rich baritone making her heart stop— Oh, Lord!

Hearing the splash of oars cutting through the waves, Lindsay darted across the sand to the lone galley and pulled back the canvas covering with trembling hands. The boat was filled with supplies, but she climbed in anyway, shifting and clearing a narrow space for herself near the stern. Then she flipped the canvas back into place, pitch darkness enveloping her, and listened breathlessly to more splashes and the sound of men wading to shore.

"Any sign of them?"

"Not yet, Cowan."

"I don't see them, either," came another man's reply.

"Well, we'll not wait with that galley. Tie the rope to her prow and shove her into the water. She's loaded so full it'll be the devil to tow, but as soon as they return, the seven of us should manage. Go on, now, and be quick!"

Lindsay gasped as the boat was heaved with

grunts and low curses from the shore, the sudden rocking of the waves causing a small barrel to shift and jam sharply against her ribs. Yet even that discomfort couldn't temper her mounting excitement, her imagination aflame.

The cove, the creeping fog, the dead of night. What better setting could there be for a gallant spy to embark upon his latest mission? And Jared clearly had an entire ship at his service. With all these supplies, it was clear, too, that he would be gone a long time, which only made her more glad that she had followed after him.

He couldn't fail to think her the most daring of women now . . . couldn't fail to see that she had a flair for secrecy that matched his—she'd successfully come this far, hadn't she? Most importantly, he couldn't fail to see that she was bold enough to face any danger they might encounter together—

"There he is! There's the cap'n now!"

Captain? Obviously one of the men she'd seen disappear into the fog with Jared was the master of the ship, although it had been clear to her, from her hiding place behind a huge rock, that they all followed Jared's commands. And, of course, that was only right. With Jared forever risking life and limb for Britain, she imagined he must need a ship and a loyal crew who adhered strictly to his orders to better accomplish his mission.

Lindsay held her breath as rapid footfalls scrunched upon the sand, but she nearly cried out when a heavy object was dumped atop the canvas, just missing her head.

"All this bloody trouble for Scotch whiskey—no, man, this galley's too full. Take the rest to Cowan's boat and let's be gone."

"Jared . . ." she whispered, her face burning at how close he'd just been to her, and now he was forging with the others into the surf. But at least he had saved her from being crushed; the man seemed fated to come to her rescue.

She heard no more but the slapping of the waves against the hull. The oars sliced with rhythmic strokes through the water, as the boat she'd hidden in was towed by the other galley, leaving behind the fog-shrouded cove, Sussex . . . England. Where might they be bound? France? Russia?

Her mind dancing with possibilities, Lindsay nonetheless couldn't stifle a yawn, the gentle rocking causing her to feel the long, tense hours since she'd left London. She was hungry, too, a gnawing ache at the pit of her stomach; she'd had no money to buy food along the way. But what did any of that matter compared with her finding Jared—she could have trudged on to Dovercourt Manor and missed him entirely, but she hadn't. They were together . . . blissfully together . . .

"Throw down the ladder! Captain coming aboard!"

Lindsay nearly sat upright, she was so startled, realizing she must have dozed off for a moment. She snuggled back into the cramped space as best she could, but was jarred once again when the boat bumped into something hard and massive.

"Easy, now; give us a bit more rope. Aye, that's it, under the prow. Pull it tight under the stern; that's it. All right, lads, swing her up nice and easy."

Recognizing the thick Irish brogue as belonging to the man called Cowan, Lindsay grabbed onto a barrel when the galley suddenly lifted clear of the water and swung free in the wind, her stomach jumping to her throat. She could hear winches and hoists creaking just as before and realized they were bringing the boat aboard, and here she was, hiding right in the midst of tins of biscuits and crocks of salted fish and fresh vegetables and, oh, yes, a keg of Scotch whiskey.

Preparing herself to be exposed when the galley came down with a hard bump upon the deck, Lindsay couldn't help wondering with sudden nervousness what Jared's reaction might be. Of course he would be surprised, but she hoped pleased as well—

"Not now, men; we'll unload when it's light. Hoist up the other galley and raise the anchor."

"Already raised, Cap'n, soon as you came aboard."

"Good. Unfurl the sails!"

Lindsay slumped onto the galley's floor, confusion vying with her keen disappointment that, for the moment, her surprise had been spoiled. She would swear that had been Jared, so why was he answering to "Captain," and so forcefully? She had heard tension in his voice, too.

"A welcome sight to have you back aboard, friend. And just in time. Roscoff was growing a bit dull—"

"Later, Walker. I'm not sure, but I think someone or something was afoot on the coast."

"Excisemen?"

"I don't know and it doesn't matter. We've been sitting in this bay too bloody long, fog or not. Get us out of here."

Doubly confused, Lindsay heard Jared stride away, then stop to utter another command.

"Cowan, get some men over here now! Have them train their guns at the shore. If anything moves to follow us, blow them out of the water."

Blow them out . . . ! Lindsay gulped, scarcely recognizing Jared's voice for its harshness. And she didn't dare move a muscle now, either, for fear some skittish sailor might train his weapon upon her instead and squeeze the trigger.

Dear Lord, what if she had found a small row-boat and tried to reach the ship or had set off swimming from shore? Would they have blown her to tiny bits? Obviously, being a military spy was more dangerous and secretive than she had imagined. So much so that Jared was even concerned about excisemen. But after three years of helping Corisande evade those snoopy fellows, she could teach him a thing or two about the King's customs men and ways to fool them, another benefit to having her aboard.

Smiling to herself, Lindsay closed her eyes and tried to get comfortable, yet she wondered how long it might be before it was safe to leave her hiding place. But at least it wasn't chilly, the canvas covering keeping things quite snug and dry.

And thank goodness she was wearing a pelisse, in case the coming day proved cool; she imagined in open water the weather might be fierce. She had no other clothes, but she trusted Jared would help her think of something.

Lindsay grew so sleepy, she paid no heed to the sails flapping in the wind and the spars creaking when the ship gathered speed. All she was conscious of was a soothing rolling motion, her sore, travel-weary muscles relaxing, her arms dropping to her sides, Jared's name upon her lips as she smiled contentedly and fell asleep.

"Is it . . . ?"

Jared didn't have to answer; he knew his grim smile was all Walker Burke had to see, his long years of friendship with the wry-witted American having fused a bond stronger than words.

"Well, well, what do you know? Couldn't think of a finer way to welcome the sun—Cooky's coffee, thick as tar and about as tasty, and a sluggish merchantman at the horizon, soon to make our acquaintance . . . unless you've decided to let this one pass?"

Jared lowered the spyglass and quickly weighed his options. He usually preferred to wait a few days after leaving England to make a first kill, so as to rule out any connection with his sudden absence, but then again, this voyage wouldn't be like any that had come before.

He had already decided it would be different; he had a record to break—thirteen vessels during his last cruise—and, with the heightened level of fervor he had seen in London for his immediate capture and execution, his immortality to flaunt.

Blast them all to hell. By the time he was done, they would pray he was no more than myth.

"You've got your wish, Walker. We attack."

Chapter 13

It wasn't so much the deafening clap of thunder that woke Lindsay; she tucked her fists under her chin and snuggled against a barrel, thinking drowsily that a storm must be brewing. But when an acrid stench burned her nostrils, she blinked open her eyes in alarm, disoriented by fading dreams and the darkness all around her.

Oh, God, Aunt Winifred's house was on fire! She had to get out—Lord help her, she had to get out!

Lindsay punched wildly at the blackness, wincing when her left elbow connected with something hard, pain shooting like prickly pins through her arm. She couldn't breathe, the stench had grown so strong, and she began to cough as she renewed her desperate flailing. Her eyes tearing, her lungs ready to burst, she clawed at the inky void, crying out with relief when blinding light poured down upon her.

Blinding light...? As a shaft of realization pierced her brain, Lindsay remembered then that she lay in the bottom of a boat but that did nothing to allay her panic. Pushing aside metal tins and loose cabbages, she lunged to her feet and stood squinting as she tried to get her bearings.

"*Fire!*"

The roared command startled her even more than the ensuing round of explosions. Lindsay spun about in place, her eyes growing wide.

The entire world seemed ablaze, brilliant sunlight glinting like a thousand mirrors upon the water, the deck alight in the blinding morning sun. And everywhere seemed commotion, teams of men—young and old—working furiously around starboard gunports to reload a row of gleaming black cannon. With a nervous laugh, Lindsay realized the caustic smoke choking her lungs wasn't proof of fire at all, but bore the unmistakable reek of gunpowder.

Heaven help them, they were being attacked! Her heart hammering, she ducked back into the boat and peered through an oar ring, supplies shifting and tumbling around her as the ship listed sharply to port. Oh, Lord, sinking, too! But the deck righted itself in the next instant, the blinding sun behind her now.

Lindsay looked out over the waves and gulped at the sight of another ship, a prosperous merchantman from the look of it, much as she'd seen on shopping excursions to the port of Penzance. But what caught her gaze was the British flag fluttering proudly against the blue sky, yet at such a queer angle, and it appeared the flag was being lowered, too . . .

She felt the color drain from her face when she spied the merchantman's shattered hull, peppered with holes. The ship was listing visibly even as men's frantic voices carried across the narrowing distance, desperate commands ringing out that longboats be lowered. Dear God, what terrible manner of enemy had they encountered? Not one but two British vessels were under vicious attack, Jared's ship and the merchantman!

She glanced over her shoulder, but the sea was blinding in the sunlight and she could see nothing, least of all some great devil ship. Her gaze flew back to the floundering merchantman, tears stinging her eyes.

It was clearly doomed. Sinking.

As Lindsay watched in horror, her heart went out to the frightened crew scrambling across the listing deck. She felt so useless, but something had to be done! No further explosions had sounded, so perhaps their phantom attacker had sailed away, the cannon aboard Jared's ship proving too fearsome, the skirmish won. Surely now he wouldn't hesitate to save those poor men from drowning.

Lindsay clambered out of the galley so suddenly that she nearly careened into a young man with a powder-blackened face. The sailor dropped back to gape at her in surprise.

"Where can I find Lord Giles? Please, you must tell me!"

To her frustration, the man seemed to have lost his voice. He stared at her as if she were a phantom herself and not a flesh-and-blood woman.

"Lord Giles—I must find him!" Her voice rising in desperation, she was almost tempted to slap the sailor to get an answer. "Can't you see that ship is sinking?"

"Th-the quarterdeck, miss."

He pointed and Lindsay followed his finger, suddenly aware that many eyes were upon her, the strangest silence settling over the lower deck. But she paid no heed to the startled faces and flew toward the stern; at the companionway, she grabbed the brass railings and climbed two steps at a time, her breath tearing at her throat.

"Jared, please, we have to do something! Those men— Oh!"

Lindsay was hauled from the companionway and swung with such suddenness to the quarterdeck that she reeled dizzily, but two strong hands clamped around her upper arms kept her from falling. Yet her knees nearly buckled when she glanced up, her thanks dying on her lips.

"By God, woman, how in blazes did you—?"

She could only stare at the man who held her, a mask covering the upper portion of his face.

A bright gold mask that shone like flame in the sun, nearly blinding her.

And she knew of only one man who wore such a guise, his name a curse upon the tongues of all those she'd heard utter it in London, a reward of ten thousand pounds announced only yesterday in *The Morning Post* to whoever captured him alive.

The Phoenix.

"Dag, take the wench below to my quarters. And see that she doesn't escape!"

With that Lindsay was shoved so roughly away from him that she almost fell again, gasping when a chafed hand as huge and red as a ham reached out to catch her. She recoiled but in the next moment found herself thrown unceremoniously over a massive shoulder.

She didn't try to fight against the fair-haired giant who now held her; her numbing shock was too great. Yet she started when she heard a familiar voice's ringing command, familiar except for the strange accent which was wholly foreign to her.

"Prepare to bring prisoners aboard. There'll be

no time to loot her, she's foundering too fast. But that doesn't mean we won't enjoy watching her burn.''

The traitorous words clamping like an iron fist around her heart, Lindsay squeezed her eyes tight against the tears suddenly threatening to spill.

Lord, what a fool! What a bloody, bloody fool!

Fifteen minutes later, Lindsay was still calling herself a fool, that and a dozen other unflattering names, as she watched transfixed in disbelief at the porthole.

Nothing remained of the merchantman but burning debris upon the waves, her seared topmast having disappeared only a moment ago. The long-boat filled with ship's officers was a dark speck against the pristine blue sky; Lindsay imagined they were rowing for England as they had never rowed before.

If they had rowed before, she amended unhappily, recalling the outraged conversation she had heard at the Oglethorpe ball. But at least she could take some comfort that the crew had been plucked from the sea; prisoners now, but alive.

The criminals who manned this ship had been quite efficient in their rescue. The ashen-faced captain and his bedraggled officers, stripped of their weapons, had been ordered into one longboat, while the rest of the merchantman's hands had been allowed to board. Lindsay had seen everything from the porthole, but now she turned away and sank to the floor, drawing her knees to her chin. She stared blindly at the Spartan quarters—a plain wooden bed, a desk and a sea chest the few furnishings in what had become her prison.

Dear God, criminals.

Traitors.

Contemptible enemies of the Crown.

And Jared Giles, the Earl of Dovercourt, was among them—no, not just among them, but their leader. The Phoenix. And less than an hour ago she had thought him the most heroic of men ... the man she wished to marry ... a man she could love ...

A lump welling in her throat, Lindsay dropped her forehead onto her knees.

Her dreams had become ashes. Her foolish, girlish dreams—Corisande had often said she was too romantic-minded for her own good. And Corisande was usually right. Ridiculously starry-eyed, seeing only what she wanted to see, believing only what she wanted to believe, Lindsay had made herself look an utter fool.

But she wasn't going to cry, she thought stubbornly, swiping at the mutinous mist burning her eyes. She wasn't so much of a ninny to believe that useless tears could help her now— Oh, Lord ...

Inhaling sharply, Lindsay rose to her feet as footsteps outside the door grew louder, the forceful stride filling her with dread. She looked wildly around for a weapon, anything, barely having time to grab a brass candlestick from the desk and thrust it behind her back before the door burst open and slammed into the bulkhead.

The fury burning in Jared's vivid blue eyes slammed into her with as much force, and Lindsay gulped. The gold mask was gone, his face so handsome that she felt her knees grow weak, but that made her grip the candlestick all the tighter.

She didn't know this dangerous man at all, she

told herself shakily as he took a step toward her. Not at all! Whatever she had concocted about him in her mind was a fanciful myth, a lie—

"Talk, damn you! How in blazes did you get here?"

She started, stunned, his raised voice so cold, so brutal, that she felt tears spring to her eyes. But that only made her lift her chin, her own voice surprisingly calm.

"If you wish to talk, sir, we shall talk. But I simply won't answer if you plan to continue yelling at me like an enraged beast—"

"Ah, so I'm an enraged beast now?" Jared had roared again, taking some perverse pleasure that Lindsay jumped. He wanted her to jump. He wanted her to know just how angry he was to find her aboard the *Vengeance*—blast and damnation, he could scarcely believe it himself!

When he had seen her running along the lower deck, her long fair hair streaming behind her, the wind buffeting her flimsy clothing against her body, every man jack's eyes upon her . . .

Jared wheeled around, a sixth sense telling him that they were not alone. True enough, Dag still stood guard just outside in the lighted passageway, his expression somber as a judge's, while Walker leaned casually against the bulkhead opposite him, a curious smile on the American's lips, his dark eyes filled with studied humor. With a low oath, Jared swung the door shut in their faces.

"An enraged beast with a penchant for slamming doors and swearing, too," came a feminine mutter behind him.

Jared turned back to find Lindsay had edged farther away from him, her face nearly as pale as her hair.

Good, she was frightened of him, he thought grimly, taking a step toward her. That pleased him, too, if only that it would help keep the reckless chit in line, although he didn't like the hint of defiance in those lovely blue eyes, which was a far cry from the joy he'd last seen in London— Bloody hell, enough!

"All right, we'll talk. Civilly. Now answer my question."

"Very well. I sneaked aboard in the galley—"

"That I was already able to surmise, as well as that it must have been your horse I heard. How did you know where to find me?"

"*That* I discovered from Della at the Boar's Head tavern," Lindsay said as rudely, although it really wasn't her nature. But this whole strange situation was so far from what she had expected, had dreamed—ah, those accursed dreams again—that she felt quite unlike herself. "I went there to speak to you, or at least to leave a note, to tell you not to come to my aunt's house on Saturday—today . . ."

She faltered, but swallowed a stab of pain and rushed on. "I feared it would be too difficult for Aunt Winnie to see you at her door, given how she felt about you, so I wanted to tell you we must devise another course." She gave a small, sad laugh. "It all seems so silly now, my even thinking that you wanted to marry—"

"Silly and as reckless as ever. You went to the Boar's Head by yourself?"

Stung that he obviously cared nothing for her feelings, and angry with herself for thinking that such a treacherous miscreant should, Lindsay hiked her chin up another notch, although she felt it trembling. "It was broad daylight and I had Aunt Winnie's chambermaid Gladys for a chaperone— so at least I didn't break my word. Not like you did to me."

"And what was I supposed to tell you, woman? The truth? That I had no intention of coming back for you in three days' time, even though my saying so was the only way I could think of to keep you from traipsing around the city like a hoyden?"

"A hoyden!"

"Yes, a hoyden and a naive chit to boot for imagining that I would take you to wife, which clearly was your misguided scheme from the very start! You would have been wiser to listen to your aunt and stay the hell away from me!"

He had yelled again, but that wasn't what made Lindsay feel as if she were reeling.

A hoyden. Naive chit. Misguided. The words echoed in her mind and she winced to herself, knowing that they were true. Yet if she had been all those things, he had encouraged her!

"Why . . . why did you agree to meet me, then?" she demanded in a strained voice, fearing she already knew his answer. "The night after the Oglethorpes' ball—"

"I was planning to seduce you, if you want the truth of it. Your aunt was closer to the mark than you think."

"But you didn't"—her cheeks aflame, Lindsay glanced down uncomfortably at her soiled slippers—"take unfair advantage—"

"No, because I realized, after you'd joined me in the coach, that you weren't the shrewd wanton I had thought, but a foolhardy miss entirely out of her realm and experience. So I decided it best to teach you a lesson."

"A lesson?"

"Not to entrust yourself so completely to someone you knew nothing about—"

"And obviously I shouldn't have trusted a notorious brigand like you!" Astonished at her indignant outburst, which reminded her of Corisande so much more than herself, Lindsay nonetheless held her ground, feeling more a fool than ever before. She swept her gaze over him, noting a pistol jammed boldly in his belt, a wicked-looking cutlass lying against his lean hip. "You're no military spy at all, but a pirate—"

"I prefer privateer."

"It's the same thing!"

"On the contrary, I hold American letters of marque, which makes me quite respectable."

"You call preying upon your own country's ships respectable? Ruthlessly looting them? Burning them? I must differ, sir. You're no privateer, but a despicable pirate and—and a traitor to boot— Oh!"

Lindsay backed up as Jared advanced upon her, but he stopped when she brandished the candlestick defensively in front of her. His face had grown so dark that she knew a moment's fear, his eyes as turbulently blue as she had seen them.

"Call me a pirate if you will, woman, but a traitor is only for God, or the devil, to judge."

They stared at each other, the long silence so charged that Lindsay felt as if a wall of intense heat had been thrown between them. She blinked when a knock finally came at the door.

"Cap'n, forgive me, but have you decided upon our course? We've the prisoners . . ."

"We'll drop them at Start Point."

"Good enough, Cap'n."

Start Point, Lindsay considered, her heart sinking. Already they were so far from London? Yet she squared her shoulders. That was as good a place as any to free herself of Jared and his treacherous crew.

"I know Start Point," she said stiffly, not daring to lower the candlestick an inch. "It shouldn't take me more than a day's coach ride to reach my father's estate in Porthleven, if I could trouble you for the fare. I'll pay you back—quite discreetly, of course."

"That won't be necessary."

"No, no, I insist—"

"And I said it won't be necessary. You're not leaving this ship."

Chapter 14

"**N**ot . . . ?" Lindsay laughed nervously, thinking she had misheard, although her pounding heart told her otherwise. "Truly, my lord, as you've made most clear to me, I've caused you enough trouble already."

"So you have, and I'd like nothing better than to be rid of you, but that won't be possible. I can't risk you revealing my identity—"

"But I wouldn't, I swear!" Lindsay blurted out, the firm set of Jared's jaw filling her with sudden desperation. "I'm very good at keeping secrets—you could ask my friend Corie, we have a secret pact ourselves . . . oh, dear, but you can't ask her, she's on her way to Lisbon—but she'll be back within a few weeks and she could tell you then—I mean, send you a letter—"

"This will be your cabin. And don't try to escape, for it's no use. Dag will be posted outside the door."

Dear Lord, no, he wasn't listening to her! Lindsay thought wildly as Jared turned to go. His jaw tensed all the more when she reached out and caught his arm.

"But you can't keep me aboard this ship, Jared.

I'll miss the London Season! I waited so long to go—"

"Obviously you were willing to forgo it, thinking I was a spy."

"Yes, but that was different! I thought you wished to marry me—and when Della told me she'd overheard that you'd gone to Sussex, and Aunt Winnie had already said your family home was near Seaford, I thought you'd been sent on a mission and I didn't want to be left behind without you. But you're not at all the man I believed you were—"

Lindsay gasped in alarm, Jared grabbing her so suddenly by the shoulders that the candlestick clattered to the floor. She thought he might shake her; instead he pulled her so close that his breath mingled with hers, his voice low and harsh.

"That's what I tried to tell you, woman, but now we're bloody well stuck with each other . . . at least until I decide what's to be done with you."

He released her as abruptly and strode to the door, while Lindsay sank to her knees in shock, staring down blindly at her hands. Yet Jared's muttered oath made her look up to see a squat redhaired fellow, appearing more a leprechaun than a sailor, jump to his feet from where he'd fallen when the door was yanked open.

"Damnation, Cowan . . ."

"Forgive me, Cap'n, I—I thought I lost a button from my shirt. Ah, me, there it is! Right where it belonged all along!"

The Irishman cast a sympathetic glance in Lindsay's direction and then he was gone, his short legs pumping fast as he disappeared down the passageway. Meantime, the silent giant named Dag,

the top of his blond head scraping the ceiling,
seemed to be frowning at Jared. Another man, with
striking good looks that reminded her of
Corisande's Lord Donovan and hair as raven-black,
hadn't budged from his casual stance against the
bulkhead.

A slow, easy smile stirred the man's lips, his
midnight eyes flickering from her to Jared. "Well,
well, friend, this is certainly interesting—"

"And none of your concern, Walker. Dag, no one
enters or leaves this cabin but you or Cooky with
her meals."

Still frowning, the big man nodded and pulled
the door shut behind Jared, but not before giving
Lindsay a look she could only describe as troubled.

Dag's size might have frightened her on the
quarterdeck, but he had been nothing if not gentle
with her after throwing her over his shoulder, although he hadn't said a word when he'd deposited
her in the cabin. Yet suddenly she didn't feel quite
so alone; perhaps some men of reason aboard this
ship might consider pleading her cause to Jared.

Either that or they might even agree to help her,
Lindsay thought hopefully, Dag's and Cowan's
kind reactions to her plight having cheered her
more than she would have imagined.

As for the man called Walker, who could say?
He had at least seemed curious, and she hadn't
sensed any ill will on his part toward her. And he
possessed the same strange accent Jared had used
on deck. She suddenly recalled that the Phoenix
was thought to be American, and now she knew
why, although she doubted that Walker's manner
of speech was a ruse.

Irishmen. Americans. A mute blond giant who

looked as if he'd just stepped from a Norse saga. Jared's crew certainly was a motley one, and perhaps therein lay some advantage. She could see already that a few aboard perceived her as a damsel in distress.

"So get yourself up off the floor," Lindsay chided herself aloud, rising to shake out her skirt. Her gaze fell on the brass candlestick and she picked it up, her face burning at how roughly Jared had grabbed her and how cruelly he had spoken.

Her sense of hurt was immediate and acute, her spirits flagging, but this served to bring to mind, like a gentle rebuke, Corisande's words to her the night before she had left: "That's not the indomitable Lindsay Somerset I know."

No, it wasn't. If she was a damsel in distress, then she would simply have to effect her own rescue with or without help.

So Jared Giles wasn't the man of her dreams. That didn't have to mean her dreams were ashes or that she must give up her search for the valiant adventurer she hoped to marry. And she certainly wasn't going to allow a ruthless pirate, a traitor to his own King and country, to stop her!

Much heartened, Lindsay actually was smiling as she returned the candlestick to the desk and went to the porthole. Yet she still felt a poignant pang of regret when she looked out onto the sunlit sea.

"Obviously London held a bit more excitement this time around. Or is that an understatement?"

Jared didn't answer, but instead stared sullenly at the darkening horizon and the distant smudge of land lying due northwest. He'd kept himself busy for hours but it was clear Walker was determined to goad him—damnation, the last thing he wanted was to discuss Lindsay.

"She's lovely, you know."

Jared grunted, saying nothing.

"Beautiful, actually, like a sea nymph with that silvery blond hair and those big—"

Jared threw his friend a dark glance.

"Blue eyes."

Walker's wry grin did nothing to lighten Jared's mood. He left the starboard railing and strode toward the prow, very much aware that Walker followed him. But he also sensed that the American had sobered, too, his face serious as he stopped beside Jared.

"What are you going to do with her?"

Jared stared out across the rolling waves, steely gray now that clouds had obscured the setting sun. He sighed heavily.

"Jared?"

"Dammit, man, I don't know what's to be done with her!"

"That's what I thought."

Walker's words grating upon him, Jared turned angrily on his friend. "So what would you have me do? Make her walk the plank? Feed her to the fish? Leave her on some deserted island to rot?"

"Easy, Jared. I have no solutions, either. It's a blasted fix, no matter what we do."

"*We*? I told you, Lindsay Somerset is none of your concern."

Walker stared at him, his pitch-black eyes narrowing; then a quizzical smile touched his face. "How long did you say you've known the wench?"

"I didn't say." Sensing suddenly where Walker was leading, Jared cursed and went to the port railing, angry with himself and somewhat startled, too, at the vehemence he had displayed. Again his second-in-command followed him, which was no surprise. Eight years of each other's company had left them both able to discern how far things could be pushed. But Walker was pushing dangerously close . . .

"So she's a hoyden, is she?"

Pleased that the direction of their conversation had shifted, if only slightly, Jared gave a snort. "That, a romantic fool and about as bloody naive as they come. But obviously you overheard everything, so I see no reason to continue—"

"I'm curious, is all. That lesson you meant to teach her—"

"Failed completely, as you can see. The first night I took her to a cellar tavern and got her drunk on ale, but that didn't daunt her. The next night she managed to find herself nearly auctioned off at a boxing match, if I hadn't offered a hundred pounds for the chit and discharged my pistol into the ceiling for good measure. I even took her to the Boar's Head and up to my room, but that didn't dissuade her. So I told her three days and I'd be back—"

"A lie, of course."

Jared threw him another hard look. "Yes, a bloody lie. I finished my business—there are enough fat cargoes scheduled for shipment in and out of London to keep us busy for weeks—and then I left the city to make our rendezvous. But as you overheard, she followed me, and now we've some Cornish baronet's daughter aboard while the whole of London is probably looking for her!"

He slammed his fist onto the railing, but Walker

merely shook his head as if perplexed.

"But why go through such trouble—"

"Because I was a rutting fool!" Jared's fingers tightened on the railing, his voice falling to almost a whisper. "She reminded me of Elise—I should have taken her home as soon as I realized I'd misread her . . . but perhaps I saw it as some small way to right the past." He laughed, the sound bitter and raw. "But we know better, don't we, friend? Revenge is the only way to right the past, and even that sometimes doesn't seem enough. It can never bring back what is lost."

Walker didn't answer, and when Jared finally glanced at him, he saw that the American was staring blindly at the sea, his face as grim as Jared felt.

He didn't need words to know what Walker was thinking. Each man aboard the *Vengeance* had endured a common loss and shared a common past as binding as blood. Each man bore a common hatred against England that sealed their loyalty. And whenever another British ship was consigned by fire to a watery grave, all of them shared the spoils and rejoiced in the destruction.

"Start Point, Cap'n, dead ahead!"

Jared pivoted on his heel, his gaze meeting his first mate's. Walker abruptly left him to see to his own duties.

"Good enough, Cowan. Order the prisoners brought from the hold."

"Aye, Cap'n."

As the stumpy Irishman disappeared into the belly of the ship, Jared turned and pulled the gold mask from his belt. Yet his thoughts weren't so much on the merchantman's crew who would soon taste again the sweetness of freedom, but upon

Lindsay confined unhappily in his quarters.

What in blazes *was* he going to do with her?

Lindsay peered anxiously out the porthole, her hands twisting in her rumpled pelisse.

It was nearly dark, but she could still see the rugged green hills of Start Point beckoning to her like the promised land; she so wished she were aboard one of the galleys heading to shore with the merchantman's crew. Yet she knew that wouldn't have worked.

Once she was free of this wretched ship, she had no desire to be implicated in any way with the Phoenix, so it was best she strike out alone. Jared hadn't accepted her promise not to reveal his identity, but she fully intended to live by it as if he had agreed. An oath was an oath. And she didn't want his capture and execution on her conscience, no matter he was a brutal pirate.

She shivered at the thought, and focused instead upon the improvised money belt around her waist which she had fashioned from the torn hem of her gown.

She had found gold guineas in the desk, a tidy sum she fully intended to repay, which would buy her a new gown and coach fare back to London. Cornwall might be closer, but she had no wish to face Olympia. Aunt Winifred and even Matilda, for that matter, would be much easier to sway with a fantastic story . . . as soon as she thought of a good one, of course. But there would be time for that later. Right now she simply wanted to be free of this cabin, and the rest would take care of itself.

She felt a bit guilty about her plan, actually, which was utter nonsense. Dag might have been kind to her—bringing in her meals himself while a grizzled old sailor, clearly the cook, given he'd been swatched from chin to knobby knees in a soiled white apron, had watched curiously at the door—but that didn't mean she owed him any special consideration.

No, not even if he had returned midafternoon with a cup of fragrant hot tea, as usual not saying a word, although his light blue eyes had seemed concerned that she had scarcely touched the meat stew he'd brought her for luncheon. Oddly, she had sensed then that something wasn't quite right with him; what, she couldn't put her finger on, but she wouldn't allow sympathy to sway her, either. Dag was a pirate, like every other crew member aboard this ship. That fact was all she must keep in mind.

Satisfied that the money belt was tied securely around her waist, Lindsay took a deep breath and straightened her shoulders. Then she doubled over and began to moan loudly, praying her plan would work.

"Oh, God, help me! It hurts . . . oh, no, it hurts!"

The door bursting open made her start, but she moaned all the louder and writhed dramatically as Dag stared at her wide-eyed.

"I fear . . . oh, no, it must have been something in the food . . . ohhh . . ."

She jerked, clutching at her stomach, then spun in a swoon to the floor. Lying perfectly still, she could sense Dag looming over her, the big man dropping to one knee. She fluttered open her eyes, her voice no more than a croak.

"Get help, Dag, please. Oh, it hurts so much . . ."

Lindsay dropped her head limply to one side,

fearing for a moment, when a huge hand covered her shoulder, that Dag might be thinking to carry her to help. She moaned as if in mortal pain when he made a motion to lift her.

"No, no, please! It hurts so . . . bring help, Dag! Bring help!"

She breathed a furtive sigh of relief when he nodded and rose, his footfalls amazingly light for a man so large as he lunged from the cabin.

That meant she had mere seconds to effect her escape. Lindsay jumped to her feet and waited only an instant before careening after him out the door. The shadowy passageways like a maze, she nonetheless knew she was headed in the right direction when she dashed through the ship's kitchen; she remembered the small galley from when Dag had carried her to Jared's quarters.

She heard a startled oath, the astonished cook dropping his spoon with a clatter to the floor while his two assistants gaped at her from their stools, where they sat peeling potatoes and chopping onions; then the galley was behind her and she was plunging into another passage. Please, please, she had to be close . . .

With a relieved cry, she spied the companionway leading out of the hold, her heart thundering against her breast as she stumbled up the narrow steps. Thundering so loud that she barely heard her name being shouted above the whistling wind, her only thought to clamber over the railing.

Then she was falling through space, icy water closing over her head before she'd even thought to catch a breath.

Chapter 15

"Damnation, Dag, she tricked you, the little fool!"

Jared dropped his pistol and wrenched off his cutlass as he ran to the railing; pulling off his boots, he scanned the dark, choppy waves in vain for a blond head. The currents were treacherous here, and unaccustomed fear gripped him. He didn't wait any longer. Grabbing a handful of rigging, he hauled himself onto the railing and dove into the sea.

Only when he broke the surface, chilled instantly to the bone and sucking air into his lungs, did he remember one of the reasons he disliked swimming so much, especially around the British Isles. The water was simply too damned cold.

And thus, deadly.

"Over there, Jared! She's swimming for shore!"

Walker waved him toward starboard. Jared clenched his teeth and lunged powerfully through the water, relief twisting his gut when he spied Lindsay valiantly struggling against the rough, foam-flecked waves. He could see that she was an accomplished swimmer but already tiring, her slim arms growing less rhythmic with each stroke. And with two hundred feet yet to go before she reached the beach, he knew she would never make it, the icy cold slowing her down.

As it was slowing him down, too. Jared squinted through the gathering night to see that the galleys returning to the ship wouldn't get to them in time. Spitting out mouthfuls of salt water, he kicked with all his might to reach her, not surprised that she didn't try to fight him when he caught a small, frigid foot in his hand. Her movements jerky, her lips blue, her fair hair plastered like a cap to her head, she barely acknowledged him when he grabbed her around the chest and began to swim with her back to the ship.

Her glazed silence chilling him as much as the sea, Jared knew there was nothing he could do for her out here. He swam as hard as he could, relief filling him again when Walker flung a noosed rope out to him. Jared looped it over his head, right arm and shoulder.

Taking care to keep Lindsay's chin well above the waves, he allowed his men to haul them to the ship, saving his strength for the rope ladder. The blasted thing nearly hit him in the head when it was dropped over the side, but he couldn't have been more glad to see it. Yet he soon found that the icy water had nearly sapped him, for when he tried to climb, Lindsay's weight, although slight, was more a unwieldy burden at that moment than he could have imagined.

He couldn't suppress a groan of gratitude when someone suddenly splashed into the water beside him, Walker flinging water from his hair when he surfaced.

"Damn, it's cold!"

Jared nodded, Lindsay more ice in his arms than

flesh, which only chilled him further, his own arms beginning to grow numb. "Quick, man, take her."

Walker did, climbing the rope ladder with little trouble while Jared waited for the two of them to be hauled aboard. Then he followed, his legs feeling like heavy, leaden weights as he forced one foot after the other; he smiled his thanks when Walker clamped a strong hand around his wrist to pull him over the railing.

"I know you said the wench was none of my concern—twice—but I thought this time you might make an exception."

With a warm blanket thrown over his shoulders by another sailor, Jared met Walker's wry smile with a weary, shivering one, though he could see that his friend's dark eyes were dead serious. The sea had long been a benevolent mistress, but they both knew she could become their tomb as well. Yet thankfully, once again they had cheated her. But where . . . ?

"Lindsay?"

"Dag already took her down into the hold. I don't know, Jared—"

"What do you mean, you don't know?" Forgetting the cold, forgetting his fatigue, Jared left Walker staring after him and dropped into the hold, regretting his sharpness even as he followed the ominous trail of seawater to his quarters.

The first thing he saw was Dag shoveling coal into the iron stove, but his eyes went to where Lindsay lay wrapped in a blanket upon the bed.

And she was so quiet, too quiet . . .

Jared went to her at once, wrenching the blanket off his shoulders to cover her, only to realize she still wore her sodden garments, which clung to her like a deadly second skin.

"Dag, go—I'll see to her."

The big Norwegian rose from the stove, his concerned gaze flickering from Lindsay back to Jared's face. "I—I s-s-sorry, Cap-tain."

"I know. It's not your fault. She'll be fine, I promise. Now go. Have Walker head us back into the Channel as soon as the galleys are hoisted aboard."

Dag nodded solemnly, but seemed reluctant to leave until Jared sensed what might be wrong and added, "I won't punish her, Dag. I think she's been punished enough, don't you? I'm going to do everything I can to help her."

A ragged moan from the bed made Dag's eyes widen, and he hastened to the door, looking stricken. But Jared couldn't worry about him now. He shut the door behind the Norwegian and went back to the bed, where he gently cupped Lindsay's ashen face with his hand. She was shivering from head to toe, her lips almost white.

"Lindsay, can you hear me?"

Her only answer was another low moan, which still encouraged him. But those wet clothes had to go, and fast.

As Jared unfolded the blanket from her trembling body, his gaze fell upon the improvised money belt at her waist and the gold guineas shining dully beneath the near-transparent lilac silk.

Blasted clever chit. Yet the heavy coins were probably as responsible as the numbing cold for dragging her down in the water. Had she truly thought she could triumph over so many elements working against her? Or had she been so desperate that she was willing to escape him at all costs?

His throat tightening even though he told himself it didn't matter one whit what she might have felt, Jared drew his lips ruthlessly together and tore away her wet clothes from collar to hem. Guineas scattered noisily across the plank floor. Limp shreds of lilac fabric, sheer white muslin and a soaked pair of slippers made a tangled web at his feet. A delicate lace corset with pale pink rosettes gave way easily beneath his hands.

Gave way to reveal the most beautiful breasts he had ever seen, ripely shaped with taunting apricot-tinged nipples, but Jared sucked in his breath and focused upon rubbing warmth into Lindsay's limbs, her fingers, her chilled toes. Yet he was a man, his eyes straying again and again to her breasts, the firm loveliness of her belly and the dusky curls between her thighs, not blond or dark, but hauntingly in between.

Nor could he seem to control his body, despising himself as he felt a tightness against the seam of his wet breeches. Blast and damnation, the chit was barely snatched from the maw of death and here he was . . . !

Focusing with extreme force of will upon the task at hand, Jared was relieved when he saw color creeping into Lindsay's cheeks, her limbs becoming warm and pliant. She hadn't moaned again, but she was breathing peacefully, which encouraged him all the more.

After wrapping her in both blankets, taking care that her feet were snugly covered, he picked her up and carried her to the stove, which was radiating a blessed heat that warmed him, too. Giving no heed to his sodden clothes, he kicked the stuffed desk chair in front of the stove, sat down and drew

Lindsay close against him. To his surprise, he felt her nestle even closer as if seeking added warmth, an instinctive move, he was certain, since she hadn't yet opened her eyes.

And if she did, he thought grimly, slumping wearily against the chair back, he doubted she would be happy to find herself in his arms. He wasn't a hero any longer to her after all, not noble and gallant and gentlemanly, but a despicable pirate.

Feeling an unsettling pang, Jared looked down at her face, at her silvery hair drying in soft tendrils, at her hands tucked like a child's under her chin.

So beautiful. So reckless. So lost in ridiculous romantic fantasies. But maybe now she was learning just how brutally realistic life could be—and the lesson had only begun.

With a low curse, Jared leaned his head back and closed his eyes.

Lindsay awoke with a start, feeling as if she were being roasted alive in front of a blazing fire. Why was she so warm— Oh, Lord!

Her discomfort forgotten, she stared with incredulity at Jared's face only inches from hers, his eyes shut peacefully, his lips slack, his breathing deep and slow. He was asleep, that was clear. But how had they come to be . . . ?

Telling herself to think calmly, rationally, Lindsay peeked over the edge of the blanket and realized they were both sitting in a chair, or rather, she was sitting atop his lap, his arms even in sleep securely around her. She glanced at her surroundings as incredulously and recognized Jared's quarters—

memories suddenly flooded back to her.

Memories of tricking Dag, and water so bitterly cold she had almost considered calling for help. Yet she had set out for shore, and she remembered her mounting fear, as insidious as the icy chill penetrating every fiber of her stricken body, that she wasn't going to survive. The beach was too far, the water too cold, dear God, the heavy coins making it so difficult to swim.

Lindsay tightly closed her eyes and swallowed back the frightening memories, the blazing warmth that had awakened her moments ago not half so oppressive now. It was so much better than the frigid cold—meaning life, not death. Thank heaven someone had come to her rescue . . .

Her eyes flaring open, Lindsay stared once more at the handsome face so near to her own.

No, not someone.

Jared.

She couldn't be sure, she'd been so cold, so numb, so dazed, yet something told her that he had braved the freezing water for her, had risked his life for her. Jared had rescued her again.

Suddenly she couldn't resist, her fingers trembling slightly as she lifted her hand to touch his face. To touch the hard, smooth plane of his cheek, then run her fingertips over the gold stubble along his jaw, the prickly sensation sending a shiver of longing coursing through her.

She even went so far as to move her thumb gently across his lips, so masculine and yet so sensual, until another vivid memory overtook her—of hunger and plunder and a kiss so powerfully possessive that her face began to burn. She snatched her hand back, berating herself even as the near-painful longing swelled mutinously within her.

Of course he had come after her, ninny! And not because he had feared she might drown, but because she knew his precious secret and might gain the shore to shout it to the farthest reaches of the British empire.

Tears springing to her eyes, Lindsay felt even more an utter fool as she blinked them furiously away. Suddenly too warm again, the blankets like a suffocating cocoon, she could see that the main culprit was a black iron stove only a foot or so away from the chair. Dismissing the thought that Jared might be sitting so close because of her, she freed her arms and pushed herself off his lap, but the blankets so entangled her legs that she fell with a startled "oomph" to the floor.

"Would you like some assistance?"

Raising herself awkwardly on her wrists, Lindsay felt her face burn with embarrassment as she glanced at Jared over her shoulder. Wide awake now, he was staring at her with the most curious smile on his face, making her even more acutely aware of how ridiculous she must look.

"No, thank you, I can manage on my own."

Emitting a small grunt, she struggled to her feet, irritably waving Jared back to his seat when he started to rise.

"Then I suggest you hold onto those blank—"

"I said I can manage— Oh!"

It happened so fast, the blankets slipping from her body to pool on the floor, that Lindsay could only stare down at herself in horror, realizing too late that she was utterly, completely naked. With a shriek, she grabbed one of the blankets and plastered it to her breasts, doubly horrified when she glanced up to see that Jared hadn't looked away as a gentleman might, but was still staring right at her. Boldly, blatantly staring, and—and he was laughing, too!

"You—you bloody pirate! What have you done with my clothes?"

He sobered so suddenly, his eyes darkening, that Lindsay almost wished she hadn't shouted at him like a fishwife.

"Curses, Lindsay? You surprise me."

She blushed at the huskiness in his voice, then raised her chin. "And you, sir, are no gentleman, but of course *that* comes as no surprise to me."

"I tried to warn you—"

"And once again I didn't listen, much to my regret, but I vow I will in the future. Now, if you'll kindly tell me what you've done with my things?"

He seemed to sigh to himself, then said matter-of-factly, "I'm afraid you won't find them serviceable."

Blanching at the unsettling realization that he must have undressed her, Lindsay found her voice had gone somewhat hoarse. "A little dampness won't trouble me, but you should have hung everything to dry above the stove."

"Not possible."

"Not—?" She went still at his arched brow, following his gaze to the bed.

To the tattered shreds of what remained of her gown, her pelisse, her corset—oh, Lord, no, even her chemise.

"You see? Not possible, just as I said. Had to be done, no help for it."

Chapter 16

Expecting another indignant outburst, Jared was surprised when Lindsay merely stared at the wreckage of her clothes, although her cheeks were aflame with color.

Clearly not aware that her fierce hold had loosened on the blanket, the covering sinking low over her breasts to expose the enticing apricot of her nipples, he was hard pressed not to gaze admiringly. With her rumpled blond hair framing her bare shoulders, she looked like the mythic Venus rising from the sea. Yet it chafed upon him that she considered him so lacking in scruples. God knows any man faced with such womanly perfection would gape like a dottering fool.

"Lindsay . . . the blanket."

She glanced down, jerking the covering into place with a gasp as she met his eyes.

"I'm sorry, but your clothing could have killed you. You were chilled enough as it was, so I did what had to be done and rid you of it—quickly. Then I wrapped you in blankets—" He shrugged and rose from the chair. "I'm pleased to see that you're obviously feeling better. You could have drowned out there."

"But I didn't, much as I'm sure to your regret,

so now you must find me something to wear."

She had spoken so softly for such biting words, and Jared didn't like how much they bothered him.

"Damnation, woman, do you truly think I would have let you drown?"

When she didn't answer, her blue eyes grown wide because he'd shouted, Jared sighed with frustration. "I may be a privateer, but I'm no barbarian. And if you're concerned that I might have taken some liberty with you while you were—"

He didn't finish, the thought disgusting him even as he recalled how his body had reacted of its own will to her nakedness. Begun to react, too, when he'd felt her fingers softly touch his face and trace over his lips, although he'd feigned sleep, wondering what had possessed her to make such an intimate gesture.

Yet in the next instant he shoved both disturbing incidents from his mind, telling himself that pure lust was no heinous crime. With an inaudible growl, he went to his sea chest and flung open the lid, while Lindsay wound the blanket tightly around her and fled to the stove, keeping her back to the wall.

"I've an old pair of breeches that should suffice, and you can help yourself to my shirts. Your slippers, at least, are still wearable."

He threw the soft doeskin breeches onto the bed, and left the lid open so she might choose any further garments herself. Then he strode past her to the door.

"There are books in the chest, too, that should help you fill your time. Some novels, plays of Shakespeare, a few volumes of poetry—"

"A pirate reading poetry? Now, *that* truly surprises me."

The sarcasm feeling strange upon her tongue, Lindsay nonetheless told herself that she could hardly be expected to act like herself under such circumstances.

Jared spun on his heel to face her, frowning. "They belonged to my sister, if you must know."

"Elise?"

She could tell she had startled him from the flaring of his eyes, yet his jaw hardened, too.

"How did you come by her name?"

She shrugged lightly, taking care that the blanket remained snug above her breasts. "Aunt Winnie. She and her husband were acquainted with your uncle Alistair—perhaps you weren't aware?"

"I scarcely knew my uncle. How would I know of his friends?"

Lindsay was tempted to say she wasn't surprised, given he'd abandoned what remained of his family to return to India—and to think when she'd first heard the sorry tale she had thought it impossible that Jared could do such a thing! Instead she added quietly, "As I said, Aunt Winnie told me. I had thought, by asking her if she knew your family, it might be easier for her when you came to call, but it only made matters worse. She thought well of your uncle . . . but the story she had to tell about you wasn't a very happy one."

"No, it's not happy no matter which bloody version you hear."

He had spoken so bitterly that Lindsay was taken aback, and confused, too. "I don't understand—"

"There's no need for you to. Think whatever you

will about me, Lindsay, the worse the better. It will probably make things easier for you." His hand went to the door but then he paused, his tone grown ominous. "Trick Dag again and you'll answer to me, woman, that I swear. He's softhearted to a fault, but that's not what brought him to his present state. Yet I'll not have you taking advantage—"

"I did sense that something wasn't quite right about him," Lindsay broke in, although she regretted her honesty when Jared scowled.

"Quite right? Three years ago he took a metal ball in the head that was intended for me, and it's still there—waiting to end his life at any moment. The physicians advised he remain abed, that any undue strain might kill him, but to keep him from what he loves would kill him, too. Like many of my men, he grew up among the fjords of Norway, the sea in his blood. So he sails with us—and we watch over him. *I* watch over him. Have I made myself understood?"

Lindsay nodded, feeling horribly guilty that she could have upset Dag so. But how could she have known?

"I'm truly sorry, Jared. Sorry, too, about what happened to Dag—three years ago, I mean. It must have been terrible."

He didn't reply, his lips locking together as he once more reached for the door.

"Wait! Don't you want to take any fresh clothes for yourself? Those look damp—here."

She hurried to the chest and dug out some clothes, not sure why she suddenly wished to somehow make amends. It wasn't as if she wouldn't attempt to escape again—but he had saved her life after all. Clutching the blanket with one hand, she held out a clean linen shirt and breeches to him. Silently he took them, yet his next words struck her like a cruel slap.

"If this is some feminine ploy, Lindsay, spare both of us. Games and fanciful illusions won't help you. No matter what you imagined we were romantically to each other, I can assure you that you're merely a prisoner aboard my ship, nothing more."

Wounded more deeply than she could have imagined, Lindsay still made herself lift her head. "Ah, so even simple kindnesses are suspect now? Then I don't suppose I'll share with you some news you might want to know—for the sake of your crew. You'd probably say it was a lie."

She spun around, but Jared caught her arm, twisting her back to face him.

"I said no games, Lindsay. What news?"

She stared bleakly into his eyes, trying not to think that only hours ago she had believed this cold, unfeeling man had wanted her for his bride—

"I said what news?"

"A reward has been posted for your capture. It was in *The Morning Post* yesterday. Ten thousand pounds."

He released his hold, to her surprise a grim smile curling his lips.

"Only ten thousand? Then my men and I haven't been working hard enough, though I already planned this cruise would be different." He sobered, his gaze sweeping her. "Yet God knows I hadn't expected you—"

"So perhaps you're the one harboring illusions if

you think no one will be encouraged by such a sum to sail against you. Just because you're known as the Phoenix doesn't make you, or your men, immortal!''

For a moment Lindsay didn't know what Jared was going to do, he was staring at her with such intensity, his blue eyes darkened to a violent hue. She was astonished when he smiled, not grimly as before, but with a calm assurance that chilled her.

"Let them come. It's never been a matter of immortality, but whose ship was swifter. And so far, the *Vengeance* has always won.''

She didn't get a chance to reply, even if she had wanted to, for Jared had pulled open the door. She took a step back when she saw Dag haul himself up off a chair, and she blushed with fresh remorse that the Norwegian's ruddy, bearded face was etched with concern. She threw him the smallest of reassuring smiles but jumped when Jared lashed out at her, his voice filled with irritation.

"Get dressed, Lindsay. I don't want you catching cold, not after I went through such great pains to warm you.''

"Oh, yes, you went through pains,'' she retorted as the door swung shut in her face. "Ripped my clothes to shreds, nearly roasted me to death in front of that stove, wrapped me in so many blankets I almost broke my leg—!''

Sighing with utter exasperation when she realized she'd been shouting at the top of her lungs, Lindsay wondered what Corisande would have thought of such a harangue. It certainly wasn't like her at all, but Jared seemed to be bringing out the very worst in her.

Which made her wonder, too, if he might be purposely goading her. He had said he wanted her to think the worst of him, and she wasn't finding that request at all difficult to oblige. But at the risk of her becoming a veritable shrew, her stomach in knots, her face aflame, her head aching, her hands shaking?

No, that wasn't going to do, it simply wasn't. Obviously if an escape wasn't imminent—and she certainly intended to take full advantage of the next plausible opportunity—at least she had found herself embroiled in more adventure than she had ever bargained for. Why not attempt to enjoy it?

Smiling to herself, Lindsay began slowly to relax as she glanced at the garment tossed upon the bed.

A man's breeches. Now, that was something new. Something unexpected and not a little daring.

And she supposed she could make her Spartan surroundings a bit more livable with a little feminine ingenuity. Humming now, she dropped the blanket and strolled to the bed.

Oh, no, she wasn't going to think the worst of him. She wasn't going to trouble herself about Jared Giles or the Phoenix, pirate or privateer or traitor, at all.

"The prisoner says she'd like to come up for a breath of fresh air, Cap'n."

Jared turned from the railing, an incredulous laugh escaping him as he met Cooky's squinting eyes. The old sailor had spent so much time in shadowy galleys among his pots and pans that daylight was almost too much for him to bear, much like a mole, but he'd obviously thought it important enough to surface this bright, sunny morning.

"She what?"

"Wants a bit of fresh air. I went to fetch her breakfast tray—she ate everything I'd brought her, eggs and fried kippers and two helpings of toast and jam—"

"A good thing we took on fresh stores in Sussex," Jared broke in dryly, though Cooky hastened on.

"Well, Cap'n, she thanked me very kindly, said it was the finest breakfast she'd ever tasted and then asked if I might find you and tell you—"

"And I say you go back to my quarters and tell *her* that she'll have to do without a morning constitutional. She's not on a blasted pleasure cruise."

"I don't see any harm in it, Jared."

He threw a dark glance at Walker while Cooky looked on uncertainly, the sailor lifting a wrinkled hand to shield his pale eyes.

"Have you forgotten we're hunting for fresh quarry?"

"No, but we haven't seen any ships yet. If we do and we attack, it'll be hours before she'll have a chance to leave the cabin, maybe longer." Walker's gaze was piercing. "Or do you plan to just leave her down there and pretend she doesn't exist?"

Jared didn't answer, but waved Cooky away. As the sailor shrugged his scrawny shoulders and turned to go, shaking his head, Walker sighed heavily.

"Dammit, Jared, she's barely more than a girl. I know you haven't forgotten how it felt to be confined in a wretched cell and neither have I—"

"That was for three bloody years, not a single day, and I say she stays. She's disrupted things enough as it is—look at the lot of you! Dag refuses to let another man guard her door; Cowan asked after her welfare the moment I left the cabin last night. By God, Cooky even ventured out of the hold on her behalf, and now my second-in-command—"

"And what of you, Jared? You're ranting about a simple request as if she'd demanded that we squire her back to London under full sail and turn ourselves over to the Crown!"

Cursing under his breath, Jared scowled at Walker, but the American didn't blink, staring right back as if daring him to deny his charge.

Which, of course, Jared couldn't. He was ranting and raving and acting unreasonably; he knew it. And if Walker could see it so clearly, what of the rest of his men?

"Cooky!"

His roar making more heads turn than the grizzled cook's, Jared lowered his voice, but not by much.

"Tell Dag to escort the prisoner to the quarterdeck."

"Aye, Cap'n!"

Stunned by the gap-toothed smile splitting Cooky's face as the old sailor disappeared into the hold, Jared groaned to himself.

Was the chit planning to cast her spell over every man jack aboard? It was bad enough that he couldn't seem to free his mind of her, what little sleep he'd gotten in Cowan's bunk—his first mate having graciously given up his cabin to sleep in the crew's quarters—plagued by scorching dreams of an entirely carnal nature.

He wished now that he had availed himself more often of Della's generous charms, or those of some

other willing wench, but none had appealed after
he laid eyes on Lindsay. And if she hadn't been a
blasted innocent, he would have kissed those beautiful breasts by now and buried himself in her
dusky woman's curls, in the heat of her, the scent
of her—

"A guinea for your thoughts."

Jared bristled at Walker's wry smile, but made
himself look out to sea at the sunlight glinting off
the water. Better that than say something he might
regret. Long, silent moments passed while he
stewed, frowning.

Blast and damnation, Walker had been right.
Confining Lindsay to his quarters and pretending
she didn't exist was a lot easier than dealing with
this devilish lust.

But obviously his men wanted none of that, the
ridiculous chit having charmed even his next in
command into championing her cause. If he didn't
keep himself and his crew well occupied, before
long she'd have them so twisted around her fingers
that the *Vengeance* would more resemble Cleopatra's barge drifting down the Nile, with them in-
dulging her every beck and call, than a ship of war!

"Good morning, Captain. My, isn't it a marvel-
ous day?"

Chapter 17

Jared caught Walker's openly admiring glance before he turned from the railing himself; he clenched his teeth against the resentment twisting his gut. But it was nothing to the effect Lindsay had upon him when he faced her, her brilliant smile hitting him like a blow.

He hadn't seen her smiling so gaily since London and he realized at that moment, much to his displeasure, how much he had missed it.

"Yes, it is a lovely morning, Miss Somerset," came Walker's pleasant reply. Jared felt suddenly like an ill-mannered school boy, that his friend had been made by his silence to answer for him.

"Forgive me," he muttered, glancing darkly from Walker to Lindsay, whose smile hadn't dimmed. "Miss Lindsay Somerset . . . my second-in-command, Mr. Burke. Walker Burke."

"So nice to make your acquaintance, Mr. Burke. I've never met an American before. You are an American, aren't you?"

"I am."

"Well, you're quite a long way from home."

"My home is this ship, Miss Somerset. And I've never met a baronet's daughter before . . . or seen a young woman dressed so fetchingly in breeches."

Jared looked, too, realizing that he'd been so focused upon Lindsay's winsome smile and the play-
ful look in her eyes that he'd given little heed to
her attire. He scowled when she spun for them as
if displaying the latest London fashion, though
he'd never seen any gown, no matter how sheer
and clinging, accent a woman's form to greater, or
more dangerous, perfection.

"The legs were a little long, so I rolled them up
a bit."

Jared sucked in his breath at the snug fit of his
doeskin breeches against her pert rump, scowling
all the more when she stopped her pirouette to
hook her thumbs in the strip of lilac silk cinched
tightly around her slim waist.

"And the shirt was far too big for me, but tying
the ends into a knot resolved that problem."

As she glanced down proudly at her handiwork,
Jared couldn't take his eyes off the ripe swell of her
breasts beneath the ivory fabric, wishing now that
he hadn't torn her corset in two.

Wishing, as a stiff breeze rippled through her
silken hair, startlingly white in the sun, that he'd
held his ground and kept Lindsay in his quarters,
where she belonged, and not on deck, where she
could tempt the very devil.

"So, Captain, what do you think? I'm quite
pleased myself. I never dreamed men's clothes
could be so comfortable."

Her sparkling blue eyes lifting to his, Jared could
see plainly that her pleasure was genuine, while he
felt as if he didn't trust himself to speak.

What did he think? Was the wench daft? Blind?
Couldn't she see . . . even sense . . . ?

Walker clearing his throat was Jared's rescue,

though his compatriot's voice held no small trace of humor.

"I think, Miss Somerset, that you might have Dag accompany you around the ship and then return you to your cabin—"

"That won't be necessary. I'll accompany her."

Lindsay gasped, Jared taking her arm so abruptly and hauling her alongside him to the companionway that she practically had to run to keep up.

"You—you don't have to rush so!"

"No, Miss Somerset? Has it slipped your mind that I've a ship to captain, my time not to be frittered away escorting a *prisoner* on a ridiculous promenade?"

His tone was so harsh, Lindsay felt much of her delight fading at being temporarily free of the cabin's confines, and she started when he shouted brusque commands that rang from bow to stern.

"Walker, see that the men continue their watch, everyone's eyes on the sea. Dammit, we've ships to hunt or they'll be hunting us! Dag, go below and get some rest. A rotating detail will guard Miss Somerset from now on—to change every eight hours. And no one enters the cabin but Cooky with her meals. Have I made myself clear?"

Apparently Dag thought so. As Jared pulled her after him down the ladder to the lower deck, impatiently grabbing her around the waist to lift her clear of the last few steps, Lindsay glanced up to see the big Norwegian hastening to leave the quarterdeck as well. And Walker was ordering sailors to climb the rigging to keep a lookout, and then he turned himself to study the distant horizon with a spyglass, making Lindsay marvel that Jared's men were so quick to obey him.

Wondering what could have earned such loyalty in a man so foul-tempered—although she imagined her presence was only making things worse—she thought to tug her arm away from him as he hustled her along the deck's perimeter. Then she remembered her determination to enjoy herself. The sun was bright with not a cloud in the sky, the sea a deep, mesmerizing blue, the weather surprisingly warm, so why not? With a deft move she wound her arm through Jared's, ignoring his frown as she drew fresh salt air into her lungs with great exaggeration.

"Ah, Jared, how lucky you are to be surrounded by such wild beauty every day! I've rarely been on a ship before, only a few times, and that was compliments of Captain Oliver Trelawny, a good friend of Corie's. He has a fine ship, a cutter called the *Fair Betty*, though I haven't the faintest notion how he came upon the name. His wife's name is Rebecca and his daughter's was Sophie, so it really doesn't make sense—"

"And what if I told you I've no bloody interest whatsoever in whether you've ever been aboard a ship and what its name might have been?"

Lindsay shrugged lightly, telling herself that she wasn't going to take any unkind thing Jared said to heart; no, she simply wasn't, not anymore. "I don't understand at all how you can be so sour on such a glorious day." She grinned when his frown only grew deeper. "I feel wonderful and these breeches are so remarkable! I'm certain more women would wear them if they'd just give them a try."

"Give them a try? That would be a revolution I doubt the world—or its unsuspecting male population—is quite ready for."

She glanced at him, as astonished by his lighter, albeit sarcastic, tone as that he had finally slowed his pace to what could be considered a comfortable walk.

"Yes, I suppose you're right. What would happen to all the poor dressmakers and corset makers— Oh, Jared, I think I just saw a fish jump! A big silvery one!"

Lindsay let go of his arm and ran to the railing, where she scanned the glistening waves. She was so engrossed that she scarcely realized Jared had come up beside her until she felt his hip grazing hers. Heat flared in her cheeks and she turned her head to find he wasn't looking for any fish but was studying her intently.

"Does it really take so little to delight you?"

She gave a small shrug, his scrutiny coming very close to unnerving her, his eyes were so incredibly blue in the sunlight. But she sensed no malice in his query which made it easy to answer candidly. "I suppose. I've always loved sunny days—we have a lot of them in Cornwall. I missed that in London, but I liked the damp and fog, too. And all the people and the bustle of the place. It was so big and grand."

"Did you like Tom's Cellar?"

She laughed, tilting her head. "Truly?"

At his nod, she flushed, wondering why he would want to know.

"Well, not at first. The noise, the smoke, but I grew used to it. It reminded me of the Trelawnys' inn in Porthleven, actually, and that was often a merry place."

"So you had been to a tavern before?"

"A few times, yes—"

"I should have known. A young woman who freely admitted to sneaking from her father's house at all hours? No wonder the blasted place didn't upset you."

Jared's tone sarcastic again, Lindsay nonetheless did not allow it to daunt her. "That's not entirely true. I did feel sorry for that doctor everyone was teasing."

"Dr. Foote."

"Yes, poor man. But I didn't want you to think I wasn't enjoying myself, because I was, truly. It was so wonderful to be with you, yet I—"

"Damnation, woman, I thought we were done with that romantic nonsense! Remember, no games, no illusions? Have you learned nothing yet from what's happened to you?"

Lindsay stared at him, stunned and doing her best to swallow the sudden lump in her throat. "You . . . didn't allow me to finish. I didn't know then you weren't a spy."

"And what if I had been? I've never met any other young woman willing to risk life and reputation to follow me into God-knows-what danger, only you! You'd have done better to pen your ridiculous dreams and fantasies onto paper and sell them as Gothic novels than to come after the likes of me—"

"My dreams aren't ridiculous!" Realizing she had shouted, Lindsay also knew she didn't care, she was so angry and hurt, too, tears jumping to her eyes. "Who are you to judge anything about me? You don't know me any better than I know you, yet you have the gall to—to—" She spun around to the railing, the lump grown so big that she couldn't swallow it down or finish what she'd meant to say. Instead she stared blindly at the waves, her joy in the morning all but fled.

So much for not allowing Jared to upset her. So much for not taking anything he said to heart.

"Lindsay."

She brushed at her wet eyes with the palm of her hand, not answering.

"Lindsay, it's true. I have no right to judge you."

Still she didn't answer. Even when she heard him sigh, she refused to look at him.

"Be angry if you will, but I've simply tried to impress upon you that your dreams have gotten you into trouble. Could get you into more trouble. You're too trusting—"

"Oh, and what was I supposed to think when I heard you were a military spy? That it wasn't true, when obviously everyone else in London believes it, too?"

"A rumor easily started and then circulated by frivolous, idle people to explain my sudden appearances and disappearances—quite credible, I'm pleased to say. The ton is so preoccupied with its own bloody amusements that it pays little heed to what is truly happening in the world, anyway."

His voice had grown undeniably bitter. Lindsay hazarded a glance to find him looking not at her but down at his hands, which were balled into fists. But it was his expression that drew her, his handsome face appearing almost haggard, as if some secret pain had been exposed. Touched in spite of herself, she felt some of her hurt melting away.

"But they're paying heed now, Jared. I heard more talk of the Phoenix than anything else in London, and with the reward—"

"They'd sooner think I had left to capture him myself than guess at the truth. Besides, the fools believe the Phoenix to be American, and never would they think him so bold as to frequent their parties, their insufferable balls."

"Funny, I thought they were insufferable, too. At least until I met you at the Oglethorpes'—"

Lindsay fell abruptly silent, realizing when Jared met her eyes that she was talking in circles. And she had no wish to hear him attack her again about how foolishly romantic she was, or to hear him reveal any more of himself to her, either.

Fearing the more she knew about him, the less likely she might be able to convince him to release her, she set off along the deck, not surprised when he caught up with her and grabbed her arm. This time she tried to wrest herself free, but he held her fast; she'd become a prisoner to him again, which stung her as much as anything he'd said.

"You needn't worry, Captain. I'm not going to take a running leap into the Channel. I tried that already and it didn't succeed."

"We're not in the Channel."

She stopped, glancing out to sea before darting her gaze back to his face. "Then where—?"

"The Atlantic. We cleared Land's End early this morning, so if you did jump, it would be a very long swim to Cornwall. But I suspect that's not where you want to be, anyway."

"What are you saying? Of course I wouldn't mind Cornwall if it freed me from you!" Desperation seizing her, she scanned the horizon, but the only thin strip of land she could see was far to the east. England.

"But what of your stepmother, Olympia? From what little you've mentioned of her, she sounds unpleasant enough. She's in Cornwall—"

"I know she is and I hate her! But that doesn't mean I'd rather stay aboard this bloody ship!"

Jared almost released Lindsay's arm, he was so surprised at her vehemence, her lovely eyes filled with turmoil and passion. He glanced up to see that many of his men were watching them, but one dark look and they quickly fell back to their work, while he drew Lindsay into the shadow of the mainmast.

"Easy, Lindsay, we don't have to talk about the witch. I take it she is a witch?"

Lindsay turned her face away, her chin trembling, which, oddly, made Jared want to press her further. He wasn't sure why, but her outburst that he didn't know a thing about her had moved him more deeply than he cared to admit.

"She must have treated you quite badly to make you feel the way you do."

"It wasn't so much me but my father," came her small voice, though Lindsay still would not look at him. "He married her five months after my mother died, and everything changed. He changed, our plans changed . . ."

A tear trickling down her cheek made Jared's throat tighten. "What plans?"

"Our grand tour. Papa had promised my mother for years we would go—it's what she always wanted. She'd never left Cornwall herself, but she'd always dreamed of faraway places. She'd read me books . . ."

A ragged sigh escaped her, her trembling fingers swiping away tears from her flushed cheeks. Flushed cheeks that Jared suddenly wanted to touch but didn't, waiting.

"A fever struck the village, Corie's mother, my mother. She made my father promise, right before she died, that he'd still take me to the Continent, even if she couldn't be with us. I heard him promise—I was hiding behind the door. But he married Olympia and she wouldn't hear of any grand tour. Only this year, when she thought it was time I found a husband, did she allow me to finally go to London. A husband to suit *her*, not me. Someone she could bully like my father, not a bold adventurer who'd stand up to her. But you wouldn't have suited her at all—"

Lindsay froze before Jared's eyes as if realizing how much she had revealed, yet in the next instant she faced him and grabbed his hands, her gaze pleading.

"Oh, Jared, please take me back to England. I promise I won't say a word to anyone about you— I swear it! And if you did, I might still have a chance to find— Oh, please!"

He stared into her beautiful, tear-filled eyes, feeling so close to relenting at that moment, even though his gut was telling him he could not.

He could not take the risk of trusting her; he had his men's lives to consider, and his own mission was still so far from being done. He had only to think of his parents and Elise . . . and of Sylvia and Ryland Potter's treachery, damn their souls to hell, to know it wasn't possible. Slowly he shook his head.

"I can't let you go, Lindsay. I'm sorry."

Chapter 18

L indsay almost couldn't believe her ears, she'd felt so sure, so full of hope that he might find it in his heart to— The blackguard! And she was such a fool!

It happened so fast, the ringing sound of a slap echoing around them even before she realized she'd struck him. Her gaze widened in horror at the bright red handprint on Jared's face. But what seemed worse was the unearthly quiet that had settled over the ship. Lindsay glanced wildly around her to see that all eyes were upon them, Jared's men as stunned as he looked.

Until his grim astonishment suddenly faded to fury. Lindsay stumbled backward when he reached out to grab her.

"Merchantman approaching from the north, Cap'n!"

She gasped; he stiffened, his narrowed gaze looking past her to scan the sea. It was her turn to be astonished when she saw a smile of such dark intent touch his lips that she felt a chill. Before her eyes, Jared had suddenly become both pirate and predator. And never had she thought him so frighteningly dangerous as when his cold gaze once more settled upon her.

"You must forgive us, Miss Somerset, but we've a hunt to commence. You'll have to finish your promenade another time."

He caught her and swept her off her feet so abruptly that Lindsay didn't have time to shriek. Nor did she think to fight him as he carried her to the hold, his fearsome expression alone paralyzing her in his arms, his roared commands deafening her.

"Every man to his station! Cowan, raise our colors!"

As the entire deck exploded in commotion, Lindsay caught a glimpse of the flag being hoisted above the quarterdeck just before Jared dropped with her into the hold.

A huge white flag with a resplendent golden bird at its center, wings outspread, the yellow silk flashing brilliantly in the sun.

But what made her heart pound was the blood dripping from its beak and claws, the emblem enough to strike fear into the soul of any beholder. As Jared strode with her into the deserted crew's quarters, she wondered if the sailors aboard the hapless merchantman had yet sighted the *Vengeance*; she could already envision their panic.

"Dag, wake up. I need you to guard the prisoner until I send another man to replace you."

The groggy Norwegian unfolded himself from his bunk with a quickness that belied his size. Lindsay winced when Jared set her down roughly and began pushing her along in front of him. She had never felt more wretchedly a prisoner than at that moment, relief filling her when they reached Jared's quarters.

She ran inside and took refuge behind the chair,

but he didn't step past the threshold. Her face grew hot as he gave a short laugh upon seeing the books she'd arranged neatly atop the desk, the pillow plumped on the bed, a pretty Indian shawl, in which she'd found wrapped two volumes of poetry, draped over the sea chest—her valiant attempt to make the cabin more livable.

"Good. At least you're keeping yourself amused."

Bristling, she would have thrown a book at him if he hadn't slammed the door shut with a finality that sounded like he had thrown away the key.

Almost two weeks later, Lindsay was convinced Jared had thrown away the key and forgotten about her entirely.

She stared bleakly out the porthole at the smoldering debris adrift on the waves, all that was left of the Phoenix's latest victim, the twelfth ship in as many days. The longboats carrying the unfortunate merchantman's crew, officers and a few dazed passengers were no longer even specks on the horizon; for some reason Jared had ceased taking prisoners aboard the *Vengeance* after that first vessel was sunk.

And she had ceased to wonder about it when she realized to her deepening dismay that she had become a prisoner in every sense of the word, with no chance for reprieve in sight.

Her requests to be granted a chance for fresh air had fallen on deaf ears; Cooky hadn't spoken to her or even cracked a smile since that morning she'd first gone above deck. The old sailor had simply seen to her needs in stony silence, bringing her meals and taking away the half-touched trays, pro-

viding her with occasional basins of hot water to
bathe and tending to the chamber pot.

Even Dag hadn't granted her more than a glance
whenever he served as her guard and stood watch
at the door during Cooky's short visits, although
his eyes had remained troubled. As for her other
guards, they had met her with the same grim silence and equally grim expressions, which had led
her to sense that these men must surely have lost
any shred of sympathy for her.

And she knew why.

She hadn't forgotten the stunned faces when
she'd slapped Jared; she now knew the depth of
the crew's loyalty to their captain. Her striking him
had been an offense against them all and she hadn't
forgotten, either, how deeply it had angered Jared.

Sighing, Lindsay left the porthole and the
glimpse it had offered of the most recent fiery devastation, her heart sinking into her slippers when
she felt the ship suddenly list beneath her feet.

Lord help any luckless vessels that might stray
into their path; Jared's search for fresh prey had
begun again.

He never lingered very long at the scene of his
latest treasonous attack. His relentless pursuit of
his next victim had horrified her almost more than
watching each ship burn.

Most vessels had surrendered without a fight,
but a few had resisted. The porthole had granted
her a view of savage, uncompromising maneuvers
by the *Vengeance* to brings its reluctant prey to its
knees. At those times she could imagine Jared's
chilling smile as if she were standing once more in
front of him and not confined to a cabin that
seemed to be growing ever smaller with each pass-

ing day. She didn't know which was worse.

Lindsay dropped onto the bed and thumbed absently through Shakespeare's *Hamlet*, a play she believed she was close to memorizing for how many times she'd read it. Add to that *Romeo and Juliet*, *Othello* and *Antony and Cleopatra*, all tragic tales of vengeance, loss and sorrow, which hadn't helped to lift her mood.

They had left her wondering, too, how Jared's ship might have come to be called the *Vengeance*, although she had told herself firmly that she didn't want to know and surely didn't care. Yet he had to have chosen his treacherous path for some dark reason, and the immense amount of time she had on her hands allowed unbidden thoughts to plague her.

Why had he grown so furious that she'd called him a traitor? He was a traitor, that was clear, yet strangely, he hadn't seemed to think so.

And if the Phoenix had been harrying British ships for three years, as that outraged gentleman had claimed at the Oglethorpe ball, then surely that must coincide somehow with when Jared had returned to England from India. Hadn't Aunt Winifred said three years as well? Yes, Lindsay was certain she had. So what could have happened in that exotic faraway land to turn Jared into a pirate? Yet if he had so ruthlessly abandoned his uncle and younger sister, maybe his character alone was enough . . .

Lindsay shoved the book away and flipped over onto her back, her head beginning to ache. It always did when her thoughts centered too much around Jared, which seemed to be most of the time.

He was such a study in contradictions, the

charming gentleman she'd met in London nothing like the coldhearted master of this ship. But was he truly coldhearted? Not when it came to looking after Dag. And what about the lengths he had gone to warm her after her misguided plunge into the Channel?

Lindsay felt a blush race to her scalp, a strange breathlessness overwhelming her when she reminded herself that Jared had seen her naked, had seen every inch of her, her breasts, her—

"And you're a ridiculous fool to feel as giddy about it as you do," she groused as she rolled onto her side and swept a sheaf of silken hair off her face. "You'd think, Lindsay Somerset, that you might have wanted him to touch you!"

She closed her eyes, it becoming no uncommon thing for her to be talking to herself. Anything to relieve the oppressiveness of her enforced solitude. Yet once more her thoughts seemed to jump right back to Jared and how he hadn't touched her, or so he had said.

Just as he hadn't seduced her in London, which made her wonder anew about his supposed ruthless character. She had certainly presented him with enough ripe opportunities; she flushed to her toes at the memory of their heated encounter at the Boar's Head tavern. And of the carriage ride back to Piccadilly when she'd been thrown willy-nilly onto his lap and he'd kissed her so thoroughly— Oh, Lord.

Her lips suddenly burning, Lindsay rose from the bed, pondering again why he had resolved to teach her a lesson. Given what she knew of him now, it made so little sense, unless . . . She went to the desk and picked up a slim volume of medieval romantic poetry, truly one of the few things that had given her pleasure these past days, although she could already hear Jared deriding her.

But if such poetry had been enjoyed by his sister, then she certainly wasn't going to think less of herself for reading it. The second volume was a lovely collection of poems by the Scots poet Robert Burns, but she preferred the other, she knew, because of the graceful handwriting in the margins that so intrigued her.

She settled into the chair and let the pages fall open to a thirteenth-century poem by Wolfram von Eschenbach:

> *Your love and my love keep each other company—*
> *   that is why I am so joyful.*
> *That your heart is constant in its love for mine*
> *   is a solace beyond compare.*

Lindsay didn't read any further, her gaze drawn instead to the jubilant musings of the young woman who Aunt Winifred had told her had died almost three years ago.

> *Oh, sweetest joy! I had hoped Ryland might care for me, but now I know it's true. He has told me of his love at last! We are to be married! I only wish Jared were here to share in my happiness. I miss him so, and fear some terrible tragedy must have befallen him. To have left England so suddenly and never written me? And with Uncle Alistair gone now, too, Mother and Father two years ago . . . Thank God for Ryland's comfort. I would be lost.*

Lindsay laid her head back against the chair, pity welling inside her.

Could Ryland have been the man who had treated Elise so abominably? Aunt Winifred had said her husband's surname was Potter . . . Ryland Potter?

Lindsay flipped through the book and read other jotted notes of a damsel clearly very much in love. But she stopped when she came to the poignant sentences that always made her heart beat faster.

> *Only two days until our wedding. I'm so happy, we'll be so happy! Sylvia has stitched the most exquisite veil for my hair. I hope Ryland finds me lovely. He's so handsome, so wonderful, everything I've always dreamed!*

The breathless words reminding her so acutely of herself, Lindsay felt her niggling intuition growing stronger.

At first she hadn't wanted to even think that Jared might have decided to teach her a lesson because she reminded him somehow of his sister, but that last line . . . She had said those very words about him! And if her suspicion was true—her every perusal of this book making her believe more and more that it was so—then Jared must have been concerned that a similar tragic fate would not befall her as it had Elise. And that would mean he wasn't cold and unfeeling at all, but more of a gallant gentleman than she could have imagined— Oh, Lord.

Very much aware that her face had grown hot as flame, Lindsay flipped to one of the last pages, but her eyes weren't drawn to the poem decrying the fickleness of love. Instead she traced her finger over a simple heartrending line Elise had written, the ivory vellum puckered and the ink smeared by what she imagined could only have been tears.

Dear God, help me. I have been betrayed. Help me!

Fresh pity tightening her throat, Lindsay stared at the page, wondering what could have happened. To go from such joy to such utter despair? It was so achingly familiar, yet different, too. Jared had deceived her, true, but poor Elise had given her love to a man she must not have known at all—

"Oh, Lindsay."

She had scarcely spoken above a whisper, but she could have shouted for how forcefully her realization had hit her. She had been ready to do the same thing, too—give her heart, her love, to a man she hardly knew.

"Only ready to give . . . ?" Lindsay murmured unhappily, struck by a piercing pang that she had felt more than once since she'd discovered Jared was the Phoenix. Sighing, she closed the book but didn't rise, not really knowing what to do.

To attempt to nap might consume the hours before supper, but sleeping only brought her dreams. Vivid, often wanton dreams of Jared, which she imagined now, given her unsettling insight, might prove all the more disconcerting.

Yet to stay awake would leave her plagued with thoughts and questions to which she had no answers, while to stare out the porthole at the gray, rolling sea would only make her wish that much more futilely for escape. Or bring her face-to-face with another ill-fated ship on the horizon soon to meet Jared's wrath. Lord help her, wasn't there some diversion to free her from being so utterly preoccupied with the man?

A sudden knock at the cabin door made Lindsay gasp and fly from the chair, the book of poetry spinning across the floor.

"Yes?"

"Miss Somerset, Walker Burke. I've been given permission to escort you above deck if it might interest you."

Chapter 19

"Interest me?" Lindsay ran to the door, startled as much by the unexpected boon as by the fact her prayer had been so quickly answered. "Yes, yes, that would be lovely!"

She had barely combed her fingers through her hair and straightened her rumpled shirt and breeches before she was staring at the dimly lit passageway, Walker and a stony-faced guard standing aside to let her pass. Yet she stood rooted in place, still incredulous that she had been granted a few moments' freedom.

"Miss Somerset?"

She started, meeting Walker's midnight eyes, and blushed at his subdued yet wry smile. "I-I'm sorry. It's been so long."

Walker's smile dimmed, but it returned when he bowed slightly and gestured that she should leave the cabin. She did, feeling oddly self-conscious as she slipped past the two men, and surprised, too, that she'd been allowed to lead. The last time she'd been down this passageway, Jared had shoved her along in front of him and none too gently— Oh, Lord. Jared.

Her heart suddenly thundering because she would soon see him again, she could not help

thinking, with exasperation at herself, that he'd
scarcely been gone from her mind for a few moments. So much for a diversion.

She felt equally self-conscious when she passed
through the galley, Walker and her guard—another Norwegian, from his ruddy-faced, blond
looks—trailing in her wake as Cooky and his
assistants looked up from their tasks. But nothing
was said, the old sailor going right back to hacking
slices from a slab of salt pork, while the other two
men resumed peeling carrots and potatoes as if
they weren't surprised at all to see her and didn't
care, her affront to their captain days ago obviously
still on their minds.

Given that, she was relieved to reach the companionway, the brisk ocean breeze pouring into the
hold lifting her spirits immensely. She turned to
Walker, but once again he gestured that she should
go ahead of him. She obliged and clambered up
the steps, her heart thudding all the harder when
she straightened and stood waiting for the raven-
haired American while her gaze flew to the quarterdeck.

To her surprise, Jared wasn't there, her disappointment so keen she felt it like a sharp stab. Yet
in the next instant she felt only annoyance at herself that she might have wished to see him.

It was ridiculous! He had virtually forgotten
about her for nearly two weeks, and let *her* not forget that he had stated she was nothing more than
a prisoner to him. And he had certainly treated her
like one, although he had finally granted permission— Oh, she didn't know what to think anymore!
Squaring her shoulders, she forced a bright smile
as Walker joined her, even though her mind was

once more awhirl with the myriad confounding contradictions that were Jared Giles.

"How truly kind of your captain to allow me to resume my promenade," she said lightly, trying not to clench her teeth. "And only two weeks later—"

"Twelve days, Miss Somerset. Now, shall we walk?"

As Walker offered his arm, the same subdued smile on his darkly handsome face, Lindsay stared at him with astonishment. Suddenly reassured that someone hadn't forgotten how long she had been left to languish belowdecks and perhaps had protested about it, she nodded and accepted his escort, proceeding with him along the same course she and Jared had taken days before.

Except it wasn't the same, the time not morning but late afternoon, the day not brilliantly sunny but overcast, the sky a somber, leaden gray. And the salt air was cool, the wind gusty, making her wish as she shivered that she were wearing more than Jared's cambric shirt.

Yet she wasn't going to complain for fear her walk would be cut short. Instead she focused her attention out to sea, noting for the first time a dark smudge of land not far to the northwest. But where . . . ? She frowned, trying to catch her bearings.

"Ireland."

She glanced at Walker, not surprised that he'd read her thoughts, although she was somewhat startled that Jared's field of attack was so vast. "So the Phoenix plagues the waters of all the British Isles."

"Plagues? Let's say we've sailed them all. North

Sea, Irish Sea, the English Channel, St. George's Channel. That's where we are now, bearing south. The hunting's always been good out of Cork Harbour. We should make another kill by sunset."

Her shiver was more of a shudder as she swiped blowing hair from her face, Walker's grimly matter-of-fact statement making her suddenly aware of the sailors standing watch around the deck, a few even sitting aloft on the creaking spars. Like vultures, waiting. Dear God, wasn't one merchantman enough for a day's treasonous work?

"I don't understand why you're doing this!" she blurted out, fixing her indignant gaze back on Walker. "You, Jared, all these other sailors, Norwegians, Irishmen, the looting, the burning—"

"Don't forget Americans. There's twelve of us aboard."

Lindsay clamped her mouth shut to stare at him, not sure if he was mocking her or being serious. His slow half smile made her suspect the former, which fueled her exasperation no matter he might have protested to Jared on her behalf.

"And we've only one Irishman, Cowan. And one Englishman, with whom you're already well acquainted. The rest are Norsemen through and through . . . the best damned sailors in the world."

His smile suddenly faded, and she heard a catch in his voice that puzzled her. In fact, he didn't seem as wittily amused as he had at the few other times she'd seen him—although anyone would appear a merry soul compared with Jared and his dark moods. Even so, she doubted she could force a straight answer from this enigmatic man, but she was certainly going to try.

"Well, I can't imagine how the lot of you came to be pirates together."

"Not pirates, Miss Somerset, privateers. I believe Jared already explained the difference to you."

"He did, and I'm no more convinced the two are not the same than when I first came aboard—even less so! Twelve ships plundered and destroyed, not including that merchantman the first morning—"

"Which makes thirteen altogether, matching the record from our last cruise. One more and perhaps Jared might consider a day's rest. I believe you've brought us good luck, Miss Somerset."

Lindsay dropped her hand from his arm as if stung and turned to face him, her frustration so great at his cavalier manner that she felt ready to explode. "Is everything a jest to you?"

Clearly, it wasn't. Walker's expression had grown as dark and daunting as Jared's, which almost made her wish she had kept her outburst to herself.

"You seem in a quarrelsome humor this afternoon, Miss Somerset. It was thought a stroll in the fresh air might cheer you, but you seem more inclined to fret over things that are none of your concern. Do we continue our walk, or is it time for you to return to your cabin?"

"My cabin?" she bit off, not appreciating being talked to like a child. "My prison cell, you mean, and contrary to your opinion, sir, I believe these matters are of my concern."

"Really? How so?"

She gaped at him, suddenly feeling a bit foolish. She truly couldn't think of a sound reply, other than that her curiosity about everything surrounding Jared was close to overwhelming her. And that was the last thing she wanted to admit to his second-in-command, and clearly a close friend, too. She had sensed that about them at once, Walker the only man aboard the *Vengeance* who didn't call Jared "Captain."

"Well, now, this is becoming even more interesting than I had thought."

She felt a slow flush creep up her face at his quizzical scrutiny, wondering if he had managed once more to read her mind. Lamely, she murmured, "I . . . I don't know what you mean, Mr. Burke."

"Oh, I suspect you do. If you've some special interest in Jared and his affairs, I suggest you pose your questions to him. I don't speak for the man. Never have."

Feeling strangely as if a precious secret had suddenly been exposed, Lindsay lifted her chin. "Very well, I will speak to him, if you'll kindly let me know where I can find him. He wasn't on the quarterdeck—"

"He's below in the crew's quarters. Dag isn't well."

"Not well?" Remembering what Jared had told her about the huge Norwegian, she felt a sudden knot in her stomach. "What's happened? May I see him? He was so kind to me . . . at least until I struck—" She didn't finish, Walker's tightening expression telling her she didn't have to.

"He took ill less than an hour ago—it's happened before. Like a spell that comes over him, the pain in his head is sometimes so bad we have to tie him down. But that didn't keep him from asking Jared if you might be allowed to leave your cabin."

"So—so it wasn't you?"

"Me? I spoke on your behalf the first time, but

after what you did . . .'' Walker laughed grimly. "I decided it might be best, like Jared, to leave things as they were. No, you've Dag to thank for your freedom. He plagued Jared every day, three, sometimes four times, never letting him forget just how long it had been."

Lindsay didn't know what to say, she was so stunned. Not Walker. Or anyone else. It was Dag who had thought of her welfare.

Touched more deeply than she could say, she still felt a telling stab that it had taken something so severe to make Jared relent. How little he must think of her! It was all she could do to force back the dismay that cold realization brought her.

"I asked if I might go to him. I doubt I can do anything to help, but—"

"Go on. I thought you'd want to see him. Just remember, Lindsay, there's no escape from this ship. You already know that jumping overboard won't help you."

Walker's reminder chilling her, she scarcely gave thought to his having called her by her given name as she nodded and hurried back to the hold, the brisk wind grown so strong she was almost glad to return belowdecks. Several sailors seemed surprised to see her clamber down the steps unescorted, but none moved to stop her or uttered a word, merely giving her wide berth to pass.

Moments later, when she entered the crew's quarters lit by guttering oil lamps, she knew at once where Dag could be found for the silent, grim-faced gathering of sailors at his bunk. But as she drew near, they saw her and stepped aside, making room. Her heart flew to her throat when Jared looked up from the stool on which he was sitting, but he spared her only a brief glance before turning his attention back to Dag.

Perhaps that indifference hurt most of all, though she told herself fiercely that it shouldn't. She meant nothing to him, he'd told her as much and he was a traitorous pirate destined one day to feel a hangman's noose around his neck, so why should any of it matter? Yet she felt compelled to move closer, to say something; the day she'd decided she wasn't going to trouble herself over Jared Giles suddenly seemed so long ago.

"Walker . . . Mr. Burke said I could see Dag. How is he?"

As if her soft words had been a command for everyone to leave, the sailors moved away and disappeared from the crew's quarters. Only she and Jared remained.

Yet he didn't look up and she was tempted to leave, too, as far from feeling welcome as a snake at a ladies' garden tea party. But at that moment Dag groaned so pitifully, his bearded face contorted in pain, that Lindsay sank to her knees beside the bunk and took one of his huge hands in her small ones.

"Shhh, Dag, it's all right. Jared's here and I'm here, too. It was so kind of you to think of me—"

"He can't hear you."

Confused, she met Jared's eyes, her heart beating faster at how vividly blue they were. At how handsome he was—the same inexplicable longing filling her as she recalled tracing her fingers over his lips. She flushed, glancing back at Dag for an instant before she could find her voice to speak. "Can't hear? I don't understand."

"Laudanum. Enough to fell three men. It's the

only thing to keep him from thrashing and hurting himself. Hopefully when he wakes, the pain will be gone."

"But it must be terrible if he sounds so wretched even in sleep."

"He has a blasted metal ball lodged in his brain, woman! What would you expect?"

Stunned by his vehement attack, Lindsay felt tears burn her eyes as she rose abruptly to her feet. "I-I'm sorry. It was a mistake for me to come here. Foolish for me to think—" She spun on shaky legs away from Dag's bunk, yet she had taken no more than a step when Jared suddenly caught her hand.

"Lindsay, stay."

Her breath stilled at the strength of his fingers gripping hers, her face aflame, she didn't readily turn around for fear of him seeing what his touch had done to her.

"Please, Lindsay. Dag would be glad you're here. Talk to him if you like. He might hear you."

Struck by the tremor in his voice, Lindsay turned to see Jared's face etched by private anguish that moved her more deeply than any apology. He released her hand as she sank down next to the bunk, but she still felt the warm pressure of his fingers . . . just as she could feel his eyes upon her when she gently lay her palm upon Dag's tortured brow.

She didn't know what else to do; there was really nothing more than the laudanum to help him. But Corisande, if she were there, would have told her reassuringly that she was doing all she could, which brought Lindsay comfort. Her friend possessed an intuitive gift for nursing that had always amazed her, making her wish she shared the same talent. Yet she had always delighted Corisande's sisters with her stories . . .

Lindsay glanced over her shoulder; Jared watched her still, his face half cast in shadow. Suddenly feeling a bit self-conscious, which was not like her at all when it came to spinning tales, she gave a small shrug. "I don't really know what to say to him, but I could tell him something of Cornwall, a favorite story of mine—mine and Corie's, actually."

Jared nodded, nothing more, but she hadn't expected him to reply. She could imagine how he must feel to see the man who had saved his life three years ago suffering so piteously. She made herself more comfortable next to the bunk, curling her legs beneath her and once more enfolding Dag's limp hand in her own.

"Well, there was a certain baronet who had a fine house and park on the coast—"

"Not your father, I trust."

Jared's voice so low she'd scarcely heard him, Lindsay still took sudden heart that her tale might give him some relief, if only for a short while, from Dag's misery. She threw him a smile, shaking her head.

"No, no, this baronet's name was Sir Thomas, and it was long suspected by the local excisemen that he had done more than wink at the doings of smugglers—fair traders, as they're called in Cornwall. But the wily 'sarchers'—that's what true Cornish folk call the excisemen—had no proof that Sir Thomas ever allowed any fair traders to use his grounds and outbuildings, though the park, as lovely and green as could be, dipped all the way down to the sea. One dark night, however, a party of men with kegs on their shoulders—"

"Scotch whiskey?"

Jared's wry query was a promising sign that his mood was lifting, just as she had hoped. Lindsay laughed and gently squeezed Dag's hand. "Brandy, I suppose. That's what Oliver Trelawny always brought back from France—"

"Your friend Corie's Oliver Trelawny? Captain Trelawny who allowed you aboard his cutter, the *Fair Betty*?"

Blushing to her roots at what she had just revealed, Lindsay glanced sheepishly at Jared, who was staring at her intently. Too intently. "It appears you had more interest in what I was saying during our promenade two weeks ago than you claimed."

"Twelve days ago."

"Well, yes, twelve days."

"And it appears I've just learned something else about you, Lindsay Somerset. Not only have you admitted to recklessly sneaking out at night and frequenting taverns, you consort with smugglers as well."

"Fair traders."

"Fair traders, smugglers. Are you admitting that, too?"

"Of course I wouldn't do such a thing. I only heard that Captain Trelawny made occasional trips to France. May I please finish my story?"

Hoping she had evaded him when Jared didn't respond—though he was still staring at her—Lindsay turned back to the bunk to find that Dag appeared to be sleeping peacefully, his face no longer lined with pain. Greatly relieved, she laid his hand upon his chest and lowered her voice.

"Where was I? Oh, yes, a party of men with kegs on their shoulders was seen stealing through the park toward Sir Thomas's house, and a short while later, they left without the kegs. That brought the excisemen down upon Sir Thomas first thing in the morning, the officer in command apologizing for any inconvenience but saying that they must, of course, make a complete search of the house and grounds."

"Of course, the bastards."

Imagining from his remark that Jared himself must have come close to encountering customs officials along the Sussex coast, Lindsay remembered, too, how he'd ordered his men to blow out of the water whoever might be following them on the night she'd sneaked aboard his ship. Which could have been she. Wincing, Lindsay continued.

"Sir Thomas was most gracious and promptly produced his keys for the excisemen, encouraging them to even look in the cellar, where the wine and spirits were kept—which they did with great enthusiasm. They ransacked the house from attic to cellar and all the outbuildings, but nothing was found."

"So where were the kegs hidden?"

Wishing that Jared would simply allow her to finish without interrupting, Lindsay eyed him with exasperation. "I'd wager a guinea, if I owned one, that you were the sort of little boy who never sat still for his lessons."

"I didn't. Drove my tutors to despair. What happened to the kegs?"

She sighed, not even bothering to ask that he guess. "The excisemen failed to look in the family coach, which was full to the ceiling with kegs. So full, in fact, that to prevent the springs from breaking or showing the coach was so heavily laden, the fair traders had propped up the axletrees with blocks of wood."

"Those bloody excisemen must have been blind."

"No, no, it truly works."

"Ridiculous. I don't believe it."

"And I know that it does! Corie and I had to use one of my father's coaches once to hide some kegs when excisemen were prowling too close— Oh, Lord!"

Chapter 20

Jared had risen from the stool, and Lindsay scrambled up from the floor, clutching nervously at the wrinkled strip of lilac silk knotted at her waist.

She wasn't sure what he was going to do—not that it really mattered he knew now she had lied to him about consorting with fair traders. He had lied enough to her!

Yet she wasn't prepared for the smile that cut across his face, Jared shaking his head as if in disbelief. She smiled, too, uncertainly at first, but when he began to chuckle, she couldn't help herself, either. It had been hilarious, she and Corisande struggling to fit all those unwieldy kegs into the coach . . .

"A smuggler, too. This is bloody rare."

She shrugged, still grinning as Jared once more shook his head, but she sobered and began to feel a little nervous again when he suddenly stopped chuckling.

"Out into the passageway. Now."

His eyes burning into hers, Lindsay gulped. "I—I think I'd rather stay here—"

"Woman . . ."

His tone was so low and ominous, Lindsay hastily decided to comply—if only for Dag's sake, she told herself, a last glance at the bunk assuring her that he was still asleep.

Her heart hammering against her breast as she hurried out of the crew's quarters, she knew Jared was right behind her. She had barely moved into the shadowy passageway when she felt his hands at her waist; she gasped as he spun her around to face him and pinned her shoulders against the wall, his voice as husky and fierce as before.

"Dammit, Lindsay, are you mad? Don't you know they hang people for smuggling?"

She was so startled she could only gape at him, his outburst not at all what she might have expected.

"Or that, at best, if you were ever caught you'd find yourself imprisoned for years or transported to some godforsaken place?"

"But we weren't caught, Jared, we never came close except for a few times, and besides, we didn't do it for ourselves. Corie used all the profits to help the people in her father's parish!"

Now it was Jared's turn to stare, his exasperation so great at that moment that he didn't trust himself to continue. Yet he was equally incredulous, his hands tightening of their own accord around Lindsay's shoulders.

"Your friend Corie's father is a vicar?"

Her quick nod almost made him start to laugh again, but not out of humor. Would this beautiful slip of a woman never cease to amaze him? Or frustrate him?

"And Corie's a smuggler—no, forgive me, a fair trader?"

"Not anymore. Her husband made her promise—"

"Wonderful. A vicar's daughter and a baronet's daughter up to their ears in contraband goods and fending off armed excisemen to boot. No wonder you're as reckless as you are with such a paragon of virtue to lead you."

"Corie didn't lead me; it was my choice to help her and I was glad to do it! Didn't you hear me? I said she's no longer a fair trader. And I don't know why you're so upset about how I spent my time in Porthleven and—and you're hurting me!"

Her outcry making him realize how tightly he held her, Jared eased his grip on her shoulders but didn't release her.

Which was his second mistake.

His first was ordering her out into this narrow passageway and standing so close to her that he could feel the sensual heat of her body as if he held her in his arms, which was almost the case. And here he had sworn when he'd sent Walker after her that he would have nothing to do with her, intending to ignore the chit at all costs. Blast it to hell, that he had failed so completely should alone be enough to upset him.

"I'm not upset," he muttered, lying through his teeth. "I can't believe you involved yourself in such a dangerous business, is all . . . though God knows you've surprised me enough times already."

"And you're not involved in a dangerous business?" came her surprisingly soft query after their spirited exchange, her voice alone stirring him more than he cared to admit. "If I never see a merchantman burn again, it will be too soon."

"Then I suggest you stay away from the porthole. We're not finished hunting for the day."

"That's what Walker told me. And that we're very near the coast of Ireland. I could get little else out of him other than that I owe my freedom to Dag."

Jared stiffened, wondering what else she might have asked Walker even as he decided it was time he left her altogether.

He was mad not to have let her go after lashing out at her about Dag, mad even to have his hands upon her, her hair soft as silk beneath his palms. Damn him for a fool, mad as a hatter, to have finally given in to Dag's constant appeals that he release her from her well-earned confinement.

"I told you before, he's softhearted to a fault." Abruptly, Jared let go of Lindsay's shoulders and strode back into the crew's quarters, very much aware that she chose to follow him. He stopped by Dag's bunk, a tightness welling in his chest just to see the Norwegian giant lying there, drugged into unconsciousness.

"I know little of these things, Jared, but I believe it's a good sign that he no longer seems in pain. If you'd like, I'll stay with him, let you know when he awakes."

Jared could see that Lindsay was truly concerned as she came up beside him, but he shook his head. "That won't be necessary. I'll have one of my men—"

"No, no, I don't mind, really. It's the least I can do and I've no wish to return to my cabin—your cabin, I mean—well, not right away. I've nothing to do there anyway, I've read all the books you told me about—"

She fell silent so suddenly that Jared glanced

down at Dag, fearing that something might be wrong. But the Norwegian, to his relief, slept on soundly. He looked up to find Lindsay staring at him, her lovely blue eyes so wide and luminous he felt his gut twist at the memory of how they had once shone with such radiant admiration—for him.

"Stay with him if you want," he said gruffly, brushing past her. "But don't come above deck unless I send someone for you."

"Jared, wait, please."

Her heart in her throat as he stopped and turned around, Lindsay knew she might not have another chance to talk to him for hours, if then. And she had to know—another day was simply too long to be left wondering.

"Please, Jared, tell me what happened to Elise."

His eyes darkened to a turbulent hue, and she held her breath, not sure if he would stay or go. He had tensed, too, and when he still did not speak, she could not contain herself.

"I know it must seem strange for me to ask such a thing, but she left notes in one of the books of poetry, and after Aunt Winnie told me Elise's husband had treated her so abominably and then I saw the name Ryland, I thought maybe he was the one—"

"He murdered her."

The bitter words striking Lindsay like blows, she was so stunned that she couldn't speak until sheer confusion overwhelmed her.

"But—but Aunt Winnie said she died shortly after you returned from—"

"The bastard murdered my sister as surely as if he'd stuck a knife through her heart—pretending he loved her so he could become the master of

Dovercourt. She knew she had been betrayed when she found him in bed with her own lady's maid only a week after their marriage. And then there were the beatings that followed for years, and the rapes—"

"Oh, God." Sickened, Lindsay covered her mouth with her hand, wanting Jared to stop but sensing, as he began to pace in front of her, his face twisted in torment, that he would not, could not, as if her question had unleashed all the demons in his soul.

"Ryland wanted to beget a son, an heir, using and abusing my sister until there was nothing left of her, four stillborn babes his only legacy. And all the while he and his mother, Sylvia, my uncle's mistress, the bloody whore, entertained the ton at their lavish country parties and no one guessed, no one knew how Elise suffered. Ryland threatened he would kill her if she said a word to anyone, so she bore the horror of what her innocent romantic notions had brought her because I wasn't there to protect her—I wasn't there!"

Lindsay sank onto the stool by Dag's bunk, her knees grown so weak that she did not trust herself to stand.

Struck dumb by the hoarse anguish in Jared's voice, she had no heart to ask him how he could have abandoned his sister to return to India, and she no longer had any stomach left to hear it. She watched in agonized silence as he stopped his restless pacing near an oil lamp affixed to a bunk and stared blindly into the flame.

"She wasn't a great beauty, but she was so vivacious and full of life, so trusting—yet when I saw her again she was a broken shell. A ghost. There was nothing I could do to help her. She didn't want to live. Ryland and Sylvia had fled, else I would have slain them at the foot of Elise's bed if it might have saved her. All she begged of me before she died was that I avenge her, avenge our family—"

"Oh, Jared, please, no more." Her eyes fogged with tears, Lindsay heard his ragged sigh and almost wished she hadn't asked about Elise, hadn't opened up such an ugly wound.

To think of the guilt he must bear—could such a terrible burden have driven him to the sea to become the dreaded Phoenix? She could never condone his traitorous actions, yet how, now, could she condemn him? And that wasn't all which suddenly seemed so clear to her, so achingly clear.

"It's true. The lesson you wanted to teach me . . . you did it because I reminded you of Elise, didn't you?"

Heavy silence stretched for interminable moments, Lindsay's heartbeat drumming in her ears, until Jared finally turned from the flickering lamp and met her eyes. His gaze was haunted, ravaged, yet his voice sounded cold and strangely hollow.

"A lapse in judgment, I fear. If all had gone well, you would have hated me once I failed to appear at your aunt's door and my lesson would have succeeded. You would have become far less trusting and more cautious in choosing a husband—not some impossible fantasy you concocted in your mind, but a man of flesh and blood . . . hopefully, for your sake, an honorable one."

"So all along you were thinking of my marrying someone else," Lindsay said almost to herself, bleak acceptance settling over her, though some stubborn part of her would not allow her to believe it really was true. "Even when you kissed me, never once did you think of me for yourself. Never once."

Anticipating his harsh reply, she looked down numbly at her hands, but when no answer came, she lifted her gaze to find him staring at her, his expression inscrutable. And in that one heart-stopping moment as she rose from the stool, she was filled with such bald hope that there might yet be a chance for them that even the slow shake of his head could not daunt her.

"Never once, Lindsay. I've no fit life to offer any woman."

His words sounding so final, she almost faltered as she walked over to him, but that same voice deep inside her insisted that his words couldn't be true. He would have denounced her at once, and if she truly meant nothing to him, why would he have become so upset about the fair trading . . . ?

She stopped just in front of him, Elise's tragic story still ringing in her mind as she realized just how unfairly she'd judged him. And here she had once shouted at him that he had no right to judge her and he had agreed, which was more than she—

"Go on, woman, strike me if that will soothe my misleading you. Lord knows I've been slapped for less."

She blinked, warmth flooding her cheeks as chagrin filled her. "No, no, I wasn't going to . . ." At the sudden wariness in his eyes, she murmured, "I wanted to apologize, actually, for slapping you the other day. I've never done anything like that before—and, well, I wanted to thank you. For thinking of me—your lesson, I mean. It was a kind thing—"

"It was a bloody mistake."

With a low curse he turned to go, but Lindsay stayed him with a hand upon his arm, surprising herself at her brazenness. Surprised herself even more, her face aflame, as she stood on tiptoes and planted a kiss upon his cheek. Then she quickly stepped away, not sure how he might react, and stared at him almost sheepishly.

"It was a kind thing, Jared, no matter what you say—oh!"

The ship listing so suddenly beneath her feet threw her off-balance, and Lindsay would have careened into a stout support beam if Jared hadn't caught her, both of them tumbling to the floor. Stunned, the next thing she knew, he was looking down at her, his hard, masculine body half covering hers, his hand swiping hair from her face.

"Lindsay, are you all right?"

She bobbed her head, his eyes so concerned that she was tempted to reach up and touch his face to reassure him. So concerned that she knew, no matter he was the Phoenix, no matter anything he might say or do, she could never think the worst of him again.

Her pulse pounding, she stared up at him, their mouths only inches apart, his gaze searching hers, and she was certain as he lowered his head that he was going to kiss her. Wild elation swept her, her lips parting, aching for him; her breath caught, gone, fled . . .

"Cap'n, we've a flagship of the British fleet at our stern, eighty-gunner! And three smaller cruisers in battle formation, the devil take 'em! We just came 'round Carnsore Point and there they were!"

Jared had risen to his feet before Cowan had even finished, Lindsay's head spinning because she'd been pulled up so suddenly beside him.

"Stay below with Dag, Lindsay, and take care you hold tight onto something. There'll be more of the same that just threw us to the floor."

She barely had a chance to nod and Jared was gone, the squat, flame-haired first mate lingering only to throw a worried glance in the direction of Dag's bunk and then he disappeared, too. Her fingers pressed to her lips, Lindsay rushed over to check on the Norwegian, doing her best to stifle the giddy breathlessness that still gripped her.

She could see that Dag had come close to being tossed to the floor as well, his massive chest and right shoulder jammed against the edge of the bunk. Flooded with concern, she spied a thick coil of rope beneath a row of swaying hammocks and spent the next several minutes rigging up a barrier to keep Dag safe and secure inside his berth.

After propping extra pillows around his head, she knew there was little else she could do. Straightening, she grabbed onto the upper bunk just in time as the deck sharply tilted beneath her feet; a nervous excitement overwhelmed her as the *Vengeance* creaked and groaned and gradually righted herself.

Danger seemed to snap and sizzle in the air. If Jared's grim expression had been any guide, their predicament was precarious at best. And if that was the case, she wanted to be with him, not belowdecks where she couldn't see a thing, forced to rely upon her imagination alone as to the peril they were facing.

His lot suddenly became hers, Lindsay felt an allegiance surge within her breast stronger than she'd ever known for anyone, so strong it spurred her out into the narrow passageway, past sailors running for the lower gun deck. None paid her any heed, not even when she scrambled out of the hold to find the upper decks a blur of commotion. Men were scurrying up rope ladders to loose the top sails, while a shout went out to prime the cannon.

Wind whipping at her hair, Lindsay dodged a pair of sailors jumping down from the rigging and ran to the starboard railing; cold salt spray lashed her face as the ship rose and fell on rolling, white-crested waves. But she barely felt the chill, her eyes widening in terrible awe at the sight of the quartet of ships looming behind them, the closest a formidable behemoth unlike anything she'd seen before.

"Damnation, woman, I told you to stay below!"

Chapter 21

As Jared strode toward her, Lindsay didn't wait but ran to him, her heart pounding in her breast at how magnificent he looked, his gait as strong and furious across the slanted deck as if they sailed a placid pond.

"Don't worry about Dag—I tied rope around his bunk so he wouldn't fall out!" she cried above the wind, sputtering as a surging wave plastered her from head to toe with icy spray. "Oh, Jared, will we be able to outrun them?"

If he hadn't been so angered that she'd defied his order, he might have stopped stock still to gape at her. *We?* Not liking how much her unexpected choice of words had pleased him, he grabbed her arm and hauled her alongside him toward the hold.

"Get back below! It's not safe—"

"No, I want to stay up here with you! If I've outwitted armed excisemen, surely a few British ships won't frighten me."

"Frighten you, woman? Blow you to bits is more likely! Now go!"

The stubborn shake of her head only vexing him further, he drew her against the capstan and out of the worst of the wind, his patience at an end.

223

"Blast it, Lindsay, I've no time to quarrel with you—"

"So let's not quarrel. I promise I'll stay out of the way."

Clenching his teeth, Jared glanced past the stern at the four vessels hot in pursuit, then back to her determined face.

"Can't you understand? I don't want any spyglass to spot you! Your blond hair is like a beacon, impossible to forget. Why else do you think I refused prisoners these past two weeks on the chance you might escape from your cabin and someone remember you?"

She broke away from him so suddenly, Jared could only curse, but when she grabbed a wool cap from a passing sailor's head and shoved it down over her hair, waving her thanks to the startled man, he knew there would be no denying her. And he had no more time to argue with her as she darted back to his side.

"See? No more beacon. And it was twelve days, Captain."

"As if I don't bloody well remember," he muttered, once more grabbing her arm and pulling her along with him. He raised his voice above the wind. "All right, you've won this time! But you'll not leave the quarterdeck and you'll content yourself with keeping your lovely head below the railing. Am I understood?"

Her nod did little to reassure him as he made her scramble ahead of him up the companionway, treating him to a fetching view of her pert rump that did little to soothe his temper. Here they were, being dogged by a man-of-war under full sail and three cruisers, and he was thinking that women in breeches might not be such an unwelcome revolution after all?

Scowling, he ignored Walker's crooked grin and Cowan's look of surprise and fisted his hand in the back of Lindsay's shirt. He heard her gasp as he steered her to the aft railing, her eyes wide as saucers when he turned her around and plunked her down onto the deck, her legs sprawled wide.

"Stay there! One move and I swear, woman—"

"Cap'n, they're firing on us!"

Breathless from Jared's rushing her across the deck, Lindsay winced as a series of explosions sounded in the distance, followed by loud splashes somewhere off to starboard, but Jared's grim laugh only startled her more.

"A waste of good shot, the fools. They're too far back now to strike us. If the wind holds to our favor, we'll outrun them, and even if it doesn't, the dark will soon swallow us."

Indeed, it was growing dark, Lindsay realized, thick, heavy clouds scudding above them that portended rain. But she was already drenched from the salt spray, so what would that matter?

Still secretly astonished that Jared had allowed her to stay, she drew her knees to her chest to keep warm and contented herself with holding her tongue and simply watching him. Another distant cannon thundered, but Jared moved around the quarterdeck with a complete absence of fear, Lindsay's admiring gaze unable to leave him. A man of flesh and blood, not a hero, perhaps, yet . . .

Almost as if seeing him for the first time, she marveled at his commanding presence and the rapport he possessed with his men—Walker, Cowan and all the others from helmsman to gunner following orders which he uttered with a cool certainty that bespoke years of experience upon the sea. The wind ruffling his dark blond hair, he seemed younger to her, too. No trace was left of the terrible anguish she'd witnessed belowdecks, Jared clearly thriving upon the dangerous exhilaration of the moment.

She almost regretted the gathering darkness which would soon hide his handsome features from her view as well as his strong, lean form, her face growing hot as she remembered the stirring weight of his body upon hers when they had fallen to the cabin floor. Might he be thinking of her, too, lying beneath him, and how close their lips had come . . . ?

"That's a first for us, Jared. Meeting a fleet of cruisers in Irish waters? It's almost as if they expected—"

"Maybe they did, but we've a record to break, remember?" came Jared's brusque reply. Lindsay hugged her knees closer as she heard Walker's low curse.

"But if they're after us, we'll meet them again at daybreak. Four ships against one are odds not even you could favor. I say we take refuge somewhere, if only for a few days until they suspect we've headed out to open sea and give up the chase. It's not worth the risk of battle, especially not now."

She craned her neck to hear Jared's reply, but he and Walker had moved away, their voices in low conference. A shiver of fear coursed through her, not because those ships still lurked somewhere behind them in the descending gloom of night, but because the reward posted for Jared's capture had jumped to the forefront of her mind.

Might it be just as Walker had said? The *Vengeance* had been expected, anticipated? That would mean ships of the British fleet were actively looking for them, probably more determined than ever, given the sum of ten thousand pounds offered, to bring the Phoenix's terrifying reign over these waters to an end. Oh, Lord, what were they going to do?

The future suddenly bleaker than she wished to imagine, Lindsay nonetheless still told herself to be calm. If Jared had sailed as a privateer for three years, he had seen tight spots before. He would know what to do, surely. Yet what about the last thing Walker had said, something about their not risking battle, especially now? Had he meant because she was aboard?

Her heart thudding faster, Lindsay recalled what Jared had told her about not bringing prisoners aboard—because he'd been thinking of her welfare. His words had warmed her more than she could say, yet right now she didn't want him to think about her, but about what was best for himself and his crew!

Lindsay jumped to her feet at the same moment she heard a curious crackling in the distance, but she gave it no thought as she ran over to where Jared still conversed with Walker.

"Oh, please, don't do anything because of me! If you think you must do battle, I won't be afraid, I promise—"

"Cap'n, did you hear? I believe they're firing muskets at us," Cowan, incredulous, interrupted her. "In the dark, the crazy devils, as if they thought they might hit—"

"Dammit, Lindsay, get down!"

She gasped, Jared lunging for her as another distant volley popped like muted fireworks, a searing pain dropping her to her knees before he had a chance to throw her to the deck. As he sank to his knees beside her, she laughed in disbelief, her right sleeve soaked in blood. Her blood.

"Jared . . . ar-aren't they too far away?"

"Oh, God, Lindsay."

She felt herself being scooped up in his arms, the pain so intense a wave of blackness threatened to overwhelm her.

"Walker, get us the hell out of here! Anywhere!"

Hearing the raw hoarseness in Jared's voice, Lindsay tried to lift her head to reassure him, but she couldn't, her body gone strangely limp. With the side of her face pressed to his chest, she could hear his heartbeat like a rampant thundering in her ear; she could hear his breath coming fast and furious and sensed vaguely that they were no longer above deck.

She heard other voices, too—Cooky's?—and something about hot water and bandages and laudanum. Then she was gently laid upon her back, Jared hovering over her.

"I have to cut away the sleeve, Lindsay. I don't want to hurt you, but it might . . ."

She saw the flash of a knife, her sharp intake of breath making him grimace as the bloody fabric was peeled away from her flesh. But at once his expression eased, his eyes moving to hers, a wetness in them that for a moment made her almost forget her pain.

"You're a lucky wench . . . only grazed. We'll probably find the bullet stuck in the mainmast."

She smiled weakly, feeling chagrined as she realized that she'd most likely reacted more to the sight of her own blood than to the fact that she was wounded, although her right arm felt afire.

"I-I'm sorry, Jared. I guess I'm not as stout-hearted as I imagined."

His answering smile fading as quickly as it had come, he turned from the bed when a tentative knock came at the door. She seemed as unable to lift her head as before, but when Cowan stepped into the cabin, twisting his stubby hands nervously, she managed to throw him a small smile, too.

"Miss Somerset's . . . she'll be all right, then, Cap'n? The men were wondering—"

"She'll mend, Cowan; give her a day or two. A flesh wound, nothing more."

"Oh, aye, that's good to hear. And there's been no more firing from the bastards, Cap'n. I think we've lost them."

"If we're lucky."

Jared's voice had suddenly grown harsh. Lindsay saw that his expression, too, had hardened as he wadded her severed sleeve and pressed it to the wound to stanch the bleeding. The difference in him was like day to night, and she wondered if perhaps she'd only imagined that she had seen emotion fogging his eyes moments before.

"Cap'n, here's the hot water and bandages, and I've tea brewing for the laudanum."

Cowan stepped aside so Cooky could enter, but before the Irishman hustled out of the cabin, he threw a last glance at the bed.

"Cowan, tell Walker I'll relieve him shortly."

"Aye, Cap'n."

Thinking that Jared would probably never allow her above deck again, Lindsay closed her eyes while he dipped a cloth into the basin Cooky set at his feet and then exchanged it for the bloodied sleeve. She sucked in her breath, but the wet cloth did feel soothing no matter its warmth, which was far less than her injured flesh seemed to be burning.

"The bleeding's stopped. Good."

She sensed he had spoken more to himself than to her, but she gave him a grateful smile.

He didn't return it. He didn't speak again until her wound had been powdered with basilicum and her arm thoroughly bandaged, though his hands had been gentle. That gave her some hope that he might not be too angry with her. But when Cooky returned with a steaming mug of tea, Jared's tone was harsh as he bade her to drink it down, once he'd helped her to sit up and propped a pillow behind her.

"But it's too hot . . . Jared?"

He'd gotten up from the bed so suddenly that she was jarred by the jostling; he strode to his desk and returned a moment later with a bottle he'd taken from a bottom drawer.

"Brandy and laudanum. You'll sleep like a babe."

As he poured a generous dose of the spirits into her mug, she felt a tension mounting in him that she couldn't place. And when he lifted the bottle and took a draught himself, a long, long draught, his expression all the harder when he'd finished, she didn't hesitate to drink, downing the lukewarm stuff.

"A pity you didn't obey me a while ago as you did just now. Keep your head down? Stay by the railing? But at least you'll have a scar to help you remember your little misadventure.''

His words cutting her, Lindsay doubted there was anything she could say at that moment that might soothe him, so she remained still. Still, except for her pounding heart. There was more than a trace of the same torment on his face that she'd seen earlier as he abruptly left her bedside. And he took the bottle with him, tossing down another draught as he headed out the door and down the dark passageway. Within an instant he was gone.

''I'll clean up the mess, miss.''

Scarcely aware that Cooky still stood by the bed, she nodded, laying her head back against the pillow as tears sprang to her eyes. Oh, Lord, why couldn't she have listened to him? But she quickly wiped the tears away with her good hand, though her arm felt like a leaden weight when she dropped it to her side.

Already the laudanum was taking swift effect, Lindsay fast asleep by the time Cooky tucked a blanket under her chin and then quietly closed the cabin door, shaking his head.

''We're heading west?''

These were the first words Jared had uttered since he returned to the quarterdeck long moments ago. He didn't look around as Walker came up beside him, nor did he blink at the cold drizzle lashing his face.

''Yes. According to the map, there are plenty of islands along the coast. We'll head for one near shallow water. Even if they spot us, they won't get close.''

Jared didn't reply, not liking what he was thinking. Not liking that if those ships were prowling Irish waters, there were bound to be more.

That bloody reward. He had scoffed upon hearing of it, but he sensed now, deep in his gut, that ten thousand pounds was no doubt spurring more than a few Channel fleet admirals and captains into straying far afield to search for him in earnest. But why now, when he had Lindsay Somerset aboard?

His gut clenching, he wished he hadn't emptied that bottle of brandy so quickly, but there were always a dozen kegs left of Scotch whiskey.

That boastful merchant's ship the fourth vessel he had sunk during their cruise, he could have brought a hundred kegs aboard before they'd set her ablaze, but he had opted for only a few. Yet better his crew than Lord Wellington and his officers in Portugal to consume what little they'd looted, though he'd scarcely given his men opportunity to enjoy a drink.

They had been too busy hunting, he'd been attempting to keep his mind off Lindsay—and look what those twelve interminable days, endless thoughts and futile dreams had brought him. She could have been killed— The devil take it, enough!

"Cowan said it was only a flesh wound."

Taking a ragged breath, Jared nodded, not liking at all how he felt at that moment. Not liking that he hadn't thrown her to the deck in time, not liking that he hadn't kept her from harm's way and protected her.

Not liking that he was starting to want something that he could never have . . . and want it badly.

Jared turned with a fierce oath from the railing, fighting the overwhelming urge to return belowdecks and see how Lindsay was faring. And it came to him again—even more forcefully than when he'd tended to her wound—that there was really only one way he could protect her. Damn him for a selfish fool, he should have done it almost two weeks ago, before they'd left the Channel.

"We'll hide out one day, maybe two, no more."

Walker didn't answer, though Jared could feel his friend studying him in the dark.

"Then we'll head north. There should be plenty to hunt around Galway Bay."

As silence fell between them, Walker doing no more than nod, Jared lifted his face to the biting drizzle, denying to himself even then that the soul-deep chill that had gripped him for so long was beginning to thaw.

Chapter 22

It wasn't the sunlight streaming through the porthole that made Lindsay awake with a start.

Muzzy-headed, she stared at the knotted planks overhead, realizing through the fog in her brain that the ship wasn't pitching and rocking, but only swaying gently. Strange. She licked her dry lips and tried to gather her bearings. The last thing she remembered . . . Oh, Lord.

A stinging like dozens of pins pricking her flesh made her groan; she glanced at the thick white bandage encircling her right arm from elbow to shoulder. Tentatively, she flexed her fingers, her wrist, grateful at least that she wasn't so stiff that her arm was useless. Her mind gradually growing clearer, she raised herself up on her left elbow, grateful, too, that the pain wasn't so bad that she must lie in bed like an invalid.

"You have to get up," she murmured thickly to herself, not surprised her voice was hoarse.

Wondering how much laudanum Cooky had added to her tea, she then remembered the brandy Jared had poured into her mug—she hadn't slept like a babe, but like the dead. She had no idea what time it might be, but that didn't matter. She had to find Jared, show him that she was all right, none

235

the worse for the bullet that had grazed her.

Groaning as she sat up, the cabin swimming a bit, she closed her eyes for a moment and took a deep breath. She imagined the queer sensation would pass soon; then she would change into a clean shirt and—

"So you're finally awake."

She knew before she'd opened her eyes that it wasn't Jared, her disappointment obviously showing as Walker flashed her a wry grin.

"Sorry. He's gone ahead into the village to make some arrangements. I'm to take you there."

"Village?" Feeling as if she'd awoken to an odd dream, Lindsay wished the last of the cobwebs would clear from her mind. She stared at him in confusion. "I don't understand."

"I imagine not, if Cooky gave you his usual dose of laudanum. Better's always been more in his book—more onions, more pepper. Anyway, we've anchored off an island—Dursey, County Cork. Been here since morning."

"Morning," Lindsay echoed, her gaze flying to the porthole. "Then what—"

"Midafternoon. I told you, Cooky used a heavy hand. I'll wait outside until you're ready."

Walker was gone almost as quietly as he had come, while Lindsay stared at the door closing behind him in consternation.

What could he have meant, Jared making arrangements? Her curiosity alone spurring her out of bed, she winced at the stinging pain her movement cost her but told herself she'd best grow used to it. She didn't want Jared to think she was suffering any worse than she was, and she knew it wouldn't hurt as much forever. She hurried to the porthole, her eyes widening in surprise.

Land. Just as Walker had said. And she couldn't believe how good it looked to her, either. The *Vengeance* was anchored no more than a hundred feet off a steep, rocky shoreline as rugged and windswept as she always imagined Ireland to be.

Suddenly itching to feel solid ground beneath her, she ran to the sea chest, almost forgetting her injury until she threw back the heavy lid. She sucked in her breath at the pain shooting through her right arm, her eyes tearing, but she focused upon pulling out another of Jared's shirts and getting herself dressed.

Her wound continued to smart and burn as she exchanged the blood-splattered garment for a clean one; an incredulous laugh left her as she realized she still wore the cap she'd borrowed from a sailor. Tossing it aside, she plunged her fingers through her hair, glad for the few tangles. Ready at last, she ran to the door. True to his word, Walker was leaning against the wall just outside.

"What sort of arrangements?" she blurted out, recalling the conversation she'd overheard between Jared and Walker about seeking refuge for a few days to make it appear they'd headed out to sea.

"A decent meal, no offense to Cooky. There's an inn in the village. I know Cowan's forever dreaming of a piping-hot Irish stew."

She couldn't help but smile, but she was puzzled that Walker didn't return it, the handsome American suddenly appearing oddly preoccupied as he gestured for her to lead the way.

Shrugging to herself, she did, the idea of a savory meat stew spurring her on. Cooky's fare had grown a bit less inspired as the fresh stores had been used up, and she hadn't eaten since luncheon yesterday. Her stomach growling in protest, she glanced with chagrin over her shoulder. To her surprise, Walker seemed to be frowning, although his expression eased somewhat when he met her eyes.

"Dag's doing much better, in case you were wondering."

She flushed, embarrassed she hadn't thought of him until now. "Oh, dear, I'm so glad to hear it! Do we have time to look in on him before—"

"He's above deck. Jared thought some fresh air would be good for him. It seems our short visit here has been blessed by one of Ireland's rare sunny days."

Eager all the more to leave the hold, Lindsay hoped the fair weather would help to finally clear her head as well. She felt a bit light-headed as she climbed the steep steps, but the fragrant spring breeze that greeted her made her spirits immediately soar. Once on deck, she smiled and saw a sky as blue as a robin's egg, a few white, puffy clouds, with the sun warm upon her face. The day was absolutely glorious!

"Dag's over there, but we don't have long."

Wondering what could be the rush, Lindsay made her way over to the port railing, where the bearded Norwegian appeared to be staring, not at the island, but out to sea. In fact, he didn't notice her standing there until she touched his arm and softly murmured his name.

She'd never seen him smile before, his expression reminding her of a shy child's as he lifted a hand to shield his eyes from the sun.

"Dag, Walker is waiting for me, but I wanted to tell you thank you for asking Jared to release me from my cabin. It was very kind of you."

As the big man nodded, Lindsay noticed for the first time the grooved indentation on the side of his head, a circular reddish scar where blond hair should be. Her throat tightening, she quickly shifted her gaze back to his face, to find his pale blue eyes upon her arm. His smile was gone, his expression the same troubled one with which she'd grown so familiar.

"You know about . . . ?"

"Cap-tain t-t-told me."

Startled to hear Dag speak to her for the first time, his voice a deep bass timbre that matched his size, she recovered to give him a reassuring smile.

"It hurts a little, but I'm fine. Truly, you musn't worry."

"Cap-tain a g-good man. S-s-saved m-my life." He turned clumsily, waving a hand as if to encompass the entire ship. "S-saved all. W-Walker, Cowan"—he glanced back to Lindsay—"y-you f-from the wa-ter. Good m-m-man."

She didn't know what to say, or even what to think of such a revelation. "Yes, yes, I know he saved me. But Walker and Cowan—in India, Dag? Is that what you—"

"Lindsay, we have to go."

She started, not even aware that Walker had come up behind her. Her thoughts awhirl, she nodded, then flashed an apologetic glance at Dag. "I'm sorry. We can talk more when I return—unless Dag is coming, too?"

"No, just us."

Surprised by Walker's subdued expression, which wasn't at all what she might have expected, given his comment about their being blessed by a sunny day, she walked with him to where a galley had already been lowered to the water. But she stopped abruptly by the railing when she saw only two sailors at the oars.

"I thought you said Cowan . . . ?"

"He's already there with Jared and a few others."

"But is it safe for us—I mean, with the reward?"

Silenced by Walker's short laugh, Lindsay stared at him in surprise, bristling. "I didn't mean that to be amusing."

"And it wouldn't be if we were somewhere along the Channel, but we're far away from England, Lindsay. Even if anyone here had heard of the reward, I doubt they'd want the money. Cowan said it would be something akin to being a traitor. There's no love lost here for the English."

"But Jared's—"

"American. At least he can pass for one. I don't know if his accent would pass in Boston, but out here? I'll go first and then help you down the ladder."

Walker climbed over the railing before she could ask another question, and she decided it would be best to wait to venture any more. He'd made it quite clear once before that he didn't speak for Jared. Though Dag's words still rang in her mind, she again focused on the beautiful day.

And on how eager she was to see Jared and show him she truly was feeling better. Her heart was already pounding.

"There they are, Cap'n, coming up the lane."

Jared had already risen from his chair to stare out the window, his eyes upon Lindsay as she and

Walker walked side by side, her lovely hair blinding white in the sun, her step jaunty, her winsome smile making his stomach knot. He downed the last of his ale and then strode from the inn, but not before signaling to Cowan and his three other men and the pair of young Irishmen drinking with them to keep to their seats.

She spied him as soon as he stepped outside, her cheerful wave making him almost regret what was to come. It was for the best, he told himself for the hundredth time as if trying to convince himself, which, it seemed, he still was. But the decision had been made. He would not retract it.

"Oh, Jared, have you ever seen such a splendid day?"

He shook his head, remembering all too clearly how he'd thought last night she would never see another. He'd found the bullet embedded in the floor planks of the quarterdeck, the flattened piece of metal tucked now in his belt, all the grim reminder he needed that what he had arranged was right.

"You look well," he said to Lindsay when she stopped a few feet from him, while he nodded a greeting to Walker. "I see you found another of my shirts."

Grateful when she didn't pirouette for him as she'd done once before, he still was astonished that she continued to smile at him as if she were truly happy to see him.

"I couldn't come to supper dressed as I was, one sleeve missing, now, could I? Is this the inn?"

When he nodded, she glanced from him to the door and back again, her eyes beginning to dance.

"It's such a beautiful afternoon, it would be a

pity to waste it. Wait here, Jared, will you?"

He didn't get a chance to answer as she hurried past him and disappeared inside. Incredulous, he stared at the door for what seemed interminable moments before he threw a dark glance at Walker, but the American merely shrugged.

"Don't look at me. I don't know what she's about. I only know I've never seen anyone take such delight in green grass and birds and flowers—"

"And fish," Jared muttered dryly, looking back at the door.

"Fish, too?"

"The big silvery kind that jump." He was scowling when he glanced back at Walker, but his friend was eyeing a comely young brunette who'd chosen that moment to step out of a whitewashed cottage and sweep the front step. And to throw a wink at Walker, which made Jared groan.

"Dammit, man, we've no time—"

"Here I am, Jared!"

He whirled around, Lindsay clearly breathless as she rushed back outside carrying a covered basket.

"Cowan told the innkeeper you'd pay for everything. It isn't much, just some fresh-baked bread and cheese and a bit of stew, but I didn't have any money. Jared . . . ?"

He must have been staring at her stupidly, but in the next instant he heard Walker's amused voice.

"Don't worry about the rest of us, Jared. I think a little afternoon picnic is a wonderful idea. We'll be here when you get back."

With that Walker sauntered over to the cottage, whistling, while Jared suddenly found a basket hooked over his arm, Lindsay's voice soft with apology.

"I'm sorry, I would carry it—the picnic was my idea—but my arm still hurts a little. Could you . . . ?"

Staring into her eyes, Jared found himself nodding; but in the next instant, as Lindsay settled her hand into the crook of his elbow and drew him with her down the lane, excitedly telling him of the loveliest spot she had seen on the way into the village, he knew he was mad.

Stark raving mad.

A lunatic.

Yet he didn't stop, at that moment wanting nothing more than to accompany Miss Lindsay Somerset on a picnic, though he told himself he was a fool.

"Isn't this grand? I can't believe we're in Ireland! I've never been anywhere before."

With the little girl shining in her beautiful eyes, Jared felt a fierce tug deep inside him that made his throat tighten.

Damnation, a bloody fool.

"There's the place, Jared! On that hill. What do you think?"

Chapter 23

Lindsay wasn't daunted when Jared didn't reply, imagining there were few men who would derive as much pleasure as she from a grassy slope covered with wildflowers. And she had sensed his hesitation from the start about going on a picnic, but he had agreed, thrilling her. It would have been a shame to spend the rest of the afternoon indoors, no matter how quaint the inn.

"I think it looks like a spot you would choose. Anyone who revels in simple things as you do."

She glanced at him, as startled as she was warmed by his words, the intent way he was looking at her making her heart race. Suddenly feeling quite giddy, silly, too, she let go of his arm and proceeded to pull off her slippers.

"You can't go to a picnic with shoes, Jared. It's not permitted, didn't you know? One must be barefoot to walk in the grass."

He frowned as he glanced down at his black boots, and for a moment she thought he might decline. But when he handed her the basket, she could have clapped her hands with delight.

"I hope none of my men see me."

"And what if they did? I've never heard that going barefoot could make someone less of a man."

Especially not a man as magnificent as he, she thought with a shiver of longing so intense she was glad Jared had leaned over to wrench off his boots. How she envied the sea breeze rippling through his burnished hair, wishing it were her fingers; envied the sunlight caressing his face—

"There. So much for my boots. Is there anything else we must divest ourselves of to enjoy our picnic?"

Caught staring at him, Lindsay met his eyes to find his gaze drifting as brazenly over her. Blushing to her toes, she started out across the field without him, but he pursued her, catching up easily within a few strides.

"The basket, Lindsay. Let me carry it."

She handed it back to him and slowed her pace, unable to suppress a smile at how boyish he looked, his boots tucked under one arm and the basket tucked under the other. Again she was overcome by such yearning, such hope that it might be true—that she might mean something to him—that she knew she had to find out. And there was only one thing she could do, but not yet . . . not yet.

Lindsay was grateful for the coolness of the grass beneath her feet, suddenly feeling so warm, so distracted, that she gasped when Jared nudged her arm.

"Isn't that the spot over there? You walked right past it."

Indeed she had. Lindsay felt twice as warm as she murmured her thanks and backtracked, delicate white and yellow wildflowers swishing against her legs. The day seemed not quite so carefree now for the import she'd given it, but she still made herself smile brightly as she whirled to face him, hoping she didn't appear nervous. She gestured with a dramatic flourish.

"How about here, my lord?"

"If the honeybees aren't vicious, I suppose we'll survive. Are you as fond of them, too?"

"Of course," she said lightly, sinking down into the grass and folding her legs beneath her. "Bees and flowers go together—they don't frighten me."

"I don't think much does," came his wry reply. Jared set the basket in front of her and then sprawled on his back, his boots thrust under his head for a pillow. He closed his eyes, swiping at a thin stalk of grass tickling his ear. "Hmm, is this how picnics go? The gentleman sleeps while the lady readies the meal?"

"I suppose, if the gentleman isn't hungry. It's usually been my experience that everyone helps themselves, because it's fun to see what's in the basket. Haven't you ever been on a picnic before?"

She was surprised when he shook his head, then rolled onto his side and propped himself on one elbow, his eyes distant.

"Never one like this. In Calcutta, picnics were grand, elaborate affairs all the English attended with their servants and silver plate and great tents spread over the lawn."

"Sounds lovely."

"Maybe. I don't know anymore, it was so long ago. Like a dream."

Never having seen him so pensive before, Lindsay was tempted to ask him more about India, especially considering what Dag had said, and that Jared would talk about a place where he'd lived until three years ago as if he hadn't been there for ages. But she changed her mind when his expression grew hard, almost as if a shadow had passed across his face . . . and their picnic.

"Shall we eat?" she offered softly, wondering what grim thoughts could have so suddenly darkened his mood. When he sat up without a word, she threw aside the linen napkin covering the basket with as exaggerated a flourish as she'd displayed moments ago, hoping to make him smile.

He didn't, but, undaunted as before, she smiled at him and drew a small crock of fragrant Irish stew from the basket, placing it on the grass between them. "I hope the innkeeper thought to give us spoons. The poor woman was in a terrible tizzy. I told her I was in such a hurry, you were waiting for me outside—ah, here we are!"

Handing him a spoon, she immediately dove hers into the thick lamb-based broth studded with pearly chunks of potatoes, her stomach grumbling so loudly she imagined they might hear it all the way out to where the *Vengeance* was anchored. Only when she popped the wonderful-tasting stuff into her mouth did she realize Jared was chuckling, which made her redden with chagrin. Yet she could hardly talk, her mouth was so full.

"Sorry. I'm . . . I'm so hungry—"

"Swallow first, then make your excuses," he said, amused, then dug into the stew as well.

Lindsay couldn't help herself, enjoying several more heaping spoonfuls to soothe her long-denied stomach before she pulled out the rest of the basket's contents. A crusty round of bread, a creamy wedge of goat cheese and a tall corked bottle the gracious innkeeper had thrown in at the last moment.

"Wild berry wine," she announced, producing

two tin cups. "Last year's vintage, a bumper crop on the island, or so I was told. Will you honor us, sir?"

Jared smiled and nodded, Lindsay glad to see he appeared to be enjoying himself again, which relieved her immensely. Deciding she wasn't going to touch the subject of India at all, at least not today, she tore off a generous hunk of bread and sprinkled one side with crumbly goat cheese while Jared poured the wine.

"Do picnics always inspire such a hearty appetite?"

Meeting his eyes, Lindsay could see that he was teasing, but her cheeks grew warm again anyway. "Actually, I made this one for you."

"Ah. Then it's only right that we should share it."

He set a brimming cup of wine in front of her and then accepted the bread, his fingers grazing hers making Lindsay feel as if her entire body were aflame. Suddenly she wasn't so hungry any longer, ignoring the torn half he offered her and reaching for her wine instead.

"How is it?"

She must have grimaced, the stuff more tangy than sweet, for he winced in empathy. Yet he raised a brow when she drained the cup, then sheepishly wiped her mouth with the back of her hand.

"Sorry. I was—"

"Thirsty, I know." Smiling, he shrugged, then proceeded to drain his cup, too. His eyes were watering when he finished, his mouth pursed as if he'd bitten into a lemon, which made Lindsay laugh aloud when he tossed his cup back into the basket, clearly disgruntled.

"A vintage year, you said? I'd hate to taste a bad year's bottling—either that or these Irish don't get off their island often enough to know what's bloody drinkable!"

"Ah, but at least the stew was lovely, wasn't it?"

"Lovely? That's a word I'd use to describe you, but a stew?"

As if he hadn't realized what he'd said, Jared rolled back onto the ground, adjusting his boots higher under his head while he stretched his long, lean legs out in front of him. Meanwhile, Lindsay could only stare at him, her heart thundering, as he finished his bread, crumbled bits of goat cheese falling onto his chest.

He brushed them away, but not all. Almost without realizing what she was doing, Lindsay moved to him, a startled look coming over his face when she reached out to brush away a last few crumbs.

"I'm sorry, you missed . . ." She couldn't finish, his eyes darkening to such a vivid blue as he stared at her that her breath caught, too, and suddenly she knew that the moment had come. She had to know, she just had to, her heart in her throat as she leaned over and pressed her lips gently to his.

At once Lindsay felt him tense, and she feared she'd been too brazen, too bold. But almost in the same instant she heard a low groan, Jared's arms encircling her to crush her fiercely against him, his fingers enmeshing in her hair.

Joy overwhelming her, she thought no more, surrendering to a kiss that belonged to Jared now, not to her, not gentle but deep and dark and powerful, her hands fisting in his shirt when his tongue swept into her mouth. Wildly she clung to him, scarcely realizing he had rolled over and drawn her with him until she felt his weight atop her, pressing her into the grass, her arms flying around his neck to draw him closer still.

"Oh, God, Lindsay . . ."

His husky words against her lips like a prayer, she gave herself to him as surely in that moment as if he'd sworn his undying love, her hope soaring, the longing she had felt for him from the moment they'd waltzed together growing so intense, so searing, she thought she would shatter into a thousand aching pieces. And when he tore his lips suddenly from hers to stare into her eyes, her breath gone, her limbs weak and trembling, she knew, she knew. Yet she found she had voice only to whisper what she wanted to shout from the depths of her heart.

"Oh, Jared, I love you. I love—"

"Damnation, woman, enough!"

He'd thrust himself off her before she could blink, Lindsay staring at him in shock as he rose and swept up his boots.

"Get up. Get up now. We're going back to the village."

Incredulous tears blinding her, she didn't think she'd ever heard him sound so harsh. Or seen him look so furious as he wrenched on his boots. Somehow she made herself rise shakily to her feet while he began to throw things back into the basket, the crock of stew, her tin cup. She winced at the sound of a bottle shattering, red berry wine seeping out onto the grass.

"Jared—"

"I said enough, Lindsay!"

"But I don't understand. I know I mean something to you, just as—"

"You mean nothing to me, woman! How many times must I tell you?"

As his cruel shout echoed across the field, Lindsay almost sank to her knees in despair. "No, I don't believe that's the truth," she said hoarsely, unable to check the tears running down her face as Jared thrust her slippers into her hand. "I can't, I won't."

He sighed then, so raggedly, turning his face to the sea, that Lindsay felt once more the slimmest ray of hope. But his voice was so cold, so hollow, that the tiny flicker seemed to freeze in her heart.

"Someday you will find someone to love you— someone who'll care for you and never let you go. But it can't be me. It will never be me."

"But you kissed me. If you don't care, then why . . . ?"

He laughed brittlely, his expression hard as stone when he turned back to face her. "Still naive, too, and as reckless. Maybe after today you might be better able to discern the difference between lust and love. I'm a man, Lindsay, like any other. You're a beautiful young woman. If you've imagined something on my part, then I'm sorry, but I don't love you."

He looked away, grabbing up the basket, but she scarcely noticed, as numb as if her heart had been torn from her breast, no feelings left inside her. The only thing that stung badly was her arm, the exertions of the day obviously too much, too soon for her.

Wincing, she glanced down at her right sleeve, not surprised to see a small bloodstain there, her wound seeping. Jared saw it, too, and he came up beside her, but she brushed past him and began to retrace their path across the field. He didn't bother to pursue her this time, yet she knew he was behind her, probably thinking what a foolish twit she was, so ridiculously romantic to have fallen in love with a pirate.

Reaching the winding lane, Lindsay faltered; to return to the village made little sense to her. Without meeting Jared's eyes, she glanced toward the distant beach, where the two sailors who'd rowed her and Walker to shore sat waiting for them beneath a stubby tree.

"If you don't mind, I'd like to go back to the ship. To lie down—"

"You can lie down at the inn. Come."

Jared's face inscrutable, she couldn't fathom what he had meant, the walk to the village unbearable compared with how wondrous everything had seemed when they'd left. Wondrous and lighthearted and so full of promise—

"So you're back. Enjoy your picnic?"

Walker was striding from the inn to greet them. His grin faded when Lindsay gave no reply, Jared steering her past the American to the door.

"What happened to the wench?"

"The wench . . . ? Oh, yes, the wench. She had a father—an old bugger, really, but he had a pistol. He thought it best I wait for you at the inn."

"Wise man."

Wondering how Jared could make sport with Walker after what had just happened, Lindsay felt her heart sink even lower, for everything he'd said must have been true. Fresh tears burning her eyes, she didn't bother to turn around when Walker cleared his throat, his voice oddly strained.

"I'll wait for you on the beach, Jared. Good-bye, Lindsay. Godspeed."

"Good-bye?" She tried to face Walker, but Jared pushed her through the door, Cowan and the three other sailors from the ship all rising as they entered, as well as two russet-haired young men she didn't recognize. Intuition suddenly gripping her, she stopped, her gaze flying to Jared's face, her voice gone hoarse. "Good-bye?"

His nod brought reality crashing in upon her. Lindsay glanced wildly at the two strangers who came forward, their eyes roaming over her as if taking in every aspect of her garb not half so jarring as Jared's sudden switch to a bold American accent.

"These are the Killigrew brothers, Ian and Michael. They'll be escorting you back to England."

Chapter 24

"**B**ack . . . back to England?"
Jared had to steel himself against the anguish in Lindsay's voice, his own as harsh as he
could make it.

"You've nothing to fear, it's all been arranged.
You'll be back in London with your aunt Winifred
within a week. You'll have to stretch to come up
with a good story, but pleading amnesia might suffice. As for your wound"—he shrugged, doing his
best not to show any concern that it had bled
again—"a sorry scrape. Good-bye, Lindsay."

Her eyes so stricken he couldn't wait to leave the
inn, Jared dumped the picnic basket on a table and
cast a last glance at the men he'd hired to do the
job. "Take care with her. Don't doubt that I'll find
you if anything goes awry."

"Awry?" echoed the taller Irishman as if affronted. "What could go awry? For the gold you've
paid my brother and me, we'd take her to Russia
to visit the Czar!"

The fellow's coarse loudness grated on Jared
without his knowing why, but he did know there
were no other men in the village to do the job. All
but the old of the male inhabitants were out on the
water for at least another few weeks, trying to fill

their boats with herring, fishermen every one. And he wanted nothing more than to be out of there, with Lindsay not moving, not speaking, as if she'd turned to stone.

Yet she wasn't stone, the tears trickling down her cheeks finally sending him out the door, a grim-faced Cowan and the others silently filing after him. He didn't look back, telling himself fiercely, as he'd done all day, that it was for the best. Blast it to hell, it was for the best!

"Come on, miss, we've the tide to catch."

Lindsay didn't answer, her eyes upon the door through which Jared and his men had just disappeared. He had left her. He had truly left her—

"Didn't you hear Ian?" the tall Irishman shouted at her, making her jump. "If we don't catch the tide, we'll be stuck here the night, and we've a mind to reach the mainland before dark. So move or I'll spur you along myself!"

"Here, now, what's all this wild ranting?"

It was the innkeeper clumping down the steps from upstairs. Lindsay cast a bleak glance at the kindly-faced woman while she was nudged none too gently toward the door by the Irishman named Michael.

"Nothing to worry your head over, Mrs. Tully, nothing at all," Lindsay's rough-mannered escort hastily explained, Ian following close after them.

"No, no, just a minute," the woman demanded, a frown creasing her forehead. "Are you leaving with these two, miss? What happened to your friends? What about your picnic?"

"The . . . the basket's over there," Lindsay managed to murmur before she was rudely interrupted, Ian piping up.

"Uh, we're escorting her about the village—while her friends tend to something on their ship. That American captain even gave us a gold bit to entertain her—"

"A gold bit to the likes of the Killigrew brothers? You shiftless pair, then out with you and earn it and take care with the young lady. You might show her our lovely little church—"

"Oh, aye, the church. Of course, Mrs. Tully, what a fine suggestion!" agreed Michael, Lindsay grimacing as he pulled her out the door by her injured arm. Only when they were well away from the inn did he spit upon the ground and mutter, "Nosy old hag—the church indeed. I'd rather burn it to the ground than step foot in the place."

Apprehension building inside her as Ian grabbed her other arm, the two Irishmen hurrying her down a path leading to a pebbly beach not far from the village, Lindsay felt the numbing daze that had gripped her slowly lifting.

Dear Lord, what sort of miscreants had Jared entrusted her to? The innkeeper, Mrs. Tully, had seemed appalled that she shared their company. Hadn't the woman called them a shiftless pair?

"Watch your step, now, pretty lady," came Michael's gruff command as he handed her off to Ian, who'd already jumped into a large, battered rowboat. The next thing Lindsay knew, she was shoved roughly onto a seat in the prow; then the brothers each grabbed a pair of oars and pushed off from the beach.

"She is a pretty lady, now, isn't she?" Ian said in a silky tone that sent chills plummeting down

Lindsay's spine. "She must be special to be worth so much gold, wouldn't you say, Michael?"

"Aye, special indeed."

Not liking the way the two men were looking at her as their powerful rowing carried the boat into deeper water, Lindsay decided it was wisest to ignore them. She glanced over her shoulder, a terrible ache welling inside her at the sight of the *Vengeance* anchored off in the distance. At least she thought it was anchored until she saw the white sails unfurling. Fresh tears clouded her eyes.

They were leaving the island . . . leaving her behind. Clearly, Jared had decided not to waste any time—

"I've an idea, Michael."

She met Ian's eyes, narrow green eyes like a snake's, as he lifted a hand briefly from an oar to brush a shock of reddish-brown hair from his ruddy face. He wasn't merely looking at her anymore but was openly leering, his gaze falling to her breasts.

"I say when we get to the mainland we find a cozy place to spend the night, the devil with finding a coach straightaway. We'll find a cozy place . . . and get to know our lovely English miss a bit better."

"Are you mad?" she demanded shakily, not liking at all how both men were ogling her now. "You heard the captain—you're to take good care of me or he'll find you and—"

Michael cut her off, his tone cruelly mocking. "Ha! He'll not find us if we decide to disappear, you can be sure. We've enough gold to take us wherever we want! We never have to return to that scrap of an island, and good riddance, I say! Just because a man doesn't like to fish, can't stand the smell of fish, that makes him worthless? No, no, pretty miss, we can do with you whatever we want, and your American protector would never be the wiser.''

Michael's tirade chilling her to the marrow, Lindsay looked desperately at the water and back at the beach, so far away now. But she would jump, by God, she would, if they even tried to touch her!

She tried one last time to frighten them. "You don't know my protector. If I don't return unharmed to London, he will find you and shoot you between the eyes with his pistol. Or else he'll use his cutlass to chop you to pieces!''

"Or maybe he'll hit me over the head with his picnic basket, eh, Ian? Did you ever see such a fine sight? He looked like he'd just come from market, the basket swinging so daintily on his arm—''

As the Irishmen broke into uproarious laughter, slapping each other on the shoulder, Lindsay knew she had failed to daunt them and seized her chance. If she could just get back to the inn and Mrs. Tully . . . Grabbing up a spare oar at her feet, she stood and brandished it in front of her like a sword.

"Stay away from me, both of you, or you'll be swimming to the mainland!''

His throat tight, Jared turned his back on Dursey Island and eyed the great sails filling with wind, the sleek schooner already skimming with ease across the waves.

He stood alone on the quarterdeck, none of his men coming near. Not Dag, who'd remained by the galleys, not uttering a word since he'd heard Lindsay hadn't returned to the ship and why. Not Walker, who stood silently between the two stern guns, his face turned as well from the island. Only Cowan approached, shielding his eyes from the late-afternoon sun, his voice as subdued as the mood that had settled over the *Vengeance*.

"Cap'n, a word if I may."

Jared nodded, though he turned to look out at the open sea, his first mate coming up beside him.

"Cap'n, I think you made a mistake trusting the Killigrews. I would have said so when you returned with Miss Somerset to the inn—they were a boasting, slothful pair—but then everything happened so fast, and you seemed so determined to get back to the ship—"

"Because those damned cruisers are probably still looking for us, man—have you thought of that, too?" Jared said tightly, though his gut twisted at Cowan's words. It was true about the ships, he knew, but that wasn't what had spurred him, his every step taking him farther away from Lindsay only making him want more intensely to rush back to her. But it was done, finished. No more!

"I warned them both," Jared added under his breath, but not so low Cowan couldn't hear him. "You were there, so you know. I made it clear my orders were to be followed, they'd be fools to do otherwise. The deed is done, Cowan. We'll not be returning to the island—"

"C-C-Cap-tain! L-l-look!"

At Dag's agitated cry, Jared tensed, thinking for a fleeting instant the Norwegian had spotted a ship bearing down upon them. Then he heard Walker's low whistle and he spun around to find his second-in-command peering through a spyglass, not out to sea, but back toward the island.

"Good God, Jared, she's just knocked one of them off the boat!"

"Dammit, man, give that thing to me!" His breath stopped in his chest, Jared stared incredulously through the spyglass at the struggle taking place only three hundred yards away, Lindsay's hair shining white in the sun as she jabbed an oar at Michael Killigrew, the man clearly trying to lunge at her. And the other man, Ian, was attempting to climb back into the rowboat . . .

"Steer to port!" Jared shouted to the helmsman, striding to the railing. "Five degrees to port! Walker, have the gunners fire a cannon. Now!"

Only an instant later, though to Jared it seemed an eternity, a deafening boom sounded from one of the carronades near the prow, the huge ball sending up a towering spout only a few hundred feet from the rowboat. At once through the spyglass he saw Michael Killigrew dive into the waves to join his brother, both men setting out at a desperate swim for Dursey Island.

Yet Jared's gaze wasn't upon them but on Lindsay, an admiring smile lighting his face in spite of himself. She stood with her feet braced wide in the rocking boat, and hurled the oar with all her might at the retreating Irishmen—following it with another until four oars had flown through the air. Then she turned her face to the *Vengeance* and Jared's smile faded, his throat constricting at how pale she looked, her eyes stricken. Cowan's words coming back to him, he swore then if those men had dared to touch her in any way . . .

The schooner slowing in the water as sails were hastily furled, rope ladders unrolled over the sides, Jared didn't need the spyglass now, the ship almost upon Lindsay and her bobbing craft. Fortunately, she hadn't thrown all the oars overboard, but she made no effort to row toward them, instead plunking herself down upon a seat and proceeding to row away from the *Vengeance*, which made Jared's jaw grow tight.

Damnation, did she think she would take herself to the Irish mainland now? Alone? With no coin to her name? He could see that her strokes were awkward at best, her right arm clearly causing her pain. But she stubbornly rowed on, not sparing them another glance.

"Now what, Captain?"

There was no amusement in Walker's voice, only an unspoken question in his midnight eyes as he stared at Jared.

"What? You think I'm going to leave her out there?"

When no answer came, Jared lunged past Walker, feeling the unsettling weight of his entire crew's eyes upon him as he left the quarterdeck and strode toward the ship's galleys. His orders were sharp.

"Lower one of the boats. If she won't come to us, we'll have to go to her."

"N-no, Cap-tain, l-l-look."

Jared did, following Dag's gaze to see that Lindsay had obviously changed her mind and begun to row toward them, the schooner drifting close enough to her now that she didn't have far to go. He turned back to the Norwegian. "Help her at the ladder, Dag."

"N-not you, C-Cap-tain?"

He shook his head, the fact that Lindsay would soon be back aboard not changing his mind in the least that he would be rid of her. Maybe not today, but soon. It was the only way to protect her.

From harm.

From him.

His jaw clenched fiercely as he strode back toward the quarterdeck, he knew bloody well they were one and the same.

"Cap'n, Miss Lindsay Somerset coming aboard!"

Cowan's animated voice ringing out over the deck, Jared couldn't help noticing that the Irishman didn't sound subdued at all, but almost elated. Which made his gut knot, too.

Didn't his men realize that Lindsay could be no part of their world, a world so fraught with danger their own survival was continually in question? But he could feel the heavy pall over the *Vengeance* lifting just as surely as the sun peeking out after a storm as Lindsay's blond head appeared above the railing.

Not only Dag, but Cowan and Walker were there to help her over the side and greet her. Jared was tempted to turn his back to the entire proceedings, although he could not bring himself to. Almost resenting the smile she gave them, no matter her heart was surely not in it, he could not stifle his wrenching relief that she was safe.

He felt his breath jam as their eyes met across the distance separating them, Jared jolted by near-physical pain at the hurt in her gaze. But he hardened his heart, Lindsay not appearing surprised at all when he voiced a brusque command.

"Walker, have the helmsman set a course for the English Channel. We're taking Miss Somerset home."

"Cap'n . . ."

Jared looked at Cowan, who had hastened across the deck to the opposite railing. A disquieting intuition gripped him before his first mate had even uttered another word.

"Cap'n, have you the glass? I think those devils may have found us."

Cursing under his breath, Jared pulled the spyglass from his belt, but he didn't have to use it. He could easily see the ships in the distance, four altogether, their taut sails stark white against a dark, angry line of clouds gathering to the west. But it was an alarmed cry from aloft that made him slam his fist upon the railing, a sailor having clambered up the rigging to the main topsail yard.

"Ship approaching from the north, Cap'n, and four at the west sailing straight for us!"

Jared lowered his head, such odds not unknown to him, but for the first time in his life, he hesitated.

They were coming for him, he knew it, coming for him and his crew, determined to capture them and win the reward. But every man aboard the *Vengeance* had sworn to fight to the death rather than face prison again or hang from a noose—so what, then, of Lindsay? His plan to protect her had failed completely, just as he'd failed to help Elise, and now they faced a greater, potentially insurmountable trial—

"Jared, the men await your orders."

First realizing that Walker had joined him on the quarterdeck, he met his friend's intense scrutiny, saw the concern there and the urgency. It spurred him, those ships at a swift glance not so close yet that outrunning them would be impossible, but he'd be a fool to think they weren't in danger.

"Loose the sails! Every man to his station!"

The words were no sooner out of his mouth than the ship seemed to come alive: sails unfurled and swelling with the wind, sailors priming guns while others scaled the rigging. Jared looked next to where Lindsay still stood by the railing, Dag at her side.

"Dag, take Miss Somerset below to her cabin and then return to the quarterdeck. We need all hands—"

"Cap'n, the ship at the north!" cried the sailor who still clung to the main yard, a spyglass clutched in his hand. "It's the man-of-war *Trident*!"

Chapter 25

indsay felt the strange hush fall across the *Vengeance* as if the sailor's cry had sucked away all movement and sound except for the flapping sails and the schooner creaking as it was steered hard to the wind. Yet in the next moment activity resumed with a furor that she'd not seen before, Jared's face grown hard and impassive as granite, his roared commands filling the air.

And one of them was for Dag to escort her below at once. Lindsay knew there was no hope of her remaining above deck, even if she had wanted to. If she'd ever wondered what it might be like for the ship to face a true battle, she felt it now, struck by a terrible sense of foreboding as chilling as the sudden cool gust of wind whipping at her hair.

It smelled of storm and rain, the sun sinking into the west already obscured by ominous clouds. Her last glance of Jared before she ducked her head into the hold was of him staring to the north, the tension in his body as palpable as Dag's nervousness. She had never seen the Norwegian so agitated before.

"What is it, Dag? Do you think we won't be able to outrun them?"

She got no answer, the big man clearly anxious

to return above deck as he led the way swiftly to Jared's quarters and shoved open the door, his agility again surprising her for someone so large. She had no sooner stepped into the cabin than the door was closed firmly behind her, and suddenly she felt as if she were reliving what had happened two weeks ago.

Yet it wasn't the same. So much had changed—everything had changed, and not simply the fact that no guard was stationed outside. Still incredulous that she was actually aboard the *Vengeance*, she knew, too, that she wouldn't want to be anywhere else, no matter the peril they faced.

She had realized that when she'd thought first to row away from the ship after the cannon fire had chased the Killigrew brothers away, but every stroke of the oars had made the ache in her heart only worse. Despite everything Jared had said to her, everything he'd done, something inside Lindsay would not allow her to relinquish all hope. She had seen too much in his eyes, felt too much in his kiss.

And she had seen enough lust on the faces of Michael and Ian Killigrew to know that Jared had never looked at her in such a vile way.

Glad that at least one of the oars she had hurled at them had struck home, the memory of Ian's pained cry still fresh in her mind, Lindsay moved to the porthole but lost her balance when the ship suddenly listed sharply to port. She cried out as her shoulder struck the cabin wall, but her pain was nothing to the dread that seized her when she heard a deafening thunderclap, the sound so close she felt the entire ship shudder.

"Oh, Lord, no, they can't be firing upon us!" She

made it to the porthole despite the heavy list, her eyes widening to see rain pelting the glass.

Nervous, near-giddy laughter escaped her; it wasn't cannon fire but thunder she'd heard, the *Vengeance* overtaken by a sudden squall. Yet her laughter froze in her throat when she saw a huge ship plunging through the rolling, rain-lashed waves toward them, her heightened sense of fore-boding almost choking her.

"They're going to ram us," she murmured in horror, thinking to run but not knowing where, and unable to tear her eyes from the terrifying sight. The words were no sooner off her tongue than the *Vengeance* listed severely to starboard and seemed to surge forward, throwing her to the floor. She could do nothing but close her eyes and wait for the impending impact, so certain the two ships were going to collide that she screamed when the cabin door burst open and slammed against the wall.

"Lindsay, get up! Come with me now!"

Astonished to see Walker grasp her by the shoul-ders and help her to her feet, Lindsay felt as if a cold hand had taken hold of her heart.

"Is it Jared? What's happening?"

"Move, Lindsay, there's no time! He sent me down here to get you out of the cabin—now!"

Half stumbling, she obeyed, the American grab-bing her arm and almost dragging her along with him into the passageway. She heard men shouting, the air crackling with tension, then the thunderous boom of cannon as if every gun on the *Vengeance* had opened fire.

A horrifying answer came too soon. Lindsay screamed again as an explosion so near to them

rocked the ship; she and Walker were both hurled
to the floor, her head hitting something hard.

Dazed, she lay there; as if from a great distance,
she heard more screams, but they weren't hers. She
tried to speak but couldn't, her last shred of con-
sciousness like a bizarre dream as she was hauled
across the floor, the acrid smell of gunpowder enveloping her, choking her. Dimly, she saw Walker's
face, cut and bleeding. Then everything went black.

It was the sound of fierce pounding that roused
her, Lindsay unable to guess, when she opened her
eyes and tried to gather her bearings, how long she
might have lain there in the bunk . . .

A bunk? She raised herself up shakily on one
elbow, grimacing at the pounding in her head
which seemed as fierce, matching her sudden confusion. The last thing she remembered, she and
Walker had been running and—

"Oh, God, help me! Help me!"

The agonized cry coming from somewhere behind her, Lindsay rolled over; her startled gaze
flew to the bloodied sailor who lay stretched out
on a table, Cooky and his two kitchen assistants
frantically working over the injured man. Recognizing the crew's quarters, she thrust herself from
the bunk, paying no heed to the aching in her head
or to her wobbly legs as she hurried to Cooky's
side despite the pitching deck.

"What happened? Can I help—what can I do?"

"Help us hold him down, miss. We've got to cut
the fragment from his leg."

As a gag made of rope was thrust into the
wretched sailor's mouth, Lindsay did as she was
told, squeezing her eyes shut as his muffled cries

filled the large cabin. His agony was mercifully short-lived. When she looked again, the man had fainted. She almost felt like fainting herself when she saw the bloody knife in Cooky's hand and watched him throw a jagged chunk of metal to the floor with disgust.

"Damn the bastards! Hit us from the stern, they did. Had to be the *Trident*, too, may her timbers rot in hell. A broadside. Most of the shot fell short—we were far enough ahead, thanks to Cap'n turning the ship to starboard—but a few did their damage, as you can see. I only wish that was the worst of it."

At Cooky's heavy sigh, Lindsay felt a chill course through her. "There . . . there are more wounded?"

The grizzled old sailor's grim nod made Lindsay look around. She was astonished that she hadn't seen the half-dozen men lying drugged and bandaged in nearby bunks.

"Thank you kindly for your help, miss. We'll manage fine now. This is the last of them."

Grateful to hear at least that bit of good news, Lindsay shuddered as the pounding through the ship continued unabated.

"They're plugging up the holes left from the *Trident*'s cannon, miss. Walker told me you'd taken a blow to the head. A bit of laudanum—"

"No, no, I'm fine," she murmured, although, in truth, she didn't feel fine for the disquiet filling her. If there were so many wounded, had anyone been . . . ? She wanted to ask Cooky, but she couldn't bring herself to, the man already busy with bandaging his patient's ravaged leg. And the other two sailors helping him looked so somber, matching the gloom that tinged the air, that Lindsay felt a sharper chill.

Cooky would have told her if anything had happened to Jared, wouldn't he? she assured herself wildly. Swallowing hard, she left the crew's quarters and its cloying stench of blood and sweat. The ship was rolling so heavily that she had to brace her hands against the bulkheads, suddenly remembering the squall that had come upon them just before the attack.

Lindsay felt her heart lurch as she remembered, too, Walker's words when he'd burst in upon her—something about Jared sending him to get her out of the cabin. And that cabin lay in the stern . . . Jared must have known it was in the line of fire—

"Miss Somerset, I wouldn't go above deck if I were you."

She turned to see two sailors who'd just come through an adjacent passageway, their faces blackened from gunpowder, huge mallets in their hands and other tools stuck in their belts. She realized then that the pounding had stilled, these men obviously the ones who'd been hard at work plugging the holes made by cannon fire.

"We're not going to sink, are we?" she asked.

"No, the damage has been fixed, at least for now," the sailor closer to her added quickly, reassuringly. "But not above, not yet. There's rigging down and sails torn and a shattered top foremast to be cleared away—"

"I won't get in the way, I promise." She turned to go but stopped, surprised, when the man reached out and caught her arm.

"Miss, it's not a pretty sight. They're still cleaning up the mess—"

"Mess? If you mean the damage you mentioned from the attack—"

"Not that. We've four men didn't make it, miss. I think Cap'n would want you to stay below, especially . . ."

The sailor fell silent, glancing uncomfortably at his companion, his face so grim that Lindsay felt her breath stop when the second man uttered a low curse. She looked from one to the other, her voice sunk to a hoarse whisper.

"Dag?"

They didn't need to answer, their grave expressions telling her all she needed to know.

Tears blinding her eyes, she fled to the main companionway, not heeding what the sailor had told her, not caring. She could think only of Dag . . . and of Jared, his anguish at Dag's side just yesterday leaping to her stricken mind. Her eyes were so clouded she stumbled upon the third step, made slick from rain and blood; suddenly she felt strong hands on her shoulders and she looked up, Jared's gaze burning into hers as he made her climb back down with him into the hold.

He was drenched from head to toe, a wildness in his eyes that she'd never seen before, a fierce desperation that touched her very soul.

For a fleeting moment he stared at her, his gaze moving over her as if ensuring that she was safe, his trembling hand grazing the painful knot above her temple where she'd hit her head. Then he shoved her almost roughly away from him. Yet his shift from poignant gentleness to harsh treatment of her wasn't half as jarring as the agony in his voice when he spoke.

"Don't . . . don't go up there."

"I-I won't," she murmured, shaking her head even as she longed to reach out to him, to touch him, to console him. "I promise, Jared. I promise."

He said no more, brushing past her and the two startled sailors, who backed up to let him by. Jared disappeared down the darkened passageway, disappeared just as surely as if his private anguish had swallowed him whole. A distant door opened and then slammed shut with such violence that Lindsay jumped.

She wanted to follow him, wanted to so desperately, but the horror of his suffering seemed too black, too deep. Her knees giving way, she sank to the floor and surrendered to the wrenching sobs she could hold back no longer.

A full day later, Jared still hadn't emerged from Cowan's cabin and Lindsay hadn't gone above deck.

She hadn't needed to, Walker telling her what she wanted to know.

Dag and the three other sailors had died instantly, a single cannon shot snuffing out their lives and leaving a gaping hole in the deck; their shattered bodies had been wrapped in sailcloth and buried early that windy, rainy morning at sea.

Serving as temporary captain of the *Vengeance*, Walker had also told her that Jared's last order had been that they make urgent course to the northwest coast of Spain, since it was too dangerous, given the reward for their capture, to venture into the Channel. For that reason, even Roscoff, Brittany, where they usually docked, was denied to them. No British ships would dare proceed into the French port, but smuggling vessels from England abounded, some whose crews might have heard of the reward.

No, it was safer for them to head to northern Spain, which was still controlled by Napoleon's army. There they would make needed repairs and decide what their next move would be.

He had said little else, except that they had managed to outrun both the *Trident* and the four other ships that had dogged them, thanks in part to the turbulent weather that had yet to abate. Walker had been as subdued as every other man aboard, all responding to the black pall that hung over the ship like a funeral shroud. He had left Lindsay to her own devices, which consisted of no more than counting the bleak hours and wondering when Jared might break his tortured exile.

Only when supper had long passed did she finally allow her mounting fear for him to overwhelm her. Cooky's several tries to get him to open the door for a meal having failed, she decided to make an attempt herself.

After fetching a plate of salt pork and dry biscuits, the weather too rough to risk lighting a fire in the galley stove for a hot meal, Lindsay thought her hammering heart might burst from her breast when she knocked softly on Jared's door.

She wasn't surprised that no answer came, and no light from an oil lamp shone, either, Jared shut away in complete darkness. She almost faltered at the daunting image, but the memory of his trembling touch last night spurred her on.

She took a deep breath and entered, the stillness

inside the cramped first mate's cabin so great that she wondered for an instant if Jared might have left while she'd been in the galley.

"Jared?"

This time she held her breath, her fumbling hand finding a table by the door where she set the tray. An interminable moment later and still no sound, she tried again.

"Jared, I've brought you some food—"

"Leave me."

She started, his voice so empty, so emotionless that her heart went out to him. No, she would not leave him! Slowly she closed the door behind her, the pitch darkness swallowing them both.

"Jared, if you would at least drink something, I've brought some water—"

"I've drink here enough . . . and I told you to go."

She smelled it then, not the sweetness of brandy, but the pungency of Scotch whiskey; she heard, too, the telling slur in his voice that warned her she might want to flee. But she thought he might care to know at least that Dag, and the other sailors who'd died, had been properly laid to rest.

"I will go, Jared, but—I wasn't there myself, I haven't been above deck—but Walker told me a prayer was said for Dag and the others—"

"A prayer? And who might be there to hear it? A God who could make a gentle man like Dag suffer wretchedly for three years, not counting the ones that came before, and then allow him to be blown to pieces? Did you know we found his severed head lodged beneath a cannon, his left leg hanging from the rigging?"

Jared's voice was so icily bitter that Lindsay

couldn't help but shudder. Sickened by his words, she shook her head bleakly in the dark.

"As for the other three, there was scarcely anything left of them to throw to the sea. But better food for fish than worms. Perhaps it won't be long before such useless words are said over me, and that's one prayer I know God won't hear."

"No, don't talk like that!" she blurted out, rushing blindly forward. She gasped when she bumped into his legs hanging over the narrow bunk, flailing her arms to find some hold to keep herself from falling, until a strong hand suddenly clamped around her wrist to steady her.

"My blasphemy troubles you, woman? You should have learned by now that I'm far closer to spending eternity in hell than in heaven—damn you, leave me, Lindsay! Go!"

She almost did when he abruptly released her, his angry words almost masking the tremor she heard in his voice, a hoarse tremor that made her heart ache for him anew. She didn't think, only acted, reaching out to draw him near and cradle his head against her breast, his tense resistance melting almost at once.

"Oh, Jared, I'm so sorry about Dag, and the other men, too. So sorry."

She heard an anguished curse as Jared's arms went around her to hug her fiercely against him, his face buried in her shirt. Tears stung her eyes, but she would not allow herself to cry. All she wanted right now was to be strong for him and hold him and hope he might find some comfort, some solace, in her arms.

Just as she felt such warmth to have his arms around her. Lindsay closed her eyes when his hands tugged suddenly at her shirt and then slipped beneath the cambric to encircle her waist, his fingers splayed against her back.

His embrace became wild, desperate. She tunneled her fingers in his hair as he buried his face deeper against her breasts, her breath stopping when her shirt was lifted higher and his stubbly beard raked the tender flesh of her stomach. She nearly sank to her knees when she felt a warm wetness against her skin . . . Jared's tears. Her love for him swelled so, she could not stay her trembling.

As his lips moved fervently from her stomach to the valley between her breasts, she lowered her head and kissed him, his hair smelling of gunpowder and the sea. And when she kissed the hard plane of his cheek, tasting the salt of his tears, she knew, no matter what happened after tonight, she would never, never leave him.

Their breathing coming faster, his hands pressing against her back to draw her even closer, Lindsay moaned raggedly when she felt him draw a nipple into his mouth, the wondrous agony unlike anything she had known. Her desire to surrender to him so searing, so intense, at that moment that she thought she might die from sheer longing, she bent her head and whispered against his hair.

"If you want me, Jared, I'll stay. Please . . . please say you want me . . ."

Chapter 26

This time Lindsay couldn't stop the tears from falling when Jared tensed, but he didn't pull roughly away. Instead he pushed her slowly from the bunk until he held her at arm's length, her throat tightening at how his hands were shaking.

"Leave me, Lindsay. Please. You deserve so much better."

She wanted to scream, to shout it to the heavens that he was the only one she wanted, but when he dropped his hands and rose in the darkness to open the door, she knew she would not sway him. Not tonight.

Somehow she made herself leave him, but as the door closed behind her and she walked numbly down the passageway to her cabin, her hands fisted in her sodden shirt, her breasts flushed and aching from his touch, she swore that there would come a time when he would not push her away. Maybe he had forgotten, but she still remembered how to pray.

And she prayed for six days, but Jared didn't leave Cowan's cabin, although she took heart when, the morning after she'd gone to him, he began to accept meals from Cooky. The heavy pall over the *Vengeance* remained, not lifting even when they finally anchored off Cabo de Peñas, near the port city of Gijón, Spain.

The only thing that had changed was the weather, the storms that had plagued their crossing from Ireland giving way to an afternoon sky of intense blue, so clear that she could see rugged mountains to the south and the formidable Pyrenees to the west, and all from the porthole in her cabin. She still hadn't gone above deck, honoring her promise. But her yearning to breathe fresh air was very close to overwhelming her when Cooky came to ask if she might like to accompany him to shore to buy fresh stores for the ship.

She jumped at the chance, not surprised he had thought of her. She'd done what she could to help him with the wounded sailors the past week, although another man had died. Lindsay was almost glad Jared remained in Cowan's cabin for fear of seeing what a fifth death might do to him.

She knew he'd been told. Walker had gone to him, the American as grim-faced upon leaving as when he had entered.

That had just made Cooky shrug helplessly and shake his head, mumbling something about seeing Jared like this once before. She could only imagine he had meant after Elise's death, but she hadn't asked him, the old sailor succumbing to a gloomy silence that had captured the entire ship.

Yet he seemed of lighter spirit when they left the hold, his eyes squinted into slits against the sunlight—until he saw the shattered deck near the ship's galleys that men were already hard at work repairing. His vehement curse blistered her ears, while she could no more than attempt to swallow down the terrible lump in her throat.

She tried not to think of what Jared had told her about Dag and the other poor victims, only too glad to leave the scene of such wretched destruction. Yet as six sailors rowed the galley toward shore, Cooky sitting grim and silent beside her, she couldn't seem to take her eyes off the shattered topmast and sails shot through with holes as if poked by a giant's stick.

"To think it was the *Trident*. There's no damned justice, none at all."

She glanced at the old sailor who was as accomplished with pots and pans as he was with a surgeon's knife, his leathery face creased by a hundred intersecting lines. But none was so deep as the scowl around his pale eyes.

"I don't understand."

When Cooky didn't answer, Lindsay saw somber glances pass between the other men, making her wonder all the more.

"Has the *Vengeance* run into that ship before?"

"In a way, miss, in a way," came Cooky's low reply. "We knew her to be far away in India these past three years, but it's clear she's finally come back to haunt us."

"So it was India, then—where you ran into her, I mean—"

"India? I've never been to the place, though Cap'n lived there a long time ago. Left when he was a lad of seventeen, and that's how old he was when I first met him. Beaten to within an inch of his life, those bastards. Just for trying to tell them who he was."

As Cooky sighed heavily, Lindsay could only

stare at him in confusion. Whatever was the man talking about? The three years made sense; it seemed everything had happened to Jared three years ago. Dag saving his life, she had thought in India. Jared returning to England. Elise dying. But the rest?

"You'd best stay close to us, miss, while we're ashore," Cooky said, interrupting her roiling thoughts. "We won't venture far, just to the market, and I doubt these folk will give us any trouble. They've probably little love for the French, but I've heard they don't care much for the English, either. At least not this far north. And gold is gold, no matter who you are."

As the galley bumped against a wharf, Jared's men clambering out to secure the vessel with a thick twist of rope, Lindsay could see that her questions would remain unanswered, at least for now. And suddenly she felt a bit nervous. Gijón was a bustling port where tens of ships were anchored, although she was relieved to see that none flew the British flag. She saw French flags and the colors of a host of neutral countries; obviously trade was trade, just as Cooky had said, no matter the ongoing war.

Given a hand up onto the wharf, Lindsay felt more than a little self-conscious, too, about her male garb, wishing she wore a gown as curious Spaniards glanced her way. Not silk or satin, just a simple one would do; the breeches didn't grate upon her so much as that she craved something feminine to wear. She blushed, wondering what Jared might think to see her . . .

"Cooky, do you think there's a chance we might

find a place that has women's clothes? I don't have any money—"

"But I do, plenty to go around. And Cap'n said to buy you something pretty first thing."

Startled, Lindsay hurried to keep up with him, his pace quite sprightly for an aging sailor. "Jared said . . . truly?"

"Do you think I would have dared to bring you ashore if he didn't know about it? He'd have my hide and then some, miss! I may be old, but I'm not blind. He's never looked at any woman as he does you."

Flushing to her toes, Lindsay could do nothing but catch up again, Cooky frowning and shaking his head as if he'd said too much, while she felt like she'd just been given the greatest gift in the world.

It was past sunset by the time they returned to the wharf, a brilliant moon full and heavy above the water, making Lindsay smile. She loved full moons.

And she loved her new gown, a simple creation of pale lemon-yellow muslin with a matching satin ribbon tied beneath her breasts. The kindly dressmaker, who'd reminded her of Mrs. Tully, except that she spoke little English, had brought forth slippers to match, and a delicate white satin chemise and drawers—and then had not allowed Lindsay to don a bit of the feminine finery until she had enjoyed a warm bath in the back room, prepared by the motherly woman herself.

Lindsay had sensed the dressmaker was appalled by her appearance the moment she'd entered the small shop; Cooky and the others had been shooed back into the street at once, where they had waited for over an hour. But their awe-struck expressions upon Lindsay's emergence from the shop had pleased her more than she could say, and she was hardly able to contain her impatience for Jared to see her, too.

If he had left Cowan's cabin, she thought hope-fully. She felt a bit guilty that she carried nothing back to the galley except a package neatly tied with string that held her borrowed clothes, while Cooky and the others were laden with sacks and bags bursting with fresh stores. But Cooky wouldn't hear of it, not wanting her to muss her gown.

Some of the men had already made a few trips from the market to the galley, which Lindsay feared might now be so full that she'd have to wait for it to be emptied at the ship first before it could come back to fetch her and whoever else was left behind. Her impatience mounting, she was sur-prised to see another galley from the *Vengeance* moored next to the one that was indeed loaded to the gills, several sailors she recognized coming for-ward to help them with their burdens.

"What's this?" Cooky asked, relinquishing a sack of potatoes to one of the men. "Cap'n sent you?"

"We're waiting for him. He went into that tavern there," the sailor explained. Lindsay followed his nod toward a two-story building right off the wharf. "About a half hour ago. Said he wouldn't be long."

So he had left Cowan's cabin at last! Wild elation filling her, she glanced back at Cooky, who had a speculative frown between his eyes. "I'll wait here for him if I might—the galley's too full anyway.

Actually, the tavern's so close, I could even meet him there—"

She tossed her package into the nearest boat and set off along the wharf before anyone could say a word, and she didn't see Cooky grab the arm of one of the men who made to go after her. Her mind consumed with thoughts of Jared, she imagined he might not be pleased that she had followed him, but she so wanted to see him . . . for him to see her. She glanced over her shoulder and saw that Cooky and the others were intently watching her progress, which made her feel safe and certain that if anyone might trouble her, help would be soon to follow.

Her heart was beating furiously by the time she reached the tavern, several men looking up from their mugs to eye her with surprise as she rushed inside. So, too, did the portly gentleman who she imagined was the proprietor from the apron around his vast middle. Lindsay hurried over to him when she didn't spy Jared among the few patrons.

"Excuse me, sir, I'm looking for a tall gentleman, an American—oh, dear, do you speak English?"

"*Sí*, senorita, a little," the fellow said to her relief, still appearing as astonished by her presence in his establishment as she was anxious to find Jared. "Upstairs, second room, but—but, senorita, wait!"

Lindsay paid him no heed, hiking her gown and dashing up the creaky steps two at a time. But she took a brief moment to compose herself outside the second door, although she could do nothing to slow her heart or cool the warmth in her cheeks. She lifted her hand to knock.

"Senorita, no, no! Wait!"

Glancing at the proprietor huffing up the stairs,

Lindsay didn't tarry any longer but threw open the door. "Jared—"

She stopped, her eyes widening as Jared hauled himself in astonishment from a huge wooden tub, water splashing everywhere.

"Damnation, woman! What the devil?"

She stared; he stared; the proprietor stared, the red-faced fellow rolling his eyes heavenward and clasping his hands together in fervent apology as Jared grabbed a towel and threw it around his lean waist.

"I-I tried to stop her, senor, but—but—"

"It's all right, man. I'll take care of it."

The proprietor appearing only too eager to return to his patrons downstairs, he mopped his face with a handkerchief and left. Lindsay almost felt like following him and she might have if her feet weren't rooted to the floor. Her embarrassment at having burst in upon Jared during his bath was nothing compared with the shock that overwhelmed her. Her stomach still lurched because of the ugly ridged scars she had glimpsed on Jared's powerful back and shoulders—a sickening diamond pattern she had seen only once before.

One of Captain Oliver Trelawny's crew had served in the British navy, and had been flogged to within an inch of his life when he'd been accused of stealing from another sailor. Within an inch of his life . . .

Jarred by the memory of Cooky saying those very words that afternoon, Lindsay licked her dry lips, something telling her by the way Jared was looking at her that he knew exactly what she was thinking. He cursed and turned away from her, not even trying to hide what drew her eyes again with sickening force as he reached for a glass of brandy set near the tub and drained it.

"Why aren't you back on the ship?"

His tone so harsh she faltered and said nothing, in the next instant she regained a measure of composure as he threw her a dark glance.

"Dammit, Lindsay, why aren't you back on the ship?"

"I-I would have been, but your men said you'd come to this tavern, and I so wanted to see you— to show you . . ." Flushing, she glanced down at her gown, spotted now from tiny droplets of water. "Cooky told me you'd wanted him to buy me something pretty. I chose this." She lifted her eyes to his. "Thank you, Jared."

He didn't reply, but his gaze slowly raked her; then, with another low curse, he poured himself more brandy. "Very well, I've seen you, now go. Have my men take you back to the ship and tell them to return for me—"

"No."

He went as still as stone, the glass freezing halfway to his lips. Lindsay had never felt her heart beat so wildly, felt herself tremble so fiercely, but somehow she lifted her chin and met his deepening scowl, scattered pieces suddenly falling together with horrifying precision in her mind.

Dear God, could it be possible? That Jared, like that sailor, might have served . . .

"I'm not going to ask you again, Lindsay. I said go—"

"No, Jared, I'm not leaving. Not until you tell me how you got those terrible scars . . . and about the *Trident* and—and— Oh!"

Chapter 27

Jared had stridden forward and grabbed her arm, spinning her into the room so roughly and slamming the door behind her that she could only gape at him, her jaw dropped in astonishment.

"Who told you about the *Trident*? Walker?"

"No, no, Cooky mentioned the ship a few times, is all. How there was no justice that she'd been the one to attack us—"

"That damn old fool."

Jared released her and strode back toward the tub just as abruptly as he had come upon her, leaving Lindsay to massage the white imprints he'd left on her arm. As he took a long draught of brandy, she tried not to let her eyes stray over his magnificent body, but it was impossible, her cheeks growing hot as flame. She tried not to think, too, of that arresting part of him which she'd glimpsed for only an instant— Oh, Lord.

"I-I'm glad to see that you decided to leave Cowan's cabin, Jared."

He gave a short laugh, but it held no humor, the sound laced with bitterness.

"I stank. Decided I needed a bath." His eyes met hers, the blue so deep and dark in the lamplight that Lindsay slowly sucked in her breath. "But I didn't expect to see you."

"Truly?"

Her query soft as a whisper, Lindsay was almost as stunned that she had asked such a thing as Jared appeared to be, though a strange intensity now burned in his eyes. She sensed the shift as surely as he had touched her, a shiver coursing down her spine. If he hadn't expected her . . . perhaps at least he had hoped she might find him— Oh, Lord.

"We have a bargain to make, you and I."

His voice was so husky and low that Lindsay felt her breath stop; somehow she nodded.

"I will tell you what you want to know and then you will leave. Are we agreed?"

Again she nodded, his jaw suddenly so tight that she felt his tension in her own body, her eyes unable to leave him as he drained the last of his brandy. She jumped when he set the empty glass on the table with a dull thunk, the sound strangely deafening to her. She swore she could hear the fierce beating of Jared's heart.

"I won these scars aboard the *Trident*. Most of them. The rest came from prison."

"Prison?"

"In the West Indies. Four years of forced servitude on a British man-of-war and three years spent in a rat-infested hole no bigger than Cowan's cabin. With two other men for company. Walker and Dag."

Lindsay was so stunned that she didn't know what to say, while Jared's voice grew only more bitter.

"I was seventeen, Elise only fifteen, when we returned to England from Calcutta to live with my uncle, Alistair Giles. But I was there only a few weeks when I was attacked on my way home from Seaford one night, two hired thugs telling me how lucky I was not to be murdered as they'd been paid to do, but that they intended to sell me to a press-gang looking for recruits for the *Trident*."

"But who hired those men?" Lindsay blurted out, horrified.

"Sylvia Potter, my uncle's mistress, because she wanted me out of the way. Out of the way so her son, Ryland, would have no impediments to one day marrying my sister. They had planned for me to die in Calcutta with my parents, poisoned by one of our family's most trusted servants—"

"Oh, Jared, no!"

"Something I learned from Elise just before she died. They had boasted as much to her after the marriage, all the while making her life a hell on earth—even told her the truth of what had happened to me, at least as far as they knew it. They said I'd been murdered, making Elise believe she was alone for all those years, with no one to help her . . ."

Lindsay's heart flew out to Jared as his voice caught, but he wasn't looking at her any longer. He stared at nothing, his eyes haunted, his face etched with such anguish she felt she could envision his terrible memories as if they were her own.

"So you see, I didn't abandon Elise and my uncle as everyone believed. That note I supposedly left behind about returning to India was forged by Ryland, the bastard. He destroyed it after the wedding, not needing it anymore because he had gained his vicious end. But more damage had been done, everyone believing the worst of me—the ton, your aunt, everyone. And I did nothing to change their minds when I finally came back to England three years ago. By then I'd had my own purpose in mind."

His words grown so icy cold, Lindsay felt as if she were staring into the farthest reaches of Jared's soul. And what she saw was so desolate, so full of despair . . .

"I fitted out a ship and manned it with those who'd suffered the same fate as I, men who'd been treated no better than prisoners aboard the *Trident*—Walker, Dag and the others—all of them taken against their will from their native ships and impressed into service in the British navy. If not for Cooky, I would have died that first week, I'd been beaten so mercilessly. No one believed my uncle was the Earl of Dovercourt—that foul play had brought me to that bloody warship. I never uttered a word about it again."

"So for four years . . ." Lindsay fell silent as Jared met her eyes, his expression as hard as stone.

"We finally managed to escape, almost fifty of us, when we set fires on several lower decks. We lowered galleys, then made it to an island, only to be recaptured and thrown into prison, since the *Trident* had already headed back to sea. And there we sat for three years, left to rot—and some did. There were only forty of us when we mutinied inside the prison, and nearly less when Dag was shot. He saw the guard about to fire and stepped in front of me—*oh, God!*"

Lindsay jumped at the agonized cry that burst from Jared's throat, watching, stricken, as he picked up the brandy glass and hurled it at the wall. Then, as if that pistol ball had seared into his own brain, he sank to his knees and clutched his lowered head. Tears burned Lindsay's eyes to see such torment. Dear God, how could any one man have been made to suffer so much?

"I swore then . . . I swore that I would do anything I could to destroy England, her trade, her ships . . . for the years, the *years* when I could do nothing to help Elise . . . for Dag, for my parents. And someday I will find them . . . I will find Sylvia and Ryland Potter . . ."

He said no more, but his voice had shaken with such hatred that Lindsay shuddered, imagining his retribution against the two who had destroyed his family. His life. She had already seen the fiery devastation wrought again and again by the Phoenix. Devastation she feared, a terrible lump growing in her throat, and a burning need for vengeance that for this man might never end . . .

"Leave me, Lindsay. Go."

Tears slipping down her cheeks, she knew suddenly what she risked if she stayed, her love, her heart, her very soul, just as she knew that her decision had already been made.

She could not leave him. She would not. Quietly, she went and sank down on her knees in front of him. He lifted his head, his gaze so ravaged it stilled her breath.

"Woman, you must leave . . ."

She silenced him with trembling fingers pressed to his lips, slowly shaking her head. "No, Jared, this time you will not send me away. I will stay."

He stared at her for the longest moment, as if not

daring to believe the import of her words. Lindsay waited, hoping, fearing, praying . . .

His hand reaching up to grasp her fingers made fresh tears burn her eyes, but when he upturned her palm and placed a fervent kiss upon the tender flesh, a ragged sigh tore from her that matched his. Her breath gone, time had fled with it, Lindsay aware of nothing more than Jared as he rose and drew her with him, pulling her fiercely into his arms.

Then his lips captured hers and she was lost, lost to the power and desperate hunger of his kiss as a searing need so intense filled every part of her that she felt her knees give way. But she didn't fall, for she was swept so suddenly from her feet that she gasped while the room seemed to whirl around her, only to still itself when she found herself gently deposited upon the four-poster bed.

Yet Jared didn't join her. Instead he stood there looking down at her, the tension in his powerful body, the turbulence in his eyes telling her even now he might deny her, even now he was thinking to protect her.

Everything Jared Giles had done had been to spare her from harm. She knew that now. Just as she knew she wanted to drown in the blazing torment only he could inflict, to drown and never again come up for air. With trembling fingers, she reached up and touched his hand.

"Jared . . . please . . ."

Her whisper driving straight into his heart, Jared could hold himself back no longer. All he could see was light, Lindsay's hair, her yellow gown, her skin, against the icy darkness threatening to overwhelm him, threatening to steal even this bright moment from him. All he craved was the warmth of her, the heat of her, as he buried himself in her welcoming arms and blanketed her with his body.

Just as he wanted to bury himself that very moment in the wondrous softness of her body, to chase away all the howling demons tormenting his soul. But he could not, would not, humbled as much by the priceless gift she was giving him as by the love he'd seen shining in her beautiful eyes.

His throat tightening, he lowered his lips to hers, so warm and sweet, so innocent, trembling with desire and perhaps the slightest hint of virginal fear. If only for tonight, he would bring her no harm, and as for the rest, with supreme effort Jared shut the looming reality of the future from his mind. Lifting his head, he stared down at her, his gut clenching with emotion so fierce for this woman even as he sought to soothe her with gentle teasing.

"Hmm, a pity about your new gown."

"A pity?"

With her voice trembling, too, her soft breasts rising and falling against his bare chest the most beguiling torture, it was all Jared could do to hold himself still atop her and not think too much yet of that aching part of him pressed against the sweet juncture of her thighs.

"Yes, that it has no buttons like one of my shirts. But I suppose there are other ways around . . ." His voice so hoarse he couldn't finish, he straddled her legs and began to ease the pale yellow muslin over her creamy thighs, over her hips, his lower body aching all the more at the sheer loveliness of her.

While Lindsay could scarcely breathe as Jared undressed her, his hands skimming her flesh so lightly that she wasn't sure if it was her clothing or his palms sweeping like a whisper over her. Within a moment the gown was gone, slipped over her head and tossed to the edge of the bed, followed soon by her chemise . . . and then she felt the full seductive weight of his hands upon her; Lindsay moaned deep in her throat when he lingered to cup and squeeze her breasts by turns.

But not long, dear Lord, not long enough, as he moved to slip her satin drawers from her body. An instant later she truly trembled, lying naked beneath him while his eyes seemed as intensely blue as she'd ever seen them in the lamp's golden glow.

Her heart thundering, she watched his hands move to the towel slung low around his waist, and then that covering, too, was gone. He loomed, powerfully muscled and naked, above her; the part of him which she'd glimpsed a short while ago taking on new and startling proportions.

"I'll not harm you, Lindsay, I promise," he whispered huskily, all trace of teasing in his voice gone as he bent over her, his mouth nuzzling at her breast. "Not tonight . . . not in this . . . I'll not harm you."

She had no chance to wonder at his words, his lips seizing upon a swollen, aching nipple making her cry out, his tongue swirling around and around and then flicking at her with a mastery of equal parts torment and sweet ecstasy. Her fingers funneling into his burnished hair, still damp from his bath, she closed her eyes, never dreaming, never knowing, such pleasure could exist. But she flared them open in surprise when she felt Jared's fingers enmesh in her woman's curls, then slip into her body and tease a secret, hidden place that already throbbed and tingled.

"Jared . . ."

"Shhh, Lindsay, shhh." His lips molded to hers, his tongue delved wildly into her mouth and she surrendered to the passion of his kiss just as she gave herself over to the sensual agony of his fingers slowly circling her. Circling and venturing ever deeper only to slide out again until she felt wet and flushed and utterly weak with desire.

Her hands fluttering to his stomach, she splayed her fingers against his taut, masculine flesh, the impassioned recesses of her mind overtaken by an instinctive yearning to touch him, too. And she did touch him, her palm grazing something silken and hard, her fingers closing around him even as Jared started and groaned raggedly against her mouth.

"Woman . . . no, enough!"

She did not heed him, would not allow herself to, sensing as he groaned again, like a dawning upon her as old as time, the potential of her feminine power to please him. And she wanted to please him so desperately, her hand slipping lower. Crisp, springy curls entangled around her fingers, his flesh grown even harder and throbbing against her palm—

"Damnation, woman, will you be the end of me?"

His voice thick and hoarse, Jared dragged her arms above her head so suddenly that Lindsay gasped, a mounting wildness in him now as he clasped her wrists with one hand and caressed her body with the other, his touch first teasing, then almost fierce until she writhed and squirmed and moaned beneath him. Again his mouth found a hardened nipple and he suckled ravenously, only to trail a brazen path to the other breast, back and forth until she was panting and whimpering, her body shaking just as he shook, their desire a raging tempest more frenzied than any storm.

She felt him part her legs with his knee and of her own accord she widened them for him, opening herself for him, not knowing why but sensing the timeless answer when his full weight settled upon her and a hard ridge of flesh swelled at the aching heart of her thighs. She heard him whisper her name, heard him whisper he might cause her pain, but only for an instant, and then he thrust himself inside her, so deeply that she cried out . . . tears stinging her eyes not because he had hurt her, but because at last, finally, she felt whole.

"Lindsay, I'm sorry. Forgive me . . ." he said raggedly against her ear.

She threw her arms around his neck to reassure him; she caressed the ravaged flesh on his back and powerful shoulders as he sank again and again into her body, his breathing coming harder, faster. She rose to meet him, lifting herself to him, craving more of him, all of him, her throat constricting and tears streaming down her face as she held with all her might onto the man she loved.

Just as Jared held onto her, the terrible darkness gone, blazing light overwhelming him as he shuddered and spilled himself into the wet, engulfing heat of her body, clutching Lindsay to his heart as she moaned wildly and found her climax beneath him.

Long moments later, he still held her, caressing the damp hair away from her tear-stained face, a wave of such fierce possession gripping him that he doubted he could ever let her go.

And when she finally opened her eyes and snuggled against him, his body growing hard and urgent for her once more, he told himself that at least for this one precious night, he would pretend that they would never be apart.

Chapter 28

"**L**indsay, are you awake?"

Jared's low query thrilling her, Lindsay didn't move, didn't flutter an eyelash, wanting simply to lie there for another glorious moment and listen to his steady heartbeat against her ear and the sounds of the wharf coming to life outside their window.

She had never known such contentment. She felt utterly, completely, his from head to toe, every inch of her body caressed by him, kissed by him, in ways she could never have imagined between man and woman. And the last time, when he had taken her from behind, his hands moving wildly over her body as if he couldn't touch enough of her at once, she had never known such a sense of consummate possession. Even now it made her cheeks flare hot to think . . .

"Woman, I know you're awake. Unless you're blushing in your sleep, which isn't likely."

She couldn't help smiling, nuzzling closer to him even as he rolled her gently onto her back and brought himself above her, staring into her eyes. She stared back as he smiled, too; she was so filled with love for this man, so filled with hope for their future. Surely now things would work out between them, they had to—

"Don't you think it's time we dressed? I'm sure my men are wondering . . ."

Jared didn't finish the thought, but he hadn't needed to. Lindsay blushed even hotter, although she shook her head, winding her arms around his neck.

"No, I don't want to get dressed. Not yet, Jared."

"Not yet?"

She shivered at the way he looked at her, shivered even more when he shifted his full weight upon her, his smile gone now, intense heat burning in his eyes. She drew in her breath sharply when she felt the hardness of his flesh nudge her softness, her thighs opening to him unbidden as Jared lifted himself slightly and then sank easily into her, her body already wet and eager for him.

As he thrust deeper, yet so slowly she thought she might scream for wanting him fully inside her, he dragged her arms from around his neck and enmeshed his fingers with hers, pushing her hands into the pillow. And still he stared at her as he possessed her, his eyes never leaving hers, not even when his breathing grew unsteady and his lean hips thrust ever faster against hers.

She felt her sudden climax coming upon her like a cresting wave pulling her under deep water, felt Jared grow rigid just as she did, her breath gone, her gaze held captive by his, until they were both lost to the sweet agony of their bodies throbbing together, finding release together.

And still he watched her as if he wanted to see, wanted to know fully, the effect of his possession upon her, his eyes as intent as she'd ever seen

them. As if he wanted to burn upon his brain the
sight of her surrendering to the ecstasy they
brought each other. Lindsay finally closed her eyes,
the aching, heart-stopping sensations simply too
much.

When she finally opened her eyes, Jared had become quiet except for his flesh still throbbing inside
her, and she wondered as wanton heat raced to her
toes if he might be growing ready for her again.
She knew she would never know enough of him,
never feel sated, and a slow smile came over his
face as if he'd read her mind. Yet it held a strange
hint of sadness, too, and she felt a niggling of unease.

"Jared? What is it?"

"Nothing. Just that the morning has come. It's
time you and I were dressed."

He withdrew from her and then was gone from
the bed, Lindsay never having felt so bereft as she
watched him retrieve his breeches from a chair
near the tub. He was so magnificent to look upon,
so beautiful, that her throat became tight, her
breasts, her body still yearning for him. She
blushed hotly at her brazenness, but she left the
bed and ran to him just as he turned to fasten his
breeches.

"No, no, it's not morning, it can't be," she said,
throwing her arms around him. "And if it is, then
let's pretend it's not, Jared—"

"Woman, I'd like nothing more," he said so
huskily she thought for a moment she had swayed
him, his arms going around her to hold her tight.
He hugged her so fiercely that for a moment she
couldn't breathe, but why did she need air if she
could forever be a captive in his arms? Yet all too

suddenly he began to release her, although she clung to him, not wanting him to let her go.

"Lindsay, how can I hope to find a vicar in this city if you won't allow me to dress?"

She froze, her mouth dropping open, so stunned she simply stared up at him.

"Yes, a vicar," he repeated, giving her a sound slap on her bare bottom, then gently pulling her arms from around his neck. "And he'll be shocked indeed if he arrives to perform our wedding and finds you looking like anything but a blushing bride. Now, shall we dress?"

Lindsay glanced down at herself, overcome as much by shock at what he'd announced as by the joy suddenly flooding her, tears of elation jumping to her eyes. She felt so flustered—light-headed, too—not knowing what to do first, that Jared took pity on her and swept up the towel he'd tossed to the floor last night and wrapped it around her, knotting the thick cloth at her breasts.

"This will do for clothing until you have a chance to bathe. I'll have the proprietor send up some hot water for you."

Lindsay was still so astonished, she didn't notice that Jared had grown tense; she ran to the bed to shake out, one by one, her muslin gown and her underclothes. The garments were a bit crumpled, but she had no others— Oh, Lord, could it really be true?

She turned to look at Jared, but he was already dressed, fastening the last button on his ivory shirt and then thrusting his pistol into his belt. He didn't glance at her but strode to the door, his impatience to be on his way overwhelming her. He couldn't seem to wait for her to become his bride. His bride!

"Jared, wait!" She flew to him, the sudden warmth in his eyes overwhelming her, too; she'd never known such happiness, and she threw her arms around his neck. "Oh, Jared, I knew it would only take some time before you realized you loved me, too. I can't believe we're to be married! It's all I've ever wanted!"

He didn't answer and she didn't see the flicker of pain across his face as he bent his head to kiss her. Kiss her for so brief a moment, she already missed him desperately before he'd even walked out the door, and after he had, she could only stand there, listening to his footfalls retreating down the steps.

Only when they had faded did she allow herself such a whoop of pure joy, she was certain the entire city of Gijón had heard her.

Lindsay had bathed, dressed and been pacing excitedly for what seemed like hours, even staring out the window at the bustling waterfront unable to divert her, when she finally heard footsteps returning. She flung open the door, her disappointment so keen when she found the portly proprietor in the hall and not Jared that the poor man was clearly embarrassed.

"Senorita, come. El Capitán is downstairs— Senorita?"

She had flown past him so suddenly, but she couldn't help herself, so near to bursting was she to see Jared again. And he was waiting for her in the main room of the tavern, a balding, bleary-eyed Englishman standing beside him who appeared even less a vicar than she was a blushing bride. Her face aflame as she remembered Jared's words, she knew she didn't care that the wedding was coming after . . .

The memory of Jared's recent possession of her as vivid as that his intense gaze now held hers, she swallowed at her sudden nervousness, taking his outstretched hand.

"Lindsay, the Reverend Charles Standish."

"Dee-lighted, my dear." The man hiccuped before Lindsay could utter a word, clearly well into his cups even at this early time of the day. "What a fine day for a wedding, haven't performed one since I left England ages ago, but better to be living among the Spaniards than deported, I always say— Oops, excuse me."

The drunken fellow had practically reeled into her, reeking so foully of rum that Lindsay wrinkled her nose and glanced doubtfully at Jared. She noticed then that he was anything but smiling, probably as dismayed by the man who would perform the sacred ceremony as was she, so to reassure him, she summoned her brightest smile.

"If he can say the words, what else matters?" she whispered in a cheerful aside, glad to see, as she looped her arm through Jared's, that the vicar pulled a prayer book from his pocket, at least having come prepared.

"Do we—have witnesses?" the reverend demanded loudly, another hiccup bursting from his throat.

As if prearranged, the portly proprietor stepped forward, already mopping his eyes with his handkerchief, while two early-bird patrons in no better condition than the vicar lurched out of their chairs. But Lindsay could have been standing in the loftiest church for all she noticed, her gaze upon Jared, her heart overflowing.

He said his vows so soberly, his eyes never leaving hers, while she could barely speak at all, and before it seemed she could blink, the vicar shut the prayer book with a thud and dropped it back into his pocket, the ceremony done. She must have looked startled; in the next instant Jared drew her against him to seal their marriage with a kiss so stirring, she was aware of nothing any longer but the impassioned warmth of his lips upon hers.

Yet just as quickly he released her and took her by the hand, leading her from the tavern while their motley witnesses sank back into their chairs and the vicar demanded a drink from the proprietor, who snuffled into his handkerchief and went back to his work. Lindsay blinked at the blinding sunlight outside, a bit ashamed of herself for thinking she and Jared might retire at once to their room.

Of course, he must have something special planned; perhaps he'd somehow gotten the word to Cooky aboard the *Vengeance* to prepare a wedding breakfast. He seemed preoccupied as they walked along the busy wharf, and they were moving away from his ship, which made her wonder, but nothing could daunt her joy. She and Jared were husband and wife! At last her dreams had come true—

"Lindsay."

Jared had stopped, his voice oddly somber as he pulled her out of the way of bustling passengers boarding a brig lying at anchor alongside the dock, Lindsay glancing from the commotion to his face. And she sensed then, from the dark turbulence in his eyes, that there was no wedding breakfast in store, her heart plummeting like a stone into her shoes.

"We must part now, Lindsay. Everything's arranged. This ship is bound for London, a Swedish neutral, so you'll be safe. I've paid for your passage, and you should be home within a week—"

"No." She had barely whispered, so stunned, so stricken that she could say no more, staring in shock at Jared. She glanced at the ship, which was preparing to sail, and clutched all the more tightly to Jared's arm. "No—"

"And I say, woman, that you will go. You will return to England and take your place as the Countess of Dovercourt. You'll not want for anything—a house, money, servants—and there you will be safe. Do you hear me? I've a man there, Simon Tuft, a good man whom I trust, and he knows of Sylvia and Ryland Potter. If they would ever dare to show their faces at Dovercourt Manor, Simon has orders what to do—"

"But what of you?" she blurted out, somehow finding her voice, although her throat was so tight she could scarcely breathe. "I don't want a house or money or servants, Jared, only you! Your love is all I want, all I need—"

"And I told you before, Lindsay, I've no love to give you."

"But we—you married me!"

"Only to spare your reputation when you return to England. No matter what story you concoct about your disappearance, people will always wonder—especially if you find yourself with child. At least now you have a husband"—he reached into his belt and pulled out a piece of folded vellum—"and what I trust will pass for a proper license to prove you're Lady Giles, the Countess of Dovercourt."

"No." Lindsay numbly shook her head, refusing to believe him, refusing to take the license, but he forced it into her hand.

"Damnation, listen to me, Lindsay! If it ever becomes known who I am, you must fashion the biggest story of your life and swear you never knew anything about my being the Phoenix, do you understand? You were just as fooled as everyone else."

He shoved her then toward the gangplank, Lindsay so sick at heart that her legs would scarcely move, while Jared felt as if he were dying inside. But, dammit, he had to make her go! He had to!

If he somehow got back to England, he would make amends to her, but at least this way she would be safe. There were too many ships looking for him, even this short stay in Gijón of imminent risk, and he planned for the *Vengeance* to sail at dark no matter if all the repairs hadn't been made. But for now, if he must hurt her to get her to go . . .

"Jared, please, no! Let me stay with you!"

She had cried out so desperately that sailors and passengers alike were beginning to stare, forcing Jared to be cruel.

"Woman, I've given you everything I can. For once, look at life as it is and to hell with your fantasies!"

He could have stabbed her through the heart, she grew so deathly white, stumbling up the gangplank. It was all he could do not to grab her back, to seize her in his arms and tell her how much he cared. Yet he would no more allow himself to do that than to abandon the vengeful path he had chosen for himself, a path too perilous to share with the woman he loved and would do anything to protect.

Unable to bear the stricken weight of her gaze upon him as she clutched at the railing above, a command going out to drop the gangplank and unfurl the sails, he turned his back on the ship and strode away.

"Good-bye, Lindsay."

His hoarse whisper lost to the noise and bustle of the wharf, he didn't need his eyes burning to know that leaving her was truly the hardest thing he had ever done.

Chapter 29

Lindsay stared at Jared's retreating back until she couldn't see him anymore. The wharf was so crowded, and even then she searched wildly for his dark blond head. But he was gone, though his words still rang in her ears—brutal words that had cut her to the quick and filled her with unimaginable despair.

It was true. He would never love her. He had room in his heart only for revenge. Maybe, just as he'd said, he had given her everything he could . . .

"No," Lindsay whispered fiercely, swiping at the useless tears fogging her eyes as she looked down at the crumpled vellum in her hand.

She had given him everything, too, her love, her very soul; there was nothing left save for her life. And if she had a choice to be safe aboard this neutral vessel or to risk death to be with Jared—it wasn't even a choice! She knew what she wanted to do; memories of his kiss, his caresses, the memory of how he'd stared into her eyes that morning as if emblazoning her rapture upon his mind—all spurred her on.

Such things couldn't be lies, she told herself desperately as she tucked the license in her bodice and climbed onto the railing, then grabbed a fistful of

rigging while nearby passengers gasped in surprise. Words might hide the truth, but she'd seen
no fantasy in Jared's eyes no matter what he'd
said—

"My lady, come down from there! Come down!"

As a dignified gentleman wearing the braided
trappings of a captain rushed toward the railing
along with several of his crew, Lindsay shook her
head and climbed shakily down the rigging.

"No, no, don't worry about me! It was all a mistake, I'm staying in Gijón—oh!"

She lost her footing and almost fell, even now
the Swedish vessel edging slowly away from the
wharf while she clutched at the rigging and fought
to regain a toehold. As more startled faces appeared at the railing, she waved to reassure them
and then, squeezing her eyes shut, she jumped, not
knowing if she might just make the end of the
wharf or find herself in the water.

She laughed giddily when she landed upon
something solid, the dock soundly beneath her feet,
and she spun again to wave at the ship. The em-
barking ship that she was no longer aboard, while
the *Vengeance* . . . oh, Lord, the *Vengeance*.

Realizing as if waking from a frantic daze that
she still had to find some way back aboard Jared's
ship, and without him seeing her, too, or she was
certain he'd lash her to the mainmast of the next
vessel to ensure she stayed put, Lindsay ducked
into an alleyway that led behind the row of build-
ings facing the wharf. An alleyway she would not
have dared venture into except for the comforting
light of midday, although she hurried all the same
for fear of meeting any unsavory characters.

Fortunately, she startled only stray cats that meowed and skittered out of her way, and a few serving women who watched her progress curiously before she reached the tavern where she and Jared had stayed the night before. After entering through a back door, Lindsay heard glasses chinking and mugs being thunked down upon tables. She took a brief moment to catch her breath before she swept into the main room and brushed past the stout proprietor, who glanced up from wiping a table, his eyes growing round.

"Senorita—excuse, excuse, senora?"

"My husband told me to wait for him here." Without even looking back, Lindsay proceeded right to the stairs. "El Capitán. He will return soon."

She heard no response; hoping she'd been believed, she raced up the steps and didn't stop until she had entered their former room, relieved to see that it wasn't occupied, though the rumpled bed had been made. Her face hot as flame, she drew the bolt quietly and then raced to the window, her heart battering against her breast as she spied Jared's ship among a dozen still anchored in the sparkling bay.

She could see men working busily on deck, the shattered topmast being replaced while sailors climbed the rigging to get at the torn sails needing repair and patching. Dear Lord, how was she ever going to find a way . . .

It was then she spied him, Cooky with two other sailors—his kitchen assistants, she realized, her heart racing faster—and they were rowing a galley back to shore.

*   *   *

"Cap'n's going to have my hide."

"Shhh, Cooky, he'll have mine first," Lindsay admonished him for what seemed the hundredth time since she'd been lugged in a burlap bag to the galley, hoping desperately she appeared nothing more than a lumpy sack of potatoes. "Are we almost to the ship?"

"So we are, and there'll be no word out of you two, either, do you hear me? Or our hides will be patching the sails!"

Lindsay bit her lower lip, praying that Cooky's assistants might not panic and give her away. She had never seen men look so startled as when she had dashed from the tavern and drawn all three with her into a shadowy alley—pleading for them to help her, declaring passionately that she didn't want to be anywhere but at Jared's side—although from the look of admiration in Cooky's squinty eyes, she had sensed his acquiescence at once.

Yet that had obviously become anxiety as they neared the *Vengeance*, and Lindsay couldn't say she wasn't nervous, too. She hugged her knees and chewed her lip as Cowan's Irish brogue rang out, ordering the galley to be hoisted aboard. Then, as the ropes and winches began to creak and groan, reminding her so much of the first time she'd sneaked aboard, she truly began to pray.

"Aye, good thing you came back when you did, Cooky. Cap'n's ready to sail. And he's in a black mood, just as a warning. Ever since that Swedish ship left the bay, so you'd better unload fast."

Oh, Lord. The news filling her with equal parts dread and incredible elation, Lindsay grimaced as she felt herself being lifted, her breath gone from her body. To think if Cooky and his men hadn't come back to shore for more supplies, her only recourse to wait until dark and then try to find a way aboard. She would have missed . . .

Shoving the dreadful thought away, Lindsay resumed praying, hard, as she was carried toward the hold. Everything had been carefully planned. All they needed to do was get her safely below to the ship's kitchen, where Cooky had promised to hide her until the *Vengeance* was well under sail again, and then she would carefully make her presence known to Jared.

"Blast it to hell, Cooky, haven't we enough potatoes to last us a year? We've eaten so many of them, I'd sooner see the damned things tossed overboard to the fish—"

"A needless waste that would be, too, Cap'n." Cooky's surprisingly calm voice did little to soothe Lindsay's trembling as she realized Jared must be standing very close to them. So close, she feared she might have to reveal herself then and there or risk drowning inside the sack. But when the light seemed to fade around her, she knew Cooky's assistants were descending with her into the hold. Only then did she dare allow herself a swamping sense of relief.

"All right, men, put her—put the potatoes over there under the table. Gently, now."

Settled on her side upon the floor, Lindsay smiled gratefully at Cooky as the sack was loosened at the top to allow her some air. She longed for nothing more than to stretch her cramped legs, but that would have to wait.

"Is there anything else I can get for you, miss? It might be a while, maybe not until morning, before we're far enough out to sea that Cap'n wouldn't be tempted to come right back once he knows . . .''

At Cooky's worried frown, Lindsay shook her head, very much aware of what the old sailor had risked for her. "I'm fine, truly. Thanks to you, Cooky, and your men, I've everything I want. I'll never forget how you helped me."

"Neither will Cap'n, I fear," the man mumbled, but he gave Lindsay a gruff smile. And he didn't leave her to begin preparations for the evening meal until he had wadded up a towel and tucked it gently under her head for a pillow.

And Lindsay slept, not realizing the depth of her fatigue until Cooky tried to wake her late that night to get her to eat something, which she did. But she couldn't have remembered if she ate the choicest stew or a dried slice of salt pork, she was so tired, the day's strain and excitement clearly too much for her.

As well as the previous night's.

At one point she awoke, the galley darkened, Cooky and his assistants long ago gone to their bunks or hammocks, the ship eerily quiet but for the creaking of timbers and the distant flapping of sails. She lay there for long moments staring at the planked ceiling, the ship rocking beneath her while her flesh burned, her breath snagged in her throat, dreams and memories of Jared's hands upon her, his mouth upon her so vivid it seemed as if he were there at her side.

But he wasn't, and she still feared it was too soon to go to him, although she wanted to so desperately.

She sensed he wasn't sleeping in his cabin at all but pacing the quarterdeck, restlessly, unceasingly, which only made her ache for him the stronger. Would he take her in his arms, think her a dream or a phantom come to haunt him or flesh and blood? Would he rouse the crew and order his helmsman to head straight back to Gijón— No, no, no, she couldn't bear to think of it!

Somehow Lindsay forced herself to be patient, forced herself to close her eyes, although the next hours were more a futile tossing upon the hard floor. Yet she did finally fall asleep, Jared once more filling her dreams: her husband, her love, her life . . .

"Miss, miss, wake up! Wake up! We're attacking, God help us, the ship barely repaired—"

"Attacking, Cooky . . . what?" Roused so suddenly, Lindsay could only stare at the grizzled sailor with bleary eyes while he threw aside the burlap sack.

"Climb out of there, miss! It's safer in the stern, for we're coming at them broadside. Now, miss, now!"

Cooky's urgency cutting through the drowsy fog gripping her, it was still the deafening roar of cannon that got her to move. She gasped, the sound bringing back the horror of the last time, when Dag and the others . . .

"Oh, God, Jared." Irrational fear overwhelming her, Lindsay stumbled to her feet, her legs so numb from being confined in the sack that she fell over, knocking Cooky to the floor.

Yet they both scrambled back up when another round of cannon fire boomed with fierce explosive power, making the entire ship quake. Although Cooky tried to hold fast onto her arm, she broke free, running frantically toward the hold.

"No, no, miss, the stern, Cap'n's quarters! It's too dangerous—great God, he'll never forgive me now! Come back, miss!"

Lindsay was halfway up the steps when Cooky caught her by the ankle, the old sailor's agility as startling as his grip was so desperate. Yet she was equally desperate, rounding on him with hoarse pleading in her voice.

"Let me go, Cooky! He's my husband now—we were married in Gijón! Please let me go!"

Cooky was so stunned that he released her. Lindsay didn't waste a moment but lunged up the last few steps and burst onto the deck, the familiar and horrifying smell of gunpowder burning her nostrils, black smoke choking her, the brilliant morning sunlight blinding her eyes. She blinked, wildly looking for Jared, but what drew her gaze before she could find him was the high-pitched screams coming from the stricken brig lying broadside, the two ships no more than twenty feet apart.

The terrified screams of women and children clambering from the hold onto the deck—dear God, and the British vessel had already struck its colors, ready to surrender.

Coughing from the smoke, she ran toward the quarterdeck and stumbled up the companionway, nearly collapsing into Jared's arms. He hugged her fiercely for a moment, then quickly thrust her away from him, his expression as grim as his eyes behind his fearsome gold mask, but she couldn't think of that now.

"No more firing, Jared! Tell your men to stop! There are innocent women and children aboard—"

"Damnation, Lindsay, the order to cease fire has already been given! What are you doing here? How—"

He didn't get to finish, a deafening blast roaring from the lower gun deck making his face go white. In horror, Lindsay saw the ominous damage to the brig's hull as the thick smoke gradually cleared, three gaping holes at the waterline. Like a great bird winged by a hunter's bow, the crippled ship before her very eyes began to list and settle.

"Walker, get down there! Tell them to cease fire!"

Incredulous, Lindsay met Jared's stricken eyes. "You said you had ordered . . ."

"I did, woman! I sent Cowan . . ."

Lindsay scarcely heard him, looking back to the sinking vessel, her gaze drawn to the name emblazoned in white upon the prow.

Industry.

Oh, God, no. Breaking free of Jared's arms, she ran to the starboard railing, her heart in her throat as she searched the passengers frantically thronging the tilted deck. Desperate shouts went up to load the longboats with women and children and lower them to the water at once, before it was too late, which only set off more screaming and weeping and frenzied cries of terror.

Yet one man's commanding voice rose above the din like a strange calm amidst a storm. Lindsay's breath caught, her eyes widening in disbelief when she recognized Lord Donovan Trent at the ship's prow, his dark head towering above the rest as he helped passenger after passenger onto a crowded galley.

And standing at his side, stubbornly refusing to

leave him even as he lifted her bodily onto the boat, was an auburn-haired young woman holding a sobbing child in her arms, the poignant scene making Lindsay's throat grow tight.

"Corie!"

Chapter 30

J ared heard Lindsay's hoarse outcry at the same moment one of his men shouted to him from high in the mainmast rigging, the sailor waving wildly at the horizon.

"Cap'n, man-of-war approaching from the south, seventy-four-gunner!"

Cursing, Jared wrenched the spyglass from his belt; his gut clenched at the sight of not one warship cruising at full sail toward them, but three—the vessels abandoning the convoy of seven merchantmen stretching behind them that, he realized too late, must have included his latest quarry as well. Now there was no time to help the people aboard the foundering ship, not if the *Vengeance* was to escape—

"Cap'n, look, she's going over the side!"

Jared spun around, his heart lurching as Lindsay grabbed a fistful of rigging from her precarious perch atop the railing and swung over to the sinking vessel. A powerfully built man with hair as jet-black as Walker's caught her and hauled her safely aboard. A man Jared knew he had seen before . . .

Terrified shrieks rent the air as the brig suddenly listed further to port and he knew, too, with a cer-

tainty as sure as that he breathed, that he couldn't
leave Lindsay behind.

Damn Cowan, why hadn't he repeated the order
not to fire? The *Industry* was sinking; there was no
choice even to be made. God help him, if they left
now, Lindsay and those innocent people could
drown before help ever arrived. And what if those
bloody cruisers chose not to stop at all just so they
might chase him?

"Walker, send our men over to help! She's settling too fast for us to lower the boats—helmsman,
bring her closer in!"

As the deck exploded in commotion, sailors
who'd served Jared so loyally for years leaving
their cannon to grab rigging and swing over to the
other ship, Jared caught a rope, too, and lunged
into the air, to land squarely on the listing deck.
Already the stricken vessel's passengers and crew
were scrambling from the longboats, now useless,
a host of frightened faces looking to the *Vengeance*
for deliverance as the schooner scraped alongside
the brig, heavy planks dropped at once atop the
railings.

"Over the side! All of you, now!" Jared roared,
searching for Lindsay, who was nowhere to be
seen. Then he spied her ducking into the ship's
hold and he knew she'd gone to see if anyone below needed help. His gut clenched all the tighter.
Damn the woman, must she think of everyone but
herself? The sea would claim this vessel in a few
moments, no more!

He ran toward the hold, tearing off his mask, but
a man lunged in front of him so suddenly that they
nearly collided. Cursing, Jared faced his strapping,
midnight-haired opponent eye to eye, the same

man who'd helped Lindsay aboard, while his hand moved to his pistol.

"Get out of my way—"

"If you care for her, man, you'll have nothing more to do with her. Do you understand? Nothing!"

Jared stared into near-pitch-black eyes as resolute as his own, every part of him fiercely aching to find Lindsay, aching to shove this man violently from his path. Only when a tall, long-limbed beauty approached them, cradling in her arms a little girl who looked terrified, did he realize that he had once seen the young woman before, too, no more than a month ago in the smuggling port of Roscoff, Brittany.

"It's you," came her incredulous whisper, her lovely brown eyes searching his face. "I couldn't believe it was Lindsay, and now to see it is you— you saved my husband's life! Donovan, this is the man who—"

"We've no time now, Corie! Take Paloma and wait for me on the other ship while I go find Lindsay."

As the woman nodded and hurried away, Jared stared once more into his opponent's dark eyes, the man's voice as determined as before.

"While *I* find Lindsay. Dammit, man, will you take her down with you? No one has to know what you are to each other. I promise we'll do everything we can to help her. Lie for her if we have to, anything, but now is the time to choose—before those bloody ships get here and slap you and your men in irons!"

The deck creaking ominously beneath his feet did more to sway Jared at that moment than Donovan's words, which he knew rang as true as the agony tearing at his heart. With a vehement curse, he turned from the hold and Donovan disappeared down the steep steps, Jared knowing all too well he was turning his back upon Lindsay just as surely as if they had never met. But what else could he do? Have her share the deadly fate that awaited him?

"Cap'n, that's nearly the last of them!" he heard one of his men cry out. Jared realized then that the sinking brig was almost deserted. Somehow he made himself cross back over to the *Vengeance*, but he whirled around on the deck when a shout went up from the passengers huddled aboard his ship. A relief so intense filled him when he saw Lindsay emerge from the hold, followed by Donovan bearing an unconscious woman in his arms, that it was all Jared could do not to rush back and help them.

Instead he forced himself to make his way to the quarterdeck as a thundering warning shot hit the water with a huge splash only fifty yards off the prow, but he paid little heed to the approaching warships. His eyes were upon Cowan, the stricken-faced Irishman meeting him at the companionway.

"I'm sorry, Cap'n. God help us, I don't know what came over me. I couldn't give the order not to fire—not after Dag and the others . . . yet if I'd known that your lady—"

"She's not mine, Cowan, not anymore." Jared silenced him, dropping his gold mask to the deck. The day had become as black as the darkness overwhelming his soul as he met Walker's grim gaze. "Strike our colors, friend. The Phoenix is dead."

*   *   *

It was a nightmare unlike anything Lindsay had ever known.

She had truly thought there would be time enough to rescue the passengers and crew aboard the *Industry* and yet outrun the approaching warships, which had seemed so far away. But she had been wrong. Terribly wrong.

Sitting now in an officer's cabin that had been vacated for her use during the journey to England while Jared and his men languished somewhere below in the bowels of the mammoth warship H.M.S. *Clementine*, she had never felt so numb. So numb or so wretchedly helpless, reliving for the thousandth time the horrible memory of watching Jared being taken prisoner, his head held high even as irons were clamped around his wrists and ankles.

And all the while Corisande had been whispering urgently in her ear. "Say nothing, Lindsay! If they know what you are to him, they'll take you prisoner, too, and then there won't be anything you can do for him. At least this way there's a chance, a slim chance, to help him."

Thank God for Corisande these past three days, and for Donovan, too, although Lindsay had sensed from the first that he held no sympathy for Jared. It had been such a shock to see them aboard the *Industry*—and for them to see her—and she'd barely had a chance to tell them anything before Corisande had hissed her to silence.

Then the deck had listed perilously and she had dashed below to see if anyone needed help; a good thing, too. That poor seasick woman would have drowned in her bunk if Donovan hadn't followed to help get her to the *Vengeance*, the schooner barely clearing the sinking brig before she slipped with an eerie groan beneath the waves.

Lindsay closed her red, swollen eyes and hugged her knees, rocking herself on the narrow bunk.

To think Jared had saved Donovan's life in Roscoff. She had long wondered about the incredible story Corisande had told her weeks ago in London—about the American and his friends who'd appeared as if phantoms out of the darkness to help them. It had been Jared all along, more the gallant hero than she could have ever imagined . . .

"Thank God they believe him to be American," she whispered raggedly to herself, that fact truly the one thing giving her any hope at all.

If it became known that Jared was the Earl of Dovercourt and an Englishman, his punishment would be death, his crimes as the Phoenix the highest treason. But Corisande had explained to her, having overheard several officers laying wagers as to the fate of their prisoners, that Jared, as a privateer protected by letters of marque, and the rest of his men—all Americans and neutral Norwegians save for poor Cowan—would most likely find their lives spared. Imprisonment would be their lot until they might be traded for British subjects held as prisoners of war in America or Scandinavian ports.

Yet Donovan knew the truth. Lindsay had entrusted the crumpled marriage license bearing Jared's name to Corisande even before they had boarded the H.M.S. *Clementine*, and later had told her how she and Jared had met, everything, so surely Corisande must have bared Lindsay's story to her husband. Would he keep her secret? Dear Lord, she could only hope and pray—

A knock at the door to the tiny cabin made Lindsay gasp, but she felt an overwhelming sense of relief when Corisande entered, despite her friend's ominously somber expression. Corisande sank down beside Lindsay on the bunk, keeping her voice low.

"It's as I feared. Donovan just told me the captain won't wait any longer to speak with you—"

"Oh, Lord, Corie, no!"

"Shhh, Lindsay, will you have them hear us? We knew this might happen, but I was hoping not until we reached Plymouth. They're planning to take your husband and his men to Dartmoor Prison, where other prisoners of war are being kept. But the captain insists he must ask you some questions now—no matter that we made it clear to him from the very start that you're no more than a poor unfortunate victim of circumstance and that you'd been desperately trying to escape when you came aboard the *Industry*."

"Sounds like a story I might have thought up," Lindsay said with a forlorn smile, tears rushing to her eyes. But if she had expected sympathy from Corisande, she got nothing more than a sigh of pure exasperation.

"For bloody sakes, Lindsay, I would have thought by now you'd cried every tear you possibly possessed! How can you hope to help Jared if you're unwilling to help yourself?"

"I'm not unwilling to help myself," Lindsay countered, her friend's unexpected dose of temper making her bristle. "How could you even think—" She fell silent, staring at the satisfied smile breaking across Corisande's face. "You. . . you said that on purpose, didn't you?"

"Of course I did, silly! You've faced serious trials

before—living eight long years under the same roof with Olympia Somerset? Braving excisemen with me? And what about that wonderful imagination of yours? I can't wait to hear what you might say to that pompous captain—"

"You'll be there, too?"

"Only if they intend to keep me away with armed guards. I wouldn't miss this for anything and besides, it makes sense, given the horrible wretchedness you've suffered, that you'll need someone to lean upon."

Staring incredulously at her dearest friend, Lindsay had to resist her sudden urge to laugh because of the hope suddenly burning bright as flame in her heart. Instead she threw her arms around Corisande and hugged her fiercely, then tensed when a loud rap came at the door. Yet Corisande's hushed voice gave her the reassurance she needed.

"Shhh, Lindsay, and remember, I'll be right by your side. You've helped me so many times, now let me help you. Are we agreed?"

Lindsay didn't dare reply, for a pair of grim-faced officers shoved open the door. But the cheering glance Corisande threw her made her feel, at least for the moment, that she might not have so much to fear after all.

Unfortunately, a quarter hour later, Lindsay wasn't so sure as she sat meekly in a leather chair while Captain Horatio Billingsley paced in front of his desk, eyeing first her and then Corisande, who had remained staunchly silent at her side.

"So you say you were abducted in London but you remember little about the incident."

The man's voice as skeptical as he looked, peering at her down a long patrician nose as angular as the rest of him, Lindsay gave what she hoped was a thoroughly distressed sigh.

"How could I, sir? All I know is that I was sitting in a carriage, waiting for my maid, Gladys, to come out of a hat shop, when a sickly-smelling cloth was pressed over my nose and mouth—oh, dear, it was so dreadful!"

"Really, Captain Billingsley, must we go over all this again?" Corisande piped up for the first time, draping a comforting arm across Lindsay's shoulders. "The poor dear was drugged, abducted from home and hearth—"

"And when you awoke, you found yourself aboard a ship," the man cut in, hooking his thumbs in his spotless white waistcoat. "Is that correct, Miss Somerset?"

"Yes, yes, yes, a ship full of pirates! Cutthroats! God help me, why must I endure another telling?"

"Because one of the passengers reported to me that they saw you embracing the captain of that scurrilous vessel, Miss Somerset—the privateer known as the Phoenix—just before you found it so necessary to 'escape' to the *Industry*. Now might you have an explanation for me?"

A tense silence hung in the opulent cabin, Lindsay realizing with a niggling of apprehension that the time for playing the long-suffering maiden was past, if indeed she was to convince this man she knew nothing.

"Embracing him?" she shrieked, startling both the captain and Corisande as she jumped shakily to her feet. "I ran to him to beg him not to fire on innocent women and children and I tripped, sir, tripped and fell against him! Yes, he threw his arms around me, and it wasn't the first time I felt his loathsome touch, God help me! I'm ruined, I'm ruined forever!''

Her hysteria mounting by the moment, Lindsay advanced wildly upon the captain even as he took refuge behind his desk, his eyes round and horrified.

''Miss Somerset, please, we don't have to continue. Pray spare yourself any further distress—''

''Distress?'' she shrieked anew, lifting her hands to tear at her hair. ''Do you know what I've suffered at that pirate's hands, sir? The gross indignities—and not only that, sir, but he allowed his men . . . his men—oh, God!''

As Captain Billingsley gasped, Lindsay collapsed to her knees and began to rock herself, tears slipping down her cheeks that were as real as the desperation suddenly seizing her. She had to find a way to see Jared—she had to!

''Don't you see, sir? I'll never know justice,'' she cried out hoarsely through her gut-wrenching sobs while Corisande ran forward to comfort her, her friend's eyes as concerned as they were confused. ''That despicable man took everything from me, everything! And I'll never be able to tell him that I hope he rots in hell for what he did—that I hope he hangs! Unless you let me go to him, unless I can tell him myself . . . Oh, please, sir, what other retribution can I hope for?''

Again silence hung, Captain Billingsley looking almost sick, his face chalk-white. And when he nodded, Corisande was ready to seize the opportunity of the moment, tears streaking her own face as she tried to help Lindsay to rise.

''My husband could accompany her, sir, Lord

Donovan Trent. It's true; what other justice can this poor woman hope for than to lay bare her pain to her attacker?"

The stricken man nodded once more, leaning heavily upon his desk as if witnessing their anguish was simply too much for him to bear. His voice, too, had lost its imperious weight, grown almost hoarse as he gestured to the two officers who had accompanied the women there.

"Help Miss Somerset to her cabin and then find Lord Donovan. They've my permission to visit the gaol."

Lowering her head, Lindsay truly needed their assistance as she rose on trembling legs, scarcely able to believe she had won the right to see Jared even when Corisande gave her hand a quick, victorious squeeze.

Chapter 31

A n hour later, Lindsay couldn't say how deep they had descended into the man-of-war's belly, Donovan grimly silent at her side while the same two officers led the way. The air was foul and stuffy, guttering oil lamps the only lighting in the cramped passageways. She felt almost as if they were entering the portals of hell, for the place gave her such an unearthly chill.

"The Phoenix is in here, the rest of the bastards further down," one of the officers informed them, stopping abruptly near a low door. "We'll be right outside if you've need of us."

"Is the prisoner chained?" asked Donovan, his voice so stern and cold that Lindsay shivered, no doubt in her mind that Corisande's formidable husband didn't approve at all of this visit.

"Chained fast, my lord, hands and feet. He can't move more than a few inches from the wall."

"Then Miss Somerset may enter alone and face her attacker. I'll wait here with you."

Stunned at the unexpected boon he'd granted her, Lindsay sensed, too, that Corisande must surely have had a hand even in this concession. As the heavy bolt was drawn with an eerie thunk, she threw him a glance of thanks, but Donovan made no expression of acknowledgment, his dark eyes unfathomable.

But what could she hope to expect from a man who had fought loyally under Wellington for years and seen countless men die for England, while inside the cell was someone he saw as no more than a traitor? Pity? That Jared had saved his life had probably brought him this far, but she would be an utter fool to imagine—

"Make it quick, miss. Captain Billingsley said a few moments, no more."

So he had, that admonishment coming just as Lindsay and Corisande had left the commanding officer's cabin, the slightest hint of suspicion in his voice. For that reason, she had to make this exchange sound convincing, though it wasn't hard to summon anguish to her breast as she ducked into the poorly lit cell, the smell of urine and sweat nearly overpowering her.

She gasped, her eyes tearing, not so much from the fetid air, but because Jared sat slumped in one corner, his arms shackled to the wall. He was stripped to the waist, dried blood streaking his powerful shoulders, and she knew then that he'd been beaten. Dear God, it was her fault, too! His capture, that of his men, the *Vengeance* commandeered now by naval officers—but what else could she have done?

Stricken, Lindsay wanted to run to him, but that would have been a fatal mistake. Somehow she made herself stand her ground just inside the door, summoning all the agony in her heart to shriek hoarsely, "You detestable bastard! I hate you for what you did to me! Do you hear me? Hate you!

And I hope they hang you and then cut you down and tear out your filthy heart—"

The door slamming behind her made Lindsay jump, her harangue obviously upsetting her escort more than it appeared to have moved Jared; he hadn't even lifted his head. She moved closer, horror filling her.

"Jared? It's me, Lindsay . . . Jared?"

No answer came, the cell so deathly quiet she realized only then that he was unconscious. Dear Lord, did they plan to kill him before they reached Plymouth? Were they giving him no food? No water?

She flew to him, unable to hold herself back any longer and not caring if those officers burst in and had to drag her away kicking and screaming. Tears nearly choking her, she sank to her knees in the fetid straw, her hands trembling as she cradled his face.

"Jared, oh, please, wake up," she whispered desperately, his flesh so clammy, his head limp. "Wake up, *please*."

She tried to rouse him by shaking his shoulders, her horror only growing when her palms came away wet from his blood, the beating obviously recent. Yet she took heart when he suddenly groaned and licked his cracked lips. Wildly she looked around her, scrambling to her feet when she spied a bucket with a ladle near the door.

The water stank, she smelled its foulness the moment she filled the ladle and rushed back to Jared, but it was all she had to give him.

"Those bastards," she said fiercely as he drank like a man who hadn't tasted water in days; she imagined Jared had more likely suffered the rank stuff thrown in his face than been allowed a sip. Finally she drew the ladle away, fearing it was too much, too soon, and he did begin to cough and choke.

He opened his eyes, too, staring at her in disbelief as she stared back at him helplessly while he wheezed and sputtered until gradually he grew still.

"Lindsay . . . ?"

"Oh, Jared, I've probably only another moment before—" She didn't finish but turned to the door and raised her voice to an agonized shout. "You bastard! Monster! I hope you burn in hell for everything you did to me! Do you hear me? Burn in hell!"

"Probably what I deserve."

Jared had spoken so somberly that Lindsay had to subdue a tender laugh, shaking her head at him.

"No, no, I didn't mean you—it's only what I've led them to believe. That you cruelly abducted me in London and mistreated me and stole my virtue—that's why Captain Billingsley allowed me to come down here. To rant and rail at you—"

"I did steal your virtue."

She sucked in her breath, staring deeply into his eyes. "You know that's not true. I gave myself to you, Jared, wholeheartedly, completely. I only wish now that I hadn't sneaked back aboard the *Vengeance*"—her throat tightened as her gaze fell to his bloodied shoulders—"dear God, that I hadn't brought this horror upon you."

"I brought it upon myself, Lindsay, years ago, just as it can no longer be your concern what happens—"

"It *is* my concern," she whispered fiercely, wish-

ing there were some way she could free Jared's
arms so she could feel them around her. Wishing
that just once he wouldn't tell her she couldn't care
about him, couldn't love him. "Damn you, Jared
Giles, you will always be my concern! I love you!
Doesn't that mean anything to you?"

When he didn't answer, she felt such a wave of
despair that she was almost tempted to leave him,
the pain was so great to think he truly might not
love her. But his eyes held hers so intensely that
she couldn't move, her heart beginning to thunder
in her ears.

"I can only cause you harm, Lindsay. Don't you
see? Even now you're risking everything—"

"Because I don't want to live without you, can't
you understand? And I'll wait for you as long as
it takes—Corie overheard you're to be taken to
Dartmoor Prison once we reach Plymouth. They
believe you're an American, so surely it will be
only a matter of time before you're exchanged for
another prisoner of war—"

"Or before they find out who I really am."

"But I've said nothing, done nothing to make
them doubt my story, Jared, so how will they
know? Surely your men would never betray you.
And the only others who know the truth are Corie
and her husband, Lord Donovan Trent. He's outside the door right now, waiting for me—"

"Lindsay, enough, they might hear you. It's best
you leave—best you forget everything, forget
me . . ."

He strained against his chains and grimaced,
clearly in severe pain, but Lindsay was certain his
agony at that moment was nothing like the torment
she felt. Her voice sank to a ragged whisper.

"Forget you? And what shall I do with the love in my heart, forget that, too? You ask an impossible thing, Jared. I only wish you would stop trying to protect me from harm and admit you might love me—"

She didn't get to finish, the door starting to swing open so suddenly that she had time only to scramble on her knees to the center of the cell, where she dropped her head in her hands, moaning to herself. Moaning and wishing so desperately she'd had a moment more to touch her lips to his . . .

"Enough, miss. The bastard will pay for his bloody crimes soon enough," came a sympathetic voice, one of the officers bending down to help her to her feet while the other cursed foully at Jared.

Meanwhile, Donovan stood outside the door, staring into the cell and saying nothing, his expression as grim as before. But she saw something flicker across his face when one of the officers gave a sharp kick to Jared whose groan made Lindsay pale.

"Come, let's be gone from here," Donovan murmured, his voice oddly strained. A second sickening thud of a boot hitting flesh made Lindsay want to turn and run back to Jared's side. And she would have if Donovan hadn't grabbed her arm and pulled her out of the cell and down the passageway while the officers laughed crudely that the legendary Phoenix didn't seem so bloody immortal now and slammed shut the door.

None of them heard another groan, pained and raw, nor heard Jared whisper hoarsely, blood trickling from the corner of his mouth, "I . . . love you, Lindsay. Love you."

* * *

The afternoon couldn't have been gloomier when Lindsay stepped from the gangplank onto the Plymouth wharf. A chill wind that smelled of rain whipped at her soiled yellow gown, the sky heavy with clouds as miserably gray as her mood.

Even the chatter of Donovan and Corisande's little daughter, Paloma, couldn't cheer her. The winsome two-year-old clapped her tiny hands and seemed to take delight in everything she saw, especially the prancing white horses harnessed to the carriage Donovan had hired to take them to Cornwall.

He and Corisande were going home to begin their life as a family, while for Lindsay, Cornwall unhappily meant returning to her father's house, where she must face Olympia. Yet her stepmother's expected wrath was truly of no consequence to her at that moment. She turned at the sound of heavy clunking of chains, her heart aching as Jared and his men—Walker, Cowan and all the rest—made their way, one by one, down the gangplank now that all the passengers from the *Industry* had disembarked.

True to his word, Captain Billingsley already had a half-dozen wagons waiting to take his prisoners to Dartmoor; jeers and curses filled the air as other passengers turned to watch.

"Lindsay, we should get into the carriage," Corisande whispered in her ear, handing Paloma to Donovan. "You've come this far unscathed, but you're still at risk—"

"Listen to them, Corie," Lindsay said in disbelief as the jeers grew louder, joined now by those of passersby and sailors from other ships who hooted and spit. "Jared and his men saved those people only last week . . . and listen to them."

She flinched as soldiers from the H.M.S. *Clementine* were forced to link arms and form a human barrier to hold back the crowd, which seemed to be growing larger and more raucous by the moment, word no doubt spreading throughout the port city that the dreaded Phoenix had been captured at last. Her stricken gaze flew back to Jared, at the haggardness of his face, at his ravaged shoulders, his captors having neglected to give him back his shirt.

"Lindsay, please . . ."

She nodded, the quiet urgency in Corisande's voice finally making her move, though she could not tear her gaze away from Jared even when she was assisted by a footman into the carriage. Tears stung her eyes because he could yet hold his head so high, not looking to the right or the left, not looking for her, which she knew was done to protect her. But she sensed from the tension visible in his body that he must have glimpsed her—

"I know that man! Stop, stop—I know him!"

Gasping, Lindsay gripped the carriage door as a woman burst through the crowd, disheveled and wild-eyed. Dear Lord, it was the same woman, wretchedly ill from seasickness at the time, whom she and Donovan had rescued from the *Industry*.

"You're Jared Giles!" came an unearthly shriek that made Lindsay's blood run cold and a startled hush fall over the wharf. "In chains, eeee! Only what you deserve! The mighty have been brought low, ha, ha! The Earl of Dovercourt in chains!"

Chapter 32

To Lindsay, it seemed no one moved for a horrifying moment while the woman danced a demented jig in front of Jared. Then bedlam erupted, none other than Captain Horatio Billingsley bellowing down from the H.M.S. *Clementine*, "Seize her! Seize that woman!"

"Oh, God, Donovan, what are we going to do?" Corisande's voice broke through Lindsay's paralyzed haze, Corisande appearing, for the first time in her life, completely at a loss. While Lindsay could only stare as the woman frantically fought off three ship's officers trying to subdue her, her outraged shrieks rending the air.

"How dare you! Leave me be! Where's my Ryland? Where's my son? Ryland, help me!"

Dear God, *Ryland*? In shock, Lindsay sank back against the seat, staring at Corisande, whose face had gone as deathly white as she imagined her own to be.

"Lindsay, she said Ryland. Wasn't that the name of the man who married Jared's sister? Ryland Potter?"

Numbly, Lindsay nodded as disorderly shouts and jeers once more erupted outside the carriage. Little Paloma began to cry, the noise surely frightening her. Which made Donovan curse so vehemently that all three of them jumped, his voice brooking no argument as he lunged from the carriage and slammed the door behind him.

"Stay here, all of you! Do you understand me? Just stay here!"

Somehow they did, Lindsay so sick at heart she thought she might be ill, while Corisande did her best to soothe Paloma, no matter the bedlam which continued outside for what seemed a very long time.

At one point a harsh cry was heard urging that all the prisoners be hanged right there on the wharf; it was echoed around them until Lindsay pressed her hands to her ears, trying to shut out the horrible racket as futilely as she could chase away her crippling fear. In her mind's eye she could see Jared standing tall and unafraid amidst the fray, just as she'd seen him aboard the *Vengeance* in the heat of a sea chase, which renewed her flagging spirits. Yet it was all so awful—to think that woman might be Sylvia Potter . . .

"Lindsay, you know no matter what happens, I'll do anything to help you," Corisande said gently when it seemed, finally, that the din was lessening, if only a little. "I can't speak for Donovan, but he knows my feelings. If not for Jared, I wouldn't have my husband, or Paloma . . ."

Lindsay's chest grew tight from the tears brimming in Corisande's eyes; she'd rarely seen her stouthearted friend cry. As Corisande hugged the beautiful little girl in her arms, Paloma amazingly having fallen asleep, Lindsay couldn't help but be touched that Corisande could already love so deeply another woman's child. Just as she so clearly loved her husband, even now Corisande craning her neck to look for Donovan out the carriage window, while Lindsay couldn't look at all for dread of what she might see—

"Oh, Lord, Lindsay, here he comes now."

With Corisande's announcement sounding both apprehensive and relieved, Lindsay lost all ability to breathe as Donovan climbed into the coach and took his seat beside Corisande, his hand tenderly caressing Paloma's mahogany curls. Yet his expression remained grim, and on a man as swarthily dark as Lord Donovan Trent, it was even more ominous to behold.

"The prisoners are being taken to Dartmoor just as planned—all of them."

Lindsay exhaled in a rush, her gaze jumping to Corisande and then back to Donovan as the carriage jolted into motion. "So . . . so they're allowing me to leave?"

"For now, but they may call you back for further questions. An official inquiry has already begun into Jared's—the Phoenix's true identity. Messengers have been sent to London. It probably won't take more than a few days to summon acquaintances of the Earl of Dovercourt to Plymouth."

"And that woman . . . the one who recognized him?"

"Mad as a hatter. Otherwise, they might have tarred and hung your husband this very day. She says her name's Sylvia Potter, though they got little else out of her before she fell into a fit. She's been taken to the Three Maidens Inn near the town square and put under guard until the investigation can begin."

"So it was Sylvia . . ." Lindsay murmured, not astonished at all that Donovan knew she and Jared were married. She slumped back, horrified, against the seat. "Sylvia Potter."

"Bloody woman should have drowned."

Stunned that Corisande had voiced what Lindsay had just been thinking, however cruel it sounded, she couldn't help but wish that she'd never gone belowdecks on the *Industry*—but there was nothing to be done about it now. And she didn't think it wise to discuss Jared further, given the forbidding scowl settling over Donovan's handsome features as he stared out the window at the passing streets, although the glance that Corisande sent Lindsay told her the matter was far from finished.

Thank God, for a short while at least, Jared was safe. But, remembering how he'd been so cruelly treated aboard the H.M.S. *Clementine*, Lindsay drew little comfort that Dartmoor Prison would be any better.

Meanwhile, she had a trial of her own to face, although it paled next to Jared's. Yet a full day's coach ride wouldn't seem nearly long enough to prepare herself for what was to come once she reached Porthleven.

"Disgraceful! Absolutely disgraceful! Just look at you, girl! Look at you!"

So weary from the journey she could barely stand, Lindsay nonetheless bore Olympia Somerset's fury just as she always had, silently, stoically, not wanting to make things worse for her poor father even now . . .

"Have you nothing more to say? This is utterly

scandalous—scandalous! We'll never be able to lift our heads in the village again! In London! Anywhere!" Throwing the train of her blue silk dress behind her, Olympia paced in front of Lindsay like an outraged pigeon, her massive breasts heaving, her double chin fluttering, her narrow, high-bridged nose positively pinched with displeasure.

"When we received word from Winifred that you'd disappeared, your father and I were beside ourselves! Who will marry you now? Will you answer me that, my girl? When everyone hears you were found aboard a pirate's ship? That you were abducted and—and—dear God, I can't bring myself to even say it!"

"Ravaged."

As stunned silence fell in the lamplit drawing room, Lindsay didn't think she had ever seen Olympia's powdered face so red, near hatred distorting her features and blazing from her cold blue eyes.

"You . . . you ungrateful girl. To think I allowed you to go to London for the Season and this—this scandal is how I'm rewarded for my generosity! You knew your responsibilities! You could have married well—won a title for yourself, enhanced our family name and position—"

"And given you someone else to bully?"

Incredulous that she had spoken up even as Olympia advanced upon her with an ominous rustle of silk, Lindsay didn't think to back away but held her ground, lifting her chin to take what she had endured a thousand times before—something her father knew nothing about, nor even Corisande. White light burned in front of her eyes as

Olympia slapped her viciously across the face, and then slapped her again on the other cheek.

"Damn you, girl, I've borne all I will from you! It's not enough I must suffer the embarrassment of having your father for a husband—wretched, spineless little man. You'll not live under my roof another day, do you hear?"

"And you will never touch my daughter again, do you hear me, Olympia?"

Lindsay gasped, her gaze flying to the doorway, where her father stood, his face ashen, his hands visibly shaking. Olympia looked startled, a flush creeping past her painted eyebrows, although she threw back her head contemptuously.

"This is between Lindsay and me, Randolph. It has nothing to do with you—"

"It has everything to do with me! God help me, woman, have you struck my daughter before this day?"

Lindsay wasn't sure if she was more astonished that her father had roared at the top of his lungs, almost incongruous in so slight and graying a man, or that Olympia seemed truly nonplussed, a bejeweled hand flying to her breast.

"Randolph, please, of course I would never— dear me, no, this is the first time, truly, and once you hear of what has happened— It's so dreadful! Horrifying! I was just about to send a servant to find you, to tell you Lindsay was home so you might know what your daughter has done, the scandal she's brought upon us—"

"If there's any scandal, madam, it's that I no longer recognize you as my wife. A pity you don't lie as well as you've a gift for making everyone around you perfectly miserable—and I'll stomach no more. Leave us! Now, or I'll summon the foot-men to throw you out!"

Lindsay had never thought she might see the day, Olympia's jaw dropping, her imperious shoulders slumping, tears swimming in her eyes. But somehow the woman managed to maintain her composure long enough to tilt her fleshy chin and sweep haughtily from the room, though Lindsay heard her stepmother gasp in shock when her father slammed the drawing room door shut behind her.

"Damned witch. Should have been rid of her years ago."

Her own eyes clouded, Lindsay gave a choked laugh, remembering how Jared had once called her stepmother a witch. But in the next instant she flew into her father's arms and buried her face in his coat as she sobbed ridiculously, for so long and so hard, that he actually began to chuckle.

That made her stop and draw back from him in surprise, but he had sobered, his kindly gaze full of concern.

"So tell me about this privateer who's won your heart. Jared Giles is his name, the Earl of Dover-court?"

So astounded she couldn't speak, Lindsay dropped her gaze to the neatly folded piece of ivory vellum he withdrew from his coat pocket.

"A letter from Corie. Seems while you and Don-ovan and their little daughter were asleep in the carriage last night, your friend was very busy. She must have slipped this to the footman somehow when they dropped you at the door; he told me she said I must read the letter straightaway—and then he informed me you were in the drawing room with Olympia." Tenderly, he lifted his hand to wipe a tear from Lindsay's face. "Corie has a plan, you know."

"She does?"

As her father nodded, Lindsay had never felt so brilliant a burst of hope, and she couldn't help blurting out, "Oh, Papa, you would like him, I know you would!"

"I believe I would, too, and perhaps someday I'll have a chance to meet him," came his reply, his expression tinged with sadness. But the next moment found him drawing her over to the far end of the room, keeping his voice low. "There's much for me to do, and much for Corie to arrange, but all you must do is wait patiently until tomorrow morning."

"Wait? But how can I wait while Jared—"

"Shhh, Lindsay, you'll have a chance to play a part, I wish not so dangerous a one, but there's no other way. At least I've a chance now to make amends for the years you've suffered—"

"But you've suffered, too, Papa."

"Yes, but no more. No more." Emotion welling in his eyes, he squeezed her hands. "I've wanted to tell you for some time that I haven't forgotten the promise I made to your mother so long ago, though it might have seemed . . ."

His voice failing him, Sir Randolph Somerset shook his head, but Lindsay didn't need him to finish to know he intended to do anything he could to help her.

He already had.

Chapter 33

The long night a sleepless torture Lindsay wanted to forget, her only relief came in the morning, after she had rushed through her first real bath since Gijón and then dressed hurriedly in one of the nicest gowns left in her wardrobe and a fine gray cloak. Her father was waiting for her at the bottom of the staircase and together they left the house, neither of them mentioning Olympia at all, as if the despicable woman were already gone from their lives.

Sir Randolph seemed disinclined to speak, in fact, just as he had become last night after telling Lindsay about Corisande's letter, except to encourage her to try to get some rest and to mention again that he had much to do. But what he had to do, she hadn't divined, the crux of Corisande's plan still unknown to her.

Even now, as they settled into the carriage, she had no idea where they might be bound, but it became clear after many long, silent moments that they were heading into the fishing village of Porthleven. Was Corisande perhaps meeting them at the Easton parsonage? Lindsay was almost relieved when they rumbled by the cozy stone house with its blue shutters, not because she didn't want to see Corisande's three younger sisters and Frances, their motherly housekeeper, but because she felt little like talking to anyone herself, her nerves on edge.

Her father was so still, so grim almost, occasionally checking his pocket watch and then staring out the window, until finally she could bear the suspense no longer.

"Papa, will you please tell me—"

"Good, she looks ready to sail."

Her heart rearing at his words, Lindsay followed his gaze to the quay down the hill and a single-masted ship she recognized at once, Oliver Trelawny's *Fair Betty*. She could see men moving busily about the deck and sails being unfurled, but what made her mouth drop open in astonishment was that Corisande stood at the starboard railing next to the burly Cornish captain, though she left him and bolted down the gangplank when the carriage rolled to a stop.

"We've no time for good-byes, Lindsay—you must go," her father urgently insisted as the footman opened the door.

Almost in a daze, Lindsay obeyed him, allowing herself to give him only a quick, fierce hug before she found herself on the quay, Corisande rushing to her side.

"Lindsay, come! I don't know how long before Donovan—"

Corisande didn't finish, instead grabbing Lindsay's arm as they both hurried up the gangplank, two sailors dropping the heavy plank of wood to the dock as soon as they were safely aboard. Everything was happening so fast, the sails flapping and swelling in the stiff breeze, the *Fair Betty* slipping away from the quay while Oliver shouted commands to his men, that Lindsay felt the only thing steadying her was Corisande's reassuring presence at her side.

Her eyes filled, her chest aching at the sight of her father sitting so alone in the carriage, but when he lifted his hand in farewell, somehow she managed a smile.

"We couldn't have come this far without him," Corisande said softly, squeezing Lindsay's arm. "Gold, enough muskets for an army, gunpowder—"

"Gunpowder!" Lindsay met Corisande's eyes, apprehension gripping her. "Dear God, Corie, what have you planned?"

"It's a last resort, but we'll use it if we have to. Oliver says it wouldn't take but a small cask or two to blow a hole in a prison wall, no matter how thick."

"Oh, no, but that would mean a battle, wouldn't it? Lord, Corie, I don't want any of his men to be hurt or Oliver or you—what did you say about Donovan? And where's Paloma?"

"Safe with Frances and my sisters, so you needn't worry for her, and Donovan's at Arundale's Kitchen. The tinners staged a mine accident only an hour ago, I hope convincing enough to keep him occupied until we're out of Mount's Bay—"

"Oh, Lord." Her knees suddenly gone weak, Lindsay wasn't sure why she felt so distressed, but there were so many people involved, so many people willing to risk their lives to help her, and if anything should happen to a one of them . . .

"Lindsay, stop, I know what you're thinking."

She shook her head, her throat constricting as her father's carriage finally rumbled away from the dock, Porthleven shrinking farther into the distance as the *Fair Betty* forged south toward the Channel.

"No, Corie, I can't allow you to do this for me— it's too dangerous—"

"Dangerous mostly for you, I fear. We'll be there as a last resort, just as I said, but it's you with the largest part to play. You're at the heart of this plan, Lindsay. Jared's life depends upon you."

Her hair whipping about her face, she looked at Corisande, her friend's brown eyes as somber as she had ever seen them. But all Lindsay had to think of was the way Jared had stared at her so intensely in his cell, and her heart began to thunder.

"Tell me what I have to do."

With darkness heavy all around them save for the lighted fortress at the distant crest of the hill, Lindsay swallowed hard. Corisande crawled closer to her friend, her voice barely above a whisper.

"Remember, if anything goes wrong, find a window and scream, Lindsay, as loud as you can. We'll be waiting right here to help you."

Flinching as a horse snorted, Lindsay nodded and glanced behind her toward the copse of stunted trees where Oliver and a dozen of his crew waited with their hired mounts and casks of gunpowder and muskets primed and ready—and once again she was nearly overcome by the odds of any of them escaping with their lives if something did go wrong. Yet she forced away her daunting thoughts; every mile they had ridden from the inlet where the *Fair Betty* lay anchored made her that much more determined to play her part, for she'd been drawing closer and closer to Jared.

"All right, you'd best go. Whatever happens, we've got to clear Plymouth harbor before dawn."

Lindsay didn't answer, simply squeezed Corisande's hand, and then she was on her feet and trudging across rugged moorland that seemed to have been crafted to shelter a prison.

Her pulse pounding in her ears, she imagined it wouldn't be long before she was spotted by guards, and she ruffled her hands through her tangled hair one last time. She licked her dry lips, tasting the dirt she had rubbed over her face and upon her pale blue satin gown, Corisande having used a knife to prick and tear at the hem to make it appear as if Lindsay had stumbled through dense patches of brambles.

Even her bodice had been torn, revealing the white curve of a breast, and she shivered at the cool night air, her cloak hanging forlornly from one shoulder as if she were too weak to protect herself from the elements. One slipper gone, she sucked in her breath as she stepped painfully upon a bed of thistles, yet it only helped to remind her she must begin to weave aimlessly and moan.

Her plaintive voice sounded eerie in such a desolate place, but thankfully, Dartmoor Prison wasn't so far removed from humanity that it would seem strange she was out wandering, lost and helpless. Helpless, that is, except for the pistol strapped to her inner thigh. The cool metal rubbing against her flesh every time she took a step flooded her with chills.

"Stop! You, there, stop!"

She didn't stop, even though the guard's stern command seemed to echo around her, soon taken up by a second man, who began to shout. It was easy for her to tremble now as she continued to weave and even stumble, dragging herself to her feet as the massive gates to Dartmoor Prison swung wide, men armed with muskets rushing toward her.

She stumbled again, hair falling across her face, hiding the burning in her cheeks as the guards drew closer.

"Help me . . ." she rasped, her throat so tight with momentary fear that that was easy, too. "Please . . . someone help me—"

"Wot the devil? It's a girl out here—and lookin' none the better for it. Give me a hand, mate!"

Lindsay dragged herself to her feet as two men took her arms while five others gathered around; she didn't want anyone to carry her, for they might discern her weapon. Instead she wrenched desperately at her cloak as if trying to cover herself, sobs washing over her.

"Help me, please. I'm so cold . . . so cold."

"Didn't you hear her, mate?" the man who supported her on the left side chided his grim-faced companion, shaking his head with sympathy as he draped her cloak around her quaking shoulders. "God in heaven, how could the wench have come to be out 'ere?"

"Wench?" scoffed the other while the rest of the guards fell in behind them, scanning the darkness and keeping their muskets lowered. "She's a lady, you fool—ain't you taken a look at her gown? The warden'll want to hear of this bit o' work, you can be sure."

Lindsay's pulse beating faster as the huge gates closed with a resounding thud behind them, she was thankful at least that all but her two rescuers went back to their posts. She made herself keep moaning, the men casting looks at each other above her head.

"Do you think the poor girl might be 'urt? Should we send someone out for a physician?"

"Warden Harford should see her first. It's a strange business, if you ask me, her being out there all alone—"

"I-I was riding . . . I fell, my horse . . . oooh, it hurts!"

"Cripes, mate, did you hear her? She's injured, I swear! This'll put an end to the warden's supper party quick enough, and with that Captain Billingsley and his officers come tonight to see after their precious prisoners, too. You'd think we had Napoleon himself here at Dartmoor and not some bloody pirate!"

Captain Billingsley? In a panic, Lindsay tried to slow the guards' progress by sinking to her knees, anything to buy herself some time, she thought desperately. But they simply hoisted her back up between them and half carried her through a doorway and into what appeared to be the warden's sumptuous private quarters, the boisterous buzz of conversation coming from an opposite room. Oh, Lord, oh, Lord, all it would take was for that pompous man to recognize her and . . .

"Please, please, no farther," she begged, emphasizing her plea with a ragged groan as she clutched at her side. "Let me sit, please . . . it hurts so terribly."

"Over there, mate—can't you see we're only making things worse? Set her down in the chair, gently, now, gently."

"C-Captain Billingsley . . . you did say Billingsley, didn't you?" she asked in a piteous whisper, grabbing one of the men's hands before he could walk away.

"Aye, miss, so I did. Do you know the gentleman?"

"Yes, yes. Oh, please, send him to me. He's a friend . . . a friend of my family's. Please bring him quickly! I fear . . . oh, God, the pain . . . I fear I'm dying!"

The guards blanching white, they stumbled into each other as they both hastened to oblige her, disappearing into the next room and leaving Lindsay, at least for a moment, alone. Her heart wildly thundering, she flew to the door and sought refuge behind it, her hands trembling so badly she feared she wouldn't retrieve the pistol from beneath her gown in time.

"An injured girl asking for me? Did she tell you her name?"

Billingsley's arrogant voice carrying to her from the dining room, Lindsay held her breath and began to pray. Please, please, may they not think she was bluffing . . . She heard the chink of fine crystal and a chair scrape, then footsteps approaching, annoyance emanating from Horatio Billingsley as he stopped just beyond the door.

"What the devil is the meaning of this charade?

There's no girl here, not a soul. The damned room's empty—"

"Except for me, sir," Lindsay said hoarsely as she reached up, grabbed the man's collar and thrust the pistol against the base of his skull, just as Oliver Trelawny had instructed her to do. "Tell your men—everyone—to stay back or I will shoot you. I swear it!"

Chapter 34

The air was still. The silence hung so heavily Lindsay could hear only the pounding of blood in her veins. Finally Captain Billingsley's subdued voice broke the charged spell.

"I believe she means what she says, gentlemen. Stand away, give her room—"

"I do mean it!" Lindsay moved closer to her captive, her back carefully against the wall. "Warden Harford. I want to speak with Warden Harford!"

A portly, pink-faced fellow peeked around the corner, eyeing her nervously. "You . . . you wish to see me?"

"The Phoenix, take me to him. Quickly!"

The fellow did, giving her as wide a berth as possible in the small room, the two guards and half a dozen ship's officers who had accompanied Captain Billingsley to Dartmoor attempting to follow the warden until Lindsay pressed the pistol deeper against her captive's head. "Stay where you are, all of you. Just me, the captain and Warden Harford."

"Do as she says! Do as she says!" cried Captain Billingsley.

Lindsay felt a rush of unease, but she could not allow herself to drop her facade. She only had to remember how brutally Jared had been treated aboard the H.M.S. *Clementine*, and she found more than enough determined resolve to allay any pity.

As they left the warden's quarters and moved into the prison yard, Lindsay continued to keep her back to the wall and the pistol firmly upon the captain, lest anyone doubt her intentions. A tense hush had settled over the place, the warden gesturing frantically for guards to lower their muskets and stand away as his little group walked to a nearby stone building with tiny barred openings for windows.

"He's in here, miss," Warden Harford said nervously, once more leading the way as they went inside.

"And his men?"

"All together in the same cell—the lot of them, miss."

Lindsay felt a shiver as they passed cell after cell from which stark, astonished faces stared out at her, but she kept her eyes riveted upon the two men in front of her, her hand firmly grasping Captain Billingsley's collar, Oliver's stern warning ringing in her ears.

"Where is he? Where?" she demanded an interminable moment later, when it seemed they had passed a hundred cells, her face grown flushed, her nerves taut, her fingers cramped around the pistol. And then she saw him, Jared rising to his feet and staring at her in utter amazement while his men gathered openmouthed behind him, only Walker Burke with the wryest smile on his face.

"Unlock that cell—quickly!"

Warden Harford was so desperate to oblige that he grabbed the ring of rattling keys from an ashen-faced guard and released the prisoners himself.

Lindsay's legs had become so shaky she doubted she could have gone another step. At once the cell door flew open, Jared and his men spilling out. But what amazed her was how silent and grim they were. Even Walker had become somber.

"Give me the pistol, Lindsay."

Jared's hand covered hers, and she was only too glad to relinquish the deadly weapon, his touch alone filling her with such overwhelming relief that she truly thought her knees might give way. Almost in a daze, she watched as Walker, Cowan, Cooky and the others disarmed the guards standing near and shoved them into the cell. Then Jared lowered the pistol to Captain Billingsley's chest.

"Undress, sir. I need your shirt."

Horatio's eyes widened in outrage, his aristocratic nostrils flaring, but he stripped hastily to the waist, not daring to utter a word. Within a moment Jared had a fine cambric shirt to cover his ravaged back and shoulders, while the captain shivered in front of them, his pasty-white physique covered in gooseflesh.

"Get into the cell."

As Horatio obeyed the terse command, Lindsay grabbed Jared's arm. "But we might need him—"

"The warden will kindly see us from this place."

His voice was so cold she felt a chill, but it was nothing compared with Warden Harford's raw panic. The man dropped to his pudgy knees and actually began to sob.

"Oh, please, sir, I've a wife and six children!"

"Then better you do exactly as I say and you might live to see them again."

The warden's reddened eyes widening in horror, he was standing the next moment, hauled roughly to his feet by two of Jared's men while Walker slammed shut the cell door and locked it.

"On behalf of His Majesty King George, I vow the English government won't rest until the lot of you are captured and hanged!" cried Captain Billingsley as they set off.

But they paid him no mind. Lindsay did her best to keep pace with Jared's furious strides, his hand firmly upon her arm. His jaw was so tight, she might have thought he would curse and denounce the man's threat, given what he felt about England. But he said nothing until they reached the main door, where he grabbed the winded warden by the throat.

"I have a wife, too, man, and I will see her safely from this damned prison. Do you understand me?"

Warden Harford's eyes darted from Lindsay's flushed face back to Jared; he bobbed his head. "Yes, yes, you'll need horses."

"Exactly. Move!"

With the pistol held to his head as they stepped from the building, the warden called out hoarsely for his guards to throw down their weapons—a very good thing. Lindsay gasped at the assembled force that had been waiting for them to emerge, at least fifty muskets aimed at the door. Fifty muskets that were quickly tossed to the ground, the guards ordered harshly by Jared to lie facedown in the dirt and not move, not attempt to follow them, or Warden Harford would die.

The next moments passed like a bewildering dream to Lindsay; she didn't allow herself to believe that they were safe even when they were riding at a full gallop from Dartmoor Prison,

Corisande, Oliver and his men joining them at the bottom of the hill.

Glad that she'd insisted that Warden Harford be blindfolded to protect the identities of her friends, Lindsay still wouldn't allow herself a shred of relief when an hour later they finally reached the secluded inlet where the *Fair Betty* was anchored, a single lantern guiding them to the sailors waiting with longboats to take them back to the ship. Their portly captive had been left trussed and gagged a few miles back in an abandoned cottage, but she knew, despite Jared's threat, it would be only a matter of time before word of the escape was carried to Plymouth and the authorities alerted, perhaps a frantic messenger riding there even now—

"Oh, Lord, Lindsay, I think it's Donovan!"

Corisande's voice was tinged with apprehension. Lindsay was so surprised she didn't think to dismount beside her friend, and neither did Jared nor any of the others, as a tall silhouette emerged from the darkness leading a heaving horse lathered in sweat. Donovan's face was both grim and weary in the lantern's dim light, his voice as somber, his gaze upon Corisande.

"I met Sir Randolph's carriage outside Porthleven, wife. He told me where you were bound, what you planned—"

"Donovan, I'm sorry, I would have told you, but I feared you wouldn't approve. I had to do something to help Lindsay—I had to!"

Lindsay shifted nervously upon her mare as a tense silence fell, her gaze following Donovan's to Jared, both men staring at each other for the longest moment while it seemed no one dared breathe. Finally it was Donovan who looked away, his eyes once more upon his wife.

"I came here only to be by your side, Corie. If the *Fair Betty* is to pass safely through Plymouth harbor, we must leave now, before it grows light."

Grateful tears jumping to Lindsay's eyes, she knew then that Donovan planned to make no attempt to stop them, but a shadow passed over her heart when she glanced at Jared. Though everyone else had begun to dismount, he made no motion to quit his bay stallion, his jaw taut as he met her eyes.

"Go with them, Lindsay. There's something I must do—"

"No!" Her hoarse cry echoing around them, she slipped off her mount and ran to him, knowing what he was thinking, knowing what he intended to do. "Sylvia's mad, Jared—dear God, isn't that vengeance enough?"

Her outburst could have fallen upon deaf ears, he looked so grimly resolute, and she knew before he even said the words what was poisoning his heart.

"It's Ryland, Lindsay. I must know where I can find him. I must know!"

"Then you will take me with you," she said fervently even as Corisande ran to her side.

"Lindsay, please, we can wait for Jared just south of the city. He'll have no trouble finding the *Fair Betty* there—"

"Jared, no, you can't leave me behind, not again, not now," Lindsay cried out despite Corisande's plea, her voice anguished, desperate. "If you love me, you'll take me with you!"

He stared into her eyes so intensely that she felt her knees grow weak. For a moment she stood, dreading his decision. Then he cursed and reached down, sweeping her into the saddle in front of him, his arms locked with fierce possessiveness around her.

"South of the city, Captain Trelawny?" he shouted to Oliver, sharply veering his mount in the direction of Plymouth.

"Ais, my lord, an' well away from those damned warships!" came the hearty response in a thick Cornish accent. "God grant 'ee be there before dawn, or I fear, for the sake of all aboard, we'll have to leave you!"

Lindsay could still hear Oliver's warning ringing in her ears. But there was no time to think as Jared headed their exhausted horse into a dark alley.

"We'll make it back in time," she repeated to herself in a fervent whispered prayer, the joy she felt in Jared's arms more profound than anything she had ever known. Yet she couldn't deny his embrace had grow more tense with each passing moment as they approached Plymouth at a hard gallop. Now, as he gave another low curse, a mail coach rumbling down the street a sign that the city was already rousing itself, she knew he regretted bringing her with him.

Undaunted, she slid from the saddle before he could dismount, and spoke up before he could utter a word of what she sensed he wanted to say. "No, Jared, I'm not staying here. We'll face Sylvia together—"

"Woman . . ."

He had dropped down beside her, but Lindsay sidestepped him, her heart pounding as she threw her hood over her hair and hurried toward the street. If he saw her urgency, that there was no time—

His hand suddenly catching her arm made her gasp. Jared drew her against him just before she could step out of the alley.

"Damnation, Lindsay, then stay close to me!"

She nodded, a lump forming in her throat at how hard his expression had become as shown in the lamplight. She knew he was thinking of Sylvia and Ryland Potter.

They moved together out into the deserted street, the palpable tension in his body growing. He grasped her fingers so tightly she winced, but she said nothing, even when they drew closer to the town square and her hand had gone numb. It seemed that they both spied the sign for the Three Maidens Inn at the same time, Jared reaching for his pistol. Yet he appeared to come to some other decision, and handed the weapon to her.

"Hide the pistol under your cloak, but be ready if I've need of it."

She nodded, apprehension filling her that light shone from the inn's street-level windows. Her anxiety only grew when they entered the establishment, but to her relief, the main room was empty except for a sleepy-eyed serving girl, wiping down tables, who looked up and shrugged at them apologetically.

"Sorry, we've no rooms. Inn's full."

"Not a room. We've come to see my aunt, Mrs. Potter—Sylvia Potter." Lindsay had spoken up before Jared could say a word. "We only just heard she was here and came to Plymouth straightaway."

"Aye, poor woman, she's upstairs. I'll show

you the way, but you'll have to speak with the guard—"

"No, no, we'll manage. You just go on with your work."

Holding her breath as the girl gave another shrug and went back to her cleaning, Lindsay glanced at Jared, but he was already moving to the stairs. As she caught up with him, he gestured for the pistol, which only made her heartbeat race. Oh, Lord . . .

With the wooden stairs squeaking, it was impossible to be quiet, but that sound seemed nothing compared with the rumbling snores emanating from the guard slumped asleep in a chair at the far end of the dimly lit hall.

"Stay here, Lindsay."

She froze at Jared's terse whisper, the lump in her throat nearly choking her when he moved stealthily toward the guard; she closed her eyes tight as he lifted the butt of the pistol, the man's snores suddenly silenced. Oh, Lord . . .

Jared was already opening the door to the room nearest the unconscious guard by the time Lindsay grabbed the oil lamp from the hall table and reached him, his broad shoulders taut with tension, his expression less hard now than tortured. Imagining his thoughts, she wanted so badly to say something to him, to let him know that she understood, but he moved so quickly to the bed that she could but turn to close the door behind them. Then a startled gasp filled the room.

Lindsay spun around, her eyes widening in horror to see Jared's hand clamped over Sylvia Potter's mouth, the pistol pressed to the woman's temple.

Chapter 35

Fearing he might slay Sylvia right there in her bed, Lindsay set down the lamp and ran to him. The older woman's wild eyes upon her gave her chills.

"Jared, no . . ."

"Damn her, Lindsay. Damn her."

His voice so choked that Lindsay felt tears burn her eyes, she gently covered his hand gripping the pistol with her own and shook her head.

"Jared, this isn't the answer—it can't be. Ask her about Ryland and then we'll leave. We'll leave England and never come back, both of us, together . . . Please, Jared."

He didn't answer for so long she wondered if he had heard her, his face so full of hatred that it frightened her. Then, slowly, he lowered his hand from Sylvia's mouth, although he didn't remove the pistol.

"Where's Ryland, woman? Damn you, where is he?"

"Gone! Gone away!" A shriek of such maniacal laughter burst from Sylvia that Lindsay could only stare in shock as a stream of frothy spittle foamed at the corner of the woman's mouth.

"Dead, dead and gone away—oh, God, my Ryland! My son, my beloved Ryland!"

Now Jared lowered the pistol, looking as stunned as Lindsay felt, while Sylvia clutched her knees and began to rock herself, tears tumbling down her lined cheeks. At first she seemed only to mumble incoherently to herself; then she suddenly fixed a look of pure hatred upon Jared.

"You killed my son! Chased us away to Lisbon—not our home, not Dovercourt Manor. We were going to come back, find you, but cholera came and took him away—he's gone! My Ryland is gone! He was to be the master of Dovercourt, not you, not Alistair!" Another burst of laughter bubbled up from the woman's throat as she grinned almost gleefully from ear to ear. "We killed your uncle, you know, Ryland and me, like your parents—oh, my, and stupid Elise. How she wept for you, stupid girl! Ryland wanted another wife, a new wife, so he beat her and beat her—"

"Damn you, woman, enough!"

Sylvia had started at Jared's tortured cry, then began to rock herself again and pluck mindlessly at her dark, tangled hair.

Jared turned from the bed. "God help me, no more . . . no more."

His voice had become a hoarse whisper, and Lindsay felt a shiver at how drained he appeared, older, his face ashen. Her heart aching for him, she went to his side, settling her hand gently in the crook of his arm.

"Jared, we should go. It's nearing dawn—look."

He followed her gaze to the window, pale light creeping beneath the shade; relief filled her that he seemed to bolster himself before her eyes. He glanced back at Sylvia, sighing raggedly as he shook his head.

"Maybe there's some justice after all."

Lindsay nodded, unable to speak as Jared met her eyes and then drew her into his arms, hugging her as if he would never let her go. But he did release her a breathless moment later, growing tense again when they moved to the door.

She sensed at once what lay upon his mind, that someone might have overheard their exchange with Sylvia, but the inn was quiet, the guard still slumped in his chair. Lindsay swallowed hard, Jared squeezing her hand as they moved quickly down the hall.

"Don't worry about him. He'll have a headache and a good-size lump to show for ignoring his duty, but he'll survive—"

"Damn you, Jared Giles!"

He turned, his heart lurching as Sylvia shakily aimed a pistol she must have taken from the guard, the report exploding before he had a chance to pull his weapon from his belt. He heard Lindsay's gasp and glanced behind him in horror to see her begin to crumple; he lunged to catch her in his arms before she struck the floor.

"Lindsay!"

Blood was streaking the left side of her head, and he was so stricken that for a moment he lost all thought of what to do. Doors being yanked open around him finally gave him the impetus to move. His eyes stinging, he bolted down the stairs clutching Lindsay to his heart, past the astonished serving girl, who shrieked in terror, and charged blindly into the street.

"Oh, God, Lindsay . . ." His jagged breath tearing at his throat, he barely dodged in time a carriage traveling through the town square, the coachman shouting out crude obscenities that Jared didn't hear. His blood thundering in his ears, he didn't slow his desperate pace until he had reached the alley, Lindsay so horribly limp in his arms, a slash of scarlet staining her blond hair . . .

Damn him for a fool, how could he have brought her with him? He'd known the danger! Yet he knew, as he hoisted himself into the saddle with her, the bay stallion snorting skittishly, that he couldn't have denied her anything for the way she had looked so pleadingly into his eyes. With Lindsay's head lolling helplessly against his shoulder, he kicked the steed into a gallop, his only burning thought to find the *Fair Betty*.

"Do you see them, Oliver? Do you see anything?"

Growing more anxious as her old friend shook his head, Corisande glanced at the brightening sky and then at Donovan, who stood silently beside her at the starboard railing. He was so grim that she felt her heart sink into her shoes, but she wouldn't allow herself to believe that something terrible had happened to Lindsay and Jared. She wouldn't!

"Corie girl, I hate to tell 'ee, but we can't tarry here much longer," Oliver Trelawny said without lowering the spyglass, still scanning the wharf, where a half-dozen warships were berthed. "It's too dangerous for all concerned, I know 'ee can understand. An' even if we miss them, Lindsay's a clever girl just like you, she'll think of a way— Lord help us, what the devil?"

"What is it, Oliver, what?" cried Corisande,

wishing she had a spyglass, too, so she might see . . .

"It's Lord Giles—there, in that longboat, but I don't see Lindsay . . . unless . . ."

Oliver's vehement curse made Corisande blanch.

"Ais, she's in the boat, too, but something's wrong, Corie. Lord Giles has her lying in the stern, an' she's not moving at all—"

"Oh, Donovan, no." Grateful for her husband's strong arms suddenly around her, Corisande buried her face against his shoulder, praying for strength. Not Lindsay, please . . . not her beautiful, indomitable friend, who deserved some happiness more than anyone she knew . . .

"Lord, now what's all the commotion on the wharf?"

Oliver's puzzled query making her leave the warm comfort of Donovan's embrace, Corisande gasped when a thunderous burst of cannon fire sounded from the direction of the H.M.S. *Clementine*, towering plumes of water erupting all around the approaching longboat.

"Those bastards are firing on him!" Gripping the railing, Corisande had never felt so frantic. "Dear God, they must have heard about the escape and Captain Billingsley. Oliver, we've got to do something—anything! We can't just sit here and watch them be blown to bits!"

"Corie, we're out of range here." Donovan answered for the burly captain, who looked at Corisande helplessly. "We'd be fools to venture any closer. Jared's rowing hard—"

He broke off and strode so abruptly toward the prow that Corisande watched him in surprise, realizing his intent only when he called for one of the

Fair Betty's own galleys to be lowered. Her heart overflowing that he would be willing to help Jared even now, she ran to him as eight of Jared's crew stepped forward to join him, including a man with hair as raven-black as her husband's.

She had only an instant to hug Donovan and then he was gone, over the side with the others. Corisande rushed back to Oliver as the galley surged powerfully through the choppy waves toward the longboat that still seemed so far away. It was torture to watch, especially when another explosive round came so close again to hitting Jared and Lindsay that Corisande once more began to pray.

She didn't stop praying even when the two boats finally met, her stomach knotting as she saw Lindsay handed over first before Jared joined them, her fear for her dearest friend mounting. But her fervent prayers didn't prevent her from cursing like a sailor when, mere moments later, the empty longboat was blown to splinters; her stricken gaze was now fixed steadfastly upon Donovan.

She prayed all the harder while Oliver bellowed to his crew to unfurl the last of the sails and to lend a hand getting the heavily loaded galley back aboard. Corisande was there waiting as Jared was the first to disembark, his face haggard, his eyes as haunted as she'd seen in any man when he turned to face her with Lindsay limp and ashen in his arms.

"Corie, please, my wife . . ."

Her gaze only for an instant straying to the dried blood matting Lindsay's hair, she swallowed hard and nodded. "Oliver's cabin, Jared. Let's take her there."

* * *

It wasn't so much the dull throbbing in her head that made Lindsay open her eyes, but that she heard someone coaxing her to, a low, husky voice that filled her with comforting warmth. Yet she panicked, crying out when at first it seemed she couldn't focus, everything appearing strangely blurred to her ... until the same baritone quietly told her to give herself a few moments, she wasn't alone, she had no need to worry.

She closed her eyes and relaxed, someone soothingly rubbing her fingers, the sensation filling her with peace. Yet the voice came back again, gently urging her to look around her once more, to see if there was anything she recognized, anyone she knew.

Her vision was not so blurred this time; with each blink it grew more focused, sharper, until a face began to take shape and form in front of her ... a handsome, beloved face.

"Jared ..."

Her voice sounded so strange and hoarse, but her single word elicited a soft ripple of laughter from other dear faces she gradually recognized: Corisande and Donovan; Oliver Trelawny; Walker Burke and Cowan and Cooky, too. But once more her gaze moved as if drawn by some inexplicable force to the man who held her hand firmly locked in his own, a wetness in his eyes that she knew she had seen there before.

"Oh, Jared, what happened?"

"Shhh, Lindsay, you needn't try to talk too much," he said, his voice nearly as hoarse as hers. "I feared I had lost you, but Corie was quick to assure me you'd only been grazed ... much like what happened to your arm. If any of us has proved to be immortal—"

His voice seemed to catch and he fell poignantly silent, his grasp on her fingers growing all the tighter. Suddenly her throat felt tight, too, and she lifted her other hand to touch his face, just to know that he was truly real, the moment real. But what convinced her was the fierce intensity in his vivid blue eyes, making her breath stop, and the words he bent his head to whisper for her ears alone.

"I love you, Lindsay. Love you . . ."

She had never known her heart to feel so full, but when a shadow seemed to pass over Jared's face, she felt a moment's panic. "Jared . . . ?"

"I've nothing to give you, Lindsay, no house, no beautiful clothes, nothing that you deserve—"

"But you've given me everything, Jared. Everything I could ever want. What else could I need?"

His expression appeared to lighten, a tender smile upon his face as he bent closer and kissed her, but not for as long as she might have wanted. Corisande clearing her throat made Jared lift his head, Lindsay's gaze flying to her friend, who gave a small shrug and glanced with mischief in her eyes at Oliver Trelawny.

"Hmm, if there's nothing else they need, I don't know what we're to do with all that gold Lindsay's father entrusted to us, do you, Oliver?"

"Well, I suppose we could put it to good use, but didn't Sir Randolph say something about telling Lord Giles that his daughter had always wanted to see the world?"

"Yes, I believe he did—something about America, too. Now, there's a big place—so big, I've heard, that you can become lost in it. And we're already planning to leave them in Roscoff, where they might find a ship to take them there, France and America friends enough that it shouldn't be too hard to do. I say America would be a fine place to start—seeing the world, of course."

Lindsay was so astonished she just stared at her friend, her eyes clouding when she saw tears swimming in Corisande's eyes. And she knew, once they reached Brittany, they would be saying good-bye to each other, maybe forever. But as Donovan drew his wife gently against him, Lindsay felt Jared squeeze her hand and she smiled into his eyes, knowing, too, that she and Corisande had both found what they were looking for . . . the men of their dreams.

"What do you think, Lindsay?" Jared's gaze full of love, his voice playfully teasing, he lowered his head and gave her a tender kiss that thrilled her to her toes. "America?"

Lifting her hands to cradle his face, she whispered against his lips, "Anywhere, Jared. Anywhere as long as I'm with you."

Avon Romances—
the best in exceptional authors
and unforgettable novels!

THE HEART AND THE ROSE   **Nancy Richards-Akers**
78001-1/ $4.99 US/ $6.99 Can

LAKOTA PRINCESS   **Karen Kay**
77996-X/ $4.99 US/ $6.99 Can

TAKEN BY STORM   **Danelle Harmon**
78003-8/ $4.99 US/ $6.99 Can

CONQUER THE NIGHT   **Selina MacPherson**
77252-3/ $4.99 US/ $6.99 Can

CAPTURED   **Victoria Lynne**
78044-5/ $4.99 US/ $6.99 Can

AWAKEN, MY LOVE   **Robin Schone**
78230-8/ $4.99 US/ $6.99 Can

TEMPT ME NOT   **Eve Byron**
77624-3/ $4.99 US/ $6.99 Can

MAGGIE AND THE GAMBLER   **Ann Carberry**
77880-7/ $4.99 US/ $6.99 Can

WILDFIRE   **Donna Stephens**
77579-4/ $4.99 US/ $6.99 Can

SPLENDID   **Julia Quinn**
78074-7/ $4.99 US/ $6.99 Can

Avon Romantic Treasures

*Unforgettable, enthralling love stories,
sparkling with passion and adventure
from Romance's bestselling authors*

LADY OF SUMMER *by Emma Merritt*
77984-6/$5.50 US/$7.50 Can

TIMESWEPT BRIDE *by Eugenia Riley*
77157-8/$5.50 US/$7.50 Can

A KISS IN THE NIGHT *by Jennifer Horsman*
77597-2/$5.50 US/$7.50 Can

SHAWNEE MOON *by Judith E. French*
77705-3/$5.50 US/$7.50 Can

PROMISE ME *by Kathleen Harrington*
77833-5/ $5.50 US/ $7.50 Can

COMANCHE RAIN *by Genell Dellin*
77525-5/ $4.99 US/ $5.99 Can

MY LORD CONQUEROR *by Samantha James*
77548-4/ $4.99 US/ $5.99 Can

ONCE UPON A KISS *by Tanya Anne Crosby*
77680-4/$4.99 US/$5.99 Can